THE OUT-OF-SORTS

Gary Fincke

THE OUT-OF-SORTS

New and Selected Stories

VANDALIA PRESS

MORGANTOWN 2017

ISBN:

PB: 978-1-943665-93-8
EPUB: 978-1-943665-94-5
PDF: 978-1-943665-95-2

Library of Congress Cataloging-in-Publication Data is available from the Library of Congress.

Book and cover design by Than Saffel / WVU Press
Cover illustrations of dogs by Victoria Novak / Shutterstock.

As Always, for Derek, Shannon, Aaron, and especially for Liz

CONTENTS

Acknowledgments / ix

NEW STORIES

Things that Fall from the Sky / 1
Roustabouts / 16
Gun Comfort / 35
What was Good for You / 51
A Day like Any Other / 58

FROM *FOR KEEPSIES* (1993)

Story Stories / 71
The Nazi on the Phone / 83

FROM *EMERGENCY CALLS* (1996)

Callback / 99
Darwin in the City / 110

FROM *THE STONE CHILD* (2003)

The Stone Child / 122
Zombies / 137
Natural Borders / 150

FROM *SORRY I WORRIED YOU* (2004)

Wire's Wire, until It's a Body / 164
The Lightning Tongues / 179

FROM *THE PROPER WORDS FOR SIN* (2013)

Somebody, Somewhere Else / 191
The Out-of-Sorts / 205
The Proper Words for Sin / 220

FROM *A ROOM OF RAIN* (2015)

A Room of Rain / 238
The Worst Thing / 253
The Visual Equivalent of Pain / 268
Roger That / 281

FROM *THE KILLER'S DOG* (2015)

Where We Live Now / 298
The Killer's Dog / 312

Credits / 329

ACKNOWLEDGMENTS

———

My thanks to the Pennsylvania Council on the Arts, Susquehanna University and the Degenstein Foundation, and the editors of the presses and magazines that have supported my fiction. A special thanks to my colleagues in the Writers Institute at Susquehanna and, of course, the creative writing majors and minors who made it a joy, every day, to go to work.

THINGS THAT FALL FROM THE SKY

———

Tim

Like she always did when we traveled to New York City, my wife Sally drove the Ohio leg from where we lived near Cincinnati. Our daughter Christine took over at the rest stop just inside Pennsylvania. Route 80 from there into New Jersey was long, but easy. They relied on me to do the last 100 miles, half of that in heavy traffic, no matter that it would be after midnight when we neared the city.

So it was Christine driving and me half asleep in the back seat when the windshield exploded half way across Pennsylvania. Christine screamed and braked hard, but it was Sally who took the rock full in the face. I sat up and leaned forward and wanted to scream myself. For all of the blood, I didn't know where her face was, but I could see her brain.

Wesley

Randy and I had an hour to kill waiting for my big brother Luke to get off work. We stopped at the DQ so we could have chocolate cones without Luke making fun of us, and after Randy turned off onto Well's Hollow Road, I let out a whoop because I knew what was coming, him plowing into Max Wagoner's corn and bumping along taking the full-grown stalks down. We couldn't see shit except all those stalks slapping at the windshield like those rubber flappers do at the car wash, and then we were out the other side away from the Wagoner house so even if he heard the car or saw our headlights, we were way too far gone for him to catch us.

Randy drove almost to the Turkey Hill before he pulled over and we picked out the leaves that were stuck in the grill and inside the fenders. If he noticed any of that, Luke would tell us that was old shit we needed to leave behind and call us pussies as if being eighteen and out of school two months made him King Daddy.

We cleaned that car good because Luke didn't say a word about us being kids, but when Randy said we should throw rocks off the Route 80 overpass, I thought Luke would tell him to grow the fuck up. Instead, he said "Cool," and we stopped where we knew a farmer smarter than old Wagoner had plowed stones out of his field and left them near the highway to keep guys like me and Randy from driving through. We each took three. I kept mine softball size and so did Randy, but Luke had three that could have passed for bowling balls pretty near. "These motherfuckers will break some shit," he said.

Christine

Dad told me later that I screamed until he got off the phone, but that can't be right because I heard everything he said when he called 911. I had the car stopped and off on the shoulder by then, and he was saying, "This is bad. A rock just crashed through the windshield from out of nowhere. My wife's grasping for life. My God, half her brain is gone."

Later, when somebody from the newspaper talked to the dispatcher, she said she could hear somebody screaming the whole time my father was on the phone. So there it was, like my voice was caught on tape for some kind of evidence.

Wesley

I threw my rocks as far as I could, and none of mine hit anything but Route 80. Randy aimed real careful-like at oncoming cars and didn't hit a thing. It was Luke who hit a truck with his second stone, and we high-fived after it bounced off the hood. "Give this big mother a heave," he said. "Let's see if one of you pussies has grown some hair."

Randy gave me a shove in the back, and I half stumbled. "Fuck you," I said, but there it was, that heavy thing that was hard to do anything with except throw it from just off my shoulder like I was shot-putting. When we heard the windshield shatter, all three of us hollered and laughed.

Randy even did a little dance instead of getting right into the car. I had to yell at him like he was going to stay there and celebrate until the cops showed up. All the way to my house he kept saying, "You hear that? You hear that? Fucking awesome." When we got to the house, Luke had to tell him to shut the fuck up.

Marvin

I heard the boys come in around midnight. They knew I'd be at the tv, so it wasn't like they had to sneak in. With my wife Leah dead and buried going on a year, I'd taken to watching a movie after the news, something to keep company with until I could settle enough to sleep. My job at the mall ended at ten, and I'd gotten into habits—getting up late, eating lunch instead of breakfast, not caring my own self about the extra pounds.

But when they seemed all keyed up, opening and closing the refrigerator, looking through the cupboards like scavengers, I waved at the tv and told them I was going to bed. "You boys help yourself," was what I told them. "Play your video games or watch a movie. Just stop all that hunting and pecking in the kitchen and remember this isn't a bar the next time you open the refrigerator."

Tim

Sally had just finished speaking with our boy Rick before the rock smashed her. She asked him to send her a selfie from where he was stationed in Texas. "It's only a week before you ship out," she said. "I need more pictures."

The picture came through and Sally showed it to Christine, who looked at it so long I had to tell her to keep her eyes on the road. "I really miss you guys," he texted.

"He's so sweet," Sally said. She put the phone in her purse and the rock burst through.

Marvin

I heard the boys leave and looked out to see my car gone. I heard them come back and leave again. I drifted off for a bit and came right up straight in bed when I heard the doorbell.

The sweat came right out of me. I checked the boys' room and saw their beds empty and wished to Christ I'd come out and locked them up for the night the second time they'd come back, even that little wingnut Randy.

There was nothing for it but to open the door to the police and, as it turned out, be thanking God when the officer told me that a car had been damaged on the freeway, nowhere my boys would be. I blew out a breath just before the cop added, "A passenger has been seriously injured."

"You think somebody lives here is involved?" I said.

"We'd like to find out. There's a car in your driveway was seen twice driving past the scene. We find that unusual."

I looked and there it was, my car back where it belonged. Randy's was there, too. "They must be around here some place," I said.

"That's what we believe, sir," the cop said, and just then all three came up from the basement so I knew they'd snuck in quiet as church mice and gone down there to filch beer straight from the case like I wouldn't count.

Doctor Wentworth

There was every chance trauma like the kind the woman had suffered from being struck by the rock would be fatal, no matter the effort that was made to save her. But even as we worked on her, hours upon hours, everyone in the room had a sense of how extensive the repairs would be, how many more operations we would be sharing before she could have any hope of leaving the hospital. She could very well be dissatisfied with her diminished quality of life. I'd seen cases less terrible than hers where the ongoing treatment created an uneasy balance between gratitude and cost. Not only the financial. That was the easy part.

Randy

It was Wesley's idea to go back to check things out, but it was Luke who said, "I'll drive," and I knew right off he thought I'd screw something up, stall the car right on the bridge or pull over to take a look down with the cops there like they had to be by now. But when he got into his Pop's car, I thought maybe it was Wesley he was worried about, what he might be thinking about the damage all that glass breaking might mean.

So we just cruised by slow, and Wesley piped up, saying, "Look at that, the staties are here too."

Though when I said, "This'll be famous," I got a look from Luke like I was a total moron.

Marvin

From the very first, when I studied on what the paper had to say about it, I expected the woman to die, one son turning to killer, the other an accessory. Like werewolves, they'd be in the papers, when she went. Brain surgery sounded like something doctors did to say they'd tried. Taking off the top of her head. It sounded like what they did for those boxers who get their brains beat in. Duk-Koo Kim, Kid Paret, and all the rest like them, though if I told my boys they'd just look at me like I was making things up. Nobody follows the fights anymore. The kids, for sure, don't know a thing except their cartoon fights they're all the time playing.

Doctor Wentworth

There are times, while operating, that I think anything can not only be corrected, but also made new. A perfect orbital reconstruction. A seamless cranial prosthesis. Things Sally Kirsch would need when she came out of her induced coma. If the stone had crushed her face thirty-five years ago when she was her daughter's age, she almost certainly would have died, and had she lived, her face would have broadcast her deformities like neon. I had a friend whose mother went through a windshield around that time, her lacerations leaving scars that transfixed people and made her keep to herself the rest of her life, something to remember each time I stand over a patient like Sally Kirsch who had already lost an eye, whose skull cap I'd removed to allow for swelling in her brain. And when I read the newspaper accounts two days after, I noticed that one of those boys swore that every rock he threw hit nothing whatsoever, as if a shooter missing his target is a synonym for innocence.

Marvin

My boys both took the blame for the rock that hit the teacher's car. Some comfort in that, though I admit I wished all along that it was Randy who'd tossed the accurate one, that my boys would be guilty because they were dumb enough to keep him around instead of the other way people would be seeing them now, Randy spreading the word about how he didn't lay a hand on that stone, and if egged along a bit with a smile or two and a handy lawyer, drifting into saying he didn't know what he was doing out there on the bridge until he was watching rocks crashing among speeding cars, hitting a truck and then the car with the teacher from Ohio. If I had to do it myself, I'd take an oath and swear his hands were covered in clay dust, that I'd heard him bragging about being the one with the idea in the first place, the one who'd thrown the first stone.

Wesley

"What does that mean, Pop," I said, "an induced coma?"

Pop just looked at me and said, "What do you think it means?"

I studied on that a few seconds until I thought I had it worked out. "They put her to sleep, and she won't wake up unless they let her."

When Pop nodded, I said, "That don't make sense. Aunt Bev was in a coma until Uncle Ray had them pull the plug. A month she laid there, and she didn't change at all."

"This lady's not Aunt Beverly. There looks to be different kinds of comas." He squeezed my shoulder. "Ones that maybe people wake up from, maybe feeling better than you might imagine."

Randy

They had all of our names in the paper, all in a row like we'd done the same thing, like some kind of circus act. Luke and Wesley Walters, Randy Osgood. I got credit for one thing that was right, driving my Mitsubishi Eclipse when we stopped on the overpass near Route 80's Midway Exit. But then there was this—"When the car below them slowed, they fled to the house where the brothers lived." We didn't flee. We just knew to celebrate somewhere else. Bank robbers do the same thing. They don't flee; they escape.

There was this, too—"They tried to watch a movie, but dying to know how much damage they'd caused, they got in the Walters' gold Honda Accord and drove past the scene to see what was happening." How does some reporter know what we were dying to do? If he'd asked me, I'd have told him I was dying to get Bonnie Roenig into bed, and I didn't much care where.

But I'll admit to the one thing—that second trip back to look yet again? That one's on me. All those extra police cruisers meant we'd done more than break a windshield, and there was the Honda's license plate in plain sight.

Tim
When I read in the newspaper what the trucker who was hit right before us said, I thought he was grandstanding. The fuck it happened like that, a thump like thunder, the rush past of something big and heavy like a meteor. And now here he is up for getting himself in the papers as the luckiest guy and all that goes with it. There's vanity everywhere was what I thought, even among misery.

Christine
Every year, Mom has an individual picture of each of her students on a kitchen bulletin board. They're arranged to coincide with where they sit in her classroom. From time to time she switches a few—because they talk too much maybe, but more likely because she's learned one of them has trouble seeing the black board or one has a hearing problem uncorrected. She wants me to see them when she tells stories during dinner. So you know who I'm talking about, she says. To help you understand.

Now school has started with a substitute, and my mother's students could be sitting anywhere. They could be disrupting class, switching seats without permission. Or one of them might be squinting from the back row, too ashamed to let that substitute know she can't see a thing.

Randy
I told the cops it's about wrecking things, not hurting anybody, but they looked like they wanted to slap my face or maybe more. Everybody I know hits mailboxes with ball bats. Everybody does a corn run, even girls sometimes. It's not like we were out drunk driving and being way stupid.

Doctor Wentworth
Two weeks in an induced coma is exactly what Sally Kirsch needed. The body requires time after thirteen hours of surgery to save its life and

reconstruct its face. It was the worst case I'd ever seen, and nothing since has changed my mind.

Wesley

Pop was always telling me, Luke too, that Randy was so squirrely he was trouble waiting to happen. Twitchy is what I'd say. Like the Alien monster was inside him and fixing to get out. Pop let us watch that movie when I was eleven. "You're about grown," he said, "and it's better than having you sneak it behind my back." He'd bought it used someplace, but the whole way through, Randy acted like he was six or something, pissing his pants for every little scary thing. Pop called him Ripley after that, even though she was the strongest one in the crew. He said he coud tell Randy had a girly side. For a while it was funny. And then Randy got big enough to whip me, so what did that make me?

Christine

Dad's told me about the trucker and his meteor. "My ass," he said. "If it bounced away and didn't hit you, you'd think it came from right here on Earth. Afterwards you'd know you could drive out there and pick up that rock and never once think it was anything except something pulled from the ground."

There's always the talk about meteors hitting us head on, ending us once and for all like the dinosaurs. Those guys with their telescopes can see them coming for a million miles so they'd know way before us we're all going to be disintegrated. And then they'd have to tell everybody, and there would be fighting back and forth about whether they had it right. They'd be like weathermen predicting a hurricane. People would hope that path might change. Them and their prayers and such. But it makes me think on what would you do once it got to where the end of everything was a sure shot. It's what movies are made of—heroes and cowards and those who turn to a few weeks of pure evil because it's been in their nature all along.

Wesley

Pop was all the time thanking the doctors for saving me from murder, but sometimes I wished that lady was dead right away. She'd have been gone then instead of all the time looking at me with her one eye half blind in her smashed up face. She's like some kind of ghost everybody loves. Like Casper for old people—they all want to give her a hug.

Marvin

Nearly every day during the winter when Wesley was twelve, he searched the sky for the first sign of space junk that was forecast to tumble out of orbit. "What if it lands here?" he asked more than once, and each time I told him that was so close to impossible there was no sense even thinking about it. "But not 100% impossible, right?" he said.

He asked to sleep downstairs in the room where we kept an old bed for when relatives visited every so often. From time to time, I caught him walking with his eyes focused on the sky. "Will we be able to see it coming?" he asked, and when Leah said, "Not likely," he had her go outside with him with binoculars. He worried that most of the late January and early February days were cloudy. By then he knew enough that the space station would break apart and mostly disintegrate before it reached Earth, but still he wouldn't let it go. "So many pieces makes it worse," he said.

It turned out the space station plunged back to Earth one night when nobody within five thousand miles of us noticed a thing. Wesley, he acted disappointed, like he wanted that pile of junk to land on the Johnson land right next door.

Wesley

Mom was nice about it the winter I was scared of space junk falling on us. Pop said stuff like that always fell in the ocean so don't be such a baby.

I looked space junk up on Mom's laptop and showed Pop the story about Wisconsin. In 1962, a twenty-one pound metal object plummeted from the sky and landed at the intersection of two streets in Manitowoc, Wisconsin. In the end, it turned out to be part of Sputnik IV, the first example of a significant piece of space junk surviving re-entry after falling out of orbit. The part I wanted him to see was it ended up imbedded three inches deep in the asphalt street.

Pop told me to shut the computer off and do something useful. "There's no point in being afraid of something you can't fight," he said.

Doctor Wentworth

A titanium implant is an extraordinary thing. The skull discarded, no longer viable, yet medical science permitting the body to re-enter the world.

Randy

It wore me down, all the talk about prison and me knowing I hadn't even touched that rock the Walters boys almost killed somebody with. I considered on some regrets I could have, but after a while, as part of a plea deal, I agreed to testify against Luke and Wesley. They would have done the same if I hadn't got first in line is how I figured. Luke always made fun of me, and their Pop thought I was some kind of handicap. "Ants in your pants" is what he always said, like he'd just thought of it after saying it since forever.

And I didn't lie. That's what's important. There's nothing wrong with telling the truth like I did in these exact words: "We decided to throw rocks at cars, just go out and be bad. When we got to the overpass, Wesley and Luke jumped out of the car with rocks ready to go. By the time I was up there beside them, Wesley had tossed a rock so there was no going back like maybe we could have done if they wasn't in such a hurry to put a hurt on something. For absolute sure, I didn't hit a thing, but there was a loud crash when Luke's rock that Wesley tossed hit glass. We all laughed as we drove away."

Wesley

"We're not a bunch of retards," I told the lawyer Pop got for me and Luke. It's just chance. And such a long shot. I knew twenty guys who'd thrown stuff off that overpass—rocks, sure, but also golf balls, and even old books. Sometime they hit cars, but never a windshield, not with rocks at least. The lawyer didn't even write it down. He looked bored. Like he wanted me to make something up. A good lie instead of the truth.

Marvin

The police questioned Ron Davenport, who lives only 100 feet from the overpass. He mentioned to them that kids had tossed rocks at tractor trailers from the same bridge about seven years ago. "Then they put the signs up, 'No standing on bridge,' and there for a while the cops were coming by on a regular basis checking. But nothing happened, so the cops stopped coming by."

Tim

When asked by the reporters, the state police said they didn't know how many times someone threw an object that struck a vehicle last year because its database lumps those in with incidents in which something lands on a highway. What they knew was troopers responded to 213 "assault-propulsion of missile" incidents last year. What else they knew was fences are erected on highway overpasses in urban areas that have sidewalks and are near a school or playground. The Willow Hill Road overpass where those boys threw from doesn't meet that criteria because it's in a rural area, with no sidewalk. The overpass, they said, is twenty-two feet high.

When I searched for other incidents of rocks thrown from overpasses onto passing cars and trucks, there were dozens of stories. Near misses, most of them, but one man, driving near Austin, Texas, was hit square in the face like Sally. He was paralyzed on his right side and was unable to talk or write, according to a television report. Three other motorists were injured in rock throwing incidents on the same highway within a month of the one that paralyzed that driver.

Marvin

I told this story to Leah way back when and to my boys once upon a time, but now it sounds like I'm the devil talking to say it:

One afternoon, just after recess ended, a corner of concrete from just under the roof of my elementary school broke off and fell fifty feet into the playground. Our teacher kept us in our seats. She told us to pay attention to what we were doing, not what was happening outside, but when school ended, everyone I knew veered out of the path to where the school buses waited to take a look at the crash site. We all knew exactly how long it had been since we had stood in the spot where the stone struck the cement. Last week. Yesterday. That morning. Minutes before.

Doctor Wentworth

When I was fourteen, I went with two friends up the winding outside staircase that led to the top of the water tower at the county park. We had water balloons, balancing two in each hand. "There's always somebody who doesn't know enough to not stand around close to the tower," one friend said, meaning other people who were there for our church picnic. By the time we reached the 100 foot-high observation deck, I was uneasy with the height and having only one way down after we tossed those balloons. My friends screamed when a balloon burst close enough to somebody to soak them. I was the only one who didn't lean over the railing to see the damage. I tossed all of mine one right after the other, and before the last few balloons were tossed, I made my way down the stairs and hoped that anyone coming up the 154 metal steps would figure I wasn't part of the group that threw the balloons, that anyone soaked would see me half way down while one last balloon arced toward them.

Christine

Nearly three months it took for Mom to leave the hospital. Dad spent half those days in Pennsylvania. He made me go back to Ohio State for my sophomore year, and I put up with sympathy that started to smell like too many flowers in a room.

Tim

Eventually I learned that there have been reports of fatalities from rock throwing incidents, including two drivers killed by rocks as big as soccer balls tossed onto a German highway in 2000. Like the boys who hit our car, all of those rock throwers were teenagers. They were charged with murder.

Christine

In November, while we were waiting at the rehab center for Mom's grand exit, one of the nurses told my father and me about the time in 1969 a big cloud formed out of nowhere over Chester, South Carolina. "Right away powder started to fall all over that place and the people were afraid," she said. "Nearly all of them went inside and closed their windows. Some who were stuck outside expected to die. But it turned out to be from the new Borden's plant. It was the stuff they make to put in coffee."

"Cremora," Dad said. He knew the name right away.

The nurse looked surprised that Dad had interrupted. "The person who told me didn't know the name," she said. "But the best part is that the day became white and sweet like the air above a rolling pin thinning cookie dough. The cloud was soluble on tongues. And later, when the whitened bathed, some of them must have stroked the film that had formed along their cheeks, can you imagine?"

"So some people down that way got to be happy for a bit thinking the world didn't fall on them," Dad said.

"Dad, Mom's alive," I said. "She's coming home."

"Yes," the nurse said, "isn't that wonderful?" and she hurried away.

Dad looked straight at me then. "You'll see Mom like she is now every day."

"Yes."

"So you can't pretend even once in a while."

Doctor Wentworth

When Mrs. Kirsch stepped out of the Medical Center for the first time since being struck, she wore a pink #KirschStrong t-shirt. Her artificial skull was covered by a pink and white knit cap. Outside the rehab facility, she was filmed ringing a victory bell reserved for patients who overcome long odds. When she first entered the facility, she was so confused she couldn't manage any of the therapy. Three months since the incident, she said she had no memory of it. Anyone watching the video will notice that as she walks, Mrs. Kirsch is braced on both sides by smiling attendants. At the victory bell ceremony, she is still lightly supported. When asked to speak, what I said was she was "nearly independent, walking with a little assistance, able to take care of herself."

Christine

My mother came out of the hospital like a prisoner, her exposed eye blinking. She wobbled when she paused at the applause, the hands of two aides on her shoulders. A woman next to me checked her phone, and my father's head snapped sideways to glare, his mouth working the way it does when he's keeping curses to himself. For a moment, the day began to lose its balance, and then my mother took a few tentative steps unaided, and my father put his arm around my shoulders and drew me close as everything straightened and held steady.

Tim

Everybody looks happy in the video of Sally's release, and so do I. But they aren't thinking about having to live the rest of what's coming without being swallowed. I can be angry, but I can't say a word about being uncomfortable. I'd be a selfish prick if I let it slip how her face isn't hers anymore, that it belongs to the doctors and the rock throwers.

Marvin

"You're good boys," I told them right after the teacher went home to Ohio at last. Luke paused the movie he and Wesley were watching, and I readied myself to accept their bodies in a hug. "You sure are," I went on, "don't let nobody tell you different."

They shifted in their chairs, but neither one stood. On the screen an actor who looked familiar was aiming an arrow at an enormous dragon. I'd seen this before and so had the boys. The outcome was impossible, but it was about to happen, and what came to me was wondering whether either one of them would have paused the movie if he'd never seen it before, whether his eyes would have stayed on that dragon, his head nodding, while I finished what I had to say and left the room.

Tim

One of the reporters, before she left me alone, said, "Where I come from, those boys would be afraid for their lives when the word got out about their stupidity."

I didn't ask her where that was, but if she was making that up to lead me along, I was willing to go. "There's some of that in me," I said. "That's one way of how some might handle such a terrible thing."

Marvin

My Wesley, he needs to be tried as a juvenile, him being sixteen at the time. That's something to feel better about, the lawyer said to me. And he wanted me to know there was certain evidence he wanted to be suppressed when the trial rolled around. Most important, he said, is not to admit as evidence the 911 call made by Mr. Kirsch. Likewise, pictures of his Missus should not be permitted to be shown. They're prejudicial, he said. Those exhibits are too emotionally charged.

Christine

My mother has a new skull. Like a crab entering a new shell. And now my father and I will examine the crease of its circumference as often as we enter a room where we find her. She will pretend not to notice until one day my brother will be back from Afghanistan all in one piece and my father will give up a smile and we will fix on her whole body, believing it will go on by itself. We will feel some small sense of what might be happiness. The reporters will be gone to other things, and it will be just our story for ourselves, all of us thinking the same thing, "Here we are, here we really are."

ROUSTABOUTS

———

Though it had been ten years since he'd worked on an oilrig and he'd held half a dozen jobs since, my stepfather Ray Ressler always told people he met that he was a retired roustabout. Said he worked out of Galveston, a town rough and ready as any you'd ever see. "I was coming up for roughneck when my accident finished all that," he told me right off. "That's the real deal. Somebody call you a roughneck, you tell them there's such a thing that's worth a good goddamn."

I liked the sound of roustabout, but roughneck was even better. "All right," I said, though I was imagining gangsters or bandits or even the highwayman we'd read about in a poem in my eighth-grade English class. You had to be a tough guy who could take charge, somebody, though I was far from it, I thought I wanted to be.

My mother, reading my mind, told me roustabout jobs were "at the bottom of the pile out there in the Gulf." When I asked how big the pile was, she shook her head. "Big enough to smother you if you don't get out from under, but Ray says it paid good."

"Wet and dirty" is how Ray put it when I asked. "Unloading crap. Carrying it around. Cleaning up after everybody. Maybe fix a few things if you're handy that way. But it was two weeks on, two weeks off, the way to do it. Like one of those regular puny vacations most get only they come around every month." He was standing outside smoking like he always did because my mother wouldn't put up with it inside. He took a long drag and grinned. "There's no sissies stay long out there," he said. "You

16

need to have some balls, Wayne, that's God's truth. And there I was a few days, maybe a few weeks, from being promoted to roughneck, and my car wreck ended all that."

Ray was about fifty when he married my mother, which would have made him fifteen years older than her, but still a young man when it came to all his retirement talk a year after their wedding, and I turned fourteen in Front Royal, Virginia, where we moved at the end of April, 1962. Because we lived outside of town and I didn't own a bike, Front Royal didn't seem to be much except a place where tourists passed through on their way to the Skyline Drive and the Shenandoah National Park. I had a month of junior high school to finish, so short a time nobody paid much attention to me, but it wasn't so bad in the tiny four room house with no basement, a sight better, at least, than Ray's crummy apartment in Hagerstown we'd moved into when my mother married him, three rooms with families on either side, always loud with radios, televisions, and angry voices. And it was way better than the two rooms and the shared bathroom my grandmother let us live in at her run down house for the six years after my father got killed because of what my mother called a "misunderstanding."

What I hated about the new house was the water that came out of the spigots. It stunk like rotten eggs. Sulfur, Ray said the first time I complained. Like he was letting me in on a secret. "It don't hurt you, so get yourself used to it," he said every time he saw me making a face. "It tastes the same as what comes from that fountain you love at the A&P."

He'd seen me go back to that fountain three times while my mother went up and down every aisle loading up a cart with all the things we needed to get us started in the house Ray told us he'd gotten "for a song." It was the only time he ever came along to the A&P, but he seemed to know I drank my fill every time I kept my mother company when she shopped.

It was the only refrigerated fountain I knew of, not room temperature or worse like the school fountains that, by second period, were clogged with gum wads that encouraged puddles full of mucus-laced spit globs. For the five weeks I attended after we moved, I never took a drink except before my first class of the day.

Ray, it turned out, was on disability, a monthly check my mother called small but steady. He was doing maintenance at the Kmart in Hagerstown

when we met, but by the time they were married and we were settled in
his place, he said he was on his way out and looking around for a new start
for all of us. "Thank the good Lord for my disability that comes regular,"
he said, as if God had a plan for us.

"Your new Pop's too banged up to work at anything he's good at," my
mother said a few days later.

"What hurts him?" I asked.

"Everything you need to do a man's work—shoulders, knees, back.
Don't you be bellyaching to him about anything that ails you unless it's
deep inside."

By the time school ended, my mother was cleaning houses three
afternoons a week, all she could manage because Ray had to drive her to
and from, and her back, she explained, was starting "to go south." Ray
chipped in by being a paperboy. He left the house at six a.m. and was home
by nine. "If folks wasn't so scattered out this way, you could deliver too," he
told me. "If they had lawns they loved, you could babysit them, but we'll
figure something before too long a fourteen year-old can do to help out."

I had plenty to do for a while. We had a yard that looked huge because
the lots on either side were vacant, but all of that space was over grown
from a spring of being uncut. Ray set me to work with a rusty scythe and
a pair of old gloves to get all the lots presentable. "Good, honest work,"
he said every time he came outside to smoke. Right before school ended,
he brought home an old power mower he said he'd found along his paper
route, the thing lying across the back seat like he'd told it to keep its head
down. "You keep that all cut and you got yourself a park to play in," Ray
said. "Baseball, football, you name it. Just make sure the mower's under
that there tarp when it's not running."

Which I did. I wanted that grass and weeds as short as I could keep
them. I had a couple of old golf clubs my mother had kept in the back of
her closet since I could remember, and now, she said, there was room for me
to give them a try. Right away, Ray noticed that one had a wooden shaft.
"Antiques," Ray declared. "Maybe worth something." But after he showed
them around, he stopped imagining any windfall out of the two of them.
No luck either with the burlap sack full of balls my mother fished out for
me like an early birthday present. Eighty-six balls in that sack, half of them
cut, which meant Ray couldn't get a quarter for them or even a dime, what

he marked the cut ones down to for the yard sale he put together in June to get rid of anything worth a damn that we didn't need lying around. "Go ahead then, all yours to waste your time with." I almost agreed with him about the waste of time because all I did, mostly, was smack line drives that hooked left if I swung any harder than half speed. There was a secret to those clubs that kept me coming back though, and I had forever to learn before ninth grade started up at Warren County High School.

Ray was short and wiry. A banty rooster, Mom called him when she was upset. "You settle down, you banty rooster," she'd say. More like Jack Sprat and his wife, I sometimes thought. I loved Mom enough to keep that to myself, but Ray was all the time acting like skinny was something to be proud of, explaining his side of things, like the one time in July when he called out, "Your Momma was a looker when we got hitched, just a little extra meat on her bones, but she's taken to forgetting about herself." He was smoking out back, and I gave him distance, but soon enough he waved me closer and started in on roustabout, acting like that was all there was to talk about besides finding some work for me to do that paid.

Ray moved his neck around the way he always did, acting like his t-shirt collar was too tight. I'd never seen him in anything but t-shirts, mostly the white underwear kind. My mother had told me he'd let slip that his first wife had broken him of forever tugging at his shirts because it ruined them. "But now he wears that crick-in-the-neck habit," she'd said.

"Your Momma says you're one that's scared of being up high," he started in.

"A little," I said, as far as I wanted to admit. Right about then I didn't have anything particular enough to be doing except listening.

"A little's too much out there on the rig. Lots of working up high when you're a roustabout, and for starters you're way up over the water to begin with. You go out on the walkways and you get yourself a good look down to where hell's waiting for the careless. You fall in the water and it'll kill you fast with cold most of the year and kill you slow with it the rest."

It sounded like something I'd never want to do, another reason to be a roughneck, somebody in charge, somebody with enough of a reputation he'd get to keep his feet right up close to the ground, even on an oilrig. "I'd get used to it," I said for something to say besides admitting I couldn't even climb the ropes in gym class without thinking about wetting my shorts. I wasn't ever going to mention that to Ray. Sissy was just about the worst thing there was to be this side of getting paralyzed or going blind. I knew Ray thought golf was a sissy game, that if I was going to end up being friends with boys who were on their way to being real men that football was what I needed to try, and practice was starting in a couple of weeks.

"Get used to it or get the fuck out," he said, and then he added, "You want to try one of these here smokes?"

"That's ok," I said, but Ray tapped one out and handed it to me like he knew I'd started stealing one almost every day since school had ended.

"It's like being up high," he said. "You get used to this here too."

A few days after that, my mother out cleaning, Ray returned with a trunk and back seat full of plants. I watched from the kitchen as he emptied them onto our scraggly lawn, and then he called me outside. "Your Momma laid down the law about all this here," Ray said, his hands motioning toward the base of the outside of the house. I counted eight bushes sitting nearby, their root balls snug and moist looking. I recognized four rhododendrons; the others looked like they were related to pine trees only smaller and rounder. "We got work to do."

I had to admit that with the plants sitting there, the house looked even uglier than usual, like it might pick up and sail away in the wind because nothing held it to the earth. Ray dug in with a shovel, turning up mostly rocks and clay. For a while he looked like someone else, a man concentrating hard on doing things right, somebody who had planned this out and had thought about improving the way the house looked in ways that I never would.

There were bags of topsoil so dark and rich it looked like it came from another planet. There was peat moss and fertilizer. We had never done any work together, but now I cut open the bags and dumped part of their contents into the first three holes Ray dug. I carried cans of our smelly water and poured it into each hole. Ray set two of the rhododendrons on each side of the front door and one of the bushes farther along the outside wall.

After that he stopped to smoke, lighting one for me off the first. "You do the next ones," he said. "Build you some muscle." When I hesitated, making what he called "my beat-dog face," he added, "and maybe you find yourself some fancy rocks to read about," because I'd shown him a brochure for the Skyline Caverns I'd picked up at the A&P and told him about the anthodites in one of the pictures, crystals you could only find right there in the Skyline Caverns and a couple of other caves in the whole country.

I started in on trying to dig a hole then, showing him it wasn't about being weak and lazy, but he disappeared into the house like I was on my own for the next five bushes. I was down about six inches into the dirt when he came back with a beer for himself and a soda for me that he set on the front stoop.

And then he watched. "Get used to this roustabout business," he said. "It's coming right on down the highway."

A half hour later I'd dug five holes and raised blisters on both hands. "You oughta put on them gloves I gave you first," Ray said as he lit a cigarette and inspected the holes. "You think on this while you're wishing you had your hands back—all these here stones you have in a pile, they bringing you nothing but sweat and blood. There's no cash money for knowing their names. For goddamn sure, nobody cared if I knew geology out there on the rigs." I waited, keeping my hands on the shovel, until he said, "I'll finish this here, and you find that whisk broom your Momma has and get to work on the inside of the car. She'll have herself a fit if she has to ride home on filth."

Instead of handing over the shovel, I leaned on it, imagining I looked like somebody who was used to work. "There had to be some men out there who knew all about geology," I said, and for once Ray looked thoughtful, like he was considering on whether I might have learned something about drilling for oil.

Finally, he said, "That's them, not us."

"I could go to college."

Ray took a drag and let the smoke out slow and easy. "I seen your grades."

"It's just high school that counts."

"Right now it's this here that counts. You get that bitty little broom now and bring me out another of these cold ones on your way back."

When I handed him the beer, he nodded. "That's the stuff," he said.

"You know what science they should be teaching you?" Me not answering didn't slow him down. "You don't need chemistry and physics and geology, you need to know the ins and outs of what's happening to you."

"That's not science," I said.

"Yes, it is," Ray said. "Don't you be fooling yourself."

"My boys," my mother said when she saw the shrubbery all in place, neat and green. "Thank you." She fished in the fridge and came out with a beer for Ray and a soda for me. Ray grinned and tapped his can against mine.

"Right about now I feel just a little bit like I did after we rode out the big one in the Gulf back a ways," Ray said.

"Hardly," my mother said right off, surprising me.

"You oughta be up in among the scaffolding looking down. Skyscraper window washers got nothing on that all harnessed in and back inside as soon as the weather turns."

"I meant the other way around, Ray," my mother said. "This is nice; that's something else entirely."

Ray downed a big gulp and touched cans with me again. I thought he was going to hug my mother, but he started in with "You damn betcha" and kept right on going. "This beauty of a storm blew across the Gulf and was working its way up to hurricane force with just me and a few others stuck out on a rig. There was nothing to do but ride it out. Ready to keel over, it was. The whole shootin' match. There wasn't none of us wasn't cursing Texaco for a few hours. But Wayne, let me tell you this about that—there ain't nothin' like it, knowing the next minute you might be done for. There's nothing like it you'll ever feel for yourself anywhere near here."

He slapped my back, drained his beer, and tapped out a cigarette, but he didn't take another beer out to the porch with him as he stepped outside to smoke. My mother followed him with her eyes and slid closer to me, lowering her voice to say, "Before you go on and think your stepdaddy lived through a hurricane out in the middle of the Gulf, you should know that was a tropical storm he was stuck in. That don't make light of it, but there weren't any big ones around where he was that summer. His old rig buddy told me that at our wedding reception. I thought he might take his fists to his friend, but all he said was, 'Anybody think it's a joy ride out there should go out and wait his turn.'"

"It would still be a big deal," I said. "The rig would still feel like it could collapse."

"Maybe so," my mother said, "but Ray is all the time wishing it was a full-fledged hurricane he could have ridden out, one with a name. Back then the big ones were named like how the army does it—Abel, Baker, Charley, Dog." She picked up Ray's empty beer can and tossed it into the trashcan beside the sink. "Dog," she said, "that had to sound dumb for a hurricane even at the start. And Easy. Imagine those that went through that hurricane and how they felt." She walked over to the window and looked out as if she thought Ray might be listening at the door. "Look at him out there. A regular chimney, he is." She turned back to me and smiled. "You know your stepdaddy smokes more than he drinks. Trust me, that's a blessing. Some have it the other way."

"Like my real Pop?" I said, and she laughed and brushed her hand in front of her face like she was fanning herself.

"We had ourselves some good times."

"And bad?" I started. When her smile disappeared, I didn't know what came next.

"Nobody wants to be alone," she said. "You settle for what comes your way."

A week later, for my birthday, my mother gave me two tickets to the Skyline Caverns. "I know you've been looking at that pamphlet you grabbed at the grocery," she said before she added the real surprise: "And Ray's ready to take you whenever you're up for going. He's been underground and can tell you stories."

Ray moved closer to me and punched my shoulder just hard enough to make me grimace. "And one to grow on," he said, like we'd turned the corner onto Good Buddies Street while my mother beamed. Right then I was sure my mother had told him to make nice if we were going to be under the same roof.

Just like that, before the week ended, Ray and I were on the way to the caverns, him talking the whole way about how his Daddy was a coal miner. "My Pap took me down just the one time to show me why I should never grow up to be him," Ray said. "He already had the cough that comes with the dust. He took me to where they were working a seam, sometimes on their knees where the ceiling was so low you'd be better off being a midget. He turned off my helmet light and his own, and we were in the dark, all hunched over like that ugly fucker who rang the bells in the big church. Never ever work underground is my advice. Pap was dead at forty, almost twenty-five years down there is what killed him. I was in the Navy by then, so I was used to being out where you can't see anything but water except right there where you're standing. It made it easy for me to go out on the rigs in the Gulf."

"I bet they turn out the lights when we get way down under," I said, and Ray snorted.

"I bet they do, boy. I bet some tourists squeal like pigs when the lights go out."

It turned out about a dozen of us followed a guide for a while where stalactites and all that were lit up by colored lights. Nothing looked real until we were in plain old white light and the guide said, "See the eagle?" And there it was, a feathered wing formed so clearly in the rock I wanted to reach up and run my hand over it. "Isn't it wonderful," the guide said, "this formation right here, and it being so close to Washington like we are?"

Ray leaned over and whispered, "They want us to feel like God made this just for the good old US of A."

The pretty, crystal-like anthodites were bathed in white light, too, but I knew enough not to ooh and aah over them around Ray. The rest of everything interesting was all in color. A chandelier. The Fairyland Lake. It reminded me of the wheel of three-colored cellophane that circled a light bulb every year near the base of the silver artificial Christmas tree my grandmother put up. A little thing about four feet high she stuck on her coffee table after she moved it into a corner. "Just right for a growing boy," my mother said every year, even when I was taller than it, table and all.

Our group walked about a dozen steps away from the Fairyland Lake before the guide said, "I want everyone to stand still for a moment like you're getting your picture taken. Ready?" All of the lights went out, and I heard Ray clear his throat, spit and whisper, "Now we're talking."

I waited for my eyes to adjust, but nothing changed. The guide didn't speak. A woman's voice went "Ohhh," startled and nervous like she'd felt a hand on her. And just about the time when I thought of the nearby lake and how somebody in a panic might walk right into it trying to get above ground, the lights came on and a ripple of undertone went through everyone but Ray and me. The woman who had called out looked like she was scraping something off her blouse. A woman beside her watched, and I wondered, for a moment, whether the nearest man had brushed her body as he reached out to steady himself in the dark.

After we came back out into the sunlight, Ray tapped out a cigarette and held it up as if he needed to inspect it. "You been sneakin' these again?" Ray said.

"Not since."

Ray chuckled. "Already a liar," he said. "Your Pap must have been a pistol. I bet we'd a been friends. Here, take one. Let's talk about ways I've been thinking to make spend money."

I inhaled and held the smoke like I'd been smoking for a lifetime. "You're fourteen now," Ray said, "starting at the high school in a month. Maybe you want something special, save up for a car you'll be driving soon enough. Maybe you want real golf clubs for next summer. You want to putt on those carpets at the golf club you're always staring at when we pass? Well, there's nothing you can do at fourteen to make any part of that happen."

"I don't get it then," I said.

"You will," Ray said, "but first let's learn you how to drive. All that's anywhere tricky is learning the stick shift. We're not going out in heavy traffic. It's thirty-five tops and just a little coming and going up there on the Skyline where what we need you to be doing is waiting for you to show up and be ready."

A week it took me to make Ray believe I could be trusted not to stall his car or over steer it into a ditch. All that time he put me off about what he had in mind. It was like I had another birthday coming, a surprise I couldn't quite imagine. Finally, he drove into the national park and started up the Skyline Drive a few miles before he pulled off at the first overlook and told me to show the road who's boss. "Easy as pie, right?" he said after a couple of miles. "Speed limit like we have here suits a beginner and keeps the hurry-ups from boiling over."

I nodded, happy not to have any trucks or horn-blowers on my tail, but

I kept my eyes on the road, and Ray laughed, short and almost a cough, before lighting up a cigarette like he'd done all week about the time I'd driven a couple of miles without anything going wrong. "Let me show you something right up around here. Pull into that there lot coming up."

There were three other cars, plenty of room for me to swing in ten feet from the nearest one. "I've been sniffing around and know not many stop here to do their hiking because it's so close to where the park starts. They figure there's better up ahead, you know?"

He had me walk into the woods with him, passing, five minutes in, a man and a woman who were taking pictures and a family with small children. "Down here," he said at last, "there's a little bitty path you can barely see the start of that looks to be going nowhere. Folks going that way know right off they made a wrong turn and give it up, but you set your mind to it, you can cut back through the woods and go straight to the road without making the big loop they have marked on the signs."

I peered down the narrow path like I might learn something worth remarking upon. "I don't think anybody would think this was the way they were supposed to go," I said.

Ray slapped me on the back. "Yessiree, boy, that's just what this here doctor ordered. Follow me."

Two minutes of scrambling over downed trees and through briars got us to the road. "Just us and the animals come that way," Ray said. "It's a half-mile hike up the hill back to where we parked, but we can use the time for me to tell you exactly how me and you are going to be a team."

Ray talked as we hiked along the shoulder. "Listen. Here's the plan. You drop me off up ahead at that lot and then drive back down this way ten minutes later and pull off where we was just standing. Anybody passing will think it's some animal you're seeing in the woods, but any kind of good timing will make it me coming out like I've been on bathroom break. I can't be prancing around in that parking lot after, that's for damn sure."

I felt my heart racing, but I said, "I don't get it" to buy some time before I knew for certain what Ray had in mind.

"I thought you was smart," Ray said, "but I'll lay it out for you. I've had me a pistol since my roustabout days. I ain't never fired it and don't intend to now, you can be sure of that, but I aim to scare a few rich people shitless. It'll be easy. They think being in a park means there's nothing could hurt them. Like the bears are toys. By the time they follow that trail back up here and find a phone, we'll be back to Front Royal. They ain't none of them going to miss what I take. It'll end up like they paid to have a story to tell back home, and we'll be a step ahead of wishing."

Instead of "count me out," I heard myself say, "Don't you need a mask or something?"

Ray smiled like he knew secrets. "I got me sunglasses and a ball cap like a tourist. You saw that outfit your Momma bought me when she thought I needed something besides jeans and a t-shirt. Bermuda shorts and that shirt with a collar like I was fixing to play golf. I'll look like nobody I'd ever be and that's good." He inspected me up and down, making sure I understood what he thought of my own khaki shorts and raggedy polo.

"And I'm driving getaway?"

"All them that hands over their cash will be scrambling back to that parking lot we just left behind. That trail loops big and bendy so they'll never know where I've been or where I'm gone to. Meanwhile, you're picking me up like a taxi driver." Ray pulled out two cigarettes, but he kept on walking and didn't light them. "I bet you like that fella Robin Hood. It's no different right here. We're poor as all get out."

"I don't think so."

Just then the parking lot showed itself as we came around a bend, and Ray lit both cigarettes, handing me one. "You don't like spend money, you don't have to do more than the once, but you got to drive like I told you so we learn how good this can be before you make up your mind."

Ahead of us, after getting out of a car, two women in shorts put on sunglasses and visors. Ray whistled softly. "I've seen women up in here by themselves while I was doing the look-around, but I ain't that kind of man. What we're doing is strictly business."

"One time only," I said.

Ray laughed, full-throated this time. "That sounds like a boy about to spark up his first cigarette." Then, before I could open the car door, he stepped up close and his eyes went to slits. "We're on for tomorrow. I don't need my partner mulling things over so long he gets hisself religion."

The next afternoon, Ray not saying a word all the way to the park kept me quiet too. Just as well, since all I wanted to say was "Let's not do this." I felt like I did every time I had to start over in a new school, only worse. Maybe how I'd feel in a couple of weeks when some senior would pick me out of a crowd because I'd give off some kind of fear smell. I started hoping Ray was thinking along those lines, but when he pulled into the lot and there were two cars, both station wagons, he said, "Good, families," and I started concentrating on doing things right.

Ray handed me the keys and put on his sunglasses and Oriole's cap. I had to admit he didn't look like Ray Ressler the roustabout. In his getup with those dark glasses, he looked blind. "Ready, hoss?" he said. "I'm countin' on you."

"Ready," I said, and he disappeared down the trail.

Three minutes to the second I was out of the car because I couldn't think of a reason, if anybody drove up, I could give for sitting by myself in a hot car in full sun. I walked just far enough to be in the shade and checked my watch, waiting for the sweep hand to announce four minutes. I kicked an old pinecone around the lot and checked my watch. Kicked it some more and saw eight minutes had passed, close enough to let me get behind the wheel, start the car, and wait a full minute before pulling out.

I thought I'd be early, but there was Ray stepping out of the woods as soon as I eased the car to a stop. "Jackpot," he said, climbing inside. "I got to do a two-for-one."

I didn't say anything, concentrating on the road, but Ray didn't need any prompting. "Both families were down the trail aways and together when I come up on them. One fella was taking a picture of the other family, kids and all, by some tree they must have thought was special. Who'd a thought there'd be a traffic jam up in there, but a break for us, just double the cash, no trace."

I drove slowly, glancing down at the speedometer to make sure I wasn't going over the limit, but no cars caught up to us and only one passed going the other way. "Pull in here," Ray said when we got back to the first overlook. We switched, Ray getting behind the wheel and lighting a cigarette and offering me one, saying, "Here you go, partner" before he pulled out, both windows rolled down to ease the smoke, me having the time to wonder if I was already acquiring that smell Ray had of sweat and cigarettes.

"Damn," Ray said as he looked at me and smiled. "Damn!"

Back at the house, my mother not needing a ride for another hour, Ray showed me $320. "See? What did I tell you? Easy pickings. And here's sixty for you," he said. "Driver's pay."

"I don't want it," I said.

"You too good for it? You all high and mighty now?"

"I was just helping out."

Ray took my hand and laid the bills on my palm. When I didn't let them fall, he said, "That's it. Take it. You and your bellyaching, but I knew you was cut out for this here."

Ray was so sure of me I started thinking of alibis and denials, but what I knew right then was that I was afraid this was something like smoking, that once this guilt and fear passed, I'd look forward to it. When he left to pick up my mother, I spread the six ten-dollar bills out in one of the set of Chip Hilton books my father had given me for Christmas just before he was killed, the only book where Chip's high school sports team doesn't win the championship. Ray was right. We were partners. He thought he'd seen something in me that I'd grow into. I was just the bellyaching one who worried all the time about what other people would think and then acted high and mighty.

My mother looked tired when she walked in with Ray, but she settled in on making dinner. Ray sat down to watch the six o'clock news, but nothing came on about the Skyline Drive. "You getting interested in where we live?" my mother said.

"Yeah," I said, and Ray snapped me a look like I was introducing a confession.

At eleven that night, my mother asleep for an hour by then, Ray switched to the news, and there it was, a report about armed robberies in the Shenandoah National Park, a few seconds of footage taken from the parking lot where I'd dropped Ray off. "Ok," Ray whispered. "Now we wait until nobody cares anymore that this ever happened."

For a week I spent all my time outside, staying away from Ray and trying not to smoke. I'd changed my grip on the clubs, getting rid of holding them like baseball bats, what felt good at first but led to all those low line drives that hooked, or just as likely skittered and bounced if I swung as hard as I could.

Once I moved my hands, I loved hitting with the pitching wedge. It didn't seem that hard to loft most of the balls into high arcs that the angle of the club provided. My best shots carried the length of the three lots and scattered just short of the road, and when, the few times a ball carried to the road, it bounced high and ended up in the yard across the highway, I pretended I'd made a hole-in-one on a real course.

"You're getting so good at that," my mother said one afternoon. "You could show the rich boys a thing or two about their game." I was using the sand wedge, which, even though it had a metal shaft, looked older, and the club face was thicker and heavier in a way that made it harder for me to loft the ball unless I placed it on a tuft of sparse grass like I'd just done while my mother watched.

"Maybe so," I said, half-believing her. It didn't seem that hard and surely would be easier hitting off the perfect-looking grass at the local course.

"Remember when we used to live by the Bon-Air Golf Course? Your Daddy found those clubs after men left them on the course. He told me he expected to find a full set like that after a spell, and there might come a day when you had a use for them. I never saw him even swing one. And all those golf balls in that dirty old sack, most of them cut up and scuffed like someone wanted to murder them. And now here you are."

"I was too little to do much except slap the balls around the yard."

"Remember that bridge they had up there on the course, how scared of it you were?"

"I always thought it would throw me off into the creek when it moved."

"The golfers would walk across that with their clubs and nobody ever fell."

"I didn't know that. Back then I was small enough to fit underneath the railing."

My mother picked up the pitching wedge, and for a moment I thought she wanted to give it a try, but all she did was hand it to me like a caddy. "You know what your Daddy said hurt him most in his life?" she said. "Being fingerprinted. He was a prideful man."

"It's hard for me to remember anything about how he felt," I said.

"He told me it all come about after a fight with a man over his first wife. He couldn't abide a man taking her clothes off with his eyes." My mother seemed out of breath as she talked, but now she relaxed and spoke evenly. "And it cost him dearly the second time," she went on. "You should know how much a woman is floored by such a devotion. One important thing like that matters more than a fistful of flaws."

Ray stepped outside like a man who'd been listening to every word. "Having a problem?" he said, and my mother's expression changed.

"I know Wayne's been smoking," she said. She looked at Ray and me like she was adding up the sum of her disappointments.

"I'm sorry," I said.

"You're so smart," she said. "It's what fooled me for a while." Ray grinned like he was about to do a little dance.

"I'll leave you to it," he said, and he got into his car and drove off.

My mother watched the road for a few seconds before she turned back to me. "Such a filthy habit. I have to believe that brains are stronger than desires in the long run. Can I believe that?"

"Yes," I said at once.

"You know Ray's not perfect by any stretch, but he's never laid a hand to me. Don't you think that of him."

"I've never thought that," I told her, which was true.

"He keeps his filth outside our house." She sounded so awkward that I knew this was about sex.

"You don't have to tell me."

"Yes, I do, or I'm going to burst." She took a deep breath. "Whores," she said, the word a near whistle. "There, now you know. He spends his money on their privates. A paper boy, and that's where the money goes."

"How much does a paper boy make?" I said, but instead of answering she began to cry.

I didn't mind her not saying. I was sure a paperboy made next to nothing. What I really wanted to know was how much a whore charged, how many days Ray had to deliver to pay for one.

Like Ray expected, the park robberies disappeared from the news after two days. He waited another week before he drove into the park to sniff around for stakeouts, and then he waited two days more before he said, "By now the cops think the bandit was just passing through. We need to do this before Labor Day when the traffic starts to thin."

"No," I said. "I've had enough." I felt committed. I hadn't even smoked a cigarette for two days.

"Hard to get, huh? You took that stash of bills after acting the saint. Like some cunt saying no until you're balls deep in her."

I pulled myself up straighter and said, "Your whores always do whatever you want, don't they?"

I thought Ray would look embarrassed or angry, but his voice stayed even. "You want to spend some of that loot to find out?"

"No."

"Maybe you're wishing you could charm some young thing. You're going to be in ninth grade. All you'll get is something to imagine from while you play with yourself."

"Last time," I said then. "For absolutely sure, and anyway, school's starting, and I won't be around when Mom's out working."

"There you go," Ray said. "We'll reconsider on everything when the time comes."

So I went, driving slow after I took the wheel in the first overlook, looking like I was wishing for deer or bears to wander out along the road. Ray smoked and said nothing, his window closed, I thought, to punish me for acting like a sissy. There was just one car in the lot, perfect for what we were up to. Ray put on his sunglasses and ball cap and got out without saying a word, dropped his stub and stepped on it before he hiked into the woods in his Bermuda's and golf shirt.

I wound down Ray's window and lit the cigarette I'd stashed under the seat, telling myself I was creating a reason to be sitting in a parked car. I didn't want to get out like I had the first time and show myself as a kid who had no business driving. When I finished, I let a few more minutes pass before I drove back to the meet spot, but Ray wasn't in sight, and every time a car passed I thought it was a park ranger or an unmarked police car.

I started thinking of how stupid it was to go back to the same trail and all that. I pulled out and drove a mile, turned around and drove back, but Ray still wasn't there. I told myself I was being smart, smarter than Ray at least, and when I turned again, facing the right direction to leave the park, I checked my mirror and saw nothing behind me so I could go really slow, school zone slow, I saw a bear slow, until, from a quarter mile away I could see Ray standing on the shoulder.

With the late August sun nearly behind me, I thought Ray might not be able to make me out for sure, and I pulled off to the side and stopped like I could be the police. I saw him light up, turn, and go back into the woods. I wanted him sweating in there, maybe scrambling up that narrow path like he was a lost tourist, his eyes off the road. When I thought he was deep enough, I drove up to the meet spot and parked like I was just late. It took him a minute to come out, so I was pretty sure he didn't see it was me sitting back up the road.

"Jesus Christ, where were you?" he said, flicking his cigarette onto the road.

"There was a car parked up there," I said. "I thought this place might be staked out."

"I saw it," Ray said. "Just a minute ago. I was waiting for it to pass." He looked back. "It's gone," he said, "but I never saw nothing go by."

"It u-turned. It went by me going the other way. I was worried whoever was in it might be wondering what I was doing pulled off the road up a ways."

Ray looked puzzled, like he was working out the scenario. He laughed then, short and air-filled, like he'd made up his mind that I was somebody who understood so little about the science of experience that I could believe in heaven.

"Step on it," he finally said. "Christ. I thought two weeks would put them to sleep about this." I drove right at the speed limit for a minute, Ray glancing around like he thought the trees were full of eyes. "$78," he said then. "I had time to count it back in there. I was ready to hide it and just walk out clean as a whistle. It's practically nothing that guy had on him."

"You keep it all," I said. "You earned it."

"I should have kept that card I saw in that fellow's wallet, you know, what some people have nowadays to buy things without handing over their money."

"I think a lot of people have credit cards," I said, though I had no way of knowing that for sure.

I slowed when I saw the first overlook, but Ray said, "Keep going." He was breathing hard. "I should burn that little box we live in and let the insurance company buy us a new one." He seemed to be talking to himself now, making plans he'd never put into any kind of motion. He'd gone out and followed through on one crazy idea, and here we were leaving the park with $78 and him all panicked about the police knocking on our door. "Get ourselves a place where the water don't stink to high heaven, right?" he finally said.

"Sure," I said.

"You damn betcha," he said, but I knew Ray was scared. Adult scared, like what he was afraid of was here to stay, and I understood then that Ray had done a lot of talking to himself to come up with the robbery plan, that he'd coached himself up the way Mr. Glass, back in Hagerstown, got our junior high basketball team to run out onto the court believing we were better than we were, and now he could see he was losing this particular game.

"Your Momma never knows about any of this," he said then. "Understand?"

"I get it," I said, suddenly happy I had something Ray had to depend upon.

"I love your mother. Don't you forget that. She told me all about giving you the lowdown, but that other stuff is just entertainment, like going to a ball game. Understand?"

"I think so."

"You will. Just wait half a lifetime and it'll come to you."

Ray, for once, didn't light a cigarette. It seemed like he'd forgotten his habit because he wasn't driving on the way out of the park like he always did, out of sync with who he was. Like he's a boy, I thought, and then dismissed it when he grabbed my thigh hard and hissed, "You keep your damn eyes on the road. No fuckups allowed."

I didn't say anything then. We were out of the park, and I was still behind the wheel. Ray said, "Take us home, you know the way," and I did, though I was sweating so much I thought if I had to turn the wheel hard my hands would slip off and we'd end up going straight ahead until we ran into something that wouldn't budge.

GUN COMFORT

———

A thousand times by now Cassidy's daddy had told her, "You live out here, gun comfort come automatic as breathing." Sometimes he made it end with "as your beating heart," but she believed it either way. A gun in her hands was second nature.

Her Uncle Walt, who'd put himself through the state college to be a teacher, said, "You take to a gun early, it's like growing up knowing a second language."

"And he's never forgot hisself," her daddy said, as if a brother could turn uppity and leave like a wife. Though mostly, she thought, it was Daddy wanting to be alone and answering to nobody, like he'd tried the world's ordinary ways and decided they weren't meant for him. She already could feel him waiting for her to leave in another year after she graduated from high school.

It didn't hardly matter, she wanted to tell him. He wasn't going to be by himself, not with the cell phone tower already close by, the rumors of the big tire burner plant getting built less than a mile away, and the gas drillers all the time looking to buy somebody out. He should be fretting about all that, not the little problem of the detour sending traffic past their house night and day while the bridge along County Road 213 was under repair. Cars and trucks times ten, according to Daddy when he cursed them for speeding.

And what was worse, strangers now, near to all of them going by. "Who knows what those people do with themselves," he'd say, standing at the front window however long it took to smoke one of his generic cigarettes down, using an empty Blue Ribbon bottle for the ash. It was how he paced his drinking and smoking, one then the other, then on to the next pair, maybe twenty minutes a cycle, sometimes less when he got going on something with nothing else to do because once it was dark and outside work was shut off, he was set, most nights, on drinking himself to sleep. He didn't read or watch television or even listen to the tiny clock radio that never played except for the ten seconds, every morning in the dark, it took for him to shuffle to the kitchen and find the button to shut off the talk radio station he had on at nine out of ten on the volume control. If she was anywhere nearby while he opened the refrigerator for a fresh beer, he'd tell her she should keep an eye out when she had the chance because with more than a hundred cars coming by every hour of the day and night, hardly a handful carrying any kind of neighbor, there was trouble so close you could smell it.

Lately, with the weather warm, he'd taken to leaving the window behind after two Blue Ribbons to sit on the porch, like he was riding shotgun on a stagecoach, like their house was a target for bandits who thought he had treasure of some sort, even though there wasn't anything about the property or the house that suggested that could be true,

When she sometimes joined him, bringing him a fresh bottle like it was a ticket to the other porch chair, he'd say something like "They're all married to their gadgets and things. Next thing you know, we'll be hearing all those whistles and bells going off right in our ears and then we're in for it."

"They can't see anything they'd want here," she'd said that time.

"Some of them want everything, what we have included," he'd said, and she'd known he'd meant her.

His other subject was work.

"You going to live on your own, you best be ready for it," he reminded her about keeping a steady job every time he thought she had "that look." Like seventeen was old maid's age. Like she didn't have a year of high school to finish plus this summer season of work at the Tasty Creem. Or like he thought she was playing around in some boy's car on her breaks.

"Your Momma had your brother Ricky at eighteen and Rafe at

nineteen," he said in June when her job turned full time. Her brothers were in the service, safe from becoming daddies, signing on together right after Rafe graduated from high school, but Cassidy could see him counting backwards until he was right beside her age. And then, as if she'd asked him the details of what he was remembering, he left those years behind. "You snuck up on us when she'd turned twenty-five, and she skedaddled at thirty."

What Cassidy repeated was "You've never even come to the TC to take a look," but there was nothing on the porch for her to do but listen and think about how, in the morning, she'd be on her way to work at ten o'clock and on her way home at six to make dinner for him while he worked outside or worse, when it rained, sat in the kitchen and watched her.

She had to ride her bike the two miles. The shoulder was narrow and rutted, so she rode on the asphalt surface, facing traffic like she used to when she walked. It didn't make sense to have her back turned to the traffic that might hit her, no matter what the bike safety people said, and now, because of the traffic, she had to keep a look out the whole way instead of just the last half mile. But what she hated most was having to ride the bike in the tan and brown uniform that made her feel ugly. "Don't you worry about ugly," Daddy had said the one time she'd brought it up, "a thing like that don't stop imagination."

Selling dessert had sounded like fun once upon a time when she was fourteen and could only work short shifts because of her age, but by her second summer, she dreamed about the soft ice cream machine, waking up at two a.m. and thinking it was already time to fill it, or worse, to clean it. Soon enough it was time to empty that goop into sugar cones and the big waffle ones that cost extra. The rest of the day was a few hot dogs, bags of chips, and being bored. There was a gallon jar that had once held pickle slices on the counter for tips. Boys didn't tip anyone except Sarah Kantz, but men almost always at least tossed their change in the jar, especially if she flirted. Fathers with children waiting at a table or even just hovering behind them would smile and make a show of it if they folded a dollar or two and pushed it through the slot.

She wondered at that, because she'd never considered herself what her Daddy called "a looker," only one boyfriend in all her years and just a few months of that and never alone for more than a few minutes, Daddy reminding her all this summer, "I wish to hell you had one over here to keep company sometimes, a boy around the house discourages the rest from their ideas. Your Uncle Walt sees girls like you every day. He tells me how the men go on and on about them, what they imagine those girls are asking for what with all their teasing talk."

When she thought about Uncle Walt claiming he knew what was in the minds of teachers way older than Daddy, she remembered the men who sometimes ordered ice cream and stared at her while she worked their chocolate or vanilla or half and half into a cone. At school she knew which girls the boys had eyes for, but at Tasty Creem, even when she worked the counter with Sarah Kantz, she felt eyes touching her.

"That's cause they're all pigs," Sarah said. Back in May she'd shown Cassidy the bruises her daddy had made on her fleshy upper arms where she'd said he'd gripped to shake some sense into her. She'd come to school a week later with the traces of a slap left on her face.

Cassidy had told Sarah her daddy had never touched her, no matter the best moments or the worst. "Cassidy Heimbach, you are the world's worst liar," Sarah had said, and when Cassidy shook her head, Sarah had stroked her hair with her fingers and said, "Next you'll tell me you never touched yourself."

"Your pop is somebody who likes to be alone so everything's his way," Uncle Walt said. "He'll never be happy until you're out of the house, too."

"That's a terrible thing to say."

"That doesn't mean he doesn't love you, sweetheart. He just loves his all-alone more."

"He's never cooked or cleaned. He made the boys when I was little, and now he has me."

"Your cleaning up after him be damned, there's just the getting used to is all."

When her brothers were still at home, they and her daddy left their dishes on the table after she cooked for them. "It's all yours in here from now on," he'd said when she'd turned ten. "You're the woman of the house." Her daddy had bought a dishwasher for her thirteenth birthday.

"There she sits," he'd said, like it was a prize for cooking for three years by then, her brothers clapping as if she'd sung or danced.

Once, when she was sick the past February, he'd opened a can of baked beans and eaten them cold. She'd found the can in the garbage. For all she knew, he'd licked it clean and was proud of saving her the work.

In the morning, even in summer, Daddy would wake her and tell her coffee would be ready in five minutes. He'd come back with two cups, expecting her to have used the bathroom and "be decent." "I don't have all day," he'd say, or "While it's hot," until she took the cup and began to sip.

"Can't have you sleep through work," he would add as if that was any sort of explanation. As if he was ashamed of saying what he meant, that he wanted her awake and alert and on her feet if anything that might happen in a house by herself began to unspool like an old movie reel. It wasn't about getting to work on time; it was about her being safe from things he couldn't say out loud.

"You leave the house, you have a place to go," he said. Work, he meant. And going outside meant she was on the way to it. Straight there, no dilly-dally. Not anywhere that he called "just out the door." Not the woods where her brothers spent all their free time growing up, where she watched them run off to like they were in a story as soon as they disappeared. Not, at least, until she thought there might only be the choice between going crazy and going into the woods.

Awake with the sun barely up and Daddy gone, she was left with hours that didn't amount to anything but time. She hated those hours between Daddy leaving and when she had to ride her bike to work. She needed voices, and the television, without cable since her brothers had gone, didn't show anything but two fuzzy channels and the old movies Daddy had bought when the video store was going out of business five years ago and he brought home twenty of them for twenty dollars. "Enough to last forever," he'd said, not hardly accurate, but what she watched sometimes were the ones on television, their stories being told by actors and actresses who must be older than even Daddy by a long shot.

The people in those old movies were, after all, doing things before she was born, when she was absent. She watched the black and white ones that

were shown early in the day and tried to imagine how the world worked
without her, their hair and makeup and clothes before Daddy was born,
too. When she asked him what his favorite movies were, he told her he
hadn't gone to one "since your mother dragged me."

"How about TV shows?" she asked.

"There wasn't time for television when I was growing up, and then
came all of you kids and there wasn't any time for it being a man."

A week ago, when he'd started in on the way time was different for
men and women, she'd said that couldn't be true, and he'd opened the
closet in his room and stepped back like a game show host presenting a
prize. "Look at all this she had time for. Your momma left half a closet-
full of things because she had more than she'd ever need, and here they
all sit forever maybe."

"They don't belong to me," she said, and then waited for him to go
on about shopping and television being like life on another planet, but
he kept looking at the clothes as if he was thinking hard on something.

"Your momma had her eye all the time on wearing what turned a
man's head."

Or yours, Cassidy wanted to say and settled on, "We're not scavengers.
We don't live up some hillbilly hollow with no running water or electricity.
There's paved road right outside our front door."

"Most days I wish the hell we was."

"It's four miles to Taylorville."

"It's not the same as when it had to be walked."

"Nothing is, Daddy, not even you."

"This is where your momma picked to live," he said. "Somewhere
between a farm and a packed-tight place."

She knew the house was planted on a six-acre plot, but to look at it
wouldn't make anybody see but an acre, tops, the rest spreading into the
field behind the house, what Daddy mowed less of each summer, and less
often on top of that, the rest going to sumac and locust and all sorts of
brambles that were nearly into the back yard now.

All they had that looked like room was the raggedy, weed-choked
lawn that her brothers had mowed with the small tractor and the twenty-
yard setback from the road with its long gravel driveway to plow in the
winter and repair every spring. But last winter Daddy had parked down

by the mailbox when it snowed, leaving the driveway untouched and slogging up to the house like someone who'd broken down on the road and needed help. Mornings and afternoon she'd tried to step in his footprints going and coming to where the school bus picked her up, the driveway untouched in a way that shamed her.

"Your momma thought she'd garden flowers and such all around and found out it was work." There were still patches of iris and hostas scattered in the field, roses and mums close by the house, and the lamb's ear and coleus that had spread into the lawn like a bad case of acne.

Except for the large picture window in the living room, the windows in the house were small and cross-hatched into smaller sections of glass, the kind, she'd said once, that nobody could get out through in case of a fire that blocked the doors. "Why you all of a sudden worried about fire? There's just the two of us. You know what happens when you have big glass in the windows like the one we have out front. You get yourself a slew of dead birds from them breaking their necks on it. Just the one so we don't hardly get them dead in our yard and both of us standing here not all burnt up."

"I hear them hit sometimes, but I never see them dead."

"I get after them, save you the looking." He turned and pointed. "You see that tower for everybody's damn phone? That's how you hunt birds without lifting a finger." The nearest tower was part of the Kratzer farm, twenty acres of corn and a plot of vegetables, but the old man had sold off an acre to the phone people five years before. "You wait for a foggy night and follow me in the morning."

When that foggy night had come on a Thursday, he'd told her to throw on whatever was handy and walked her out first thing Friday morning to show her twenty-six dead birds, all the same. "All these beauties got led right to slaughter. These monsters are serial killers for things that fly."

"You can't stop what everybody wants," she said. Daddy nodded like he agreed for once, but his lips set tight, and she could hear the suck of air as he inhaled through his half-clogged nose as if he was inflating himself. "I feel sorry for you having all this nonsense to live with," he said. He tilted his head slightly as if he was reluctant to give any more acknowledgment to the nearby towers.

She wanted to tell him the tower was twice as ugly when you didn't have a phone to carry around. That if those towers were going to be planted everywhere, you oughtn't be left out of their magic. "So there it is," he said. "The half of you listening without both ears." She felt his eyes on her chest. "Ready yourself up like you know how the world thinks because every day there's more shit spreading every whichawhere." He stared at her then until she tugged her blouse together.

He'd walked off straight to the car and driven to work, and before she showered, she opened her blouse and slid her jeans to the floor before she lay back on her bed, imagining a boy's hands sliding up her thighs to where she began to touch herself, inserting one finger, then two, until she gasped with joy.

Afterwards, she was afraid it might be strange that it took her only a few minutes to get off. And lately she wondered if Sarah Kantz enjoyed herself as often as she did, but sometimes she just remembered Daddy telling her that dreaming during the day was cursing yourself.

In July, before she even ate breakfast, she walked into the woods for the first time and came across two chairs, one overturned as if the owner had walked away angry, and farther along, a Phillies shirt and pink socks soaked and faintly rotten as if they'd wintered there, and she believed, when the shirt hung her size against her chest, that its wearer had screamed the summer before, that a girl missing a hundred miles from the state game preserve could be found nearby if she, Cassidy, had the courage to search instead of returning to those chairs and righting the fallen to sit and listen like a schoolgirl for a calamity of footsteps as if someone would return, months later, to where his crime had ended, driving for hours to retrieve those clothes.

She set that chair up, sat down on it, and waited like she expected that somebody until she began to shiver and the trees turned flint-colored, her Daddy's favorite shade. He was all the time telling her how there are more plants than people, how it was intended by God. She touched a rock at her feet, but in the early morning, it felt cold and damp. Nothing here was like the road with its gradual curves, with its straight lines, everything able to be measured.

A few minutes later, on the way out of the trees, she stopped twice, listening for footsteps, but each time she thought she heard the sloshing of her heart murmur, the little squishy sound the doctor had said she'd grow out of, but she hadn't been to the doctors for six years.

At Tasty Creem the next day, Uncle Walt brought her Taco Bell. "You're all the time saying you only get the hot dogs and the cones and those god-awful slushy things."

"There's microwave," she said. "And we chip in sometimes, but for sure, I don't want to see another hot dog for a while."

"Your dad wants me to come shoot with him Saturday. He thinks I'm turning into a town boy."

"He has his ways of looking out for people."

"Your dad thinks a man without a gun in his house is a man who looks and wishes more than he does. Hah!"

Cassidy smiled like she always did when Uncle Walt added "Hah!" at the end of his opinions that had a hint of sex in them. Like he meant her to know he was just being funny, that right then he wasn't explaining exactly how small-minded his brother was, but it sounded like a period to her, not an exclamation point. "That's a lot of lookers," she finally said.

"Half the men I work with. Your dad wouldn't do well among them."

"I thought every man looked and wished, to hear Daddy tell it."

"He's only right five times out of ten, but that there's plenty of miserable men working themselves into a fret. Hah!"

When she didn't answer, squinting at him the way she'd seen teachers look at boys who hadn't done their homework, he laughed. "Stupid, right?" he said. "Don't tell your dad I said so."

She heard Sarah laughing at something a boy at the counter was saying. Uncle Walt smiled. "Who you know that likes you serving him?"

"Nobody."

"That can't be true."

"I don't mind," she said.

"I know you know better than that. Hah!" When she didn't smile, he added, "Just you wait," and after he left, she imagined herself living in her daddy's house alone, a woman in her forties, as old as daddy now, who would be dead by then, she thought, and her brothers with teenage sons and daughters living somewhere far away. "Impossible," she said aloud, and thought she sounded like a crazy person.

Before her brothers left, when they called her into their room, Cassidy had been excited. A surprise goodbye present, she'd thought, something handed down like the cable bill paid for a year in advance, because for weeks they'd been teasing her about how, twelve days after they boarded the bus, the television would turn to snow. "What?" she'd said, the two of them grinning. "Come on, what?"

They'd showed her their porn magazines. "We know you've been looking," they said. But she hadn't been. She hadn't even known they had those magazines, but they were so sure she'd been peeking, she knew it had to be her Daddy doing the looking.

That day, she'd looked at the pictures of the naked women, wondering which of them excited her brothers most. What she'd done, at last, was examine the expressions on the faces of the men and women, and she'd shuddered when none of them looked like they cared about anyone else in the picture. No matter what they said, calling her inside, she hadn't gone back in their room until they were gone to the army for a month.

Now, when she looked for those magazines, they were gone from any place in that room where somebody would hide anything larger than a postcard, and was left without knowing whether her brothers had burned them all or whether her Daddy had moved them to his own secret location, a place she didn't want to find.

For a whole week she went into the woods and sat on the same chair until she could feel herself growing so excited she hurried to her room to undress and lie naked on her bed. Afterward, each time, she told herself she wouldn't go back in the woods, but all she did differently, by the third day, was lie on one of her brothers' beds, first Ricky's and the next day Rafe's, putting the face of a boy from school on her memory of each brother's body.

Pushing herself up from Rafe's bed, she remembered Uncle Walt telling her once, "You'll know when you're in love. You'll give up your secrets nobody else will ever know." She'd nodded then, polite, but now she shuddered, imagining the words.

Sarah Kantz told her all week she looked pasty. "You know," she said, "like you're sick. Nobody looks pasty in the summer except old people."

The next Monday, the weather turning hot even at eight o'clock, she lay out in her two-piece bathing suit, choosing something besides the chair in the woods.

All those cars with somebody's eyes inside. What they did after she lay out three days in a row was tell her how many would never stop. She wanted to tell her daddy that nobody noticed, not even a horn blowing. She'd bet nobody would remember even passing by, even after using the detour for weeks. And nobody would even remember her on her bike in her stupid, ugly uniform.

The third morning, when the sun moved behind a set of thunderheads, Cassidy walked through the house in her bathing suit looking at photographs. There were dozens of photos of her in frames and albums. She smiled when she saw that in three of them she was wearing a bathing suit. But it was the most recent one, from last summer, where she was wearing the bikini she'd been wearing three straight mornings, her breasts in the picture lifted by the bra, and she remembered being surprised by the camera, that the surprise made her look like a stranger, like a girl her father might be looking at, imagining. "See there," her daddy had said when he'd first set the picture out. "See how somebody could see you wrong?" as much as he could get out of his mouth except, a minute later, like he'd expected her to be standing there waiting, "I don't ever want you outside like that."

"Like what?" she'd said. "Like what?"

And he'd managed, "Half naked."

"Like every girl I know," she'd said.

"You cover yourself before you leave your room when I'm gone. You don't flounce around just because nobody's around."

"Nobody means empty."

"There's never empty," he'd said then. "Not when you're showing yourself off."

Like always, Uncle Walt had his cooler in the truck when he parked it on the back grass the next Sunday. The only mystery about it was how many cans of beer he had on ice and how many he'd already slugged down before he arrived so he could slow down to match her daddy's pace and still have that head start to keep him. It made no sense at all. Daddy was so set on safety, and yet they finished one after the other. "You can drop the sour face," Daddy said. "When our six packs are gone, we stop."

She kept her mouth set exactly the same, counting to ten before she said, "Until you're back on the porch."

"Hah!" Uncle Walt said, starting with the period before he added, "You're getting sassy as that hottie Carrie Bradshaw."

Her Daddy snorted like he'd just heard a fart. "I know who that is," she said. "Just cause we can't see her here on our TV doesn't mean I don't know. Anyway, that's not who she really is."

"Make believe," Daddy said, looking at Cassidy. "The TV keeps him wishing."

"It's not from watching," Uncle Walt said. "It's teaching teenagers keeps you in the know. And it's the girls who tell me, so there you are." He headed for the cooler.

"Ten years ago by the sound of it," Cassidy called after him, and her daddy laughed out loud.

"Here," he said, handing her his rifle, "show Walt how it's done."

Cassidy hesitated. Not since teaching her to shoot when she was twelve had Daddy put one of his rifles in her hands. A weekend he'd spent with her, and on Monday morning, at breakfast, he'd given her a Remington 700 just like the ones he'd given to her brothers when they'd turned ten. Like always, it was loaded right now, one bullet in the chamber, but locked above her bed just like the two still displayed in her brothers' room.

"The clip's full," Daddy said. Cassidy thought about saying she wasn't used to the Savage 99, her daddy's favorite that he'd had forever, but she knew not to make an excuse. She swung it up and readied herself.

"A girl looks so sexy when she's shooting," Uncle Walt said.

"That's no kind of talk," Daddy said, but Uncle Walt didn't apologize and he didn't crack open his fresh beer or hand its partner to Daddy.

"The truth is always the right talk," he said, and she felt her daddy's eyes on her as if Uncle Walt had given him permission to just outright stare like some kind of contest judge.

"All the time with the fear of God," Daddy said slowly, like he was trying to make the words out on a page.

"Sunday sermons," Uncle Walt said.

"And all week long," Daddy said. "There's worse than God to fear."

She steadied and squeezed and a jelly jar a hundred feet away on the stone wall exploded. Walt whooped like she'd done something hard. She shot again, shattering another. "That's enough," Daddy said.

"Your pop can't let go of his antique for more than a minute," Uncle Walt said. "They haven't made a new one of those since when you were born."

"A gun proper cared for lasts forever," Daddy said.

"Truth in that," Walt said, "but a girl shoots like that ought to have herself a beer. Hah!"

"A man old enough to have hisself grandkids ought to know when he talks too much."

Walt whistled. "Listen to Warren the proud poppa."

"Exactly," Daddy said. "Do that."

"All right then. I know my place, but it's a powerful thing to watch a girl handle a gun like that."

After they ate the hamburgers she fried up for the two of them, Uncle Walt hugged her and whispered, "Remember—what you see," before he drove off in his truck, but Daddy kept his eyes on it as if he intended to follow it the six miles to Uncle Walt's apartment. "He keeps his learning to hisself, that's for sure," he said, still watching the empty road.

"It's just the beer talking," Cassidy said.

Daddy spit off the porch. "Walt teach you that there bit of wisdom?"

"He just talks."

"In a circle how he goes."

"No different than other teachers."

"Then they should be looking to hire more women at that school."

"Uncle Walt has a girlfriend, Daddy. Miss Davis. She's as old as he is, the way you like it."

"The way it's s'pose to be." He tapped his empty bottle of Blue Ribbon, the one he'd pulled from the refrigerator and sipped while he was eating, against the porch railing. "Some Sunday Walt can play house with Miss Davis and we'll shoot, just the two of us, and leave the drinking until after."

The next morning, the coffee sounding its alarm as always, she had to pee after Daddy left. When the flushing stopped, she was left looking at herself in the mirror, a minute, no more. Her shift was hours away, and already excited, she came down the hall in her nightgown, wanting to lie down on one of her brothers' beds, undress completely. And then she listened hard because she thought she heard the slow rhythm of careful footsteps downstairs.

When the footsteps stopped, she glanced over the railing to make sure she wasn't imagining. A man was standing at the base of the stairs, one foot on the first step as if testing it to see if it would squeak. He didn't have anything in his hands that made him look like a thief, and so she knew he had come for her. Someone, maybe, who'd watched her in the yard, who'd learned when her Daddy left every weekday morning. He looked young, maybe not even thirty. Just a ball cap pulled low so she couldn't make out his face as he started up the stairs.

There was time to back up to her room while those footsteps took the stairs slowly. Whoever it was, she thought, expected her, a high school girl, to be sleeping at six a.m. He figured her to be in her room, that maybe he could watch her for a while lying in her bed in her flimsy summer nightgown. He didn't know her daddy brought her coffee before he left, that he drank his second cup with her in the half-light to make sure she was up, all last summer and now this with her brothers gone, no argument from her that he would abide.

She stepped into her room and closed the door before she lifted the rifle from its rack. She had it down in a second. She waited. The man took his time, maybe ten seconds, before the knob turned and he stepped through the doorway, a ski mask over his face now, and stopped. She felt his eyes on her nearly bare thighs, and then she brought the gun up and his head jerked as he stiffened. A detour man, she thought, like Daddy expects, or somebody from the Tasty Creem or even some teacher friend of Uncle Walt. Because up close, she noticed the would-be attacker had the soft stomach of an older man.

She let the safety off so he could hear. His eyes went to the gun rack and back to her hands. He was deciding, she knew, whether she was someone who could fire a gun at a man. He said nothing, and neither did she. The room was in full sunlight now, the drapes open the way Daddy always left them year-round when he said goodbye. "Fuck you, bitch," the man finally said, but he took a step back. "Fucking cunt," he said, and he retreated into the hall and she listened with the gun still pointing until she heard him on the stairs. She went to the window then and watched him walk to the car he'd parked out front, facing away from the house. The car was at the road before she thought to look at the license plate.

She kept the gun with her as she went down the stairs. She saw that a screen had been popped out. It was propped, slightly bowed, against the dining room wall. They didn't have air conditioning, the windows open day and night all summer except during thunderstorms.

Still in her negligee, she carried the rifle into the back yard, walked to where Daddy had started that stone wall years ago, getting it waist-high for fifty feet before it stopped. She brought along two of his beer bottles, both of them full, and placed them there, the slippers she'd pulled on before coming downstairs crunching the crust of broken glass. She backed up and stood ten feet away, the distance to that flabby man in the ball cap and ski mask, and fired, exploding one bottle and then the other, beer spraying in a quick arc.

She stood in that spot for a minute, her eyes scanning the edge of the woods. She had all day to decide whether she would tell Daddy, but she knew for sure she wasn't calling the police, standing in her room in her tan and brown Tasty Creem uniform while they inspected her weapon and asked her to hold it just the same as she was telling them she had—as if that were some sort of proof her story was true.

She wanted to call Sarah and tell this story so it would do some good maybe, but it was so early, not even seven yet, that a ringing phone wouldn't set well in anybody's house. She knew Sarah's house didn't have any guns inside, and then it didn't seem as if it would do a bit of good to tell her anything.

The urge passed. She hurried into the house and locked the door behind her. She checked every ground floor window. Back in her room, she dressed quickly in her uniform without taking a shower. As alert and focused as she'd ever been firing the rifle, she felt just as tired now. Exhausted. As if she'd worked an eight-hour shift at the Tasty Creem from right after school to eleven at night the way she had in April and May when customers, on those first hot days, stood in line for cones and sundaes and shakes. In a month, when school began, she'd feel that way every Monday, Tuesday, and Wednesday until the place shut down for winter.

If she told him, Daddy would ask, "Were you dressed?" and he would know she was lying. He'd look at her body like it belonged to him. "What did I tell you?" he'd say, and she'd hate him for it.

Maybe it was enough to have lived through this, to think that she was glad the man had entered the house, that he looked as soft as Mr. Hartman, the old biology teacher who had just retired. Now she knew one more thing about herself. She began to clean the gun, plenty of time to do it right. She had another year to live with Daddy, not too long to keep one more thing to herself.

WHAT WAS GOOD FOR YOU

———

From November to March, as soon as you and your older sister Vanessa climbed the stairs and entered your Grandma Ruth's bedroom, you could always see your breath. Through the next door was Aunt Sophia's bedroom, where it was even colder. Gradually getting warm in Aunt Sophia's bed under a thick down comforter, that's where the two of you slept every other Friday night while your mother took what she called her holiday.

Years and years ago now, when you both put your pajamas on downstairs where the ancient furnace heated the three high-ceilinged rooms, your clothes were stacked by the living room door, Vanessa's on one side, yours on the other. In the morning, you'd dress right there in the clothes you'd worn the day before, handing your pajamas to Grandma Ruth, who put them in a shopping bag from the A&P "for next time."

"Your mother loves you," Grandma Ruth would say every time your mother drove up after breakfast. "She's always here at nine on the dot."

You were ten years old, and on those Saturdays your mother always had laundry in three baskets on the back seat, sheets and towels and a week of clothes folded and stacked in each because, she said, "It needed to be done first thing before the Laundromat got crowded." On the other Saturdays, you had hot dogs or a hamburger at the diner next door to the Laundromat while everything tumbled in the dryer.

Six months ago, when you'd found a comb under a chair, your mother had said, "Where did that come from?" and thrown it into a wastebasket. Three months ago, when you'd discovered a pair of dark socks under your mother's bed, Vanessa had said, "Put those back and shut up about it" when you showed her.

Your mother had two jobs because your father, according to Aunt Sophia, was "wherever the grass is greener." She sat in the kitchen and drank coffee for an hour with Grandma Ruth while Aunt Sophia kept busy running the vacuum, dusting the furniture, and shooing you ahead of her work if you weren't in a chair reading a book.

When it came time to tend the furnace, she had you gather up the three wastebaskets and dump all the paper, wrappers, and tissues into one to throw into the fire. While you waited with the empty basket, she shoveled coal inside the furnace, sometimes hauling buckets of ashes away, her thick arms straining. The coal was shiny but dusty, so strange that you still loved to touch it, turning your fingers black. Nobody you knew had a coal furnace.

For the past two years, each time you handed Aunt Sophia the wastebasket after she opened the furnace's heavy iron door, she said, "Don't get too close now and end up a pile of cinders like Melvin Ruckdaschel."

Melvin Ruckdaschel had been a boy in your class until he'd burned up in third grade. He'd lit a candle in his room and fallen asleep. Nobody else had been home. "Who leaves their boy like that?" Aunt Sophia said to your mother the day after the fire. "I bet they were out getting stewed, and they come home to that."

"I know you won't even think about matches," your mother said when you had started to cry. "Your Aunt Sophia talks like that because she loves you."

Two weeks ago, Aunt Sophia hadn't said a word about Melvin Ruckdaschel. Instead, she said, "Before you know it, you'll be eleven. That's when I started doing this." She looked you up and down as if she expected you to grow six months older right there in the cellar. "But first you have to stop that mouth breathing of yours. You sound like a dog."

Even though Aunt Sophia said not to, the first thing you did when you got into bed those Friday nights was pull the curtains apart on the window that was right where your knees reached when you were lying down. Aunt Sophia slept on the couch downstairs, so you could watch as long you tugged the curtain back exactly even. All Vanessa did was wrap the comforter around her and tell you to hurry up and look. You'd be shivering almost right away, but you had to peek because the house was built into a slope so steep the window looked out from the second floor exactly at street level with the alley behind the house.

Ten o'clock was bedtime on Fridays, but you always hoped to see a person outside, somebody who wouldn't know he was being watched through a window that stood right on the street like a door. Three years now, and all that had ever happened was a dog or a cat nosing around while Vanessa said, "Come on" and you pressed so close to that single pane of glass, it fogged up as you breathed like a dog.

Saturday morning, if Aunt Sophia noticed the curtains were out of place when she came upstairs to wake you, she'd say, "You'll leave them shut if you know what's good for you." For as long as you could remember, when you asked why, her answer was, "Somebody will see how little you are and break right through and grab you," but the last time she'd noticed the curtains were moved, Aunt Sophia had said, "The two of you have just about outgrown this bed."

One Friday near the end of January, the house across the alley, as always, had the television on. Mrs. Kordesich lived there. She and her husband, Aunt Sophia had told you, were drinkers, and Mr. Kordesich had died during the summer, falling down the stone steps from the alley to the street below Grandma Ruth's house, the ones you weren't allowed to go down unless you had one hand on the railing the whole way.

You didn't know who lived in any of the other houses along the alley Aunt Sophia called "Hell Street," but a blind man lived above Mrs. Kordesich. Whenever you checked to see if there were lights on in the blind man's upstairs room, it was always dark, but after dinner on Fridays, he sometimes sat in Grandma Ruth's kitchen, and he always touched you and Vanessa in order, he said, "to see you."

"Come closer," he said, laughing. "Let me get a good look at you."

You both stood right in front of him, and sometimes you still curled your fingers around the blind man's white cane and tried to see through his dark glasses. "You're getting so big," the blind man would say to you. "You're getting so beautiful," he'd say to Vanessa, his hands moving across her face and settling on her shoulders for a moment until he squeezed and let go.

"One of these days he'll take a tumble getting himself down here," Aunt Sophia would say after the blind man left, and Grandma Ruth would make a face.

That night you settled back to watch your breath until you fell asleep, but before fifteen minutes had passed, you heard a man's voice right beneath you in the kitchen. Vanessa was listening, too, because you both knew it was the Czar talking. The Czar was your grandfather, and he hadn't been at Grandma Ruth's on any Friday night you'd slept over since before Vanessa's eleventh birthday, nearly a year.

The Czar's voice was loud and so was Aunt Sophia's. Only Grandma Ruth's voice was soft. It sounded like the way she talked to you when you slept over sick, standing by the bed with castor oil or milk of magnesia or something else your mother didn't have in her medicine chest.

When the Czar got even louder, you moved closer to Vanessa, but she said, "You're not allowed to be up against me."

Twice Aunt Sophia said, "You old stew."

Both times the Czar answered, "Damn it to hell, Sophie," as if Grandma Ruth, who he'd been married to for the longest time, wasn't in the room.

Nobody ever said where the Czar lived now, but Aunt Sophia said he didn't drive since he'd wrecked his car with a snoot-full in him, so he had to be in town somewhere. You could have seen him and never known. If there were any pictures, they were locked away some place. He'd been kicked out when Vanessa was three and you were just beginning to walk. But Aunt Sophia had told you it was his voice coming up through the floor two or three times a year "when he forgets his Fridays."

Grandma Ruth always called him Nikki in her thick, German accent. Nobody called him Nikolai, his real name. He was the Czar because, Aunt Sophia said, "He thinks he rules the roost, expecting everybody to take care of him no matter what."

In February, after the last time you heard the Czar downstairs, Aunt Sophia had told your mother, "Somebody ought to give him what's coming to him."

"Now, now, Sophie," your mother had said.

"I can wish," Aunt Sophia had said, nudging the ship-in-a-bottle the Czar had won years ago in a fireman's raffle. It sat on the floor in the corner of the living room. "That old thing," Aunt Sophia always said. "It's so big I can't find room in the trash for it."

You thought it was wonderful. You'd looked at the bottle a hundred times trying to figure out how the ship had gotten inside. It was the *USS Constitution*, which you'd just learned was famous in history class.

"That was bought and paid for with your grandmother's money," Aunt Sophia said. "The old stew bought fifty tickets. It would have been a surprise if he hadn't won."

You'd been told what else the Czar had bought with the money he'd stolen from Aunt Sophia and then your mother and then her little sister Nina when she was eighteen, twenty one-dollar bills she kept hidden in her underwear drawer. After that, Aunt Sophia had locked him out. "The drink is a weakness," she said. "Stealing's a sin."

Now a glass shattered. "In the sink," Vanessa whispered, as if she could see with her ears like the blind man said he could.

Two hours earlier, Aunt Sophia had washed your hair in that sink because she said you never scrubbed hard enough. She'd told you to keep your eyes shut if you knew what was good for you. And then she'd pushed your head under the faucet for a hot rinse followed by a cold rinse, reminding you the whole time not to wriggle like you were still a baby in diapers.

"You're going on eleven years old," she said. "When your sister was five years old, she took care of her hair herself."

You wanted to hear if the Czar would punch the kitchen wall like he had three years ago, the holes covered by framed pictures of The Last Supper and the Titanic going down. It wasn't being fixed until he paid for it, some cold day in hell, according to Aunt Sophia. You and Vanessa were told not to look behind the paintings, but back then even Vanessa had tipped Jesus and the disciples to the side and pressed her face against the hole and found out that there was nothing to see like Aunt Sophia had said. She'd even picked you up so you could look without dragging a chair across the room, bringing Aunt Sophia in from the dining room where she played gin for an hour every Friday with Grandma Ruth. Afterwards, she made sure the picture was level so nobody would know.

You lay there waiting for what came next. The front door slammed just after you heard the Czar shout "Gott im himmel!" as if talking in Grandma Ruth's language would make a difference. After that Aunt Sophia's voice turned soft, so you knew the Czar was locked out.

"She took the broom to him," Vanessa said, and you remembered how Aunt Sophia had waved one at Mr. Kordesich during the summer before he died. "I'd take a broom to every last one of them if I could," Aunt Sophia had said after she'd chased him out of the yard.

"Your Aunt Sophia took the broom to all of the boys when we were growing up," your mother had said when you told her. She smiled like you were supposed to know what that meant.

Maybe that's how the glass had broken, you thought, Aunt Sophia sweeping a cup over the edge as she swung the broom at the Czar. Maybe he'd picked up a bottle and she'd batted it out of his hand. You knew never to ask. There had been arguing, and now there was silence.

You counted to yourself, trying to fall asleep, but at three hundred and eighty-seven, you heard a noise in the alley. "Don't," Vanessa said, but you knelt and opened the curtains. As soon as the breath from your mouth hit the glass, it steamed, and when you jerked your face back, you could see crystals forming around the edges.

You closed your mouth, trying not to fog the rest of the window, and then, leaning forward, you could still see the man who was pacing up and down in the snow, the alley never plowed because nobody drove a car into the dead end between Grandma Ruth's and Mrs. Kordesich's. Breathing through your nose made you feel like you were smothering. Finally, you sucked in enormous mouthfuls of air and blew them out on the window, but for a minute you could still make out the man slogging through snow half way to his knees, and you wondered if he could die out there on a night when Aunt Sophia had said it was cold enough to freeze shut the gates of hell. You wondered if Mrs. Kordesich was watching the man from her living room where the television flickered. You wondered what was on television at eleven o'clock.

Half way through his fourth lap between the houses, the man walked straight over and leaned down, his face six inches from the glass, but by then the glass was so covered with ice you couldn't make out the details of his face. You were so sure it was the Czar you wanted to scrape the ice away, but Vanessa said, "I bet he can hear you through the glass," and after another minute, "Close the curtains" just before you heard footsteps on the stairs.

You bunched the curtains together, and the Czar turned into a shadow. You lay back and pulled the comforter up to your chin, but you couldn't close your eyes. You faced the wall beside the window and knew, because of the small limp she tried to hide, it was Grandma Ruth you heard come out of the bathroom where the space heater glowed.

Grandma Ruth turned on her light and shut it off before you could hear her taking off the girdle she still wore even though your mother had thrown all of hers away when you were seven, declaring herself free and hugging you. Like it always did, the girdle snapped and made slithery noises before it was quiet. You listened for the sounds the rest of her clothes would make, but you didn't hear anything but Grandma Ruth's footsteps move away from her bed.

You heard the window open and knew the only reason for that would be to let the Czar climb inside. You smiled, glad that Grandma Ruth was saving him from the snow and cold.

You heard two shoes drop onto the wooden floor. You heard the bed creak and were sure the Czar was under the blankets, that he was getting warm.

You felt Vanessa stiffen and heard her draw her breath in like she was about to sink underwater. You counted almost to two hundred while you listened to the Czar breathing hard, panting like a dog until Grandma Ruth said "Nikki" one time and the sound disappeared.

"He was told," Vanessa whispered, but she was facing away from you, and you thought she hadn't meant to say anything aloud.

Now you lay quiet, your lips pressed together. You knew what was good for you, the wall so thin the Czar could put his fist right through, the Czar so close he could hear you if you took even one breath through your mouth.

A DAY LIKE ANY OTHER

———

He's up and gone.

There it is, a use for that old chestnut, the truth being that nobody, including me who should know, has any idea where Louis has gone to.

If the local television did one of those interactive polls, inviting viewers to log on and vote, Louis would no doubt be a declared suicide, what with his car, a Mini-Cooper S, so distinctive it was found within hours, being left behind near a river deep and wide.

Those voters would guess money trouble, a woman, criminal behavior, terminal illness, but aside from that last one, these are all reasons, good or bad, for disappearing rather than ending yourself.

Sick of it all is one thing. Dying for it is another.

I was the one who reported Louis missing. The same day, too early for getting any sort of action about the disappearance of an adult. The police were sluggish. I could hear their boredom surrounding me at the station where I'd gone in person.

"He called," I said. "From the road. Said he'd be home in three hours."

The policeman checked my hand for a ring. Eyed me like I was telling this story from a bar stool. Deciding what it was about my body that had me living with a successful man twenty years older than I was.

He suggested car trouble. Something work related. The cell phone gone dead. A chance meeting. I could hear "affair" in his tone, already sorting out what to call the situation when a man was unfaithful to a woman with whom he was being unfaithful to his wife.

Poetic justice. The phrase settled between us like a spider spooling down from the ceiling. He didn't care that Louis had lived with me for nearly three years, that Louis' divorce was so far down the pipeline that his version of the scenario was obsolete. "These things usually resolve themselves," he concluded.

"Pardon me?" I said.

"The odds are with you is all I'm saying."

He looked at my hand again, the sort of poker player who'd check his hole cards after the flop, giving away the possibilities of his hand. "How long does it take before the odds begin to shift?" I said.

"Forty-eight hours," he said at once, like an actuary with a spread sheet full of statistics, numbers for a test he'd taken so he could answer as if something like that could be measured.

I saw that cop's face on television the next day. He was standing beside Louis' car like a salesman. Six hours after I'd reported Louis missing, his car had been spotted parked outside a row of specialty shops in the town from which Louis had said he was calling. A local patrolman had phoned in the license when the lot emptied. "There's never a car in there after 10 o'clock," he'd said.

Those specialty shops are near the river. Nobody remembered Louis being in any of the stores. "He carried a laptop everywhere," I said to the reporter who'd showed up at my door that morning. "It wasn't in the car."

"So?" was what I heard in the silence.

"You don't jump into the river with your laptop," I added.

The reporter kept professionally quiet, but her lips pursed for a moment, and I could hear Louis explaining "tells" while we watched the Texas Hold 'Em championship together. This one let me know she saw Louis hurling his computer into the water and following close behind it, and I had to admit she got me thinking about what it was I could leave somewhere if I disappeared.

But listen.

Louis had walked into the sporting goods store where I worked in the shoe section wearing a referee's shirt. The manager didn't even pretend when he hired me. "Men love women in uniforms," he said. I was thirty-one years old, but men, he assured me, would take me for twenty-five.

Louis was busy buying golf shoes, the kind with plastic spikes on the bottom. He wanted to hear how they looked on him, as if their style and colors mattered more than fit and comfort. It put me off at first, him walking the aisles, shifting his weight in three different sizes but not even looking in the mirror until he heard my opinion. "You pick," he said at last, and I chose the better looking of the two pairs in the size of the shoes he'd worn into the store. He wore them twice before he came back to tell me how perfect they were and ask me out for dinner.

Because Louis is a prosecutor, what it came down to with the police was a coin flip between murder and suicide. You make enemies with dangerous people that way, they said in the newspaper, sounding as if they were speaking to children. If the reporter had come back to question me again, I'd have cautioned against both conclusions, quoting Louis, who liked to say, "Nothing is ever clear until you look again."

He'd explain cases that had been resolved after playing out in the newspapers for months, how the reports never got past the obvious. "It's like marriage," he said. "You don't know yourself until you live with somebody else for a while."

The worst were the sex offenders. They're compulsive, he said. You know it even as they claim remorse, and when the girls are young, they end up dead.

When I said I remembered one of those cases around here, Louis said, "Marilyn Haney" so quickly that I thought she'd been in the news the day before. "You were a girl then," he added. "Weren't you frightened?" Marilyn Haney had gone to the high school that was our big rival; she'd vanished walking home from field hockey practice in tenth grade.

"They never found her," I said. "Isn't that right?"

"Missing is dead in those cases," he said, sounding so certain I wondered how he'd spoken to the girl's parents, what he'd mentioned to them about taking a second look. I knew what I wasn't going to say to Louis, that even then, when I was fourteen, I thought Marilyn Haney was foolish for using a short cut through the local park, that she was asking for trouble and found it.

Our last Sunday afternoon together, Louis finished the *New York Times* he had delivered every day even though we live 200 miles from the city. "What should I do next?" he said. "The crossword puzzle?"

"If you want to," I said without looking up, and he never answered.

He disappeared into the house and left by another door. I didn't know that until I heard his car pull away. It made me stand and watch as the car turned north toward Allenwood. When I gathered up the *Times*, I saw that the puzzle was practically finished, that he'd filled in every space but three.

You'd think everything like that from those last days I spent with Louis would be indelible as an ink stain, but they're not. Nobody prepares to remember. The hours of an evening aren't items to memorize for a test.

The truth is Louis stayed late at work and I watched television. Law and Order, don't laugh. The reruns from seven to nine, and after that doubleheader of legal dilemmas, I'd sit outside with a glass of wine and wait for Louis as if I loved summer evenings alone on the deck, not anything hard because he came home just before ten each night, as punctual in his lateness as a man walking into the kitchen on time for dinner at six.

Except for the last night, when ten o'clock passed without him, and I poured a second glass of wine and then a third at 10:30, nodding off in the deck chair and waking to see Louis inside.

"I didn't want to startle you," he said.

It was nearly midnight. He might have been home for five minutes or fifty, already in a dress rehearsal for disappearance. I had a headache; the light in the kitchen was sun off a cement sidewalk. I felt so thick tongued and muddled I shuffled to our bed, and except for that phone call the following day, heard his voice only once again.

Once Louis was legally gone, the police talked to his wife. Had conversations with his co-workers. Of course, they questioned me. If he was dead by a hand other than his own, I was as likely a suspect as anyone, even some criminal who'd spent twelve years planning revenge in the nearby federal penitentiary.

"Was there tension?" "Was there problems?" "Was he upset? "Was you?" The policeman questioned everything in the singular, as if one-size-fits-all grammar could keep things focused.

"Walk me through this again," he finally said, and when I didn't answer right away, he added, "The last day."

"There's nothing much," I said.

"You let me worry about what's nothing and what's not," he said.

He wasn't looking at me. Instead, he seemed to be doing a kind of inventory of the living room, assessing the furniture and the bookshelves and the lamps as if they'd let him know the kind of man who lived there. As if he'd already decided who I was.

"He had whole wheat toast and coffee for breakfast," I said. "He had his tie draped around his neck, not tied, just lying loose like that. He read the *Times* while he ate."

"What's that?" the policeman said.

"The *New York Times*," I said. "It's a newspaper."

The cop nodded, but I was distracted again. The rest of that final morning with Louis fogged up until I could see him standing in the doorway, one hand on the screen. "See you sometime," he said.

I waved. I could have crossed the kitchen and kissed him or at least said something, but I waved like you do to your neighbor when you both go out for the mail at the same time.

"And then he called and said he'd be home in three hours."

"A day like any other," the policeman said. "That's what you're telling me?"

"Until he didn't show up."

"Right. Of course." He was finally looking at me, his eyes running over my skirt and blouse and shoes like he was deciding whether or not he wanted to buy my outfit for his wife or girlfriend. It was easy to wish him dead.

Did you ever stop to watch men dragging a lake or divers enter a river to search its bottom? I hadn't. Not until Louis vanished. "That lawyer," people were saying. "The one with the funny car. He lost his own case, it's looking like."

There were camera crews. I watched where they directed their lenses—a shot of the action, men entering the river in their wet suits, a shot of the crowd, newscasters holding a microphone near a sheriff or a rescue captain. It didn't feel at all like news, which is something that happens to others.

A week passed. The investigation side-stepped toward the conclusion of suicide and began to dry up. When his body wasn't found in the river or any of the wild places within a ten-mile radius, his disappearance drifted along the front-to-back current of the newspaper until it tumbled out of sight. One day there was no mention of him.

And in all that time the police had asked only the sorts of questions they thought might lead to knowing what had separated Louis and me, prefacing them with words like "recently" or "lately" and "within the past several weeks." Not once did they think to ask how we'd met or what followed to bring us together, as if the beginning of something had no connection to its end.

Before we ate dinner that first time, Louis asked me to take a picture of him standing in the doorway of the restaurant. It's done every day, something like that. Somebody shows you what button to push, the focus automatic so it's guaranteed to be a decent shot as long as one or the other of you doesn't move. "Get the sign in the frame," he said, and then "Thanks" after I'd taken three shots to be sure. When I gave the camera back, he backpedaled and snapped a picture before I turned away. "So I know who my photographer was," he said, smiling.

"Take me when I'm ready then," I said.

It made me nervous. That's what I would have told the police—I remember how I was suddenly nervous, that I struck a pose that I thought replicated indifference or mystery, but Louis snapped a moment before I was ready, when uncertainty seemed to flicker across my face, when I looked like a woman who thought she was making a mistake.

Of course I didn't know that until Louis showed me the photo. "I love this picture of you," he said. He'd had it enlarged to a 7 X 10 and framed as a one-week anniversary of meeting me.

You want to know one thing I wouldn't have told the police? Louis loved to watch me sleep. At first, when I'd open my eyes and see him sitting up and gazing at me, I'd feel a rush of warmth and desire. "What?" I said a few times, and he'd smile and say, "Go back to sleep." It was only when I woke to Louis standing and staring that I caught my breath and stiffened. "You scared me for a second," I said the next morning.

"Why?" Louis said, smiling in a way that made me doubt myself.

"You know why," I said, and let it go. A week later, when I opened my eyes, he was standing over me on my side of the bed, his body so close that I couldn't see his face until I rolled onto my back and looked straight up.

I felt like a photograph.

After the second week, when it looked as if Louis would never be found, Joanne, who had worked with me in the shoe department until I quit two years ago, asked me to lunch. She reserved a table on the deck that overlooked the same river that had been explored by divers for three days, and when I looked out over it as we began to eat, she laid her fork down and said, "I'm such an idiot. I wasn't thinking when I asked you here for lunch."

I could tell she believed I was picturing Louis being washed along toward Harrisburg, maybe right that minute passing by, twenty-five miles downstream from where his car had been abandoned. "This is fine," I said. "I've always liked this place."

"Good," she said, but she didn't pick up her fork, and for half a minute I kept eating while she watched like someone expecting a compliment on her cooking.

"It must be hard," she said at last, and when I didn't answer right away, she added, "the not knowing," as if I was the mother of an abducted child.

"What's worst is the smugness," I said, and she looked baffled. When she lifted her fork, the sun glinted off it into her face, and she laid it back down.

"Imagine that," she said, as if she was just now understanding something important about me.

"The police," I said. "The reporters." I meant her to understand she wasn't included, but I didn't say the words. Her uneaten pasta salad looked like a plate of glistening larvae. When the sun briefly slipped behind a cloud and reappeared, the coiled strands appeared to move.

"Remember that frat-rock CD we had to listen to every day at work?" she said.

"Sure," I said, though nothing registered except seeing her in uniform. She began eating again, recovering herself. "That awful Gary Glitter song. God. And the one that said 'What I like about you' a thousand times. And always they came around in the same order."

"Like following a band around the country and going to a hundred consecutive shows," I said.

She frowned. "I don't know what you mean by that."

"You'd know the set list."

"No, you wouldn't. The band could play anything they wanted. They could surprise you."

"It would be worse," I said. "They could change, but they wouldn't because they'd think they were playing in front of a new set of strangers."

"Louie, Louie," Joanne said. "Remember that one? When was that made? A hundred years ago? It was always the first song. After that, you knew what was coming." She shoveled in another forkful, and I said "Uh-huh" as if I could name the list of tunes like the Ten Commandments, the two of us in our striped shirts acting like we wanted to be invited to drink beer with every guy who took off his shoes for us.

"If you come by the store," Joanne said, "we could do something."

"Sure," I said. "If I'm in the neighborhood, sure I will."

She smiled the way my mother used to on the day after Christmas, asking me to hurry back and knowing it would be Christmas Eve the following year before I showed up at her door.

The very next day, I was asked to take a lie detector test. I'd expected it sooner, to tell the truth. They give these things when they're stuck, and no surprise to me, I passed. What else could I have done, unless they lied with the results? In the newspaper, the article about me passing was four column inches on page twelve, right below the two stories continued from page four, so nobody would notice unless they were reading every word about the typhoon in Indonesia and the spread of AIDS in central Africa.

Louis' wife passed hers as well. Without her results right below mine, the article would have been three column inches

After I passed, I told the cop it's not uncommon for prosecutors to be killed by criminals and he nodded like he was listening to traffic. "They're just as likely to be killed by dirty cops," I said, sitting him up straight, his mouth working for just a second, letting me see he wanted to slap my face. I wondered how he would do on a lie detector test if he let himself slip so easily. I could hear Louis explaining how, if that cop had a good hand, one that needed him to risk all his chips, he'd make that face and I should fold, waiting for the hand when his tongue stayed still, when I knew he was betting beyond his strength.

Look, I know I'm expected to be devastated. What's more, I'm supposed to be angry because who among us wants to be seen as a suspect? And though no one has asked me how I feel, when they do, I will say it's what I expected.

It's like sorting things out in your bedroom, knowing the inevitability of it becoming a mess again. It has to be cleaned in a week or two or even the simple things will get misplaced—a change purse, receipts, lipstick, a bracelet. They all have in-plain-sight life spans. And so does desire and how it leads to a belief in love.

Louis was fifty-two when we met. "I feel blessed," he told me. I used to imagine him out drinking with his friends to celebrate being admitted to law school while I was being born. "I'm counting on you not to change," Louis said after we'd been living together for a month in the house where his wife had lived until three months before.

"Everybody changes," I'd answered.

"Except every so often they don't."

You think that's strange? Think about singing hymns in church. You have to open your mouth and let the words out. Look around next time and see who's just forming the words with their lips, or worse, who's not even pretending, their lips sealed. If you don't keep singing, there's all those verses full of God and Jesus and alleluias to stand still through—a long time to be thinking. By the time of the communal amen, there's no way you can feel in tune with anyone in that room.

And think about this. Louis always made up stories when we had sex.

"I pick you up hitchhiking," he would say. "We park at a rest stop." I'd sit beside him on the couch and wait for his hand to rest on my thigh. When he opened my blouse, I could see families walking across the parking lot toward picnic tables. When he slipped off my bra, I could hear voices.

Those scenarios always had us having sex for the first time. We were different people, but still the same. Actors.

Afterwards, he had me dress for those parts and took pictures so he could remember them. A sports bra and short shorts for a jogger in the park. A bikini for a swimmer at an abandoned quarry pool. With and without the top. A woman with her eyes closed in a bathtub, her lingerie scattered on the floor.

I'm naked in half the pictures he took, but those photos aren't pornographic. Louis made sure of that. Mystery makes you go back and look again, he'd say, and he'd show me which shots he stored on his computer. In every one, there is some part of me in shadow or turned away or covered.

Nobody understood what a sacrifice Louis made, leaving that car he loved behind. He did that for me, I think, so I might believe he hadn't disappeared just for a simple new affair. With the Mini-Cooper S abandoned, I could believe he'd really died.

In all the time I lived with Louis, he only let me drive once. I had my own car, an old Honda Civic I'd bought with 80,000 miles on it the year before I met him. But he owned the kind of car you buy to turn peoples' heads, the souped-up, extra forward gear version, something that jumped when he pressed the gas even though it looked like, just sitting there, one of those cars you expect a half dozen clowns to tumble out of. He loved shifting through all six gears both up and down, taking back roads so he could run it fast through curves with approaching traffic just a few feet to the side.

You're thinking, maybe, that the one time was when he was drunk or sick or been up for twenty-four hours, but it was after we'd had dinner with his law partner, Steve Arlen, and his girlfriend. I say "girl" because Amanda was fresh out of college, twenty-two and so tanned and toned she looked like she'd been playing beach volleyball for the past four years.

Steve kept talking about the car she owned. "Can you believe this girl came with a Corvette?" he said. "The first time I picked her up, I saw it parked along the street and she just said, matter-of-factly, 'That's mine.'"

The girl barely smiled while Steve talked. She ordered lobster, two tails, nothing else but a side salad and sparkling water, and Steve laughed like he couldn't be more pleased she'd chosen a double tail at "market price."

Louis, when we walked outside, handed me the car keys. "The Honda is a stick," he said. "This is just the same to get started, left and down, then up, then right and down. That will get us into traffic."

"Steve," he called out across the lot as I climbed in behind the wheel and the top slid back and down. Steve and the girl looked our way. "See you Monday," Louis shouted.

"Down and left," he said, and I let the clutch out like I was sitting beside a state trooper with a clipboard in his hand. The car leapt forward, and I shifted straight up, slipping through the stop sign like it was there only for cars with automatic transmissions.

Louis didn't look back, but I saw him check the side mirror. "Twenty-two," he said when we'd turned into traffic. "Steve's four years older than I am." He told me to turn onto the back road to his house. "Let it run," he said. "That's what it's built for." He looked in the side mirror twice more as we swept through the curves, but there were never any headlights behind us.

When they found Louis' computer in the river, the hard drive was missing. I wasn't at all a suspect by then, and neither was anyone else, at least not literally.

Remember when Billy Joe McAllister threw something off the Tallahatchie Bridge in that old song and everybody tried to guess what it was? Photographs? A baby? Something he stole? Bobbie Gentry knew how to keep people guessing, all right. How else could a song she recorded before I was born come up on my radar screen? Here it is more than forty years later, and you can find an "Ode to Billy Joe" chat room where people insist they absolutely know it was an aborted fetus.

A man like Louis knows there's somebody who could retrieve anything whatsoever from his hard drive. Deleting isn't enough. What's gone is gone isn't true anymore. It's still there like your DNA years after your death. Instead of a shoebox full of letters, there are electronic messages, and somebody always wants to retrieve the past.

One more story about Louis. A week after I moved in with him, he said he needed to show me the room where he worked, the one he kept locked even when he was inside. "I don't want you to imagine something that isn't there," he said.

What was there? A gallery of heads. "I have them made for me," Louis said. "They're defendants I put away."

I counted seventeen faces, all of them men's. The room reminded me of a store that sold wigs, rows of mannequin heads draped with varying shades and styles of hair. "I don't have every defendant made. Just the ones who have taken a life."

I thought of his wife in that room. I imagined her dusting those heads. "I don't know what to say," I said.

"They're fiberglass," he said. "I know a forensic sculptor who reconstructs for the police. He's very good."

"He makes faces? From what?"

"Skeletons. Whatever's left that gives him clues. For identification. You know."

I looked around the room to see if there was anything else unusual, but without those fiberglass heads, it was an office. "You don't ever have to look at these again," he said. "I just wanted to make sure I had no secrets from you."

I thought he was about to turn off the light, but he tugged a book loose from one of the shelves and turned to a page of photographs of wax figures of faces with diseases and injuries. "All of these faces were made for doctors," he said. "You can tell what their problems were just by examining them, but the faces in this room all hide what's wrong. Not one of them looks frightening unless you know his story."

The police, when they searched the house, didn't say anything to me about the heads, but I thought they talked about them plenty among themselves.

I saw the policeman I'd first spoken with one more time. He wasn't in uniform. He was filling a plastic container with gasoline and sweating so hard his t-shirt was stained half way down his chest. I imagined that he'd run out of gas in the middle of mowing his lawn.

I glanced at the numbers rolling up on my pump and heard him mutter

"Fuck." The gasoline had roiled up out of the container and was puddling around it. He slapped the nozzle back onto its hook and bent down to twist the cap into place before he moved the container to a dry spot and walked inside the convenience store.

My own hose clicked off, and I rounded up seventeen more cents so I wouldn't get any change. On my way inside, I walked past his pump and saw that it read 1.16 gallons. What was he thinking to let it overflow so much? Though I wasn't wearing sunglasses and my hair was combed the same way it had been each time we'd spoken, he showed no sign of recognizing me when I passed him as he came out of the store.

The hard drive missing—what's that about, people always ask each time Louis' case comes up again, and now that months have passed, don't you think that means he's alive? Don't you think there will be sightings, some of them true?

That's why his story, with a photograph, needs to return to the newspaper. His face needs to become as famous as Elvis'. Every day somebody sees Elvis, even though we know he's dead. And here's Louis likely alive and still, I'd bet, looking exactly like the picture taken the day before he left. He wouldn't grow a beard. Not Louis who shaved twice a day. He wouldn't let his hair grow. Not Louis who had it cut every three weeks. The phone is bound to ring. People are always on the lookout for a myth.

What would bring him back, I think, is enough time to go by to enable fantasy. He will begin to imagine my sleeping body, all those times he watched me, how, after the first time I woke with the t-shirt of his I wore to bed up around my throat, I closed my eyes each night expecting to feel that sliding shirt tug me out of sleep.

He acted as if he could lift those t-shirts without waking me. But what I never told him was I would wake when he pulled up those shirts, that I loved being watched like that.

Soon, Louis will reappear and see I still wear his shirts to bed. "Oh yes," I'll hear him whisper. "Your sleep is perfect."

STORY STORIES

———

I saw Bob Cook standing by himself behind the speakers that were singing "Twist and Shout." Holding a drink. Assessing the room as if it were empty. There were three hundred people massing and splitting, at least half of them busy reattaching themselves to as many old classmates as they could find in six hours. The fat and the bald. The gray and the tan. The fit and Bob Cook standing there like Jack Nicholson among the hotel guests in *The Shining*.

"Fitch," he murmured when I stepped carefully over the sound system wires.

"How's it going, Bob?" I said for a start.

Cook allowed a couple of beats to go by. He might have been waiting for the Isley Brothers to wrap up, but after ten seconds, I was wishing I'd tripped over the speaker cables and said the hell with Bob Cook before I'd reached him.

"I'm in transition," he finally offered. "I'm between ships." He stared over my shoulder.

I heard the Ronettes start "Be My Baby," sounding like they were singing from under the floor, and though common sense prompted that the recording was thin because we were behind the speakers, I was suddenly thinking somebody had turned the volume down so all the members of our class could learn what Bob Cook and I were talking about. I didn't blame anybody; I wanted to tell whoever it was to shut it off entirely because I couldn't understand it either.

"Bad question?" I said.

"No."

"Your wife here?" I tried.

"No." He lifted his glass, positioning it in front of his face as if he remembered it was full of something with a bouquet. I wondered how I appeared through four inches of mixed drink, and then he lowered his glass to waist level again.

"Well, not the best of times or what?"

Cook watched me drain my drink. He might have meant to be generous, allowing me my excuse to pull away, a trip to the open bar both of us had paid for in advance. I jiggled the ice cubes. "Gin and tonic," I said, relying on the names for things like somebody who slept in a crib.

I held up the glass, but I kept myself from naming it. I said "Well" instead. The Ronettes were nearly finished doing their part to bring back 1963.

"Have a good one, Fitch," Bob Cook said as I retreated, back-stepping over those wires as if they had forked tongues, fangs, and rattles.

On Sunday afternoon, the class reunion fifteen hours behind us, I was happy to have Bob Cook to talk about with my wife when all of the Pittsburgh radio stations had faded, half the trip home in front of us with only top-forty, country, and evangelism up and down the dial. I let the radio run through *scan* one more time, but I was already saying, "I'd guess Bob Cook if somebody asked me who should have gotten the prize for being furthest into outer space."

"Bob Cook," Laura said. "I talked to his wife while you were disappeared there for half an hour."

I watched Hollidaysburg inch along, stoplight by stoplight; I saw Bob Cook staring over my shoulder, watching a strange woman sharing secrets with his wife. "What was she like?" I said.

"Fine. She was a whole lot easier to talk with than your classmates. She was just standing around like I was in a room full of aliens."

"Cook was out of it. He was burnt or something. He was wasted."

"He doesn't have a job," Laura said.

"I guessed that much. He was using code, but it wasn't that hard to crack."

"He left the Army."

"Twenty years and out."

"He didn't have twenty years."

"If he went in at the end of college, he had twenty years."

"She said he had eighteen years and ten months. She said he left early. Last October. Almost eleven months ago."

"Maybe he had his reasons," I said. "Maybe he was feeling guilty about becoming a double dipper."

"She didn't spell it out."

"Cook didn't even have an alphabet."

"She said enough as it was. What else should she admit to for her husband?"

"She could have spent the night keeping him moving. She might have led him round by the arm or something, kept him circulating for the six hours."

"They have a brain-damaged son. They have a daughter who's learning disabled."

"There's a difference?"

"Apparently."

I thought about the distinctions you'd make if both of your children were impaired, how you'd search for classifications, for fine tuning. Bob Cook had been in Vietnam; maybe he'd spent his tour in a cloud of Agent Orange.

"She said they're living with her parents in Pittsburgh."

"Old Bob Cook sounds like he's sliding down the tubes," I said. We were in Geeseytown, less than a hundred miles to go now. After a cemetery, a legion hall, and a closed gas station, we would be nowhere at all until Water Street where there were two closed stations and a Sunday flea market.

We reclaimed our children. We had a late dinner, and they let me talk about the reunion all the way through dessert. I flopped on the couch and had worked from Friday's paper, through Saturday's, and into Sunday's as far as Arts and Leisure, winding down, when the telephone rang.

"Fitch?" I heard.

"Uh-huh."

"Is this Fitch?"

"Yes."

"I don't have the wrong Fitch, do I?"

"I don't know."

"I think this is the wrong Fitch. You don't sound like yourself."

Whoever was trying to make a positive ID from a vocal lineup of Fitches hung up. I felt like Bachelors Number Two and Three, finding out I was somebody besides another person's fantasy because my voice didn't sound like it should, but I shut off the light in the kitchen before I looked outside to see if there was a strange car, shadows moving. The phone rang again, and I began doing an inventory of things someone might demand from me.

"Hello," I said. There was someone sane who might be calling; it was ten-thirty, a while yet to the hour of the wolf.

"This is the real Fitch, isn't it?"

"I don't know."

"If this is the real Fitch, this is Bob Cook."

"Ok."

"I got your number. It took a while. I threw the damn thing away, and then I only remembered the name of your town without having the reunion program in front of me."

"You all right, Bob?" I said, a rhetorical question, what I might have asked if I knew I needed a prelude in order to hear a ransom demand. "Let me hear my wife's voice," I could just as easily have asked.

"Fitch, how do I sound to you? Do I sound like the old Bob Cook?"

"It's been twenty-five years, Bob. We don't know each other anymore."

"Give it some thought, Fitch. Think about it and let me know."

He hung up again, and I stood there wishing somebody had just described what he wanted to do with my wife's body or mine. I wished I had just heard heavy breathing and the length and thickness of what the caller was stroking with his hand while he talked. I didn't want to think about whether Bob Cook was himself, or worse, whether I was the real Fitch.

He'd punched a girl in high school. That's what I remembered while I was waiting for the demons to tell Bob Cook to trial-run my number again. Cook had been the only guy I had ever seen slug a girl.

We'd been standing in the hall after lunch, a couple of minutes to kill before plane geometry. Maybe doing some furtive leering. Maybe just some sports-wish talk. Whatever we might have done with two minutes in tenth grade, and what I could see clearly was Sue Voller walking towards us looking good. "I hate her," Cook had muttered.

I didn't know how anybody could hate Sue Voller as long as he could watch her walk. I gave Cook a raised eyebrow and kept staring. "She spread stories about me to her friends," he said.

"What stories?"

"Story stories."

"She went out with you, Cook. I'm the one who ought to hate her. She turned me down."

But Bob Cook was all clenched teeth and reddening face. "Hi, Sue," I said, ready to forgive any story she might have told about me.

She smiled. "Hi, there," she answered, maybe not even remembering she'd told me NO six months before.

"Voller?" Bob Cook had said.

"Bob?" she said, stopping as if she were trying to place him.

He stepped up to her and rammed his fist into her stomach, a solar plexus shot, doubling her up. "Oh," she breathed, all exhale followed by the silence you hear when somebody lands flat on his back. Cook ran, leaving me to explain to Sue Voller why I was the kind of person who'd hang out in the halls with a psychopath.

Nobody else had seen it happen. I didn't, five minutes later, think I'd seen it happen either.

Finally, then, the third call, fulfilling the omen. "Fitch," Bob Cook started, "we ought to get this over with."

"Sure," I agreed, calculating how close a sniper might need to be.

"Reunions are lies," he said, and I relaxed, moved, in fact, in front of the kitchen window.

"It's a given, Bob. We just leave the shit in our lives unspoken."

"I have problems with that, Fitch."

"Ok."

"I thought I remembered you, Fitch. I thought I recognized you last night. I thought you were somebody I went to school with."

I didn't answer. I decided that Bob Cook had used up his three tosses at the milk cans of sense.

"I'm not calling anymore, Fitch. You won't have to wonder if I'm on the line the next time the phone rings. It won't be me."

"Ok, Bob."

"Count on it, Fitch."

And for the rest of the night, at least, he kept his promise. The next morning, because all three of our children were old enough to sleep through their last week of summer mornings, I had breakfast with Laura, a chance to fill in details for her about Bob Cook. "He's not a curiosity anymore," she said. "Who are we dealing with here?"

So I told her a couple of neutral anecdotes, reassurances because I had to run through the Sue Voller fiasco. She drank her coffee and looked like she wanted to answer the phone the next time Bob Cook called. "He's done now," I said.

"Don't bet on it. This guy's a loony."

"He's depressed. The reunion made it worse. He probably called ten people yesterday."

"He picked you, Doug. For some reason, he picked you."

"Hardly," I said, but I agreed.

"What else do you remember about him from high school?" Laura asked. "Maybe I'll hear a clue if you keep the stories coming."

Other than things that wouldn't even leave fingerprints, I could recall only one other Bob Cook story. "He was my lab partner in chemistry," I said. "I hated chemistry. It was the only C I got in high school."

"Stick to Cook," Laura said.

I nodded. "You have to understand how numb I got in chemistry, how little I remember from that class so you appreciate the specifics of this story."

"Fine. I understand that chemistry was not a good experience for you."

I was stalling. I'd thought of something to tell her, and now I was stuttering.

"Ok," I said. "One day during lab, right out of nowhere while we were heating compounds or whatever we did, Cook said to me, 'I've got a boner, Fitch.'"

Laura blinked as if I'd just turned on the overhead light, but I had things started now and kept on rolling. "Well, I just looked at him or something. After all, what do you say? And he said it again. 'I've got a boner.' And I really don't remember if I said anything then or not, but I know that what he said next was 'Don't you ever get a boner, Fitch?'"

Laura was looking through the doorway to check for our daughter. "What did you say to that?" she managed.

"'Not in chemistry lab, Bob,' I remember saying. And then he said, 'Sure you do, Fitch. You get a boner in here.'"

Laura was staring at me now. "That's not the end, is it?" she said.

"That's it."

"No, it isn't. You're just embarrassed."

"Really. I think all I said was something like 'Why don't you go take care of yours?' and he didn't say anything else."

"You didn't tell your friends?"

"No."

"He never said anything like that again?"

"Sure he did," I said, surprised when I heard myself say it. "Maybe three other times. Always in chemistry lab, I think, so it got to where I tried to work far enough away from him he'd have to say it so loud even he wouldn't have that kind of nerve."

"You didn't think he was trying to lead you on?"

"I didn't think anything. I thought it was a stupid thing to be saying; you keep those things to yourself."

"He never said anything else afterwards?"

"He always started up as if he'd never mentioned it before."

"Well," Laura said, "at least he's married now. He's living with a woman."

"To tell you the truth, I never thought about it that way. If I thought about it at all, it was sort of neutral, a kind of abstract horniness."

"How can you have abstract lust?" Laura said.

"It just seemed that way."

"Not a very good explanation, Doug."

"I suppose not," I said, signing off. I had to get to work. I had to get back to selling insurance to pay for all of the college expenses that were one year away from chewing up my income. And I was already tired of dealing with explanations for other people's lives. I had enough trying to account for myself, for three children and a wife I had to answer to. I was willing to be responsible for whatever totals I'd accumulate after another twenty-five years, give or take a decade, but the hell with Bob Cook, I was thinking, the hell with his boners and his retarded children and his out-of-work insanity. We'd been set into motion by the same community and the same high school, and all I wanted to do from here on in was go back and visit every ten years until my name went from the list of Classmates Attending to the list of Classmates Deceased. I wished him well; I wished him less pain. What else could Bob Cook expect from anybody listed on that program?

When the doorbell rang at eleven o'clock that night, I opened the door without thinking about whether or not terrorists were running spot checks on foolishness in our neighborhood. I lived in a small town in central Pennsylvania; I had a house on a street where the lawns blended into each other in color and texture as if there had been a communal decision to purchase identical seed.

At my door stood Bob Cook.

"Come on in," I said immediately, sounding like somebody who didn't wish he'd picked some other classmate to haunt.

"Fitch," he said, following me into the living room. "I'm only staying a minute."

I was relieved to hear that. I wanted to learn he had a reservation at the Holiday Inn in Allentown or Reading or Harrisburg, at least an hour more of driving in front of him; I wanted him to say he was on his way to Boston or New York or Baltimore and there was a natural reason for him to be pausing at my house before he disappeared.

And because I believed none of those things, I said, "What's up?"

"I've been doing a lot of thinking since the reunion. I've been checking things over with our class."

"That's what reunions are for."

"Non-stop thinking, Fitch. Two days now. Thinking and calling, thinking and calling, thinking and driving here because thinking didn't seem sufficient."

"You want a beer? You want a drink?" Bob Cook was sounding like he needed at least ten beers to disconnect his circuits.

"Nothing like that, Fitch. I'm out of here in a minute. I'm back in the world."

"Ok." I badly wanted a beer, but I had a sense I was stuck on my couch until Bob Cook stood up again, getting out of the director's chair nobody in our family ever sat in. I wondered if Laura was listening from the room behind me, lying in bed in the dark and concentrating to discover who'd shown up so late, who was talking after eleven on a Monday night in our living room. The police, she'd think. She'd lie there worrying the police were delivering a sudden horror story—our older son a drug dealer, our younger son a thief, nude photos of our daughter in the wallet of her old social studies teacher from middle school.

"I've been deceived, Fitch. I've been betrayed. You know what I'm talking about here? I've been thinking about how many lies a man can take before he's transformed into somebody else. Like being x-rayed too many times. There's a limit. You keep track of how many times your dentist has x-rayed you? You don't count until you feel a little polyp on your tongue. You don't keep track of lies either until you feel you're not yourself. I've been thinking about this for two days, and I'm not happy, Fitch. I've stopped being Bob Cook. I'm not who I was anymore." He paused. He stood up so suddenly I had to stay seated and look up at him from the couch like a child might if he'd just been caught carving FUCK on the legs of his fourth-grade teacher's chair, one letter per leg so the obscenity could be a year-long giggle.

"What do you think, Fitch? Do I seem like Bob Cook?"

"I don't know. Honestly. It's hard to get a grip on something like that so fast."

"My wife told your wife a lot of things about me, about my children. You think you know who I am now, but that's not enough, Fitch. You can never know enough about somebody to know who they are."

"I understand," I said, trying to pick the phrase that would defuse him. I was wishing very hard that Bob Cook would turn into somebody else right then and get in his car.

"Fitch," Cook said. He jammed his hands into his jacket pockets and stepped toward me, a combination of gestures so unnerving it made me sink back into the couch, bring my hands up in front of me. I knew, at that moment, why the victims of madmen in movies acted so foolishly, cowering and covering, giving themselves no chance to survive.

"You're one lucky son-of-a-bitch, Fitch," he said, backing up.

I was lost. I had to wait a breath longer, my hands still raised.

"Really, Fitch. So goddamned lucky." I saw he was heading toward the door, and I leaped up to follow.

"Your luck will change," I said, all congeniality and platitude.

Cook opened the door and turned to stand on the porch as if he were recreating his stance from five minutes before. "It would be somebody else's luck then," he said. "That's one thing I know for certain."

"Well, good luck anyway," I tossed his way, and I watched him get in his car, watched him pull out of my street, and watched for ten more minutes to make sure he hadn't turned around, intending to drift his car back into the lane with the lights extinguished and pitch bricks through my windows or set fire to everything I owned.

"It was Frank Miller," I told Laura when I had to go to bed or stand guard all night. She didn't answer. "Just Frank Miller from the office with a contract he didn't think could wait until morning," and she sighed and rolled over, asleep, I remembered, because she had an in-service day tomorrow, her first day back at work. If Laura could will herself to sleep at eleven as soon as her vacation ended, I thought, I could decide to let Bob Cook vanish.

In the morning, she was gone before I got out of the shower. I trusted my children to sleep until lunch, and I drove to work. The receptionist, when I passed her, said, "There's a man waiting in your office," and when I looked at her, she added, "I hope I haven't inconvenienced you. He said you were old friends."

Bob Cook was looking at the art poster next to my desk, and I wondered what he was formulating from the not quite circular red ball hovering over what appeared to be the abstraction of a destroyed city. I didn't know the title of the work or the name of the artist; I'd picked it up ten years before because it had struck me as interesting one afternoon, and now it hung there like my routine job. Right then I thought that if Cook asked me to explain either one, I'd throw the poster away and resign.

But he was only getting something in order before he spoke. The poster could just as well have been an eye chart diminishing from large red E to an incomprehensible scramble of alphabet. "I found out you were never in Nam, Fitch. I checked it out, and you were never in country."

"That's right, Bob. But it's no secret. I could have told you that."

"You said you were. I took you at your word."

"When did I say that, Bob?"

"At the reunion."

I silently cursed the receptionist. Aloud, I said, "The subject never came up, Bob. We hardly said anything to each other."

"Rick Davidson asked us to stand up if we were in Nam."

"Maybe he did. He asked us to stand up for a lot of things."

"You stood up for Nam, Fitch. You lied like some rotten scumbag."

"I stood up for having gone to Glenshaw Grade School. I stood up for living in Pennsylvania. I stood up for having three kids. I stood up for being in the Army once. Those are the things I stood up for."

"Fuck you, Fitch. I remember when you stood up for Nam because I was standing and twelve other guys were standing, and you were the only one I remembered ever knowing. All the rest were the guys who spent their high school locked in wood shop. I was thinking, 'That's who went to Nam. Wood shop guys. D-A haircut guys,' and then I said, 'There's Doug Fitch standing. Fucking-A, he was in Nam.'"

"I don't know what to say, Bob. I wouldn't stand up for something like that unless I'd done it. I was in the Reserves, for Christ's sake; I was dodging and weaving to stay out of combat."

Cook went back to the poster, and for the first time, I saw Hiroshima under that red sun. If Bob Cook stared at it a little longer, I'd be able to see the faces of survivors, their arms flung up to the heavens. If he stayed in my office for another ten minutes I'd be seeing boat people eating each other to stay alive, the end of life after the ozone layer dissolved in an acid bath of my daughter's aerosol sprays. "I'm disappointed, Fitch," he said. "Last night I had every intention of shooting you for lying about something like this." His eyes worked through the devastation in the poster. I thought I was going to throw up.

"I'm glad you didn't," I croaked. I might as well have been some idiot psycho-babbler spouting, "I hear some anger in what you're saying, Bob," and it seemed that office and the poster I had carelessly bought and tacked up had been all along a scream of "Liar" or "Fraud" that I needed to address before justice emerged from the jacket pocket of somebody one hair further into dementia than Bob Cook.

"I decided it's more of a punishment for you to have to live with yourself."

It was a sentence I would have plea-bargained for on my knees. It freed me to start calculating how Cook could have confused me with somebody else standing up as proof of combat. What I remembered was the invitation to stand to show you were in the Army had preceded the one about being in Vietnam. Maybe I hadn't sat down fast enough? Maybe I'd been looking around to see who all had managed to miss the Army altogether, while Bob Cook was searching the room for a face he recognized? I might have stood for an extra second between questions and triggered the time release of Bob Cook's despair.

It was all I could find among the clutter so indifferently packed in my mind.

"I don't think I'll see you again, Fitch," he said then.

I thought about whether or not I should make any gesture that might seem less than admirable, whether I should trust him to let me serve my sentence. "Fitch," he said, "you ever run anymore?"

"Run?" I said, as if he'd spoken in Cree.

"You ran in high school. You sprinted."

"I run from my car to this office when it's raining," I said, giddy with escape, but Cook didn't smile, so I added, "No, Bob, I know for a fact I don't sprint anymore. My hamstrings would snap."

"I know what you mean, Fitch, I gave it up myself."

I couldn't remember Bob Cook on the track team, not even in junior high school. I had no idea what he was getting at, unless it had something to do with establishing the common bond, the hope that conversation would luck onto something that resonated. And I wanted Bob Cook, as soon as he left, to find at least a little bit of good fortune; I wanted to feel better about anything I'd luck into by knowing his life was improving.

THE NAZI ON THE PHONE

———

"Hhaaah," Carol Dawson said at the end of every yawn. *Hhaaah*, as if yawns were sneezes, audible bursts of breath that deserved something like "God bless you." Fifteen minutes didn't go by without Carol yawning. *Hhaaah*. You could count on it, a kind of simple-minded, one-note carillon that told you life was getting shorter.

Maybe she was perpetually tired. Or anxious. Maybe she'd lapsed into a stupid habit, vocalizing her yawns the way some people nail-bite or ear-tug. What I didn't do was ask her its origin the whole summer of 1970 when I stayed with the Dawsons three nights a week because, like me, my high school friend Dick, her husband, was doing graduate work at Kent State University, six years after we'd left Pittsburgh behind.

It was better than driving back and forth, four days a week, to my apartment seventy miles east. It was better than renting. And I'd already learned what coincidence was before the summer began, standing around gawking at Kent State's plunge into history as if I were one of those benign faces you see on the television news, the ones looking at the camera and the candidate while a gun pokes out of the crowd an arm's length from where we're gaping.

And every time I think of watching the guardsmen kneel and fire, I hear Carol Dawson go *Hhaaah*, as if she hadn't slept in weeks or was giving the code-sound for *Why didn't they shoot you, too, while they had the chance?*

I knew our eleven seconds on the firing line was *history*. It hadn't just rippled through the newspapers with the peristaltic motion of the news, front page to back, a few bumps along the way to remind you what things had looked like in their undigested state. By mid-summer, the Student Unrest Commission had set up shop in Kent, and now all the accidental witnesses like me were being drawn over the mountains of our memories to see what we could see.

And so Dick and I listened to a self-interest catalogue of theories: from conspiracy to snipers to terrorists to murder to convergence of the planets. It was like hearing Nixon explain the powder burns on his hands from his *Bums* speech, the one he'd been so proud to deliver on May 1 because it told people what they wanted to hear about students like Dick Dawson and me who milked 2-s deferments for graduate school—we were the reason this country had hit the skids like a Third World Goon Squad.

"Christ," Dick said after we sat through those first sessions, "they could have wrapped this up months ago. They could have put the guardsmen up there where they belong and grilled the fucking truth out of them."

"Sure," I answered, as if I were agreeing with my Middle English professor after I hadn't read any of the secondary work for class.

"They're putting housewives on the stand. They're interviewing landlords and shopkeepers. They're letting General Del Corso break out the sniper theory again. It's like listening to a lecture by the Flat Earth Society."

"They're putting their fingers on the pulse," I said, but Dick wasn't through.

"They're letting Mayor Satrom talk tomorrow. We'll get the 'Anarchy in Portage County' speech again."

"Brought to you by the same people who send you all that fellowship money," I said, though I wondered where my subpoena was.

Dick kept all the articles from the *Akron Beacon Journal* in his bedroom and had a file on everything. He had a hundred pictures he'd taken on May 2, May 3, and May 5. He grilled me a dozen times, and at the end of every session, after we watched the slides again, he told me the biggest regret of his life was that he hadn't been on campus on May 4. "Who could have seen it coming?" he said each time, and I had to agree. I hadn't thought anything was coming except another big waste of platitudes and self-serving. The only reason I was standing in the firing line was my class didn't start until twelve-thirty, and I was sick to death of reading articles about the history of the Miracle Play.

Maybe ten times he listened to my sketch of the noon rally, where I'd been standing, how far from the nearest dead student. "Fifty-three feet," he prompted each time. "I went back and measured. There's enough landmarks in your story; you don't forget things like that."

And then, while we were eating lunch, he told me about the Nazi on the phone, how you could call the white-power hot line and listen to somebody tell you the revolution's here and it was time for people who qualified for the Aryan Nation to kick some tainted ass. "Listen to this," Dick said after he dragged me to a pay phone outside Arby's.

"America is weakened by the genetically inferior. The colored must be kept from the white. America is poisoned by the morally inferior. The heathen must be kept from the Christian," I heard, so I knew what would follow: "Black, brown, yellow, red must leave or perish. Jew, Muslim, non-believer must leave or perish," it went on, and then the tape ran out as if it were supposed to be a cliffhanger and maybe I'd call in next week for a fresh loop. The operator asked for thirty-five cents. I hung up like I hadn't heard her, and Dick waited for me to say something.

He was looking for shadows and darkness in my expression, and I didn't think I was giving him any. "Well?" he said.

I was puzzled, too. It was just a tape. It hadn't made me any more angry than a film villain who snuffs out a few extras' lives. "It's grotesque," I tried.

"That's it?" Dick said.

"Nobody takes this stuff seriously. It's like the promises that go with phone numbers on a men's room wall. Nobody calls those numbers."

"These guys are real. They originate from a place in Akron. There's a street number and everything. People know."

"In that case, we ought to go down and clean them out," I said like a ten year-old.

Dick beamed. "That's talking. That's what I wanted to hear."

"They're the army, not us," I retreated.

"Why don't we call the Ohio Guard then? Why don't we call General Del Corso?"

"The house number's bogus. Nobody gives up a number like that."

"Why don't we call General Canterbury?"

"I've been close enough to foolishness for a while. I'm on R&R."

"Vacations end."

"What's to see?" I said.

"Who knows? Some moron. Some redneck."

He wasn't going to find any Nazis, I thought. Nobody publicizing the virtues of white power would have any address but a post office box. Dick Dawson was always getting hot tips; he was a regular on the stairway to wealth. When summer school started, he dragged me down to the IGA Market because we were going to win five thousand dollars in their Cleveland Indians Lineup Game. All we had to do was complete the infield for the big money, the outfield for one hundred dollars, or the battery for instant small cash.

We stole hundreds of game pieces, lifting them from the shelves beneath the registers of empty check-out lanes. "It's like five-years-worth of trips to the grocery store," Dick said. "It's like we've gone to the IGA every hour of every day since the contest began."

After we opened the first twenty game pieces, we already had Eddie Lion 2B, Greg Nettles 3B, and Jack Heidemann SS. In the outfield we had Ted Uhlaender CF and Vada Pinson RF. Catching, we had Duke Sims. All we needed, with 300 pieces to go, was a first baseman or a left fielder or, if we didn't mind the small change, a pitcher.

"Come on, Tony Horton," Dick kept saying. "Come on, Hawk Harrelson." I was counting Eddie Leon cards. Pretty soon we had sixty of him, forty-five of Vada Pinson, forty of Duke Sims. "Come on," Dick was pleading, "give me Sam McDowell; give me that ten dollars."

Duke Sims was gaining. He passed Vada Pinson and nearly overtook Eddie Leon. When we reached the last peel-off piece, there were sixty-eight pictures of him in his crouch, seventy-one of Leon crossing his body for a backhand stab. The last picture showed Ted Uhlaender shading his eyes from an imaginary sun. "It's fixed," Dick said. "Look at all these pictures of Sims, and he doesn't even start anymore. How come they don't have Fosse on these cards?"

"They guessed," I said. "They went with the status quo."

"When the hell did they print these things?"

"February," I said right away. I thought I was right; I thought the picture of Hawk Harrelson, if there was one in eastern Ohio, wouldn't show him with the leg he'd broken. The Hawk, while we were looking for his five thousand dollar face, was getting votes for the All-Star Game even though he was disabled.

Four hours later, after a lecture on the psychological states of Wordsworth and Coleridge at each moment they wrote, after two more citizen witnesses, I followed Dick into his apartment. "Look at this kitchen," he said.

It had only been two days since I'd been in that kitchen, but I looked, wondering how large a damage deposit Dick put down when he signed the lease. The baseboards were gone, peeled from the walls. The tile was lifted and loose, as if it had been set back in place after a week of flood water worked it over. In one corner, there were eight scattered blocks, and among those pieces of tile stood Dick Dawson's dog, a pure-white Samoyed. It looked from me to the tile and back again, growling, sizing up, probably, whether I was someone who would ignore its kills or someone who'd come about discipline.

"That dog's been busy," I said, remembering the baseboards in place two nights before.

"We decided to keep the damage to one site. We're sacrificing the kitchen instead of scattering ruin around the house."

"Your landlord approve that plan?"

"Samoyeds do this. You can't stop them except to fence them off from the things that matter." It looked to me as if Dick's dog could leap this gate if it wanted to start on the essential things. "Ok, Thor," Dick said, releasing the catch.

The dog bounded over and rushed through the open front door. In a minute it was back, but Dick didn't lock it in the kitchen again or slam it with his fist for destroying an entire room. "Thor won't hurt anything while we're here. It's not like he's gone crazy. It's only when he's left behind he eats things."

"Last time I was here, it was only doing a little chewing, a little nip and tuck around the doorframes."

"Right," Dick said. "Here we were trying to keep him from marring everything in the apartment by giving him the kitchen to teethe on, a room with nothing we thought he could hurt. He must have been working on this place every minute we were gone yesterday. It's amazing what a dog can do when he sets his mind to it."

The Samoyed appeared satisfied. It wasn't cowering near any of the tooth-ridden walls. It was staring straight at both of us with the what-else-can-you-do-to-me glare of the death camp. "Live free or die," I said, but Dick didn't laugh.

"You're giving yourself one strange sense of humor," he said. "All your fear is getting misplaced."

I'd bought us two six-packs of Hop 'N Gator, a lemon-lime malt liquor Iron City was test marketing in western Pennsylvania and eastern Ohio. "Fag beer," Dick announced after taking his first swallow, and I had to admit it didn't taste like it could be delivering a malt liquor's worth of alcohol.

When she got home an hour later, Carol said she loved it, and Dick handed her one and searched out a Stroh's. Already the Hop 'N Gator wasn't sitting very well. It left an aftertaste that made me think of cyclamates. I thought maybe if you drank a dozen Hop 'N Gators every day for a year you deserved bladder cancer or whatever else the test mice acquired from diet soda. What I was accumulating, however, was an enormous headache, a cheap wine or bad gin sort of throbbing while Carol was drumming up dinner and the television was telling us about Angela Davis on the run after she supported one more anarchic tragedy in California.

I sat up when the newscast finished with a feature on somebody named Mrs. Pat Palinkas, who, it turned out, was the first woman to play in a professional football game. I'd never heard of the Orlando Panthers, but I was interested until the announcer admitted she was the holder for placekicks, that it was her husband doing the kicking. "You should have had Carol on one knee in the back yard," I said. "You should have kept practicing that sidewinder you picked up playing soccer."

Dick grunted. "Nothing about the hearings," he said. "We've dropped off the national news."

"We're in reruns," I said, and followed him back to the kitchen where Carol was about ready to feed us. She owned a thick, hardback cookbook with a green cover that said *McCall's*. Each night I'd eaten there, she picked a salad, a meat, and a dessert recipe from its pages and sent them our way. She didn't seem to care whether the vegetables were in season or the foods complemented each other. This time it was pork chops in the middle of the table, sweet and sour probably, because they appeared to be dipped in rust-colored tar. They reminded me of how fossils might originate, stuck in glop for a billion years. And I knew, glancing at the page where she placed her bookmark, that I could look forward to Old-Fashioned Applesauce Cake, Favorite One-Egg Cake, or McCall's Best Gold Cake for dessert. *Now to find out how good a cook you really are*, it said on the first page of the Perfect Pies section. *The really good cook makes really good pie crusts.*

Thor circled the table throughout the meal. The Samoyed's nails clicked on what was left of the tile, and I wanted to tell it to sit by me so I could slip it all of my Old-Fashioned Applesauce Cake. "Why do you put up with this dog?" I said.

"He's ours." Dick sounded like a father who'd just spent time talking to a police sergeant about his son and heard the words *Next time it'll go hard on the boy.*

"Hhaaah," Carol said at the end of her yawn.

I examined that kitchen again, saw how maybe that dog could worry the dry wall loose and then strip the panels right back to the wiring. "I know a guy back home who lost his dog," I said.

Carol stood up and walked to the refrigerator. She rummaged through the jars on a couple of shelves as if she couldn't finish her pork chop without something that hadn't been important when the meal began. "So how did he lose it?" Dick finally prompted.

"It barked at everything. It kept the guy up all night, so he tried putting it outside on a long leash, and it would fly off the porch and lunge at cars or whoever happened by on the sidewalk. It turned out, though, the leash was long enough for the dog to reach his bedroom window, and now it kept him up all night snuffling and growling."

I paused to see if Carol was finished. She was standing in front of the open refrigerator as if its light were an evil eye. "The dog hung itself," she said to the shelves, and Dick raised his eyebrows at me. I gave her a few seconds to complete the story for me, but she didn't turn around.

"Well, the guy shortened its leash," I started back in. "He decided he couldn't have the dog breathing under his window every night, and then the dog flew off the porch the next evening and didn't quite touch down. Snapped its neck. He found it dangling there in the morning after the best night's sleep he'd had in months."

"Maybe one of the neighbors tossed it off the porch," Dick suggested.

"Could be."

"Hhaaah," Carol exhaled, coming back to the table at last. "Maybe that fellow measured that leash to get things exactly right."

After the applesauce cake, Dick and I ended up standing near the edge of the grass lot he shared with the other tenant in the double. The Hop 'N Gator, by then, had given me something that seemed like what I'd feel when the aneurysm of the year 2000 struck me down, my version of the millennium of every religion that promised an ending both concrete and dated.

"Look at all the fireflies," Dick said, and I had to agree. There were thousands. They blinked on and off as if excited to be out there in the middle of August, as if they didn't know it was just about the witching hour for fireflies in that part of the country. I waved at every one of them, trying to think of the collective noun for fireflies—a host, a swarm, a throng—but I heard Dick say, "You're thinking frontal attack is stupid, right?"

I didn't have to answer. "I'll tell you how stupid I think it is," Dick said. "I'm going to drive right into Akron with or without you. I'm going to Light-Brigade the Nazis with or without any plan."

I looked at the flat Ohio countryside. Nothing I saw appeared threatening or evil. The landscape was monotonous. I didn't want to live here, but I didn't imagine people or objects inherently awful. "The Nazi on the phone," I said, "shouted, 'Dare to be great.'"

"Sounds like somebody raised on Dr. Spock," Dick said. "Like somebody who failed everything he was allowed to try and then was too dumb to grow up."

I nodded, but Dick was drumming on his bottle and staring at the yard as if it were pocked with sinkholes, and I was left behind to chew on what he'd already discarded. Like Thor in the afternoons, I was staring over the locked gate of the future thinking, *Well, that's it. Nobody's coming back.*

The fireflies seemed to be disappearing, as if a sort of low-lying cloud cover had moved in. The yard split where the light from inside cut it; the door slammed and the lawn was whole again. Thor bounded between us, choosing to leap against Dick's thigh before it nosed along the back fence for the perfect place to take a leak. If I had been staying with any other couple, Carol would have followed the dog outside and brought a beer. Or Dick would have called for her to join us.

The next morning I walked to campus from Dick's apartment. I was feeling shaky from the unknowns in the Hop 'N Gator and imagined the mile would do me good before class. Halfway, things hadn't improved, so I stopped and had coffee and a doughnut and the morning paper.

Mayor Satrom speaks today, it said on the front page. *The real story of the trashing of downtown Kent gets its day in court.* I turned the page. I knew what Mayor Satrom had to say, so I followed a column's worth of quotes from Melvin Laird, read his assurances that the nerve gas the army dumped into the ocean off Florida two days before wouldn't hurt anything because it was 16,000 feet deep. *Regardless,* the Secretary of Defense explained, *such a dumping will never happen again.*

Sure, I thought, paging to the Want Ads, checking to see if the Nazis had placed a recruiting notice. The columns looked as benign as the restaurant menu; I was as fueled as I could stand. I left a dollar on the table and started to do what I could about completing my pre-Shakespeare requirement. In two hours, I'd meet Dick Dawson at the hearings. I didn't want him to do all the translating, adding his interpretation to the Rashomon of August.

A woman and a teenage girl approached. From a half block away, there was no question the girl was the woman's daughter, but suddenly the woman steered the girl left, guided her off the curb and across the street to the other side. Although she was probably fifteen, the girl didn't resist. She acted like she was on a Trust Walk, like she was willingly blind to demonstrate there was at least one person in the world she would follow without question. She stared at me from across the street, and I thought the Hop 'N Gator had turned me green. "It's your hair, fella," I heard from behind me.

I pivoted. The man who spoke wore jeans and a sleeveless t-shirt. His hair was slicked back and smooth. Valentino, I thought. My father, twenty years ago. "And that dipsy-doo mustache. You look like somebody oughta got hisself plugged a while back."

"Thanks for the insight," I said, but the man kept on.

"You look like you been whupped with the shit stick, fella. The short end."

The woman's daughter still stared from the opposite sidewalk, the kind of look you might receive from the last passenger to cram into the lifeboat as it was rowing away from where you were bent over the railing of a fire-swept ocean liner.

Somebody like her mother had testified the week before. She'd said she was afraid to walk the streets of Kent because she didn't know what the students might do. I hadn't blamed her. I didn't know what I could do either. I'd been there when those fifty-four rounds were fired, but if they called me to the stand, they'd have at least one witness who wouldn't testify he was sure of himself, unlike Del Corso and Canterbury and the briar hopper looking at me with his I-want-to-kick-your-ass face on because my hair was two inches over my collar.

And when I found Dick after the morning hearings were over, saw him working his way back from the front rows where he must have sat for an hour before Satrom started in with *The disturbances were planned*, I said "I've given some thought to Akron."

Dick brightened. "Malice and mayhem," he said.

"Maybe," I said. "I've been thinking, that's all. We have a round of golf to play."

"You're screwing with me."

"We have plenty of time. Nine holes in two hours. I'll give you yes or no when we're done."

"The therapy of the leisure class," Dick said.

The first hole on the university course, a par four, was only 305 yards, and every time I teed off I imagined a hole in one, a couple of bounces on the fairway, the roll onto the green and down. Somebody would do it, but it wasn't going to be me after I rotated early and over-swung, hooking the ball so I had to search for it in the deep rough while a foursome stood watching as if they were thinking of teeing off and maybe matching my shot yard for yard with right to left spin.

I laid up short. I chipped to the back of the green and three-putted while Dick dropped a six-footer for par. And then, on the next hole, I let go a banana hook that drifted off the course entirely. "Nobody hooks like that," Dick said. "Those cows don't see golf balls, not on a short par three."

"What the hell," I tried. "There's no out of bounds." I figured I was forty yards left on a 140-yard hole. From outside the fence, the cows seemed stupidly passive, background for all the boring two-lane highways I'd been driving in the eight years I'd had a license. As soon as I stepped into the field, though, they raised their heads and pawed the earth. I knew dairy cattle weren't supposed to be aggressive, but my ball lay less than twenty feet from a cow eyeing me like I was something that would feel good under its hooves.

I worked my way into position. I used all the excuses of the unusual recovery to account for pivoting slowly, addressing the ball as if it were plugged in sand. And when I heard the cow shuffle, I imagined it striking me from behind, a cow's version of the grade school behind-the-knees trick, and kicking at my face when I fell.

Despite whatever good sense I had, I stepped back and turned to look. The cow was maybe a step closer, but it wasn't moving. "Watch out for Elsie," Dick said. He was leaning on his bag by the green.

There was nothing to do but step up and slap the ball quickly, a line drive that rolled through the green and stopped in the fringe on the opposite side. Not bad, really, I thought. The cow began strolling toward me, and I turned my back to hurry toward the fence like all the idiots in failed-escape stories.

"They're killers, you know," Dick said as I approached the green. "They take advantage of people who think they're stupid."

"Sure," I said. I'd visited a dozen farms. I'd ridden horses. There was nothing frightening about a field of cows. I used the putter from the apron, guessed the speed so lucky the ball died a foot from the hole, and heard, "Good up, Tex."

I tapped in. I wanted to tell Dick about the difference between walking through a field and hitting a golf ball from it. "I'm rolling now," I said. "I'll play you even up for the trip to Akron. You win, we go; I win, we drink beer like sane people."

Dick made par and smiled. "You giving me the three strokes I already have?"

"Sure."

"Ok, cowboy."

Behind us I heard one of the cows make a sound that, had I not known what was in that field, I would have called a growl. An hour later I'd made up the strokes, was plus one as we teed off on number nine. With maybe 120 yards to the flag, though, I flopped my approach under the lip of a trap, barely escaped, and three-putted from fifty feet to lose by one. "Here we go," Dick said.

"I guess."

"They're not cows," Dick said.

"That's right."

"They're not going to stampede."

It turned out we had to walk fifteen blocks, crossing and recrossing South Arlington Street, because Dick admitted, once we parked on Market, he only knew the Nazis were "on Arlington between the expressways." It was two miles of hunt and peck in a neighborhood where you save up for a down payment so you can move away. Planes skimmed overhead as they approached, I hoped, at the right altitude for the runways a half-mile away. And though I knew better, I thought maybe it was the air quality from the Firestone and Goodyear plants making me sick of the afternoon.

We'd covered about a mile and a half, closing in on Route 224, when Dick said "There." I looked where he was pointing and saw a door that said *So. Arlington Services.* Whatever Dick knew, that door wasn't giving it away.

I followed him inside before I had a chance to tell him this looked like a long shot. There was a tiny foyer and a flight of stairs leading to Christ knew what. The walls were black with a few white graffiti etchings somebody probably carved after pissing in the stairwell. I searched for *Kill Kent State Students*, but there was only stuff like *I give good head/ 555-3472.*

It reminded me of the stairs I had to climb to reach the dentist on Pittsburgh's North Side. *Dr. Mendel/Dr. Murray* it said on a door at the top of those stairs, but you had to trust those names to be there each time you returned six months later for another checkup. The door across the hall said *Allegheny Talent Associates.* Who went in there? I wondered for ten years. For all I knew, *Allegheny Talent Associates* was auditioning tap dancers, ventriloquists, and accordion players while I was accumulating fillings, was auditioning, even now, another generation of vaudevillians.

"Here we go," Dick said.

I thought there'd be nothing at all up there but abandoned offices, that Dick had gotten some ludicrous directions because nobody would expect anyone to follow-up on a tip like *Upstairs at So. Arlington Associates.* I shrugged and said, "I'm ready for the crazies."

"Hitler's finest."

I figured Dick, by now, understood there was nothing upstairs but emptiness because there we went, right to the dead-end landing that offered us the three doors of a thousand fables. All of them had smoked-glass windows. One said *Rubber City Enterprises*; one said *Akron Planning Systems*; one, improbably, claimed it opened to an *M.D.*

"Let's try Dr. Siejka," I said. "Maybe it's Rumanian for mass murder."

"That's thinking," Dick answered, turning the knob on *Rubber City Enterprises* before I could tell him I'd changed my mind about this trip.

It was locked. I twisted Siejka's doorknob to make sure he was out for the day as well, and then there was only one more chance we'd get slaughtered by idiots planning for the second coming.

Dick pushed on the door to *Akron Planning Systems*, and it opened so easily I thought for a moment normal people might be inside writing government proposals to renovate South Arlington Street.

"Can I help you?" a woman asked Dick from behind a solid-looking wooden desk.

"Is this where the call-line originates?" he asked her.

"Pardon me?"

"The recorded messages. Dial-A-Hate. Gestapo hit parade."

"Do you have an appointment?"

The door behind her opened. The man who stood in the doorway was dressed to sell insurance. "What can we do for you?" he said.

"Is this the Nazi hotline headquarters?"

"I'm afraid you're mistaken."

"What if I said we wanted to join? A haircut and brain damage would turn us into brown shirts."

The door at the bottom of the steps slammed. Five minutes ago, I hadn't been able to imagine one person ever entering this building, and now we had a traffic jam. I was waiting for Dick to look like he heard it, too, something that would jog him into common sense. "I guess I'll pass on the trim," he said then, so I knew he'd picked up on the two sets of footsteps on the stairs, could subtract the locked doors from the chances they were headed elsewhere.

"I understand," the man in the doorway said. "Where do you think you are, friend?"

Dick said, "I'm right here," but he'd already let himself glance back at the outer door.

The two men who entered wore long-sleeved white shirts and dark ties, dressed by the Mormon Church. They seemed harmless. Like the students who handed out leaflets in the snack bar, but neither of them greeted us with a sunny phrase. "And who might you be, friend?" the insurance agent asked.

"Come on," I said to Dick as if we had a choice.

"It's a sunny day, friend, and very dark on the stairs. Perhaps you've made a mistake," and both of us kept quiet, acting like we were at gunpoint or had been caught plagiarizing our junior high school social studies project.

The stairway was dark as the manager of *Akron Planning Systems* described. We walked down in a world that had turned to sound and touch: the shoe on wood, the hand on wallboard, the back of our heads sending sonar up the stairs behind us to sweep for echoes of clubs or knives or guns. When we reached the sidewalk, we treaded water for maybe ten seconds until Dick said, "See?"

I stood where somebody impatient with my tainted blood could have shot me from the stairwell. Enough of my brain activated to force *Walk* to my feet. If Dick wanted to know what I'd seen, he'd have to keep up.

"Right out in the open," he said, matching my cadence. "That means the cops let them. That means they have support."

The real street returned then. I listened to each building we passed and heard nothing but the white noise of traffic. We headed south, adding another block to our return trip, but crossed the street before we started back toward the car. Across from the *So. Arlington Associates* front door, Dick stopped again, and I had to wait for him to make a gesture.

Whatever he was going to say, I would have to disagree. I knew that as soon as he started clenching and unclenching his fists. He said, "We have an obligation here. We have to do our part for civilization," so disagreeing wasn't hard.

It was as easy to smirk at as the *McCall's* recipes that relied on adjectives. Puffy. Crispy. Perfect. A month before, when I read the Justice Department's memo after it was released by the *Akron Beacon Journal*, I'd been smug for days. "I shot two teenagers," a guardsman had been quoted, and I wanted a little frontier justice of my own. Listening to Dick's certainties, however, I was lost.

"So what are our choices?" he pushed.

I wanted to get us moving north, guide us toward the punctuation of yawns and another savory dinner. "What does that mean?" I said.

"Our choices. We have to do something now we know they're really here."

"They'll move on. They won't stay in one office more than a month or two."

"They want to be found. They want confrontation."

"And we're required to provide it?"

"Yes."

"By some force."

"Something like that."

"By decency."

"Yes."

I wanted to say, "Hhaaah." I wanted to talk Thor into spending the night in the *Akron Planning Systems* office. "And if we don't do anything?" I said.

"That's not in question here. Do you think it's in question?"

"Sure it's in question."

"So," Dick said, and he unraveled his fists. "You haven't been moved."

"I didn't say that."

"That's what I'm hearing."

I began to walk north. I knew Dick could recruit a commando squad and leave me out. I thought about the simplicity of action, that I was willing to walk all the way back to Kent, where the improbable volley had suddenly been fired, that I could stand being left behind by Dick, that I could watch him set out alone to invade the lair of the goon squad.

So I stayed shut up when I reached his car and turned to see him closing the distance between us. And I stayed shut up as he pulled onto Eastland Avenue for the drive through Tallmadge, out Route 261 into Kent. I didn't care what he had to say about the Nazis. I thought they had as much chance at success as a couple of hundred protesting students. For all I knew, the Akron Nazis had four members, as far on the fringe as some loonies making bombs in a basement to free white rats and hamsters from a laboratory.

"You're thinking all of this is stupid, right?" Dick said at last.

I didn't have to answer. A few seconds of silence was all Dick could listen to before he'd start in again. "I'll tell you how stupid I think it is," he said. "I feel like turning around right now and laying some waste to that office. I feel like dropping you off halfway through my U-turn."

"Whatever," I said, although I agreed with him there was something wrong with somebody like me who couldn't find intensity in things. And as soon as I thought it, I didn't believe it was a terrible thing at all.

CALLBACK

———

Each time Laura stirs, half-awake in the night, she pushes herself up on her elbow, leans forward over my head, and squints at the numbers on the clock radio. I know this because I'm certain I've never slept through one of her time checks. And I know, because I'm awake for half an hour afterward each time, that she sighs and drops onto her face, rolls slightly right, falls asleep within three breaths, and leaves me alone at 1:28, 3:14, and 5:06 as if her body were a conductor on a train tumbling nearly nonstop through desolate, stationless country.

She's waiting for work, the alarm set for 5:45, Top 40 music in the dark, the news, the weather, the sports, and the charted tunes again at 6:15 when she finally stirs, props herself, and stares at the numbers as if she hasn't heard the announcer repeat the time thirty seconds ago.

And then, for forty-five minutes, while she drinks coffee and works herself over in the bathroom, I sleep like the drugged, sprawled and heavy and dreamless until she returns to get dressed.

On weekends, though, since our son turned fifteen, she's lunged up at shorter intervals: 1:07, 1:39, 2:06, 2:34. She's on the local now, waiting for Darren to come home, surprised, she claims, each time he shows up at 2:59, 3:22, 3:47.

As if the dog doesn't tell us. As if she doesn't begin to growl whenever a car pulls up into the driveway. The low cough in her throat. The stammering yips when the car door slams. And then, when the side door opens, the full bark, the race into the kitchen where she plants her feet and yelps herself into recognition and silence.

So Laura will flop and roll and, finally, stay out. A half hour later, I'll lapse into something more than a nap because she won't be up and down from the worry of unconsciousness. So my son is home again without injury, and, if the phone rings, I can say, "To hell with that," knowing everyone who lived in my house is alive.

For nearly four months now, Darren has lived in another town, in a dormitory. You'd think some things would change. That Laura would sleep through Friday and Saturday nights. That I would wake up groggy with excess rest. Instead, the phone has rung a hundred times too late at night for anything but pranksters or the police calling from the college town where Darren is keeping no hours at all.

I've refused to answer the first weekend call. If it's the worst, I say, they'll call back, and I know Laura will rush to all of them, that when horror keeps her on the line, I'll extrapolate disaster from each assent and dissent of her monosyllabic litany. And now that my son is home again, now that he's been here for three weeks with another five days to go before the second semester begins, the dog is more frenzied than ever because Darren arrives in a strange car each night, having lost his driver's license to the law against underage drinking.

He's borrowed rides with the one girl he enjoys or any boy who's driving toward a party. All of them seem charmed except Darren, who has three years, now, to wait for the return of his license. Three offenses in four months—you'd think something would be learned. Camouflage. Restraint. Effective lying. I tell Laura he would have been better off doing drugs, that only alcohol steals your license, and she looks at me as if I were revving a chain saw.

After dinner, I look for leftover Christmas candy, and Laura tells me she's put all of it in the downstairs freezer. "To keep it," she says. "To slow you down."

I'm halfway downstairs when I smell a trash fire, my son's carelessness turning my house to rubble. I open his door without knocking. "It's patchouli," he says.

In the center of his room are three old beer cans, two with ashes on top, one with its lid on fire. Scattered on the carpet are tight, brown cones.

Something like Hershey's Kisses. Something like an experimental, long-lasting chew. Burning, they smell like something you'd light to disguise another odor. Contraband, I think. "Your friend was in the newspaper," I say.

"They print anything," he says. "They think anything's news."

"It's on the public record."

"It's her business. It's her mess."

"Now neither of you can drive."

The smell of patchouli makes me remember the times I stuffed dog turds into paper bags and burned them on the front porches of people I thought I hated. In Darren's prom picture, the girl is wearing a strapless gown, and I can understand why my son would risk her drunk-driving him into a stand of trees.

"She has to do rehab classes," he says. "She has to sit in a room with a bunch of hicks who spot for deer and pound each other with cue sticks in the parking lots of country and western bars."

"DUI is DUI," I tell him, like some smug asshole behind a desk. The girl is in the hospital. She has a cast and some facial stitches to worry her for a while. She'd waited, two nights ago, to leave the highway until after she'd dropped Darren off to the yammering of our Eskimo spitz.

"In a way," I try, "she's lucky."

An hour later, in the kitchen, before Darren comes upstairs, I ask the boys who have come to pick him up about school. "It's OK," each one of them says.

"I'll tell you what I like best," one says. "I'm not going to college in goddamned Pennsylvania. If I was here, I'd be on foot like Darren. I'd be hitching rides."

It gets them rolling for a while, all three complaining about the government, the police. One of them lost his license for three months last summer. None of them is a three-time loser who won't be driving until he's a senior in college. I wonder if whoever is driving is the one who's likely to drink the least. Without the help of beer, Darren has had two accidents. The insurance company, with the logic of greed, dropped the family even though Darren wasn't on the policy anymore. Some guy who gave us free calendars and pens each year mailed us the news.

I tell all three of these drivers what I'm thinking about velocity and how the human body maintains its speed independent of the vehicle. "Last year," one of them says, "I found out about that. I was fooling around in the basement where I used to play Nerf basketball when I was in middle school. I went up for a jump shot and smacked my head on the ceiling. I'd forgotten how low it was. I was maybe six inches shorter then. I went down. Just like that. Maybe out for a few seconds. I don't know. It was like I'd died. You ever feel like that? Like you'd been killed and maybe weren't going to get back in your body again? I've read about out-of-the-body travel. Sometimes I think everything I've done since then was done by somebody else, that I'm already in another world."

"Maybe," I say.

When they leave, my son following them to wherever they choose, Laura tells me their names. One of them, she footnotes, is known to be suicidal.

"Who announces something like that?" I say.

"People know," she says, as if that were a geometric proof.

I wonder how such things get to be known. Who decides it's not just the stupid talk of locker rooms and keg parties, what might come up if you got bored with bragging about whose breasts you'd fondled in the last twenty-four hours. What surprises me is the suicide watch isn't out for the guy who'd head-butted his way to limbo. "He's fine," Laura says. "He made his grades."

She's reading another article on the teenage psyche. Every magazine in the house is dog-eared where the ways to ruin are documented and discussed. Depression, drugs, alcohol, suicide—she's created a private reader's guide to despair and apprehension.

In one of those magazines, just before Christmas, I read about the dreams women have when they're pregnant. It listed the most common dreams by trimester: first—frogs, worms, potted plants; second—cute, furry animals; third—lions, monkeys, dolls. I asked Laura, "What did you dream with Darren?"

I expected her to say "How would I know?" or "Who remembers something like that?" but she answered at once: "I dreamed about my father. And sometimes about my grandfather," and I nodded and thought she'd prepped herself for that question, that she'd already made some sort of self-study of premonition and omens.

I know I'm not dreaming about much of anything, that I'm starting to miss Laura's earliest wake-up calls at the digital clock. Since September I've been reading, doing crosswords until 1:00 A.M. Since Thanksgiving I've been going downstairs and shooting an hour's worth of pool, enough to get me to the exhaustion of 2:00 A.M.

I've gotten past the run and gun of eight ball, the splash and fire of nine ball. I shoot straight pool now, play "safe" when the shots aren't there, and take seriously the shots of my imaginary opponent. I don't want to be playing with anyone who doesn't concentrate, who doesn't approach the game the same way I do. It's boring playing against people who aren't paying attention, who, after a while, aren't even watching you run the table and turn it over by breaking the rack off your first shot. My best run has been thirty-eight. Not bad, though I still miss shots sometimes, the table open for my ghost player or myself left dead after a simple shot.

When she asks, I tell Laura that sleep is overrated, that it's less necessary than she believes. I've read that there's no evidence sleep restores the body, that tissue isn't repaired because of rest.

People don't break down from sleeplessness, I tell her. People recover in a few days and get on with their lives. Meanwhile, they've lived more than usual.

I know Darren sleeps past noon each day, and he doesn't act refreshed. One afternoon between Christmas and New Year's, I talked him into a game of straight pool. After two racks, he was distracted. He splattered the third rack off an impossible combination and put his cue away when I ran the easy table. "All I ever play is eight ball," he said. "On coin tables you don't play finesse."

This time, when the phone rings, it's 2:19 and Darren isn't home. When Laura doesn't hang up, I listen. When she carries the phone into the bedroom, I say, "Shit."

"You take it," she says. "You deal with it."

So I know he's alive before I put my ear to the phone, manage "Hello" to get things going. It's not one of the guys from the kitchen. It's one of Darren's friends whom I recognize, and he tells me there's a problem. Darren is throwing up blood.

"What do you mean, blood?" I say.

"Blood."

"How much blood is that?"

"We put garbage bags around him. We called an ambulance. He told us not to, but we called anyway."

I try to decipher how drunk this boy is, how much I can rely on his judgment. "Where are you?" I say, and when he starts giving me directions immediately, I multiply the blood by two.

Laura watches my eyes and finds my calculations there. She says, "You see?" as soon as I hang up.

"I don't know anything yet," I say.

"You can call," she says. "No matter what."

"OK," I say automatically, but instead of leaving, I wait for her to add something.

"You don't mean that," she says.

"What else would I do?"

"You'll walk in on me. You'll hope I'm sleeping."

"Only if it's not the worst," I say, recognizing the truth.

It wouldn't have mattered if my son's friend had forgotten every landmark and left turn in his directions. All I have to do is drive until I see an ambulance parked in front of what looks like a decaying motel.

Thrifty Apartments, the sign says. The dashboard clock reads 2:37, the time of morning I'd expect a place like this to have at least one police car busy with wife-beating, disturbing the peace, assault. The ambulance fits right in, something with a flashing light arriving before dawn. I pull behind it, park it in like a fool in an active fire lane, but when I reconsider, it's because I don't want to see my son's emergency room face from behind a windshield, turning him into some car-crash victim being loaded like produce.

I back up, park the car between two old pickups, and walk toward the ambulance where two men are standing together as if they're sharing a beer in the parking lot. "You the manager?" one says.

"No."

"What's the problem?"

"You know anything about this call?"

"I'm the father."

"Of the caller?"

I look at him to see how far forward his forehead protrudes, whether or not his hands swing below his knees. Behind one of these doors my son is hemorrhaging, and so far, neither man has knocked.

I see we're at number 4. "We don't know which apartment," he says. "We'll be here all night. There's twenty units."

"The call came from number 1," I say. "Starting at the beginning would have had you out of here by now."

"Whose father are you?" he says, but I walk around the corner, backtracking to number 1, and knock. It's dark and silent. I knock again because the boy who called had given me the number, and none of the teenagers who'd been drinking in that apartment would have waited for the ambulance. At best it would be Darren and the girl who lived there, toughing it out in the darkness, refusing the legal complications of rescue. Something to think about, my son bleeding to a bandit's death in this dump, his hand over the mouth of the party hostess.

I knock on the next door, number 20, and when nobody answers, I try the knob to prove it's locked. When the door swings open, I walk inside to ask a couple looking at me over the back of the couch why they don't bother with their door when people knock.

"Yo, asshole," the guy says, and from halfway across his living room, I can see the woman isn't dressed, the man no one my son would be interested in drinking himself to death with.

"Sorry," I say, like somebody watching a missile silo empty its contents toward heaven.

"Get the fuck out," I hear as I lunge at the door, regretting turning around, sorry indeed that the shotgun blast would rip me apart from behind. But when I hear, "Get the fuck out" again instead of the last roar of existence, I breathe in the doorway, turn, and get to number 2 alive.

The attendants are inside. "It's not our man," one says, coming back out. An eyewitness isn't good enough for me. I step past him and into the bedroom. A fat man is sprawled naked across the bed, not responding to the overhead light.

"We thought it might be number 2," one attendant says when we're all outside again. "The door was open. The light was on in the bedroom. Sometimes people use the number next door, give themselves a minute to get things in order, make sure their stories are straight."

I don't believe him, but I let it pass. I realize I'd grown up trusting ambulance drivers to be sober men who could be counted on for lucid behavior. Now there's no sign of number 20's tenants, no sign it's anything but stupid to have faith there's a reason to stay here.

"Listen, we'll do a callback," the attendant says. "We'll call the number where the original call came from." I want to pat him on the back, say "Way to go," but I wait between number 1 and number 2 while he leans into the ambulance. The phone rings in number 1.

"There's our emergency," the other attendant says. "There's our reason for standing out here in the snow. Your kid's got some explaining to do. If you're not up to kicking his ass, you let me know." He motions to the ambulance with a thumbs-down sign. "They've flown the coop," he says. "They're patching him up someplace else."

When I get home, it's 3:14 and Darren is in the shower. Laura is lying on the bed, and when I say "What's the story?" she refuses to answer. I wait for the water to stop running. I sit at the kitchen table doing nothing at all until Darren walks out of the bathroom in shorts and a T-shirt. "U.S. Open, 1990," it says on the shirt. In six weeks, he's supposed to try out for his college tennis team.

"I was a little rough," he says. "But I'm OK now."

"Your friend says it was more blood than he'd ever seen. He said they put trash bags all around you to keep the blood off the floor."

"He's an alarmist. I'm OK."

"No, you're not."

"I don't know what got into me."

I think of the fat man lying across the bed in number 2, of the woman in number 20, both of them naked at 3:00 A.M. I think of my son in number 1 a couple of hours ago, before his body gave out, whether or not he'd been naked with the girl who rented that apartment. Last spring, she'd turned her hair into a fifties two-tone car; she'd had a ring looped through her nose. She'd been told to repeat her senior year in high school, and her parents had thrown her out. "Here's your college," my son told me they'd said. "Here's your tuition," handing her six months' rent and three suitcases to fill.

I'd seen that girl a few times since the summer. She'd taken to wearing clothes that reminded me of animal hides—leopard, zebra, tiger. I'd never seen anything like them on sale in our small town. I want to tell Darren about a cartoon I'd seen, a caveman standing in front of his tribe saying, "With this fabulous new invention, the knife, you no longer have to wear whole animal." I can't imagine him spending ten minutes of his life with this neo-troglodyte.

"Your mother's going crazy," I try. "She's catatonic."

"I'm sorry," he says. "She shouldn't worry so much."

"She runs to the phone in the middle of the night. She thinks you're dead or in jail every time it rings after midnight."

"This never happened before," he says.

"You don't even live here, and we get calls every weekend. Breathers and people who hang up without giving their names."

"Some of those phone calls are my friends," Darren says.

"So why would they call when you're not home?"

"They don't know that," he says. "They don't know if I'm not home for the weekend."

"Why not call in the daytime? Why not call when people are awake?"

"They think I'm home. They think I'm up."

"They think his mother's up," Laura says when I slide into bed. "They think she's sitting in the kitchen drinking coffee as a chaser for every adrenaline surge their phone calls jolt."

"You stop answering, they stop calling," I say, with all the certainty of the gods of platitudes.

"You start bleeding for no reason, you start going to the doctor's," Laura says, and she rolls over to face her dresser.

I wait for the phone to ring to see if she'll get up to answer. After twenty minutes, I ask, "You want me to take him?" When she doesn't flinch or say a word, I add, "OK."

Darren sleeps until two o'clock on Sunday. Nobody tries to wake him; nobody calls Sunday night, either before or after midnight. On Monday I take him to the doctor, then drive him to the hospital for X-rays of his digestive tract: cautionary fluke, ulcer, an esophagus ruptured by retching. After he drinks his barium, he goes off to machinery and I settle down to find a magazine.

The man beside me moans. He moans again, and I see he is trying to read *Field and Stream*. "They always have it for me here," he says. I go back to the pile of magazines, and he says "Ohhh" as he reads from a page opposite a picture of a man standing in a stream wearing hip-high waders. "You know what I hate about this place?" he says. "I can never get a parking place. I park on the street and walk, and when I get here, I think to myself, 'Where is everybody? Where the hell are all the people who filled the lot with their cars?'"

On the elevator, when we're leaving, Darren tells me about the X-ray procedures. "I didn't know I'd get to watch," he says, and I'm surprised as well, think perhaps it's part of a scare technique for young, careless patients. "I could see myself. I could see my stomach, how it moves. It was like personalized PBS."

"We'll see how things are working in there by tomorrow," I say.

"There's nothing wrong with me, Dad."

"That's what the X-rays are for."

"All I got was another talk."

"That ought to tell you something."

"Right. Nobody knows anything."

"They're concerned. The doctor's known you for years. Two more days and we have to believe you can take care of yourself."

"I don't even have a car. I don't even have a license. How can I get hurt?"

The next time I get home from another committee meeting in the state capital, all the outside lights are on: the front porch, the side porch, the twin bulbs that flank the garage doors. They're shining like a three-in-the-morning phone call, and I sit in the car in the driveway where it's bright enough, it seems, for baseball. Finally, I walk to the side door, turn the handle, and find it's locked.

From inside, the dog begins to bark, and I know before I get the key in the lock and open the door on the surprised and suddenly silent spitz, that a neighbor will be sitting at the kitchen table, that she'll be drinking coffee, that she'll settle her hands in front of her, holding a cup, and begin by saying, "Your wife wants you to call her. The number is by the phone, and it's very important."

Which is the dream I have every night while I wait for Laura to rise and fall. Which is what I wake to at the intervals she provides. And I tell myself, pulling from a space in the hospital parking lot, that when Darren is back at school, when we've reclaimed the house and her schedule for waking and sleeping is regular again, I'll ask Laura what she dreamed about before she was pregnant. And, if she's willing, I'll ask her what she dreamed about just before we were married, giving her a chance to work her way back to those nonstop nights, waiting for her sense of what she didn't listen to when the oracle spoke in the darkness.

DARWIN IN THE CITY

———

John Tomlins drove. His wife Rachel sat in the back between their two sons to ensure they didn't rake and claw at each other in retaliation for some insult. His daughter sat beside him listening to her portable radio through tiny earphones, doing something with her hands she'd seen on *Solid Gold*.

Tomlins was trying to see far enough ahead of his moving car to keep from crashing into the next darkened object that was carelessly out of place. He squinted. He pressed his glasses against the bridge of his nose to stir up the coagulated soup of his vision. They were riding up this unfamiliar road in a Harrisburg suburb to find the movie theater that was showing a film about a man who takes his family into the jungle to discover the meaning of life.

"It's must viewing," he'd said, when his children had groaned and suggested Eddie Murphy doing a cover version of Indiana Jones. Tomlins had read the *Heart of Darkness* version of *The Swiss Family Robinson* months before and been relieved for a few hours that someone else, even if he was fictional, was sensing the end of life as everyone in America had come to know it.

The man in the book hadn't gone crazy until he'd been foolish enough to sail for Central America. There were plenty of alternatives Tomlins was considering that would deal with disaster. He just had to think of one that was suitable.

He followed a lane that was merging with a crowded highway. A strip of franchises and shopping centers glowed ahead of him, throwing the middle of the highway into obscurity. Tomlins slowed and pulled left when the headlights in his side mirror broke slightly. At once he felt the car rise on the whitecap of a medium strip he'd thought was flat. His daughter clutched at the air above her head, transformed by the sweet horror of the roller coaster simulation.

The car dipped and then rose again, completing its small tumble into traffic. "Good job," his fifteen-year-old said from behind him.

"You can't see," his wife said. "You're blind and you won't admit it."

"It's all these lights, the way they saturate the road and forget about what it does to vision."

He saw what had to be the sign for the multiplex of cinemas and slid into the left lane to look for the entrance. "Anyway, we're here," he said, seeing the full-scale median end, nothing to block his way so there had to be an entrance over there in the gloom. He turned hard left and knew by the shouts from the backseat that he was in the midst of error.

No road to anywhere appeared. There was only a curb that was high enough to cave in the front axle, so he swerved right, facing the oncoming traffic while his wife screamed and his children sat silently. There was nothing to do but accelerate, drive up the slow lane, and pray for a break in the curb before the nearest headlights exploded through the windshield.

He heard his name and God's repeated twenty times in three octaves before he pulled the car left at the first open space, a drive-through bank, as it turned out. A chorus of horns faded into the Harrisburg evening.

"Get out from behind there," his wife said, and Tomlins opened the door and stood beneath a sign he could read from this distance. "First Northern Bank," he said to himself, listening to bells tell him he'd left his keys in the ignition.

Better.
Better.
Worse.
Better.

Tomlins stared at the tiny letters that ran across the screen like illegible subtitles from films distributed in foreign countries. Not something showing in France or Spain, not some country where he could at least catch familiar words as they scrolled across the screen. This was profoundly foreign, like Urdu or Pashto: B J D S H, nothing but consonants in the tough rows, the ones you were supposed to make out unless you wanted to be stuck with Coke bottle glasses that made your eyes swim into the center of your face each time you tried to arrange yourself in the mirror. All of the vowels seemed to be near the top: A E D U F, he read to get things rolling, something like the openmouthed wail of an infant ending in the thud of its head against a wall.

Better.

Worse.

Within minutes, Tomlins had lost the sense of how he stood, whether or not the lines he failed to identify were ones meant to be read by anyone still sighted. He took longer pauses to decide if things looked worse with each succeeding lens; he turned dry-mouthed when, for three consecutive changes, he saw nothing but the diffused light of the sun behind an inversion smog. Were their glasses that weak?

"He couldn't find a problem," he told Rachel twenty minutes later.

"Are you getting new glasses?"

"Sure, but the prescription's not much different."

He caught her staring at the way his face notched inward behind his glasses. She was sizing up the possibility that his eyes might actually touch when they were seen through the next set of lenses, but all she said was, "Of course it is. You'll see. Wait'll you put them on."

"He said this was the best he could do. He said there's no return to Eden in this business, but I should at least be able to see through the fence."

A week later, Christmas behind him, Tomlins picked up his brand new glasses and took a test drive into the country, closing one eye and then the other, measuring the difference in acuity. He took off the new glasses and put on the old; he put himself through ten miles of vision tests and decided he couldn't see well enough to be trusted driving, at least at night, when his eyes, apparently, lowered their power like the AM radio stations near the rural town they lived in, suddenly, at sunset, reverting to static. Whether or not he was going blind couldn't be settled, not yet, anyway, because the optometrist was probably second-rate, the guesses Tomlins made in his office probably out of sync because his judgment had been marred by fear. Perhaps he had simply called out his choices one click late, like a student sweating over his SATs, skipping over number 17 on his answer sheet and filling in hours' worth of BDCCBABDCC that validated idiocy.

For the next two days, he wore the glasses and smiled, waiting for the headaches and the tunnel vision that would verify the approaching end of the visible world. He watched television from five feet further back and began to imagine himself booked on a round-the-world cruise, taking his last sighted fling like the children he read about who flew to Disneyworld a month before they died of previously unheard-of diseases. His favorite was the syndrome that turned nine year-olds like his younger son into doddering, wrinkled miniatures of antiquity. He remembered that as soon as someone had flown one of these rarities in from Asia to shake hands with Mickey Mouse, another one had popped up in Texas and been airlifted in for a reunion of sorts, the two withered children riding a golf cart with Goofy. Tomlins had never heard of a third case, so perhaps it hadn't been the start of some exponentially spreading epidemic.

He was very nicely coming apart, but he managed to drive his family one-hundred and thirty miles to Philadelphia on New Year's Eve before he became disoriented at a confusing intersection in King of Prussia, making a desperate, guesswork turn that took his wife and children, in near daylight, toward the lanes marked Wrong Way in letters just large enough for him to see as he entered the double barrel of oncoming holiday traffic.

"Oh Christ," he said, swerving and jolting one tire over a safety island and back into lanes that held cars pointed in the same direction as he was. Nobody said anything, so Tomlins knew this mistake had been committed by someone who was beyond criticism and ridicule. He limped to the parking lot of the Howard Johnson's where they had a reservation and maneuvered the car carefully into a slot.

The headache he decided would be permanent began as soon as he turned off the ignition. "Give Mom your keys," his daughter shouted from behind the wall of sound in her ears. "You drive like you're drunk."

Reflexively, he glanced in the mirror. There didn't seem to be a police cruiser emerging from the gloom.

"That's it," his wife said. "That's the absolute end. I know what it is now; it's not even that dark. You know what it is?"

Rachel was hunched over the seat, leaning from between his sons with an expression that suggested she was their moronic older sister, baggage carried for a lifetime by a mother who'd conceived her as a preteen alcoholic. Tomlins couldn't think of what "it" was.

She was triumphant. "You know perfectly well what it is, John," she said. "Someone with your eyes can't be getting his glasses from a department store." Tomlins went ahead and nodded because his best hope was agreeing. He heard the unison cheer he imagined all the world's great misunderstood must have heard as they collapsed for the final time.

In an hour they were back on the highway, Rachel driving them to a shopping center five miles away to see a movie about a singing, man-eating plant. Tomlins had seen the original years before when he could still make out the details, tell one character from another even when they weren't being filmed close-up.

For the first two miles, he touched the brakes every time something rushed out of the fog. He slammed the pedal to the floor and tried to prevent destruction ten times before he gave up his family for lost, nothing he could do from the passenger's seat except listen to the squawks and squeals of his children who had been reunited in the backseat. He took off his glasses and started getting acclimated to the way his corrected vision was going to be just before the light went out forever.

Moons and void. The landscape reverted to Genesis, the first day, when it was good just because there was light and darkness. Tomlins felt as if he was flying, his life in the hands of a stranger. From several feet away, Rachel shimmered through the translucent curtain that had been drawn between them.

"Let your father decide," Rachel told the children in the theater, so they sat in the fourth row, six rows between them and the nearest people, two couples who were obviously drunk. The men yelled at the beginning of each preview. "Oh God, grant me one more," Tomlins heard when the third trailer came on. "Oh God, I am blessed," he heard when the fourth preview began. The women giggled at everything the men said, but five minutes into the feature, just as a shelf collapsed when a nerd flinched as his tyrannical boss shouted, the screen flared into a white dazzle of blankness.

"What happened?" his nine-year-old whispered.

"The film snapped," Tomlins said, and immediately there was laughter from behind him.

"Yo, asshole!" one of the men shouted. "Yo, shithead!"

His son turned in his seat to look back. "Not you," Tomlins said to him as the houselights went up.

After the hero achieved happiness thirty-five minutes late, they ate dinner and watched the Times Square apple dangle while Dick Clark explained its construction. By the time a girl-group called the Bangles had finished showing everyone how to "Walk Like an Egyptian," the apple had started to fall and Tomlins could turn it off for another year.

"It's OK," he said in the morning. "Look, it's broad daylight. It's just cloudy. It's calm. It's not icy. There's no sun reflecting off snow. It's as good a day as you can get for New Year's. I can drive in these conditions."

Everybody was busy with the unlimited doughnuts Howard Johnson's had provided for breakfast. It was going to save them time to make the best of this hospitality room and get on the road to Philadelphia as soon as they could.

At 8:00 a.m. New Year's morning, they'd already lugged their suitcases outside and returned for the doughnuts without seeing or hearing anyone. His children each took one for the road and humored him by allowing him back behind the wheel.

"We're not dead yet," his daughter said. "We're not even dented."

"We're off to see the Mummers," Tomlins shouted, "the wonderful Mummers of Phil."

"Philly, Dad," his oldest said. "You can't just drop a syllable and pretend you have a song. It wasn't the land of Ozzy."

"Like Ozzy Osborne," his daughter added. "Like the bat eater."

"A dove's head. He bit off a dove's head," his son said.

"That's gross." His daughter was horrified. "A dove's pretty."

"Wait'll you see these guys," Tomlins said. He was almost happy. The signs were clearer in daylight; he knew the way downtown, a place where they could park so they'd have to hike only half a mile to the parade route.

Thirty minutes later, they were on Chestnut Street, the Delaware River at their backs. "Over there is Independence Hall, the Liberty Bell, all that stuff," he explained. "You're walking beside history."

"Where's the parade?" His youngest son was the only one listening.

"A couple of blocks. It's not far once we get up to Race Street. You watch the signs and tell us when we turn."

"What's wrong with those men?"

"They're street people. They sleep on those grates for the heat." Tomlins was feeling worldly, at one with the experience that separates fathers from their children.

The next corner was Race. "Left or right?" he asked his son, but Tomlins didn't have any audience at all now. A Vietnamese family was gathered beside a rolled-up red blanket printed with a design meant to suggest cave drawings. They spoke singsong queries to each other, all of the questions, he was sure, about what sort of horror had expired inside the blanket.

He paused. The blanket wasn't near any grate. It was unsheltered, almost on the curb of the intersection four blocks from where the all-day parade would pass for the next ten hours, men in feathers and sequins, wings and dresses. Here was death, most likely, Darwin in the city, but he didn't want to see it just now, the new year still in swaddling clothes. Already those strutters and dancers were swaying toward them, perhaps only minutes away. Other people were walking by without comment; there was no guilt here, no unrolling of the blanket to confirm about subtraction.

Tomlins turned, and they left the Vietnamese to deal with the answers. "That fellow didn't have a happy new year," he said, getting the air cleared.

"What fellow?" his youngest asked.

His older son was beaming. "The dead guy in the blanket," he said.

"I didn't see any dead guy. Did I miss seeing a dead guy? Can we go back?"

"He was inside the blanket; we can't go back."

"How do you know he was inside?"

"You can tell. You don't have to see everything to know it's there."

They were two blocks from the parade route when he realized with the certainty of the condemned that the Mummers' Parade had been postponed. The intersection at Broad Street wasn't clogged. There hadn't been any clots of people slogging along the arteries of Philadelphia, no bleary-eyed, nauseous parents scuffing slowly behind their children.

Three strides later, his wife said, "John," using his name the way she did to introduce a plugged toilet or a melting freezer. He took four more steps to form his announcement.

"The parade's been called off," he said cleverly.

His children constructed their own pronouncements of his

worthlessness as a tour guide and a father. Not one person on the street, they could suddenly tell, looked as if he thought a parade would be passing any time soon. "Let's hear it for the jerk family," his teenager said. "Let's hear it for the hicks. Let's hear it for the hillbillies," he went on, beginning to applaud, slowly and steadily, refusing to stop even when Tomlins shot him his evil-that-men-do look.

Rachel got them moving again. "Let's go make sure," she said, sounding to Tomlins like someone who wanted to unroll the red blanket and kiss the gray face inside.

He saw the return trip stretching out in front of him like an epic miniseries, one of those blockbusters that had evolved into a television staple for people foolish or bored enough to spend six nights of their lives watching decayed or talentless actors lusting and betraying and finally, in gauze-effect, the soundtrack noodling along, screwing each other under sheets pulled exactly halfway down the woman's breasts. There were world wars to be filmed again, Communist takeovers, mother killers, wife slaughterers, mass murderers, family sagas of reds and yellows, blacks and ethnic whites, preferably downtrodden and tormented and pathetically heroic.

He completed the next block and stared up the blur of Broad Street, which looked as if it was being used for location shots for a neutron bomb story, a weeklong series in which one survivor of each major race and sex is introduced hourly until Thursday, when this re-creation breaks down into rape and murder, leaving only, on Friday night, the white woman and the black man, both so perfectly chiseled that all will be well in the gray new world.

"It must have been announced," Rachel said. "Why didn't we listen to the radio? Why didn't we watch television?"

"We watched last night. They said it wasn't going to snow until tonight, that the parade was on."

"We could have parked right here," his daughter said. "Then we wouldn't have to walk back to the river."

His oldest began to applaud again. "Let's hear it for the farmers," he said. "The guy on TV last night said they would decide in the morning if they were going to have the parade."

When they passed the corner with the red blanket, a moaning man was sitting on it with his hand extended. "Is that the dead man?" his nine-year-old said. "Did somebody help him?" Tomlins imagined this wino unfurling last night's casualty into the gutter, taking over this space like an urban squatter.

"It looks like all's well," he said, and started a diagonal through Independence Mall, cutting past the grounds full of patriotic memorabilia. Open year-round, it said on the one sign he bent over to read, but everything was locked.

When they got into the car at Penn's Landing, he turned on the radio. "Winter storm warning," the announcer said. "Most likely it will arrive by early evening, perhaps sooner. The Mummers' Parade," he added, "has been delayed for the eighth time in eleven years."

"How come we didn't know that, Dad?" Tomlins heard.

"They always had it when I was little," he said, not turning, realizing that for the first time in weeks nobody was asking him not to drive. He decided on Route 30 instead of the turnpike. They had all day; they'd wasted enough money, and so he drove through one dead town after another, the neutron bomb route winding west from Philadelphia, all along Business Route 30 after he missed the sign for the bypass.

Coatesville, the sign said at the largest and bleakest of the towns. It looked, to Tomlins, like a reconstruction of his boyhood home. It had a steel mill and thousands of yellowing frame houses set inches from the road so children could leap suicidally in front of cars from their front doors.

By now people had returned to the street, the ones who had been sleeping inside lead-lined rooms and were blinking at the miracle of their existence. Every survivor here was black. It was nearly eleven o'clock and snow was beginning to flurry, sweeping back and forth in eddies on the street.

Immediately, Tomlins had trouble making out the limits of his lane, the landmarks that would orient him to the approaching Dutch Country. As soon as the last black man disappeared into the rearview mirror, the Amish were conjured up out of the landscape.

They were as far as Paradise when he couldn't see anything but oversize, something like the huge billboard for Zook's Hex Signs. Tomlins imagined old Zook inside printing up thousands of identical symbols, but the road was turning slick, and he was struggling to make sure they didn't die.

"You having trouble up there?" Rachel said. "Your eyes holding up?"

"It's light out. I'm OK in the light."

"Boscov's," his older son said.

"I didn't get them from Boscov's. They don't do prescriptions at Boscov's."

"Sears."

"There was a real optometrist. He even checked me for glaucoma."

"JCPenny."

"That's not what your mother meant by a department store."

"Gee-Bee's."

"She meant a franchise."

"Kmart."

"A vision franchise."

"Let your father concentrate," his wife broke in.

Tomlins waited. He started counting and reached eight before he heard, "I could take over, John."

"This is snow. I don't have problems with snow; my problems are with night."

There was an end to it, a remission. For the third time since they'd left the city, his daughter found "Walking in the Rain" on the car radio. "You're dismissed," the singer said again, and Tomlins wondered how you acquired a tone like that which would make someone react, perhaps, as if you'd suddenly shoved a handgun under his nose, promising to deliver him from the age of anxiety.

Now they were in the heart of Amish Country, just outside Lancaster, a few miles south of the neighboring towns of Bird-in-Hand and Intercourse where all of the sexual energy of these people was printed on road signs that were obliterated by the snow.

The world outside was full of whirling hex signs. Tomlins studied the indistinct lane in front of him with the despair of a lung cancer victim invited to read his X-ray by some trendy doctor. Somewhere soon his malignancy would be confirmed.

"You want to stop?" he said to the windshield. "You want to pull over and wait it out at one of these authentic Dutch Country restaurants? Get your fill of corn soup? Potpie? Get some died-in-the-wool homemade apple butter?" He would have read the whole menu except for the car that was suddenly backing up in his lane.

Tomlins laid on the horn, and the car in front of him lurched forward and then spun sideways, drifting onto the shoulder, down an embankment, and out of the tunnels of his vision.

"You've killed them, John," his wife observed from the backseat. "You've gone and run somebody off the road with your blindness."

In another moment she said, "You're not stopping, are you? You're leaving it all behind."

"Hit and run," his teenager said. "This is like television."

He answered by pressing on. It was crunch time for natural selection; it was his reflexes verses the oncoming darkness. There was nothing he could do for anyone but watch them tumble briefly in the near reaches of what he could still decipher.

He slowed and stopped. He edged the car around and retraced his path back to the tracks that plunged over the rounded shoulder of the highway. He turned again, parked with his flashers blinking dismally, and made everyone get out, sure the car would be struck within seconds.

Tomlins peered down the short hillside to where a shape moved like a stunt man in a flaming asbestos suit. "Hey!" he shouted.

"You tell me," a man's voice said, the shape climbing toward them, "how come Eldon Pace isn't dead?"

Tomlins could sense there was more to his problem with balance than the recent accident and the four inches of snow he was laboring through. He'd come back to see about the welfare of a morning drunk.

"We wanted to make sure you were all right," he said, as the man gained the shoulder and blew gin breath into Tomlins's face.

"Sure I'm all right. Would I be dragging my ass up this hill if I was anything but all right? Though I don't mind telling you old Eldon Pace nearly bought the farm."

"Well, Eldon, I'm glad to hear that."

"Sure you are. Now you don't have to do anything but give me a lift to the nearest phone. Triple A'll tow me out in no time. All it did was get itself stuck down there."

"Well, we can do that, Eldon. We can get you in out of the snow."

"Goddamn, but you were Johnny-on-the-spot, waiting for me up here almost before I could get myself out of the damn car. You see me go over, maybe? You see the fool who barreled up behind me so fast I hit the gas hard like a little kid would do? Surprised the hell out of me is what he did."

Tomlin's children were paying attention to Eldon Pace, deciding whether or not to slip him clues about the identity of the driver. "I wouldna thought anybody could be goin' that fast in this stuff. I was sorta creeping myself along I was so blind."

"That's two of us."

"Yeah? I'll bet there's more out there. We ought to get ourselves in your car and move on out of here before the next blind man runs us all down."

They piled back in the car. His children had decided on blackmail, some future innuendo about how they'd saved him from the contempt of Eldon Pace. His daughter, without complaining, crammed herself into the backseat so Pace could settle in beside Tomlins, happy to be alive after getting gin-paralyzed on snowbound Route 30.

"I don't mind telling you I've had myself a snootful this morning, but I don't for damn sure know how anybody can speed after drinking. It's alcohol that lets you see the precariousness of it all. You see how one false move will settle your hash for good."

Tomlins let him talk, looking through the snow for the first service station.

"Jesus, I about had the goddamned thing parked back there, just about inching my way through the wilderness. But what I didn't take into account was the nature of fools with the hurry-ups, how they go on and give you the horn like they're about to turn you into the core of a fireball if you don't give it the old gas. I feel like I oughta look that fellow up somehow, let him understand I think he's a real shit-for-brains maniac."

Tomlins felt a distant need to identify himself, but all of this snow had displaced them. They were simply heading for the next telephone inside something roofed and heated while the road entirely vanished.

There was no horizon, he thought. Wasn't that one of the universal starting points for orientation, for finding your place on the planet? It would have been the last thing to go before everything in front of his eyes turned into a uniform, frameless white.

THE STONE CHILD

——

"They're going to induce it," Syl said. She poured a bowl of whipped eggs into the skillet, covering the chopped jalapenos and chorizo. She nodded at the juice and coffee on the table. "To be safe." I checked the clock over the stove. Ten thirty-five, and already so hot I thought about taking breakfast into the basement. "I wanted it to just happen," she added.

"Of course." I watched her slide a spatula under the omelet. She was so big her elbow was hardly bent as she reached toward the burner.

"Maybe it will," Syl said. "There's a chance. There's forty-five hours yet. I'd like that. He should get to choose something."

"Christ, it's hot. You must be roasting."

Syl fiddled with the eggs and smiled. "You know what I'd like?" she said. "Sitting in the movies. It will feel good inside."

"There's something that's over by three?"

"It's summer, Bobby. They have matinees. That war movie starts at noon. You'll be able to get to work on time."

"Whatever you want," I said.

"I love history," Syl said, and then she glanced down at her swollen belly. "And it will take my mind off things. You know."

"I know."

"Maybe it will make me feel better, too."

"Maybe," I said, but it was like pretending shrimp cocktail and a steak makes a death-row prisoner feel better the night before the needle goes in. Twenty minutes into the movie, Syl asked for my shirt. "You cold?" I said.

"No," she said, but I peeled it off and handed it to her, sitting back in my sleeveless undershirt. I watched her open her blouse and slide off her bra. The light from the screen flashed across her swollen breasts. Her stomach was enormous. For a moment I thought about whether or not she'd look like she had last summer after this was over.

"I can't get comfortable," she said, and pulled the shirt over herself and rested her head on my shoulder. By the time the Japanese showed up, she was asleep. The explosions were the only parts of the movie worth a damn, but she didn't wake up. I had to shake her when everything got sorted out and Doolittle bombed Japan and the credits rolled. "That was so boring," she said. "I bet I know everything that happened."

"You'd be right," I said.

"Why do they write stories where you can see what's coming?"

"That's the way things are," I said.

"That's not history, Bobby."

"Okay," I said, and nodded like I thought she'd won an argument.

"You don't mean that," she said, tugging at my shirt as if it made her as uncomfortable as the bra. I thought for a moment she was going to give it back to me, but she settled, finally, and said, "So what's next?"

We stepped outside into the rain so fine it felt good on my bare shoulders. The gutters were flooded, though, and the traffic splashed up waves from standing water. Off to the east, where our weather usually disappeared, it was so black and green I expected to see a funnel cloud set down. "We get through this," I said. "And then we start to take care of ourselves."

"Just like that?"

"As close as we can."

She kept the shirt pulled against her as we walked outside. I thought of what she looked like underneath. What people in the crowd would think if she handed it back to me and didn't bother to cover herself.

That was one more impossible thing, I thought. And then I started looking at the couples we were walking among, their expressions, their gestures, the way they moved toward or apart from each other. Something made me so sad about the future of all of them that I put my arm around Syl and pulled her against me so tight we both stumbled. "Whoa," she said, and I turned her toward me so I could feel her belly. She lifted one hand to touch my face, the one that was holding her bra, and I kept looking at her and hoping that some smart-ass in the crowd was enjoying us.

I made it to work with five minutes to spare. Though with the foreman, Sal Tamarelli, hovering like it was my first day, that time clock looked like it might be in a mirror, saying five minutes past the hour. "Go down to Hemmerline Hall," Sal said. "They got water."

The clock settled back to three minutes before the hour while I nodded. I'd been in that basement after a gully washer before. I loaded fans and the vacuum. I looked around to see if I had a partner on this one, but Sal shook his head. "It's all yours, Bobby," he said. "We're still working while you're mopping up."

In Hemmerline, I unlocked the corner office first, using it to judge how many doors I'd be propping open. The carpet sparkled, the water that had soaked in nearly to the door, reflecting the late afternoon sun. Three offices, I guessed, maybe the fourth. By the time I saw that the fourth office down was dry, the professor from office 1, Jack Spicer, was standing in his doorway. I noticed his blue flip-flops, the Jane's Addiction T-shirt. I wondered if Spicer wore that outfit when summer ended, whether he walked around campus as if he could leave the scent of hipness for some coed to sniff. "I'll stay out of your way," he said. "You got work to do here."

I shrugged and plugged in the wet-vac, dragging it to the corner where there was still standing water. When the door across the hall opened, I had two professors standing guard. "Has it been raining?" the second one said, and I smiled, turning on the machine.

Jack Spicer stepped into his office, bringing up water from the soaked carpet. "This place," he said. "I was watching it pour from my kitchen window, and I called in an office flood before I even drove over." He squished three more steps, acting as if this was a demonstration rather than a chance to inspect what I was doing about the water.

"Go for it, Noah," the professor from across the hall said.

"Is that the only way to take care of this?" Spicer asked.

"It's one way."

"So there's another?"

"We could open the windows and wait for nature." Spicer looked at the sopping leaves of the school's rhododendrons that leaned against his two windows and snorted to show he got the joke, but I wasn't through. "Or we could set fire to it, dry things out quick."

The second professor tiptoed across the soaked carpet and stopped. "Or have a faculty meeting in here and trust all the hot air to dry it out."

He looked my way as if he was inviting more sarcasm. I wondered if Jack Spicer was the kind of man who would call his boss and complain about "the janitor's attitude." If there was a hearing, I decided, that second professor would size up his choices and agree I'd been a smart-ass, and I'd be out of work. I shrugged and set the vacuum as far under the stilted bookshelf as it would reach.

There was enough water and furniture moving to take me right through till break. By the time I pushed the vacuum out the back door, I had fans running in three offices and both sets of outside doors propped for cross-ventilation. Spicer stepped out of the department library as if he'd just thought of something he needed by the back door. "This place will be wide open when you leave," Spicer said.

"That's how it works," I said.

"What about security? I'm the only one around, and I'm ready to walk home for dinner."

"It's summer," I said, lifting the vacuum into my cart as if that explained everything. I drove off before I told him he could call security from his house when he knew his office was being robbed.

After break, Sal saw me pull into the maintenance shack and gestured toward the spilled stack of pipe I'd just passed coming in. "I need you and Ron Steinbach to get that mess the hell out of here and up to the ball field where it's worth a shit to somebody."

I looked back and saw Ron parking a truck beside the scattered pipe. "Who dumped it?" I said.

Sal spit into the dust and shook his head. "Don't matter how it got there," he said. "Nobody doing drainage up there gives a shit about anything but having that pipe up there with some daylight still in the sky."

I waved to Ron to let him know he had a partner in this sorry project, but Sal took a step closer to me. "You have a problem in those offices?"

"They're healing," I said. "There's no miracles for soaked carpets."

"A people problem."

I kept my expression steady. "No," I said.

Sal shrugged. "I have to ask when I get a call. I have to say I talked to you and there's an understanding."

"I got it," I said.

"You got the baby just around the corner. I'll file this one under Jackass. A file like that can't get too thick though."

I nodded and walked over to where Ron was deciding which length of metal pipe to tackle first. I let him take his time deciding. Tumbled like they were, the gray pieces looked like the beginning of that old jackstraw game. It was clear to me we needed to hoist them in the right order or we'd jiggle the whole mess into an ankle-breaker.

Halfway through the load, Ron leaned against the truck bed and took off his hat. "You get one of them brain-boys riled over to the dorm?" he said. I bent down to lace a shoe, taking my time with the knot. "I took the call," he said. "He started in afore I could pass it on to Sal."

"It's over with," I said.

Ron stuck his cap back on, tugging and twisting it like he was fixing a bow tie on a tuxedo. "Your wife teaches here, don't she?" he said.

"Ex-wife. She's remarried."

Ron whistled. "That's a shit pile, then, ain't it?"

"We don't hate each other."

"No, I mean her getting it from some other guy and you seeing her day to day. I couldn't truck with such." Ron moved back to the remaining pipe section, and I bent to take an end. They were so heavy I was thinking forklift, and why it wasn't doing this work instead of our arms and backs.

"I've met him half a dozen times. That's not my life anymore."

Ron grunted as we lifted the pipe together. "Sure it is," he said. "I'd want to kill the lousy fuck if I was in your shoes."

I guided the pipe onto the truck while Ron shoved. I wasn't about to tell Ron what I felt about Sarah and Lou. "Let's just take care of this pipe," I said.

Ron nodded and tugged his hat. "Sure, I get you, but let me ask you one more question—is her new husband a professor here?"

I bent to the next section, and Ron, to my surprise, backed up a step as if he thought I might find the strength to lay him out with it. "No," I said, feeling it was true. Lou was a fund-raiser, an associate vice president in the development office.

"You're still awake," I said, when Syl was sitting up in bed reading at 11:30.

"You ever hear of the Stone Child?" she said, holding up a book with a picture of Siamese twins on the cover.

"No."

"There was a woman, once, who was pregnant for twenty-eight years."

"Really."

"You know. She was pregnant and had labor pains and then didn't deliver. All of a sudden people thought maybe she'd ballooned up for some other reason. All those years," she said. "People thinking she was a fat, hysterical idiot." She looked at me. "You should never have told Sarah."

"You told your father."

"I thought he needed to know. So it wasn't a shock. Sarah wasn't going to be shocked; she was going to preach."

"So Sarah called?"

Syl waved the book as if she meant to fling it at me. "She said she just wanted to wish me well now that it was close. That's not what she was saying five months ago."

"You don't think she meant it?"

"Back then she did. When she was going on and on about anencephalic babies. When she talked to me like I never heard about what I was dealing with."

"She assumed it was religion."

Syl waved the book again. "She assumed I was an idiot. 'It's incompatible with life,' she said. She talked like I was somebody whose case was in a book."

"The people in that book you're waving at me are once-a-century cases," I said.

"And I'm one in a thousand. I told her to wish you well if she wanted to. You're the one she knows."

Because my days off are Sunday and Monday, I always make breakfast on Sunday to start the weekend off right. Syl sleeps in and wakes to me carrying in a tray that starts with juice and ends with coffee. This

Sunday, though, she walked into the kitchen before I could even open the refrigerator. "Don't bother yourself," she said. "Cereal will do."

"OK," I said, but when I opened the cabinet, there were only two boxes, and neither one had enough left in it for two bowls. I held them up and shook them to let her know how low they were. "Pick one," I said. "Whichever you choose decides which one I eat."

"You look like my father that day he made breakfast for us the week before we were married. Remember? He gave you the choice between two meats he was cooking."

"I remember."

"You chose the kidneys. 'Well then,' he said, 'my daughter gets herself a mess of brains.'"

"I picked the kidneys because I could tell what they were. I didn't want something that looked like nothing I'd ever seen on a plate."

Syl lifted the box of shredded wheat from my left hand. "Those brains tasted like surgery," she said.

"You finished them."

"We should accept what the world gives us," she said.

"That's your father talking. We weren't kids, Syl. He acted like we were sixteen and ready to elope."

"You don't like being tested."

"There's enough trial in this world without being asked to breakfast jury duty."

"That's resolve," she said. "That's what you've lost."

"It's been replaced by realism."

Syl dumped the shredded wheat into a bowl. "It's resignation, Bobby. They're not synonyms." Half of her bowl was filled with scraps and broken pieces. They looked like straw, something that should be dumped in a trough. "I want to be out today," she said.

"Where?"

"The park. Just a short walk. We can sit most of the time."

Ten minutes into our walk, Syl started looking for a bench to rest on. The park was crowded. We'd passed two benches already full when I spotted an empty one just past where a couple walking a black lab were coming at us from the opposite direction. When they got closer, the woman flung her arms up in a sort of mock horror and said, "Syl, what are you doing on your feet?"

Immediately the dog bared its teeth and snarled, tugging at the leash the man tightened. "It's Julie," Syl whispered to me. "I work with her," and she walked right up to that dog, reached down and patted the black lab's upturned head.

"Wow," the man said, "you must have grown up around dogs."

"No, we didn't have any pets."

I saw the man hesitate, uncertain where to go next without Syl leading him. "You're so big," Julie said. "It's only been three weeks since I last saw you. Ready to pop?"

"Any day now."

To my horror, the woman stepped closer and laid her hand on Syl's belly. I saw that Syl didn't step back, that she smiled as if a curtain had gone up. The woman pulled her hand back. "So quiet, that one."

"Saving his energy."

"He'll be wearing you out soon enough," the man said, and I wondered what he'd say if I told him there wasn't enough of a nervous system in Syl's baby to get legs kicking.

"Syl's getting herself a baby-sitter," Julie said to the man. "Thinks we can't live without her at work."

Julie tugged Syl's arm enough to move her a few steps. She leaned in close to her and and whispered. I kept my eye on the black lab, taking a step back to make sure that leash didn't reach.

When Syl broke away from Julie, she walked to the empty bench thirty feet down the path and sat. I dropped beside her as the black lab, spotting a squirrel, dragged the couple away. "They think I'm coming back to work in a month for the money," Syl said. "They think I'm terrible to even think about coming back and asking for an eight-week leave. 'Your job will always be there,' Julie said. 'You don't have to make it official like teachers and such.' They act like I'm not going to care for my baby."

"They'll know soon enough."

"I couldn't tell them, least of all Julie," Syl said. "I didn't want them being sorry and talking among themselves about me every day I wasn't there."

"They do anyway, right? Just a different topic and a different attitude."

Syl shook her head. "You know what Julie said to me the last week I was on the job? 'You're like the teachers at the college. Your husband bring that day-care shit home from work?'"

"It's called maternity leave. It's been common for a generation."

"They know you were married to a professor."

"And now I keep house for her," I said, and I looked away, but the black lab and the couple had disappeared, and there was nothing along the path that gave me an excuse to stare at it. "I'm so tired, Bobby," Syl said. "If I go home and rest now, maybe we can go out later."

Syl laid down on the couch and fell asleep so quickly I felt apprehension swirl up inside me. As soon as I walked outside, I knew I had to see Sarah to work things out while there was still a day left. I didn't want to be warning her away from Syl after the fact. I thought if she called next week to offer sympathy I'd walk into her office and slap her in the face.

Sarah invited me in, but I hesitated on the doorstep when Lou stepped into the room behind her. "It's okay, Bobby. We're adults. Lou and I are just recuperating from the wedding we went to yesterday."

"You should have been at the wedding," Lou said, his voice pitched up a notch as if he were hearing background noise. "There was a karaoke singer."

I looked around the room, stopping at a picture of Sarah and Lou standing on a beach that looked like somebody had cleaned it before they posed. Sarah was wearing a two-piece, and I was surprised how flat her stomach had become, as if Lou had ordered her to work out for six weeks before the vacation.

"Some people like that stuff."

"Not at the reception. At the wedding."

My eyes dropped to her waist, imagining that taut midriff. "You can't have karaoke at a wedding."

"Before the ceremony. A woman sang to karaoke tapes. Every time she had to switch tapes, the organist played a minute of classical."

"Change the tapes?"

"She had the four songs on four different tapes. Don't ask me why."

"Celine Dion?"

"Yes."

"Faith Hill?"

"You sound like you were there," Lou said. "A church full of rednecks." He sidestepped from the room, and for the first time I noticed he'd been holding a glass against his hip.

I smiled, thinking of the woman lifting a tape from her boom box, inserting the next while Wagner thundered from the church organ. "I came over to get something straight with you," I said to Sarah.

"Bobby," Sarah said, "you made this call long ago. You know where this is going."

I heard Lou dropping ice cubes into a glass. "This?" I said.

She sighed. "Bringing a child like this to term."

"It was Syl's call," I said, wishing for the words back as soon as I heard them trickle out like drool.

"But you're stuck, too," Lou said, walking back in. He lifted his fresh drink to his lips and swallowed. "You have time for one?" he said.

I shook my head. "I remember when you said you were against this," Sarah said. "Ultrasound doesn't lie. There's no repairing a brain that isn't there."

"A fucking tar baby," Lou said.

"A what?" I blurted. Sarah looked stricken. If she'd been drinking, I didn't see another glass in the room.

Lou took another swallow. "Fucking Uncle Remus—Zip-a-dee-doo-dah."

"I'm lost here, Lou."

"I hear that."

"Lou," Sarah said, but he wasn't finished.

"The little organ recipients will buy her Mother's Day cards in a few years. They'll send her fucking flowers and a cake."

"Let me talk to Bobby alone," Sarah said.

"The good old days," Lou muttered, but he went back to the kitchen, busied himself with the refrigerator.

"What the fuck?" I said to Sarah.

"Lou has his ways sometimes. He thinks you're going to have the baby harvested."

"He *thinks*?"

"What's this always been about, Bobby? Religion?"

"Syl's no more religious than you are," I said. "That's one reason why I enjoy living with her. She's carrying that doomed child because she thinks it's right, not because she fears God. It's no different than caring for a defective child once it's born. You wouldn't throw a retarded baby in the river, would you?"

"It's not for religion and it's not for science," Sarah said. "There's no other reason."

"She set her mind to it long ago," I said. "Those are side issues."

"Call it what you want, Bobby. It's religion. Nobody but fanatics would blame her for aborting."

I wanted to tell Sarah she was so religious in her science it made me sick, but instead of comparing statistics to anecdotes, I said, "It's about knowing. It's about choice."

"No, Bobby. You know that baby could just be DOA, not viable at all."

"You're the educated one," I said. "You're the expert."

"Yes," she said, her tone making me think of every spitball I'd ever thrown in high school, every homework assignment left undone. And then her expression softened, and she rested her hand on my forearm. "Bobby . . ."

"Forget it," I said. "You teach at a college; I fix it when it's broken."

"You paint. You do cleanup."

"I could fix a drunk for you."

"Still a child," she said.

"If I wasn't, I'd set Lou on fire and make you watch."

She pressed her lips together, and I waited for her to tell me to never come back. When she spoke, she said, "This whole business is hard on everybody."

I opened the door and stepped out. "Just keep telling yourself it's only a movie." And when I was halfway to the car, I wondered whether she could name the films that line had advertised. Any of them, including, years ago, two we'd seen together.

"You said you had something to get straight," I heard her say from behind me, but I didn't even raise a hand to show I was ignoring her.

Syl was still lying on the couch when I got back, but she was awake and reading. "You still stuck in that book?" I asked.

"You went to Sarah's, didn't you?"

"I thought I could explain if I was looking at her."

"I'm okay, Bobby. There's so many things that can go wrong. Mine's already happened. I don't have to worry." I lifted the book from her hand and thumbed through the chapters: Pig-headed women. Wolfmen. Egg-laying mothers.

"I always read out loud to him, Bobby."

"He's not going to learn anything."

"So he can hear my voice, Bobby. It's what I can do for him. Everything that's alive can listen. I haven't watched television in two months."

"The TV has voices," I said, but she closed the book and let it rest on her belly.

"The husband of the stone child's mother had has wife dissected after she died," Syl said. She looked out the window as if she expected to see visitors. "Like a frog in biology class. He said he wanted to know for sure."

"Autopsies aren't immoral."

"You remember cutting up a frog when you were in biology?"

"And a worm and a cat."

"A cat?"

"I took advanced biology."

"And then you didn't go to college."

"I thought I'd learn something in Vietnam, and then we gave up before I got there."

"People go to college when they're older."

"I didn't."

Syl looked out the window again, and I realized she was examining her reflection, that standing where she was, in the light, she could look at her profile. "You know what those doctors found?" Syl said, without turning toward me.

"Tell me."

"A fetus, Bobby. She really had been carrying a baby all those years. But first they found something like a big coconut. A goddamn giant shell they could hardly crack open and inside was a baby made of stone."

I wanted her to stop looking at herself. When I spoke, my voice was a croak: "Doctors said this?"

"Yes, Bobby, a real baby, all right. One that had been alive and had grown—it calcified." Finally, she turned back to me. "Let's go out to dinner, Bobby. Tomorrow's a big day."

I watched her getting dressed. After the first few weeks of our marriage I'd never watched. I'd discovered my impatience with her care, that I grew angry watching her apply makeup and brush her hair because it seemed she took too much time readying herself, that her preparations expressed a lack of confidence I found disgusting.

But now I watched without counting the brushstrokes, without checking my watch to measure the minutes until an argument. I looked at myself in the mirror. She could see me looking, but she didn't shut her eyes or pause until I saw her take a breath and hold it, getting ready to push off the dresser, stand, and walk to the car.

When I turned down the alley that ran behind the five blocks of businesses in town, two dogs were busy tearing at a garbage bag. They turned and barked at the car, and then they ran alongside, growling and yapping as if we were there to steal that bag. Syl glanced at me as I slowed for the lot behind the restaurant, the dogs still busy with chasing us. "They'll run off when we open the doors," she said. "You don't show fear and they understand who's boss."

"Maybe."

"I saw you cringe today," she said. "Where does it come from? You're so afraid of dogs, and yet you were never bitten."

She'd been attacked once when she was twelve. The police had driven her back to the neighborhood, and she'd pointed at the dog. "I didn't know that meant it was going to be destroyed," she'd told me. "They killed it to find out if it was rabid."

"I keep my distance. You keep the law according to your father."

Syl patted my thigh. "Look them in the eye."

"And you have the scars," I finished for her.

"Yes."

"More great advice."

"There's nothing wrong with Dad's advice, you've just been lucky."

"He might as well have been preaching the gospel of Hair of the Dog. You should have seen Lou today—he was living that gospel like a disciple."

Syl lifted her hand and opened the door. "Just remember," I said, "it's only a movie."

The dogs turned and trotted off as if they'd been paid. "*The Last House on the Left,*" Syl said, looking back into the car. "I snuck into that movie when I was fourteen, and it scared me for weeks."

I was invisible in the restaurant. There were so many smiles and heads turning back into conversation that I felt like a celebrity's husband.

You read about those guys sometimes—a carpenter or a plumber married to a movie star. You wonder how it's all going to work out for him, what he does at parties.

When we were married, I'd stood beside Sarah and listened to professors talk about books as if that made it okay to be suggestive. They knew I worked physical plant. Everything in books, according to their innuendos, was politics or sex. Either way, the characters were getting fucked or being the fuckers. The more those professors talked, the more it seemed like literature was pornography for the educated. I wondered if Syl would go back to television again after the baby was born or whether she'd become a reader.

"You know what I'd like to be," she said.

"What?"

"A grandmother."

"There's no sense wishing the years away."

If she'd heard, she didn't acknowledge. "Then I'd know my child had grown up safely."

"There, now," I said, and got stuck.

When Syl shook my shoulders at 4 A.M., I thought, for a moment, that it was happening, and I was surprised at how pleased I was. "I've been trying to will it," she said, "but there's nothing."

I propped myself on one elbow and looked at her. "You've done more than your share," I said. "There's no shame."

I sensed her shrink back in the darkness. "Shame?" she said. "You think I've ever felt ashamed?"

"I meant about the willpower."

"No, you didn't."

"Let's not quibble," I said.

"Quibbling is for the lucky," Syl said. "It's like jogging on a treadmill and thinking you can run a marathon."

"Let's not argue, then." When I sensed her relaxing, I smiled though she couldn't see it.

"Right," she said, rolling over and pushing herself up. "It's his day. Let's not spoil it." She sat on the edge of the bed while I waited for her to decide what came next. "That stone baby had hair," she finally said, and I tensed, staring toward where the ceiling had to be. "It had one tooth."

ZOMBIES

———

Boys didn't get killed on the highway during the winter. A hundred and fifty inches of snow, on average, slowed them down. The drift-forming wind off the two nearby Great Lakes saved them. Even when there were three days of thaw in February, sending them out to the east–west straight stretches of highway that opened first, they survived the nightly patches of black ice, careening off in 360s that called up the stress astronauts simulate during training, but slamming, eventually, into cushions of plowed snow in front of every telephone pole and tree trunk and bridge abutment from Buffalo to Rochester.

Spring was fatality season. It sprouted a new crop of licensed drivers who hadn't yet gone over a hundred miles an hour or used the formerly drift-clogged back roads for racing. They accelerated through curves with a beer in one hand while three buddies cheered and chugged and cranked Van Halen and AC/DC.

Bon Scott Lives they carved in their desks all winter. *Teacher Leave Them Kids Alone*, they scratched out, quoting Pink Floyd in a variety of hand-designed fonts during study hall. In the spring of 1980, it was hard to make out the old messages like *Frampton Comes Alive!* and *Disco Sucks Like Mr. Elmann.*

Elmann was the Spanish teacher who inspected boys' rooms while his students translated passages about the wonders of Spain and the pleasures of each season near the Mediterranean Sea. I was the English teacher with a master's degree who was looking for a job somewhere else, preferably with students more than eighteen years old. By late April, when Dave Reeder left county road 1284 and broadsided a tree directly into the driver's side door, I was losing confidence in making any sort of change besides one that was barely a step up the hill of universal education.

Reeder was killed instantly—severe blunt-force trauma. The crash happened so late on a Saturday night the accident didn't make the paper until Monday morning, the news spreading by the ancient method of word-of-mouth.

Please Delete, it said beside his name on the absentee list when it was delivered during second period. *Deceased,* it said in parentheses. "He wasn't drinking," a boy in Dave Reeder's section insisted at the beginning of class last period that afternoon. "He was mad at Shelly. They had a fight."

Shelly Kantz was absent, but the class didn't need details. They wanted to talk about how the whole disaster was passing by without a mention by the school, and I listened to them for half an hour until, with ten minutes left in the period, a woman from the office walked in and laid a short story anthology on my desk, patting it twice with her hand before she left without speaking.

Every student knew that textbook belonged to Reeder. Nobody said anything for more than a minute, and I started to think that book might levitate from being stared at by twenty-six students. And then, just after the minute hand lurched forward for the second time since that woman had exited, a girl in the first row muttered, "This fucking place fucking sucks," and the rest of the class murmured, "For sure" and "Yeah" and "Right on" before they settled and waited for me to decide where the last few minutes of this day were going.

"Sorry," the girl finally said, "but it does."

"Maybe they'll come on the P.A. now," I said. There were six minutes left before the dismissal bell.

"Not hardly," the girl said.

The minute hand lurched again. If the principal was going to ask for a moment of silence or even just mention Dave Reeder, his time had just about come and gone. "Doesn't this piss you off?" another girl said.

"Yes," I said at once, because it was not only true, it was better than saying, "Here's another life skill lesson for you, a boy's death going unacknowledged because he was the kind of student the school wished it had fewer of."

Life Skills. It's what I taught to twelfth-grade non-regents English. They learned everything from tax forms to credit card applications to resumes. The students role-played. Some applied for loans; others approved or disapproved them, explaining the reasons in terms of collateral, interest, and income. They learned those words had something to do with them. Letters of reference. Renter's insurance. A lease. By pretending to deal with all of these nuisances, they learned the vocabulary of the everyday.

The stories they read in that anthology, one per week, called for choices—to exact revenge or not, to lie or not, to reveal the identity of a wrongdoer or not. The students talked heatedly about where lines should be drawn; they offered anecdotal evidence and considered the argument won.

And the papers they wrote, one per month, were constructed from firsthand research. They interviewed people with jobs and families, people who lived in public housing, people who worked night shifts, and those who'd been laid off. In a school the size of this one, there were enough non-regents seniors to fill five classes like the one Reeder had been in, and I taught all of them. In a community the size of ours, there were enough former non-regents students to supply oral histories about disappointment to every succeeding class.

The memorial service for Dave Reeder was Tuesday evening, held at seven o'clock so as many students as possible could attend. I counted two teachers and the vice-principal, and then I stopped looking for things to make me angry and listened to students, most of them mine, tell short, sentimental stories that featured Reeder.

Wednesday afternoon, Shelly Kantz was back in class. "Mr. Cose," she said, shifting from one foot to the other in front of my desk while the room emptied after the bell. Thin to begin with, she was so skinny now I thought she'd fasted since the moment she'd learned Reeder was dead. Eighteen, she could pass for fourteen, her rust-colored hair in tight curls that reminded me of Little Orphan Annie.

"Mr. Cose," she said again, and now that the room was empty, I said, "Sit in my chair, Shelly, if you want to talk."

She sat down so carefully, learning on both chair arms like someone expecting pain, that I thought she'd been in an accident of her own. When she glanced up as I pulled a graffiti-choked student desk chair close to sit in, she was crying.

Shelly told me right off that she was pregnant. "That's why we were fighting," she said. "Dave was mad and then so was I. I told him we'd talk the next day when he wasn't drinking; I told him we'd figure this out." Shelly paused, and I looked at where her white blouse tucked into her jeans. I thought if I lifted that blouse up I'd see the muscle definition produced by a million sit-ups.

Shelly looked at the clock above the door and then at the open door itself. "I want the baby so Dave stays alive," she said. "And I don't want the baby because I'll always see it and remember that's why he's dead." She stared at the door now as if she expected the class to return for an extra-credit session. "How do I choose?" she said. "If I wait much longer, they won't give me an abortion. And don't tell me to ask my mother. I know exactly what she'll say, so there's no sense telling her until I have to."

"Can you wait two more days?" I said. "I don't know what I'll say, but I'll say it Friday."

"Sure," Shelly said at once, "but if it's any help, every girl I've asked has said, 'Have it.'" I nodded like I understood. "And every one said name it either David or Davis when it's born."

Wednesday was my weekday night out with Claire Ellis, who I'd been seeing since Christmas break. Claire was a waitress who had off Monday and Thursday, so she considered Wednesday night a Saturday.

She'd been sitting in the Scoreboard Lounge, the bar I'd chosen among the four bunched on the two business blocks of Lissum, New York, eighteen Wednesdays ago, and here we were keeping that midweek streak alive in the Carnival Bar, two doors down from where we'd met.

"They're role-playing job interviews tomorrow," I said. "It's the highlight of the year."

"You save that one for near the end of the year to keep them coming back?"

"It's the one they practice for."

"The great motivator."

"Me and Ronald Reagan."

Claire looked puzzled, one step, I thought, from boredom. She seemed distracted by a man in a flannel shirt and jeans at the bar who I thought, by his age, might be her father. "What?" she said.

"That's what he's using as a qualification for president."

"You ought to run then," Claire said. "You play to a tougher crowd than that waxworks phony."

She glanced away again, and when I followed her look, the man was making his way toward us, taking a sip from his Genesee Cream Ale bottle, shuffling two steps, taking another sip and then shuffling. I started imagining that bottle, once he'd emptied it, breaking over my skull. "This ought to be good," Claire murmured while the man tilted his head back as if the cream ale had stuck to the bottom of the bottle before he came to attention and slapped the bottle down on the table next to us.

"I've been told you're Shelly's English teacher."

"Mr. Kantz?" I tried.

"You been speaking with her?"

"She's in my class."

"I mean speaking. A funny thing to be sitting down with a young girl after the last bell." He looked at Claire. "I know you. I've seen you around."

Claire nodded. "I get out some," she said. "I've lived here all my life."

"My oldest boy went to school with you. He just turned twenty-three—I heard your name at our dinner table."

"That would be Chester," Claire said.

"You have advice of your own for Shelly? You know, where she should be seen with teachers and such?"

Claire laid her hand on my arm, but Kantz looked at me. "Don't you have school tomorrow?" he said. "Or you planning to call in sick?"

"Two beers are healthy," I said. I kept to myself the two I'd had before I'd picked up Claire and the two I intended to have before we left.

"What's that supposed to mean?"

"Your daughter's life is her own. I don't live in it except when she's in the building."

"My Shelly was this close to being in that car with that boy," he said, holding his thumb and forefinger nearly together. "I hear you let them kids talk about their driving and their drinking and such in that class of yours."

"We talk about a lot of things."

"You know Charlie Reeder?"

"Dave's father?"

"Stepfather. He come to school about his boy?"

"No."

"Charlie Reeder, he has a fondness for guns. You think he knows what goes on in your class. You think he'd like to know who was learning his boy the ins and outs of alcohol and him sitting over to the far window there and maybe with a problem if I go over and point you out?"

I glanced over Claire's shoulder at a man in overalls who looked the image of Jack Sprat. Despite Kantz's threat, I conjured a fat wife for Charlie Reeder, a woman astonished by the power of her husband's metabolism. "Why don't we talk after school some day when everything's settled a bit?"

"But not tomorrow? Tomorrow, you're calling in sick."

"Next week Mr. Kantz. I'd welcome it."

"If you're not busy in there right after school."

Kantz moved away, heading toward the skin-and-bones man he'd said was Dave Reeder's father. When he passed him, he turned and grinned, and then he walked out of the bar.

"His boy's a talker," Claire said.

"The gene pool is a powerful thing."

Claire frowned. "That girl needs a baby like her father needs stupid pills."

"Is it that simple?"

Claire looked puzzled. "You asking me what I think?" she said. "Yes."

Greg Newton, the principal, called me to his office during my free period on Thursday. "Word is you have all your classes up in arms about Dave Reeder."

"Word is?"

"An assembly. They expect one."

"The students were disappointed nothing was said by the school. I let them talk."

Newton looked at me. "Are you not looking for a new position?" he said.

I hesitated and then managed, "I'm thinking about it," sounding as lame as any no-homework excuse maker.

"There's no need to be vague," he said. "This office receives calls when the process moves along."

I wanted to ask if he'd heard from someplace else besides the next county's community college, if a dean had called from a school where students stayed past their sophomore year, but I opted for a silence that could stand for "I'm pleased to hear that."

"You've been here just these three years," Newton said, "and you're ready to move on. If you had a regents position, do you think you'd be in such a hurry?"

"I'm not applying to high schools."

"Exactly. Doesn't that speak to your real feelings?"

"I'd be applying even if I had a regents job."

"Of course," Newton said. "And you with tenure just a month old." He pushed his chair away from the desk and stood up. "If that boy had killed himself five weeks ago, would you be so bold?"

"The class is called Life Skills. Talking things out is something they should learn."

"Is there a test coming up? Do you get to correct anything?"

"Another six weeks, and they'll have all the tests they need. Those are the ones they need to pass."

Newton folded his hands and hesitated so long I thought he was preparing to ask me to pray with him. "My experience with these situations," he finally said, "shows me they move on with their lives more quickly than the regents students. There's more where that accident came from, so to speak, and it's approaching rapidly. You could disagree, but tell me, how many cases have you witnessed? The two boys last June? We were in final exam week by then. The boy your first year? He was over Easter break, so he was in the ground when we returned. And that boy two weeks later the same year who was a regents student? He was a class officer—the students requested the tribute."

I wanted to tell him the reason why I had to leave: that I couldn't stand to lie to people like him, that I was worried I lacked the courage to be honest, and so I needed to find a place where there were fewer of his kind, or where I could start in new with the intention of being who I imagined I was.

And it wasn't just him. It was the teachers who joked about the serious books they never read and the television sitcoms they preferred. Ernie Lauver, who talked about getting laid to the Bee Gees. "Those screechy voices get her hot for some reason. She comes faster than I do when they're singing."

"That would be instantly," Roy Stockard said. He had the English regents job; the Bee Gees lover had the history regents position.

"And you know what she says every time?" Ernie Lauver went on. "'I don't know what gets into me. You ever get like that? So wired up you don't care about anything but yourself?'"

"Did you tell her that happens to you every day at the beginning of every class?" Stockard said.

Which was one time I smiled out loud, nothing I had to do in front of Newton, because all I was required to do was not argue.

Thursday night I went to the Empire State Diner, the restaurant where Claire worked. I ordered the hot turkey sandwich and a root beer, and when she brought the drink with no ice to cut me a break, I said, "I have an interview in Batavia next week. It's just the community college, but it's a step up if it happens."

Claire didn't look unhappy. "Good for you," she said.

"I thought you should know."

"We're not married."

"An interview's not a job offer."

"We're not committed."

I was ready to say the community college was only thirty-five miles away, that I didn't have to move in order to take the job, but I let everything suggestive of the future drop. It hadn't taken me eighteen weeks to decide Claire and I were a couple whose closeness depended on nothing changing. As long as we didn't move in together. As long as we saw each other three times per week. As long as each night out pointed toward sex. As long as we had food and alcohol in front of us beforehand.

As long as we could talk about what had happened to us rather than what we thought.

It was a list of qualifiers in large print, but I knew I was willing to make that forty-five minute commute each day to keep things steady. The danger was that, like my students, we were both selfish enough to read those messages and then ignore them.

In the faculty room, over lunch, George Lavin, who taught chemistry and physics, watched Elmann slip into a corner chair with his brown bag before he said, "Watch out, Larry, Cose here is soliciting for the Dave Reeder memorial fund."

Elmann looked grim. I guessed he hadn't laughed at a school joke in so long he wasn't required to. "My job is that much easier these days," he said.

I lifted my turkey sandwich to give myself something to do, but Lavin wouldn't let it go. "A plaque, Larry. For the school lobby."

"We'll see about that," Elmann said, rustling his bag open as if he was frightening off the spirits of bitterness before he reached inside.

"Ten dollars," Lavin said. "Everybody's in but you, Larry."

"I'll pay to have it taken down," Elmann said.

Lavin grinned like his favorite song had just come on the radio while he was drinking in a speeding car. "The drive-in opened this week," he said. "*Dawn of the Dead*. The zombies are back. Is that an omen or what?"

Elmann fished out a tub of yogurt and a banana. He folded the bag and creased it flat before he tucked it in his pocket. A woman's lunch, I thought, but I left it to Lavin to bring something like that up to Elmann.

As Elmann peeled the banana, I remembered the afternoon Dave Reeder lit a cigarette as I approached him on the sidewalk outside. He'd said. "You can't tell me what to do."

"You going to be a senior?"

"Yes."

"I'll see you in the fall."

Reeder had exhaled, watching the smoke in a way that said *Go fuck yourself.* "Maybe I'll quit," he'd said as the small cloud drifted away.

"School or smoking?"

Reeder had slipped the cigarette between his lips, letting it angle slightly down and to the side so naturally I figured him for practicing in front of a mirror. "When I'm in your class," he said, the cigarette barely bobbing as he pushed the words through his lips, "am I required to act like you're cool?"

When class ended on Friday, Shelly didn't get out of her chair. She looked even thinner, and I caught myself, as I sat in a desk across from her, wondering if a fetus would abort if the mother failed to eat enough.

"I went to the drive-in last night, Mr. Cose. A zombie movie. A bunch of the girls thought it would be good for me. Zombies. It started me thinking."

I glanced toward the door, half expecting to catch her father listening. "I heard the zombies were in town," I said. "I saw my first zombie movie when I was in college."

"Really? Are you sure? This one's new. It has to be because the zombies go to the mall where the four people still alive are hiding."

"They built a mall in my town when I was seven years old."

Shelly didn't seem to hear. "The one girl who's left alive is pregnant," she said. "It was so sad when her boyfriend turned into a zombie."

"But she gets away?"

"Yes. That was the good part." Shelly smiled like the animals do in children's books, and then she went dark and quiet. This time, when I looked toward the door, I expected Charlie Reeder and one of the guns he loved, its barrel as big around as his wrist.

"The movie I saw was called *Night of the Living Dead*," I said. "Yours is called *Dawn of the Dead*. See?"

Shelly nodded like someone who wouldn't admit she needed a translator. "Mr. Cose," she said, "you know what? If the dead come back they'd know who to kill. Who deserved it. They would have been watching us and they'd know."

"The zombies don't know anything," I said. "They kill everybody."

"That's a movie," she said. "In real life they wouldn't. They'd know who the liars were. They'd know who cheated and who stole and who was a pervert. All we know are the ones who get caught, like Mr. Fisher, my fourth grade teacher, with his pictures of little girls."

It came to me that Shelly's zombies would still kill everybody, but I didn't say anything, and Shelly seemed to be slowing down. In a minute,

I thought, she'd ask me my opinion about the baby, but then she looked out the window and said, "There's no way the dead are allowed to see us. The longer you were dead the more you'd know about how awful people can be. It would be hell. Dave can't be watching me kill his baby."

"He won't know," I said, confident of one thing I was telling her.

Shelly stood and sidestepped into the aisle that ran along the wall. I pushed myself up, but I didn't move away from the desk. "But the baby has a soul. And when it goes to heaven, Dave would know."

"He won't blame you. He'll understand." I felt like I was going to throw up if I said another word, but Shelly began to back toward the door, pausing for a moment with one foot in the room and one in the hall. "My Dad talked about you last night. He called you a sot. He said you consorted with whores. He talks like he's in the Bible when he's mad. I had to look up *sot*. I had to look up *consorted*. I think we're all going to hell, Mr. Cose."

When Claire and I each had a beer in our hands Sunday night at my apartment, I said, "Were you a regents student?"

Claire hesitated as if she was trying to decide which answer I preferred, and then she said, "No. I was in a lot of classes with Chester Kantz."

"It doesn't mean anything."

"Yes, it does," she said.

"I mean in the long run."

Claire turned the beer bottle in her hand the way I'd seen women do who hated the taste. "You know what we did when I was in senior English? British literature."

"See," I said, "you really were in the regents class."

"No. We had the same books as they did, but we skipped half of them. Instead of five poems, we read two—that sort of thing. I used to look at the other poems and wonder what those classes talked about after they read them."

She stopped turning the beer, put it down on the carpet beside the couch where we were sitting. "The teacher read the stories and poems to us," she said. "He had a nice voice. I liked listening."

When she paused, I started to tell Claire about the zombies, how every last one of them needed to eat those who were still alive. "That's so stupid," she said. "They'd run out of food and that would be the end of everything."

"The zombies don't care. They have to eat."

"If I was two years younger," Claire said, "I would have had you for English. You ever think of that?"

I nodded. "I read a review of *Dawn of the Dead* after Shelly told me the story. It said the zombies come to the mall because they remember it was a place they loved."

"We wouldn't have read any of those poems if you'd been my teacher. We wouldn't have had that book at all."

"It said the movie starts where *The Night of the Living Dead* ends, but Shelly had never heard of it."

"Neither have I." Claire picked up the beer and drank so long I thought she was trying to see if she could chug a full bottle. When she took it away from her mouth, she gasped. "Do you read to your classes?" she said.

"No," I said, and this time I waited to hear if she was going to add anything.

"What happened?" she said. "There's always survivors in monster movies. What did the last living people do?"

"They fly off in a helicopter. They want to go to a place where nobody else ever lived so there won't be any zombies." I was ready to keep going, but she stopped me.

"That's so sad," she said.

"You sound like Shelly," I said. "They get away."

"But everything's lost," Claire said. "All the dead will be forgotten except the ones that the survivors knew."

"I don't think you're supposed to think about that. It's supposed to be a happy ending. The girl is pregnant. Everything can start over."

"That's corny," Claire said. "Nobody would believe that."

"It's not that simple" I said. "The one guy who gets away isn't the father."

Claire brightened. "Good," she said. "That's better. It's so terrible I believe it."

"Maybe you should call Mr. Kantz and ask to speak with Shelly."

"They should make zombie movies for every time of day," Claire said.

"*Noon of the Zombies. Twilight of the Zombies.*" She laughed, and then she leaned toward me and said, "You should read to those kids in your classes."

"Not really."

She straightened again, and though I didn't catch her at it, I thought she'd sat up to see the clock on the wall behind me. "No wonder you want to change jobs," she said. "You think everything's a metaphor, even that stupid movie."

She stared at me as if the word *jerk* was condensing out of the vapor of doubts she had about me. Suddenly, everything I had prepared myself to teach to college students seemed as boring as Adam and Eve flying a helicopter to Eden.

"Chester Kantz always let me drive," Claire said. "He knew he'd get home alive with me at the wheel." Claire finished her beer, sucking at the foam stuck to the inside of the bottle before she hissed, "Life skills," without taking it from her mouth.

"None of this is my fault," I said.

"You could have told Shelly to have the baby."

"It's better for her to decide."

Claire set the bottle on the carpet and stood so she was looking down at me. "You could have told Mr. Kantz you were ready to settle up with him right there."

"You pressed on my arm."

"That was to shut you up," Claire said, stepping behind the couch so I had to lean back to see her.

"I don't get it."

She vanished then, either ducking down or retreating, and when I arched up, leaning farther, I heard her murmur, "Because I knew whatever you were going to say wouldn't settle anything at all," the words sounding as if they were seeping through the wall.

NATURAL BORDERS

———

When Buck Keister and his former nun of a wife Merle took to riding their his-and-hers motorcycles naked, word got around so quickly it was as if a suicide watch was posted. Folks found reasons for themselves to be out the county road and all along those unpaved local lanes that crisscrossed the reclaimed strip mines where Buck Keister had set his trailer a quarter-century ago just after the coal played out.

Excuses for such drives were necessary if Buck and Merle were to be eyeballed by the reliable, an honest-to-God confirmed sighting, not another rumor like the years-old one about blood sacrifices of cats and chickens inside those spray-painted red pentagrams in the back parking lot of the boarded-up elementary school.

"Merle had some catching up to do" was how most neighbors saw it. And she'd surely chosen a righteous path to follow for that when she married Buck; he'd been left by two wives who were unwilling to accept that trailer on uncertain land and the possible mayhem Buck brought to them as the last stop on their life's tour.

Maybe it was about Buck being the tallest man in the county. Shot up as a teenager towards those heights you only hear about during basketball games telecast from cities nowhere near our stretch of the woods. Buck had made the down payments on the motorcycles. He'd been seen giving Merle pointers, as understanding, it looked like, as any well-heeled golf pro at the three private courses tucked into the prosperous corners of the county.

The naked part, according to some, had been Merle's way of keeping Buck sober. Once she'd got the hang of things, she'd seen her chance to raise Buck's bet of speed, power, and danger with sex. And what's more, she had Buck lugging her arts and crafts all over Pennsylvania, sitting for hours in booths they rented to sell sliced and varnished cross sections of tree trunks Buck harvested from the oldest of the coal company restock.

Some had landscapes pressed on. Some deer or eagles. The kind of scenes most folks display on the sides of vans. Mostly, she turned them into clocks. "Good for Merle" was what most said about her way with wood. She didn't put smut under those big and little hands; Buck set up and took down, so it slowed his drinking down some, fidgeting in a chair or slurping Cokes and checking the other booths for ideas and prices.

The story got out, though, that it looked like he'd turned into a darkness drinker, swallowing that first gorgeous beer as the blue blinked out toward Ohio, another festival ended on the outskirts of a town loaded with antique stores, tie-dyed shirt shops, and three sidewalk restaurants where you couldn't get anything but flavored coffee and sweetened dough. What's more, you watch fifty sets of those clock hands stand still all day, and anybody'd get antsy.

"Hey Buck," I heard Roy Hollenbach at the hardware say last week. "I hear you're Buck naked now."

"Before God," Buck said, "like everybody."

"You giving him more than a fair chance to size you up."

"You run that fat woman of yours out-of-doors and see if it don't get her to leaving dessert to the kids."

Roy shook his head, knowing the truth, but Buck looked a bit peaked to me, like that nun of his was going to roll over more than her months-old Harley.

And who am I to speak? My wife Dorene buys things with the Coca-Cola label on them. Doesn't matter what, long as it's got those words in that old fashioned script they use. "Bill Hauck," she says each time she catches me looking funny, "you just don't know the pleasures of gathering."

I grunt some but leave her be. Coca-Cola shirts, they're common. Coca-Cola lamps, they're everywhere. But you have to be hunting to find six different waste cans, four different picture frames, all those little jars filled with spices and what-not. And those weeble-wobble people she owns, families of them dressed in Coca-Cola outfits from around the world. Russians, Dutch, Italians, all dressed up like they were about to folk dance a tribute to sugar and water.

Buck's wife, that nun, she sat me down over coffee four days back and started telling me about giants. Buck's a big man, she said, big enough to turn most men's faces up to him, but the Bible tells us that the big don't fare well in life.

"You know about Goliath?" she said, beginning like an evangelist, and then, backpedaling from whatever she saw in my face, "Of course, excuse me."

"That's okay," I said. "I couldn't make him out, them figuring him in cubits."

"And spans," Merle said. "Nine and a half feet to as much as eleven, depending on whose arms and hands were doing the calculating."

"That kind of measuring makes a man any size you want him remembered as," I said right off, thinking that might bother Merle some, my complaining, but she was set on something else.

"It's the Nephilim that's most interesting," she said, "the angels who wanted to sleep so badly with women they gave up heaven."

"That's one I understand," I said.

"Do you now?" she said, smiling so I wouldn't take offense. "Their sons were the big boys of Genesis. They were the original 'giants in the earth.' And no sooner they grew up than the Giant Flood ended all of that nonsense."

I considered on that, whether or not those giants were such a reminder about the power of lust that God said "enough."

"Buck is just six-foot-eight in his bare feet. You can't count the soles of his boots when you measure a man." I didn't say anything. She was leading me somewhere, and I gave her enough room so I could step off that path if need be.

When she started up again, she was in a different part of the forest: "I was officially a nun," she said, "if you want to know, for exactly one thousand days. I kept at it those last weeks just to make the round number. It was nothing else but vanity took me most to the end of that third year. I was long past seeing myself as the property of God."

"That's no territory of mine."

"Well, you come by our way, Sheriff," Merle said. "You'll see how Buck's gotten the Lord in him stirring up his insides over what he has title to."

When I got home, Roy Hollenbach's wife was heading to her car carrying matching Coca-Cola mugs. "Look here, Bill," she said, "aren't these cute as a baby's smile?" I gave her my version of a grin, not cute at all I could tell, and watched her turn her back to the Ford before dropping into the front seat, both of her thick legs swinging out from under her at the same time, the faint whoosh squeezing out of the seat, sounding like a last-breath.

Lately, Dorene's taken to giving away her Coca-Cola things. To everybody who visits, for starters. As if she was repaying them for kindness. And her with her nurse's job for the baby doctor, spreading Coca-Cola all over the county like it was the name of infant formula. "Maybe," she said, "they'll remember at election time the sheriff is married to the woman who loves Coca-Cola."

"'The Sheriff,' they'll be thinking, 'lives with a crazy woman,'" I said.

"Crazy's who keeps everything to herself. Crazy locks it all up and puts in alarms to let her know thieves are interested in her key chains and mugs."

I thought about Merle and her Bible stories. "Crazy's the woman who gives up God for the tallest drunk in the county."

"Don't you imagine God as tall," Dorene said.

"I can't imagine him at all," I said. "He might as well be wearing that Coca-Cola sweatshirt that promised peace, love, and harmony to the whole world if only all of us would shove our coins into the soda machine."

The next afternoon I swung out County Road 4012. I didn't have a reason to stop. I didn't have a reason to be up their dirt lane. So I wasn't surprised Buck bounded out of the trailer. "You know you're trespassing there, Sheriff. Just cause I drive across my front yard don't mean that patrol car of yours can go any whichaway."

"You fussy about your lawn now?" I said. "Besides, if someone was to come around, would you know where your property line starts and stops?"

Buck spit and took three steps and spit again. "There's a property line—me standing here saying it's so."

"Dogs do that, Buck. They piss and move on and think every dog will respect their mark."

"It's money you're talking about."

"It's the law."

"Yeah, right. I'm talking about protecting what's mine."

He nodded back at the trailer as if I'd know what that signal meant. I saw Merle step into the doorway carrying her motorcycle helmet and wearing a robe. The sight of her made me look at Buck again, his loose shorts and undershirt, his helmet already looped over a handlebar. Buck smiled then and pulled his shirt over his head. For a man who drank too much, he kept after his stomach and chest muscles. I thought if I wanted to see them naked I had only to stand there like a chained dog.

Buck backed up until he was maybe six steps from the trailer, Merle and the cycles just behind him. "Right about here is line-drawing time," he said. "The rest can sink."

Merle touched the velvet belt that was looped around her robe. She looked as much a former nun as any of the women who welcomed the fallen angels of Genesis.

"You know," Buck said, "there's always a way to set up natural borders."

"Fences," I said. "Dogs."

"Beehives," Buck said. "There's them who does it."

Merle climbed on her motorcycle with a flourish, that robe sliding up her bare thigh as if she'd decided to invite me to ride behind her. "Dried cornstalks," Buck went on. "You step in them and you're heard forever."

"I imagine."

"Mint," Buck said. "You think of that one, Sheriff? A prowler steps in mint and he's good as caught. You smell him out and kick his ass, and he knows he's brought on his own deserving."

That night at dinner Dorene shook her head. "Buck couldn't keep a dog off his property."

I thought of how I'd looked in the mirror while I drove off Buck's yard that afternoon, seeing Merle toss that robe behind her as her cycle crossed that line Buck saw underfoot. "Back where I grew up," Dorene went on, "fellow thought up using a hedge as a wall."

"We have a hedge, Dorene. Neighbor kids jump it."

"Not this stuff. It has long, skinny needles that rip you easy as pie. It gets way up to twenty feet or more, thick and scary with those thorns. So thick it stops a jeep. Government came down to take a look. They were thinking terrorists."

"It doesn't grow this far north, I take it."

"I don't know. Never seen anything like it except in Tennessee. But you want to let nobody through, there's plenty of ways to choose from."

I nodded and lifted a Coke from the refrigerator. Dorene smiled. "I ought to give Merle a Coca-Cola gift," she said. "Maybe start her towards something."

The following day I had reason to trespass out to the strip mine. Merle had managed to phone in an official invite before I heard Buck holler for her to "put that fucking phone down."

Buck was outside the trailer, dressed, I was happy to see, and Merle fully clothed as well, but things had gone so poorly since Merle's call he had a gun up to her head and his arm wrapped around her throat from behind, just like I'd seen in a hundred movies. In all those movies, the lawman figures out a way to disable the crazy guy, but I couldn't remember one method just then, when I needed to. I'd never fired my gun at anything but paper targets and tin cans. The only psychology I had faith in was making the punishment fit the crime, and right then it looked like it was up to me whether I was working toward the death penalty or locking down Buck for a month or two of rehab. Worst of all, some horse's ass in a dirt-crusted pickup took to parking a hundred yards over to the woods, so Buck knew he was on the grapevine.

"I need your help here, Buck," I said. "I'm looking for a way to save Merle and you at the same time."

"I don't want to be saved," Buck said, but Merle held her peace.

"Everybody wants to be saved."

"That's exactly the problem."

"You want to be different."

"A man's got to have something just his. All I got is my own way to damnation."

Merle was getting to me with her quietude. Somebody in her position, seemed to me, should be offering up her own version of a solution. "You married a nun," I said, inviting her into the dialogue.

"I saved her from hell fire. She was living in sin, her with her vows and all."

"You fooling with her when she was still a sister?" I said, Merle's silence starting to do me in.

"There's no make-up for things I've done. I might as well be dead shooting Merle," Buck said. "And I might as well be dead facing anybody but the blind, deaf, and dumb when the word gets out on this here state of affairs." He squinted off to his right toward that truck I hoped would turn pillar of salt, and then he looked Merle in the eyes so long I thought he might be working toward goodbye. Merle gave him back a stare until he said, "I might as well be dead if I lay this gun down like the all-time jackass of Sharpersville."

There it was, what the union and management people call an impasse. Buck saw himself the fool any which way, and it seemed uncertain if he was going to pick the least of his evils.

"It's Merle you have to live with, Buck. You're not under the same roof as the citizens of Sharpersville."

"That don't make it easier."

"Merle's likely as anybody to be the forgiving kind," I said, my face flushing so fast I thought Buck would read it as a signal to stop this foolishness and shoot me for lying. And rightly so, I thought, as he drew the gun away from Merle and swung it halfway in my direction before he knelt to lay it on the packed earth.

"I deserve these handcuffs, Sheriff," Buck said at the station. "I need to wear them until Merle has a mind to speak again."

"Give her time."

"It's looking more and more I've a mind to do everything wrong."

"You put that gun down, Buck. You did that right."

"I don't rightly think so. That was another lie."

"Nobody means something like that, Buck."

"There's one of them eternal circles, then," Buck said. He shifted his eyes away from me and fixed on the wall. "You got one of Merle's clocks," he said.

I smiled and followed Buck's look. "That's right, Buck."

"You just one fucking liar, Sheriff. That there's store-bought. You can see it for your own self if you stick your nose behind it and pry it away from the wall."

What is it that we bring ourselves to do sometimes? I clipped Buck a good one alongside his ear where his beard stubble turned into the bristles of where sideburns would start if he ever had a mind to them. He didn't seem to have paid one bit of attention to that billy club, but now he said "Unhh," and his hands lifted and jammed on the cuffs, letting me choose which part of him I wanted next.

I rammed that billy point-first into his belly, driving it up into the solar plexus like we learned twenty-five years ago when the long-hairs were asking for it. I lifted him a little because I had the time to get my legs behind that jab. Buck sat down where there wasn't a chair. With his hands cuffed behind him, he just rocked back like a baby and went feet-up. I waited, but Buck was focused somewhere above my head. "I had that coming, Sheriff," he said at last. "We're all square now."

"See?" Dorene declared when I told her the news, and then she started sweeping it under the table by saying, "You know why polio erupted in modern times?"

"We're not old enough for polio," I said. "They did the Salk the year I was born and I'm older than you."

"Because things became too clean. It was on the television this last hour."

"Everybody knows then."

"PBS," she said. "It's still a secret. We used to be exposed when we were babies, mild cases made us immune later on when we needed to be. And then we cleaned things up."

"What things?"

"Fecal matter."

"Shit?"

"You become a nun, you ought to stay a nun," Dorene said. "There's things worse than polio you need to know early."

In the morning I heard Buck taking his forearms to the holding cell wall.

He was right-handed, and after a while I could call the right, then the left, as it thudded, because he threw himself behind his blows better with the right. For sure, what a jackass, I thought, and then, after I'd listened for longer than I expected, I started hoping each thud was the last one and that I'd never hear that sound again.

He wasn't going to hurt that wall, but he was strong enough to make me imagine a groan starting to hum inside it. When I placed myself in front of the bars to put a stop to those thumps, Buck picked up the copy of *The Book of Lists* Dorene had me put in each cell—"to calm their souls," she'd said—and held it open to me. "This here fella's a sight bigger than any of Merle's Bible people," Buck said. He pointed at a picture of a man named Robert Wadlow. "He got himself big and then he up and died."

So Buck had heard the gospel of giants, too, but I had to admit the guy in the picture looked the part of a world's record; it said right there he was eight feet, eleven inches. The parents of Robert Wadlow were standing beside him, looking up as if they'd never seen their son before. "How did they manage?" I said.

Buck whistled between his teeth. "That's you, all right, Sheriff. You and your woman with no kids trying to take care of the world for other peoples' children."

"Yours are long gone, Buck."

"But they're mine. And here you are knowing the grown men of this world are past help, so you and the missus work on the young. You have yourself kids you'd know there's no saving them from themselves neither."

"That's my lookout, Buck," I said.

Buck kept up with that whistling, shrill and thin, like he was talking to dogs. "Head up, eyes open, Sheriff. That's the ticket."

"You want to make yourself bigger?" I said. I studied Buck until I saw him glance at my holstered gun. "You look up in there the one about the man who could grow himself. Six inches. He just heaved himself up somehow, breathed different, shrugged his shoulders and tensed his muscles."

"Bullshit," Buck said, but he was turning pages, looking down and then up at me like a child who'd been caught pretending he could read.

Dorene was the expert on all those lists, but I'd taken a mind to this fellow. "It says right in there he didn't use lifts in his shoes. It seems there's plenty of parts of yourself you can work upwards."

"Meaning?"

"Hips. Knees. Chest. Throat."

Buck stopped thumbing the pages and thought it over. "I could easy make seven feet that way," Buck said.

"Pretty near, I imagine."

"Pretty goddamn near. I don't have to be no expert. I don't need the whole six inches."

"Control, Buck. That's what all this is about."

He tossed the book onto the cot, and it flopped open to the pages about unusual deaths of celebrities. "I never raised a hand to none of my women," Buck said. "I ain't started now neither."

"Nobody said anything about raising a hand, Buck."

"It don't matter what's been said. It don't ever matter what's been said."

"That's got the rightness of common sense," I said. "Surely it does. But nobody's thinking that way either."

"Lying's what you got to swear to for that badge."

"You raised a gun to Merle," I said. "You put that weapon behind her ear like she was an old dog."

"That don't bruise her none. It don't raise a welt or break a bone. It's over when it's over."

"Meaning Merle and myself ought to see that gun as a sort of verbal abuse."

Buck nodded. "That's it exactly. The gun's just talking. It don't mean any harm."

"There's words in this world we can't ever take back, Buck."

"I surely know that, Sheriff," Buck said, seeming to settle. He stepped back from the bars and looked up at the ceiling as if he expected it to pop open like a beer can.

"Consider on that, then," I said.

He made a gun with his index finger and thumb, pointed it at me. "A man takes nothing back, Sheriff. You either know that or you turn into one sorry sack of shit," and he held that gun on me until I turned and walked back into my office.

When Merle showed up before noon, I closed off the door between my office and the cells. Buck didn't need to be encouraged right off. She didn't need to hear him if he took a mind to put a fresh series of forearm shivers to his wall. "You don't have to follow the church on this one," I said.

"Everything has a reward in the eyes of God," Merle said. "When I sang in the junior choir, I got candy. When I vowed I loved Mary the mother of Christ, repeating the exact words of the priest, I got a reduced price, Three Rivers Stadium grandstand ticket, and a seat on the parish bus to nine innings with the Knothole Gang on a Saturday."

"I remember those trips," I said, swimming through the syrup of our nostalgia.

Merle brightened. "You a Pirates fan?" she said.

"We lived too far for Pittsburgh," I said. "The only time one of our bus trips went the hundred miles was to the Police Circus at the Hunt Armory. I'd made a fire scene poster, and my mother paid three dollars to enter my safety slogan in a contest. So I got a pass to the circus, a bag lunch with grapes and a bologna and cheese sandwich I heaved out the bus window when we pulled out of Altoona. Before we boarded that bus, all of us poster kids had to listen to fire lessons, the consequences of smoking in bed or playing with the pilot light or toying with the shiny red can for gasoline."

"Lucky you," Merle said. "All my lessons were about eternal flames. Hell was a kind of scoreless tie, inning after inning of three-up, three-down, because God was a fireballer who could smoke them past sinners forever."

Merle laughed then. "Father Joe was a fan," she said. "You wonder how even a child could have believed such silliness." She looked at the clock on my wall as if she were deciding something. "Buck wears diapers when he's into the bottle," Merle said.

"Nobody does that," I said. "I'd quit drinking altogether before I put up with that kind of humiliation."

"It cuts down on wasted time when he's shooting pool and such," she said. "That's the philosophy of Pampers."

"You buy him the baby kind?"

"Drinking's his own purchase, Sheriff. He can't bring himself to buy Depends. People would get the wrong idea."

I measured around Buck's waist in my head and decided Merle was giving me a test I was about to fail. "There's no baby has half Buck's big ass," I said.

Merle glanced at the closed door. "He's got adhesive tape for that, Sheriff. The double width. It doesn't come away easy off a man's skin."

I went home for lunch. I couldn't sit in that office with Buck's empty cell and the sight of the two of them disappearing into Buck's old ratty Chevy. "It's not Buck getting out got you down," Dorene said right off.

I put my feet up on the chair opposite me at the kitchen table, and Dorene leaned on that chair. "Buck ran off at the mouth about us not having children made us ignorant of our good intentions."

"We had children," Dorene said at once.

"Most would say miscarriage."

"We gave them names. Stephanie. Stacey. You don't give names to blood in the toilet. You give names to babies."

"They were too early, Dorene. Even for science."

Dorene drew her hair up with both hands and held it so long I thought she meant for me to fetch something to tie it with. When she pulled it tighter, that hair looked stretched for shearing. "That cruel bastard," she finally said, "him knowing I delivered two dead girls. And you letting him go."

"I don't make the law."

"Listen to yourself. You sound like a television sheriff."

"It's Merle has to live with him."

"Lucky her. We have to live with ourselves."

"Enough, Dorene," I said.

"It surely was," Dorene said. She leaned across the table, her hair tumbling back down as she tested my Coke can with her hand. "You want another?" she asked, and when I shook my hand, she carried the empty to the sink. "The girls would have loved their Coca-Cola," she said, holding the can under the faucet. "They'd be that age right now when you practically carry a Coke with you all day."

Six hours later the dispatcher had me heading out County Road 4012. "Trailer fire," she said, "fully engaged."

Nobody but a stranger would have thought anything but Buck and Merle, though I was making a list, one by one, of the other trailers out that way. Six, I came up with, and more to come if I'd had the time to recollect before I saw Merle step out of the scrub oak and sumac, staring at my cruiser as if she expected to mental-telepathy it into a four-wheel drift.

A stone's throw up ahead was the elbow joint of a curve where that girl who was a cheerleader killed herself and nearly four others speeding into the sycamore been standing guard since before cars were a twinkle in God's eye. Merle didn't know that, more than likely. Less than two years out there, half of it spent at carnivals. She didn't know anything except what Buck let on was important.

"I knew you'd be coming by," she said.

"That's what I do."

"It's not anything like you think," she said.

"We got to be checking to find out which way we're thinking."

I was hoping Buck wasn't in that trailer as much or more than Merle might have been at that moment. Or leastways Merle was maybe about to tell me the census had dropped a notch the last hour gone by, because Buck had up and thrown his own self in among his television and Lazy Boy, that all she'd done was start things up and let Buck decide where they were going.

I'd seen the aftermath of trailer fires before, the rubble so folded up on itself you think of people who drive those tiny cars at high speeds, the consequences of economy. You were out of there immediately, TV or no TV, or you were in there forever. Anybody eyewitness to a trailer fire wouldn't lay down to sleep without twice checking every source of possible fire.

The weakening daylight didn't keep me from sniffing gasoline. I got out and came around to the passenger side. "I smell like it, but I didn't burn him up," Merle said. "Ask me right out—I'm not going to lie to you."

"That's good, Merle. Truth is what we need right now."

"A body's got only one cheek to turn, Sheriff. Isn't that right?"

"I don't recollect Jesus like I oughta."

"One side and then the other, Sheriff. You look at yourself and see if I'm right."

"I'm thinking on that Bible story, Merle. There's more to it than that. God's not that easy."

"You keep that up, Sheriff, and you'll be running for priest. Folks always have a mind to elect somebody makes everything seem hard."

Merle leaned back against the door, lifting her arms above her head like a flirting schoolgirl. For a moment, I watched the way her breasts lifted inside her thin sweater and imagined her on a motorcycle, more than those few inches of stomach exposed. Mosquitoes were rising into the twilight. Merle slapped at the side of her neck, and she folded her arms where the material settled back down over her stomach.

"What are you thinking, Sheriff," she said. "We ride in that car of yours, we'll both be naked?"

"Not this minute, I'm not," I said.

She tugged at the sweater, drew the toe of her shoe through the roadside dust. "Buck says he owns all the way to here if he says so."

I looked past her into the woods. It was more than a hundred yards straight through to Buck's clearing. I heard a siren skidding our way, but I was thinking about what sort of booby traps a man like Buck would use to border his privacy.

"You're misunderstanding," I said.

"But you want to know if Buck's dead."

I heard the fire truck brake a bit as it passed, getting ready for that curve, but I didn't look at it, not even when whoever was driving honked. "No," I said, keeping my eyes on the woods behind her, "that's not what I want to know."

The light was different now, as if the fire a quarter mile up the road or a hundred yards through the woods had taken the shadows out of the air. I breathed awkwardly, almost panting. Fire fed on oxygen, I thought, and then I squinted at the sun just above the tree line, where the head and shoulders of giants would reach if they chose to reveal themselves.

WIRE'S WIRE, UNTIL IT'S A BODY

———

Coming home from his father's funeral, late spring twilight settling in, Ray Salter felt a small jounce just outside of Lewiston. "What was that?" his wife said, slowing.

"Nothing," he said, but Cindy pulled onto the shoulder, looked in the rearview mirror where nothing, he thought, could be visible but the dark. "I hit something," she said. "You felt it."

"A small rock," he said. "A crack in the road. A tree branch."

"No, Ray. Something." She put the car in reverse and backed up a hundred yards.

"OK," he said, "maybe a rabbit or a squirrel. What can you do?"

"I want to know what I've done."

Cindy stepped out and looked, walked back and forth, checked both shoulders. A car passed. Another.

"Satisfied?" he said. "Some little piece of debris was all it was."

"OK."

Something strange, Ray thought, settling back into the passenger seat. An incident to talk about with his wife at breakfast the next day, but ten miles later, Cindy stopped again, crying this time, and searched the road for the dead body she was sure was just off in the shadows. Five minutes he helped her look, and then Ray took the wheel and told her to rest.

"Maybe I should do the night driving if it worries you so much," he said the next day.

Cindy sat across from him at the kitchen table. She'd started a second cup of coffee, but she hadn't touched it for ten minutes. "You don't see well enough at night to make out everything," she said.

"Nobody's night-blind at forty-two," Ray said. "Not even down at Eyeland. I'm not the one stopping for bumps in the road."

"You haven't had a checkup in years. You'll hit somebody and not know it."

"Of course I would."

He reached across the table and touched her hand, but she pulled it back. "A glancing blow," she said. "A little quiver and they'll spin off into the shadows someplace where you won't see them."

"If you think that way you won't be able to drive."

"I'll be more careful," she said. "I can drive as long as I'm cautious. I have to get to the office. You have your own troubles to worry about."

"That's old news," he said, but she shook her head. Over a year ago now, in early May, he'd been surprised at the tenure decision. Shocked. Everybody but the incompetent got tenure, he'd thought. Lousy teachers. Those who never published and didn't show up for committee meetings. He had decent evaluations. He'd put out a couple of articles. He'd hit a dry patch the last two years, but he thought it was the pressure of needing an article at a crucial time. It would have all sorted out. The point was there had been no black marks in his book—three adjunct jobs and six years of full-time—and yet the dean had called him to her office a week before graduation to break the news personally before the registered mail arrived the following day.

He had a year, of course, to pursue a new position. She was sure he'd find something suitable, but the year had come and gone, and here he was, the last week in May, eligible to file for unemployment.

"The old news needs to be updated," Cindy said finally. "You go take care of that paperwork. All I need to do is fit a pair of glasses, help somebody pick the perfect frames, and I'll be good as new."

Ray drove to the social services office, passing the college on the way into town. He wanted to get in and get out as early in the day as possible. As long as nobody he recognized saw him, he could stand it.

The line, he was happy to see, was short. The woman who handled the forms looked at his personal information and said that she'd see to it his checks were sent in the mail. Someone like him wouldn't have to report in person to receive compensation. An hour of his time and he was assured an income for another year. He'd need it, Ray thought, because if he didn't find a teaching job by August, any department head would know he'd been fired, and nobody would ever hire him again.

For the last quarter mile of his trip home, he could clearly see the police car in his driveway. From a distance, his house already looked like it was on the news, like it didn't belong to him.

Cindy was alive. Unhurt. She was calmly sitting at the kitchen table, the untouched coffee cup centered on the smooth pine. The policeman was standing in the kitchen, his arms folded across his chest, evaluating, Ray thought, the way he approached his side door.

"I called the police," Cindy said at once. "You weren't here, and I thought they needed to know. Hit and run is an awful thing. I wouldn't be able to live with myself."

"Your wife believes she injured a pedestrian with her vehicle," the policeman said.

"Of course I did. I hit him," she said. "A jogger. Running uphill the way he was, he had his head down. I only saw him when I came over the crest of that hill a mile down the road. I put two tires over the center line to make sure I missed him, but when I looked in the mirror after I passed him, he was gone."

For one second Ray was relieved. "He took off into the woods," he began. "He went back over the crest of that hill." He looked at the policeman for reassurance, and panic settled in. "Cindy?" he started again.

"He's in the woods, all right," she said, "but he's hurt in there, or dying. God help me, I've killed somebody."

The policeman shrugged, "I'm sorry," he said. "We looked for twenty minutes. I wish there was a better story for you to hear."

Ray nodded, and the policeman shook his hand, holding it so long he wanted to slap the cop's complacent face. Ray watched him get into his patrol car, and then he turned. "Christ, you had me worried, Cindy, but now I'm terrified."

"You don't think I hit anybody."

"Of course not."

"And now you're in a dither because somebody else knows."

"That's not it."

"You had a year, and you couldn't even tell your father you lost your job."

"He had his heart problem. He didn't need me to make things worse."

"I think he knew. He sensed it, and you not saying anything made him worry more."

Ray looked at her. "I'll tell you what he knew," he said. "The last time we visited he had me walk with him to the end of the street."

"Where was I?"

"Asleep. It was first thing in the morning. We walked into a field just behind the last house, and he said, 'Look at this.' All those years and I'd never been to that spot. There was an open mine shaft with a piece of sheet iron over it."

"I don't understand," Cindy said.

"Subsidence problems. My father wanted me to know there were abandoned mines underneath our street, that the next plan over had twenty houses with cracked foundations, three yards with sinkholes. 'You never know what's right under your feet,' he said. He had a map the county had given him. That's what he knew. It showed where all the mines were."

"And?"

"He said he couldn't read the map without his glasses, so he didn't put them on."

"Did you read it?" Irony had slipped into her voice. It made him wary.

"No. What difference would it make? Why the hell would he want to know?"

"I bet he peeked."

"He didn't need a map. Once a month, my father walked every backyard on that street. He patrolled for shifts in the earth."

"Nobody does that, Ray."

"Everybody does everything. Like this tenure bullshit. They think they're doing you a big favor giving you a year's grace, but it's dreadful. Going to work every day knowing you're fired. It's like being in the stocks."

"The students don't know."

"The hell they don't."

"You're wrong."

"As long as I think I'm right it doesn't matter if I'm wrong."

She picked up the coffee cup, and for a moment Ray thought she was going to drink from it. "Come on," he said. "Let's get you right back in the car. I'll drive, and you'll see we can go all the way to Harrisburg, forty miles down and forty miles back, without hitting anything."

When they reached Harrisburg without Cindy once telling him to stop, Ray was beaming. "See?" he said. "We made it."

They stopped at a tavern, ordered beer and wine and nacho grande, sharing globs of cheese and beans slathered over toasted, salty chips. Ray ordered a second beer, Cindy another glass of wine. He picked, finally, at the onion and jalapenos, the only things left on the plate, while Cindy started a third glass of wine.

"You know," she said, "maybe I've always had something like this. I used to pretend I was dead."

"Every little kid does that."

"You're just saying that."

"Cowboys and Indians. War. You know."

"I was always by myself," Cindy said. She swallowed half her glass and leaned back. "The time I remember best was in Wisconsin, at this man-made lake. We were on vacation, and I was six or seven years old. My father was really happy because the lake was so shallow. You could walk out thirty steps and still be only up to your knees. Another thirty steps and it would be just chest high."

"That doesn't sound like much of a lake."

"I liked it, too, but then, the second day, my parents went inside and left me there. 'Be good,' my father said. I thought they'd be back in a few minutes. I started backing away from the shore, feeling the water come up almost to my neck. I couldn't swim. My father knew that. And then I just sat down in the water and let it cover me. I counted to twenty and popped up, but nobody was looking. I sat down again and counted to thirty. It was hard, but I made it and stood up. Nobody."

"You didn't tell them?" Ray said.

"Of course not. I tried to count more, but I could only get to thirty-three before I stood up. It felt like my head was never going to get clear. I think I backed up a little more each time, and I could barely touch bottom. I remember thinking I was going to drown for real."

Ray pushed the last three jalapenos together, but he didn't pick them up. "There were people staying in the other cabins, Ray, but not one of them was outside that morning." Cindy dabbed at her forehead with her sleeve as if she were blotting beads of sweat. "You can disappear," she said, "just like that."

"That was thirty-five years ago. That's not you anymore."

"Everything I did is me. Not having children is me."

"You can't think like that and be happy,"

"I've never even had one to lose. What do you think my parents were doing in that cabin while I was sitting in that lake?"

"This kind of talk can't help anything."

"They were always at each other, but I was the only child. What do you think about that?"

"What do you want me to say?"

"I've only been crazy a few days, Ray. It'll stop."

Halfway back, Cindy screamed. "Stop," she said, "there's a body on the shoulder."

He braked and pulled over. "Come on," he said, but she was already out of the car running. He walked behind her. He hadn't gone more than a hundred yards from where she'd screamed. He saw her slow and then bend down. He saw something dark and round and quickened his steps.

A garbage bag. "Well," he said, "at least you had a reason this time."

"Open it," she said.

"Why?"

"To see what's inside."

"Garbage is what's inside."

"Somebody could be in there."

"A midget," he said, but he pushed the bag with his foot. It skittered away so easily he said, "Midget dolls."

"Please?"

He opened it and pulled out a handful of frozen dinner boxes. "OK?" he said.

"All of it," she said.

He lifted the bag and let the contents spread out on the side of the road. Chicken bones, apple cores, some sort of vegetables gone bad, but

mostly paper, thank God. She took the empty bag from him, hefting it
as if she believed something was still inside.

"This isn't funny," he said.

"Of course it isn't."

"You know what I mean." By now, though, she was turning the bag
inside out, the last crusts of bread and greasy napkins slopping onto the
shoulder.

"Wow," she said, something he could agree with.

"Now what?"

"Put everything back in."

He thought about who might have gnawed on those bones, what kind
of person would be tossing bags of garbage out of a moving car. "Put it
in the trunk," she said.

"We're not a road crew."

"Somebody else will see it and panic."

They drove a mile, and she screamed, "My God, stop."

He drifted along the shoulder this time, slowing gradually and trying
to reason with her. "That was a tire," he said.

"It's a body," she said. "Back up or I'll run the whole way without you."

He cut back onto the road and accelerated. She turned away, gripping
the door handle, and he kept the speedometer at sixty-five, afraid that
if he slowed down she would throw herself out the door. Every time he
looked in the mirror he thought of the bag in the trunk, how much room
there was for debris on the backseat.

The next morning, when he refused to drive her to work, Cindy called in
sick. By midafternoon he'd watched two movies and listened to her slap
cards on the kitchen table, playing one solitaire game after another. The
thought of eating dinner on that table, seeing that deck of cards stacked
on the edge, seemed unbearable. At 4:00 he started walking, following
the highway, facing traffic. The cars hurtled by at fifty and sixty miles per
hour. If one of them hit him, he'd either be killed or crippled, and for
sure he wouldn't be staggering off into the woods to avoid any help that
might be offered.

None of the cars seemed consciously to avoid him. Every driver,
for over a hundred cars, steered straight in the oncoming lane, and he

imagined what his wife would look like approaching him, going forty perhaps, straddling the center line, panicked. A pedestrian would think she was drunk.

After twenty minutes he turned into the campus. The first two weeks following graduation, before summer school began, was always the most deserted, but he saw a physical-plant worker sweeping the sidewalk through the center of campus as if he'd been told there was an academic procession scheduled for 6:00.

"Hi there, Dale," he said. Dale smiled.

"School's out, professor," he said.

He knew the students called this man Bubba because he was fat and stupid. He did the jobs for which no training was required. Sweeping. Raking. Weeding. In winter, chipping ice and shoveling snow.

"For sure," he said.

"They'll be back, sure as shootin'."

"Right."

He stepped to the side in order not to disturb the small piles of twigs and pebbles Dale had formed along the curb.

"'Fore you know it, school's in."

"Right."

"Have a good one, professor," Dale said.

"You too, Dale."

He walked by the building where his office was, but he didn't go in. Somebody might be there. He had until June 30 to clear out. He'd come in on a Sunday morning when he was certain nobody would be there. For an hour, he sat in the library, deep in the stacks, thinking he was going to research phobias. When he finally pushed out of his chair, he walked outside and headed home.

A mile from the house, he saw her car on the shoulder. Cindy was behind the wheel crying. She breathed wine when he leaned through the door. "I thought drinking would relax me," she said.

"I backed to the end of the driveway and had to get out to check a dead azalea that tumbled over," she said. "I had a quart of wine, Ray. A quart. I checked the street, looked under the car, and then I got back in and managed to creep to the stop sign."

"Let's get you home," Ray said.

She didn't slide over. She stared straight ahead over the steering wheel. "On the main highway," she said, "I stayed in second gear, looking for walkers, for deer and rabbits and whatever might flash in front of me. The mirror filled up with cars. Half of the cars that passed blared their horns. It's still light out, Ray, and I'm drunk and paralyzed."

She kept her hands on the steering wheel. He saw white spots where the force of her grip cut off her circulation. "'Third gear,' I said to myself, and I shifted, accelerating to twenty-five, then thirty miles per hour. 'Fourth gear,' I said, shifting, but I stalled because I'd taken my foot off the gas. I got started again, but only in second gear, sweating, driving on the shoulder, looking for a place to turn.

"There wasn't any place, Ray. In a minute I felt something. I didn't get out, though. I said, 'No, you don't get out for every bump. It's nothing.' But I slowed down, Ray. I drove so slow I had to put the car in first and just started creeping along the shoulder for three minutes. I don't think I made a mile altogether. And nobody paid any attention. Cars must have gone by, don't you think? This is a road."

"How long do you think you've been here?"

"Not long. You're the first person who's stopped."

"OK," he said, but he got into the passenger seat. They sat there for two minutes, then three, and then Cindy crawled over him and flopped against the door.

"What am I going to do?" she said the next morning, a Saturday, neither of them needing to go anywhere. "I thought if you recognized how irrational you were you couldn't be crazy."

"I don't know."

"Isn't that what they always say? That if you know you're absurd then you can't be insane?"

"I guess that's not always true."

"I guess not."

She faced the front window, looked straight ahead so long he thought she was seeing an approaching army of zombies. She turned. "We tried for fifteen years to have children, Ray. When did we know?"

"Let's talk about what's in front of us."

"We don't have money for a psychiatrist."

"I'm on the dole."

"A week of that is an hour at the psychiatrist's. I can't tell anybody, Ray. If somebody finds out at Eyeland, they'll fire me, too. Dead bodies—it's absolutely crazy."

"Starting Monday, I'll drive you to work and back. On the way we'll look at everything you imagine is a body until you see how silly it is. Two birds with one stone."

"Yes."

"We'll hit bumps and circle back. We'll see the hole in the road. We'll see the sticks and stones."

"Yes."

He walked over to the window, looked out where he could see the dead azalea bunched against the mailbox post. "I don't know why I wanted to teach at a college," he said. "Nobody teaches anymore. They encourage."

"Maybe it's for the best then."

"The best would be if I'd never done it in the first place."

"Well, then, you're going to get second best."

He raised his chin a little, looked over the tree line to where the state highway followed the base of the tree-covered hills. When his eyes came back to the azalea, he smiled. "Look," he said, "there's the bush you had to stop for yesterday."

"Yes," Cindy said, "it's the old azalea."

He brightened. "Good," he said. "That's good. Say that when we see a bundle of old wire."

"A bush is a bush if I'm not in a car, Ray. Wire's wire, until it's a body."

He pressed his face against the glass. "You think I haven't earned the right to be angry?"

"I don't know, Ray."

"You don't think this is anger, do you? You think I'm afraid."

"You tell me, Ray."

His words seemed weak. He was explaining himself instead of being somebody. In another minute just being a husband would be out of reach. "Remember how I called my father every night because I knew he would only answer maybe one time out of ten because he couldn't hear the phone unless he was in the kitchen?"

"Yes."

"How many times do you think I called that last year?"

"I don't know."

"Almost every night—that's about three hundred. And sometimes twice or three times a night. Another hundred."

"There's no need for a total."

"That's what you think."

"The 'what if' story never helped anybody."

They both smiled. "Cindy," he said then, "I know just enough about everything to try the wrong things."

She looked as if she was going to take his hand then, and he thought, "If she does, this will be over." But when her fingers, at last, brushed his arm before they settled back against her side, he knew she was closer than ever to never leaving the house again.

"Let's get you driving around campus," Ray said, putting his dishes in the sink after dinner. "Nobody's ever around on a Sunday in the summer. There are six speed bumps. You can feel what a read bump is."

Cindy wiped at the table. He watched her make three ovals with the damp cloth before she said, "Drive us there, Ray. Get this off on the right foot."

He parked in an empty lot behind a dorm. "OK," he said. Cindy slid over, and he walked around and got inside. "Take it away," he said, trying to sound jaunty.

She managed to reach second gear, the speedometer standing at fifteen. They passed the field house, the front of it glass enclosed from ceiling to floor so prospective students and their parents could gaze, as they passed, at the enormous room full of exercise equipment.

"First bump," he said.

"I see it." She slowed, and the car reared up and settled twice, thumping down even at ten miles per hour. He waited, but she didn't stop.

"See?" he said.

"That was a big bump."

"And nothing's there but a ridge of asphalt." She looked in the mirror as he spoke, but she didn't stop. "That's it," he said.

They passed the library, two classroom buildings, thumped over two more speed bumps. "Now we're getting somewhere," he said, and Cindy smiled.

"We're going all the way back around to your office."

"Yes, we are."

"There's a girl on the sidewalk."

"Yes."

"She's not looking."

"She's on the sidewalk."

Cindy drifted into the middle of the road as they approached the next bump. "Oh God," she said, looking up at the mirror. Ray stared straight ahead. The car, going so slowly in second gear, threatened to stall. "Oh thank God," Cindy whispered, "that girl's all right." She pressed the gas just enough to steady the car.

"We made it," she said, pulling in front of his office building. "You want to go in?"

"Not now."

"You should maybe go in and bring some stuff home."

"If nobody's around," he said.

"Nobody's around except that one girl."

"You never know."

She turned off the ignition. "Come on," she said, "I know you have boxes stacked up in there."

Ray filled six boxes with books while Cindy arranged photographs and his manuscripts in a separate carton. He saw four versions of himself, from each of his teaching jobs, lying on top, and then he walked down the hall to the bathroom. When he came back, Cindy had his computer turned on. "I knew your password," she said. "I thought it might be fun."

"It's not."

She clicked on IN-BOX and the screen filled with hundreds of messages, all of the files unopened, 328 UNREAD. "Oh Ray," she said, "Look at all these e-mail messages from your students. And these memos. And forms to fill out. How do you know what anyone wants?"

"I know when I see them."

"Oh Ray."

"I don't turn it on," he said. "I have office hours, more than anyone else in my building. I have a phone. I walk around campus. I'm always here."

"But how do they know?"

He reached over and pushed the POWER button. He didn't need to close down any of the systems. Let somebody else take care of that. "What did they ask you to change, Ray?" Cindy said.

"What?"

"You know, before they fired you. What did they suggest you do differently?"

"Nothing."

"That can't be true, Ray."

He looked at the blank screen, imagining all of those messages taking voice and jabbering. "If they'd already decided, it could be," he said, and as soon as he uttered the words, they sounded true. He'd heard about editors who rejected articles immediately, filing them by date, waiting six months to return them in order to keep from getting new submissions from failed writers. He saw his dated file moving methodically toward the notification date. For a year? For two? He tossed everything he hadn't packed into the middle of the floor and taped his key to the outside of the door.

"Oh Ray," Cindy said again as he pushed it shut.

A heavy rain had fallen while they were in the office. With the boxes in the backseat, Ray felt so strange he decided to take the back roads home.

There were a handful of houses, and then the road turned rural. He remembered enjoying the extra mile because he didn't have to worry about traffic. Alongside the road, a runoff ditch churned with maybe six inches of muddy water. Cindy grabbed his arm. "Ray," she said, "there's a body under that water."

"Don't do this," he said. "There's nothing."

She had the door open. He had to stop before she pitched onto the asphalt. "The last time," he said, but she waded into the ditch, kicking slowly to feel her way along. It was almost a mile forward to where the ditch shallowed and ended at the crossroads with their street.

"Nothing you want to save could be under that water," he said.

"I can't save anything. I just want to get the body out of the water."

Cindy pulled a gallon milk carton up from the water. "That's the body of an old dead jug," he said.

"Of course it's a jug. It's only a dead body until I touched it."

"You can't touch everything," Ray said, standing at the edge of the ditch now, watching her feel with her feet.

"I know that," she said. "That's what makes it so hard."

She fished out something dreadful then, stiff and furred, like an inside-out, frozen glove. "There's your body," he said then, suddenly glad.

"Take it," Cindy said, holding it out to him.

"Christ, no. Throw it the hell away."

"It's a body," she said. "We have to take care of it."

"It's a squirrel or something. It's long past being taken care of."

She looked past him then, her eyes flying open in fear. He sidestepped as he turned, bringing up his hands.

"Sorry coming up on you like that," the man Cindy had noticed said, "but I saw the two of you and pulled over back there by your car and walked over to help."

"We're looking for something," Ray said.

"In that ditch?"

"Yes."

"What, exactly?"

"My husband won't take this," Cindy said, extending her hand again.

The man took the dead squirrel at once and put it on the shoulder. "There," he said, "it's out of the water at least."

"See?" Cindy said. "That's all you had to do, Ray. Be civil."

The man put his toe to the squirrel and flipped it over once. He looked at both of them and shrugged. "Well then," he said. "Everything's all right." And then he was walking back toward his car.

Ray picked up the dead squirrel between his thumb and one finger. "What are you going to do now?" Cindy said. He climbed down into the water and extended his arm and flung the flattened squirrel into the woods. "That's the best I can do," he said. "It's back where it belongs."

They stood ankle deep in the water. "There's so much water," Cindy said.

"Yes, there is."

"That was a good thing you just did. It was almost perfect."

They watched the stranger reach his car, turn his lights on, and drive away. "We can stand here all night," he said. "It's June. It's warm."

"I'm not that crazy, Ray."

His balance seemed unsteady. He slid his feet a few inches farther apart and tested his stance. His wife sloshed backwards a few steps, moving easily, but she didn't bend down to check the water. "See?" she said, taking another step and then another, almost jogging backwards.

Surely, he thought, she was going to fall, and he raised both his arms to the side to steady himself. If he tried to catch her now, he thought he'd tumble face forward into the muck. "See, Ray," she said again, and then he felt such a sentimental longing well up that he took a step, lurched, then pushed off, leaned forward, and began to run, throwing up splashes of brown water to his calves, then his knees, and finally, when he accelerated, onto his thighs, soaking and staining himself like a child.

THE LIGHTNING TONGUES

———

One of the pleasures of working day shift at the newsstand at the mall is popping open the paper bundles, arranging them by local, state, and national, and then taking one of each into the back room to keep me company through a large coffee and a Long-John from Donut Queen.

I don't mind not getting paid for the first fifteen minutes, but the second fifteen are on the clock. And though it isn't, I'll admit, a fringe benefit anybody I know would be pleased to have, the truth is I would read through the whole half hour for free, saving the local paper until last. Which was why I didn't find out, until five minutes before I had to unlock, that Stacey Long, who worked at the pet store next to the newsstand, had left for lunch yesterday at 12:30 and hadn't been seen since then.

I'd eaten lunch with her more than a few times, even when she was still married. By then she was happy to have me sit across from her at Arby's or Burger King because Wade, her husband, though she'd moved out, let it be known she still belonged to him and he wasn't about to truck with her shacking up behind his back.

"It might as well be you he imagines, Danny," she told me. "He knows who you are. He remembers you from high school."

I didn't think my having been a linebacker was any protection to her. I'd added thirty pounds of unhelpful fat in the ten years since I'd worn a helmet, and I'd never even been in a shoving match around a pileup. But if it made a skinny loudmouth like Wade Long keep his place, I was pleased to help, meanwhile trying to believe something real for him to fret about would sometime or another arise.

I stopped reading and looked at the picture her mother must have given the reporter because I didn't remember her hair long like that since she was married to Wade. He must have had a hundred pictures of her looking like she did in the here-and-now instead of five years ago, but I admitted to myself there were more reasons than guilt for not giving up such a photo. And when I saw it was 9:02, that I was already late with opening, there was Wade Long himself fidgeting at the door.

It was daylight. I equated sunshine with safety. A well-lit place like the mall made me relax. I unlocked the door as if Wade were there to buy lottery tickets or a cigar or a sack of candy bars. "Don't this beat it," Wade said.

"You tell me, Wade."

"You ain't taken a mind to bein' one of them search party faggots?"

"I don't know anything about a search party, Wade. I have a job right here for the next eight hours."

"You don't have that much to do. I seen how you work your own damn self right over to where them puppies yammer all the damn day."

"You're mistaking lunch for sex, Wade."

Wade bounced from one foot to the other, tapping the set of keys in his right hand against the doorframe. "I got to give it to you getting to the point, Danny. That's why I'm here—clear the air and all."

"The air here is clear, Wade."

"She could have herself sitting in a motel somewhere watching the television and laughing at Wade Long getting hassled by the police. They talking about my involvement, and there ain't nothing happened far as I can make out."

"The paper says her car's still out in the lot."

"With all that yellow tape and shit around it like the front seat was covered with blood. With the police standing around looking at me like I had her stuffed up my shirt." A group of old people walked by, finishing the walking trail they followed each morning before the stores opened. Wade looked them up and down as if he were checking for a plainclothesman.

"Listen up, Danny," Wade said. "Guilty men don't come back. That's mythology made up by cops. You see me standing here. You see proof."

"The ex post facto alibi."

"Yeah," Wade said. "Whatever. You can see I'm investigating on my own. Looking for the weak links is looking out for my own self in this sorry mess where the bullseye's on my back."

"I'll tell everybody you're looking for clues," I said.

Wade settled down and smiled. "There you go," he said. "Though she fucked with me, I'll admit to thinking. She done me wrong."

"You don't kill somebody for being unfaithful."

"You best be careful making such judgments. I didn't say nothing about her fucking another man. I took care of her needs. I did right by her. It was her all the time being smart."

"It's not something that comes and goes like lust."

"You weren't so smart in school. I remember you, Danny. You just kicked ass on the football field and waited for the girls to think that was some kind of foreplay. You went in the navy like any hick jackass. You didn't go to any college, even for football."

In front of the pet store, under glass, are toads and lizards you can waken with a quarter, dropping crickets or flies to their lightning tongues. I did it once and threw away two dollars in three minutes. It was like being drunk and feeding a one-song jukebox, listening to eternal heartbreak driving down the booze-sloshed two-lane to hell in a nasal twang. Stacey, a week ago, had sold a pair of hermit crabs to my sister's boy Dale. She'd given him 10 percent off for being under twelve, and before he showed me the crabs, he described the last seconds in the life of the cricket his quarter had paid for.

When I left the mall for lunch, I walked by Stacey's car. It was like looking at a black hole, all of it dark with vacancy. I kept going, set on ending up at Hardee's at the end of the lot, but just like that, passing it, I started imagining one of those chalked outlines of her body in the driver's seat, set it upright, one foot on the brake, so maybe she could climb back into that shape, fitting it so exactly she could reclaim herself. And as soon as I turned my back to that car, I was sure she was dead.

On the television news at 6:00, the police said they'd had Wade Long in for questioning, but no arrest had been made. Their big news was a film clip from a security camera at the drive-through teller at the mall. Stacey's car was parked a couple of spots down from the window, and they'd watched the film until a woman showed up beside that car at 12:32.

"A man walks into the picture," the police chief explained. "It's fuzzy because the two of them aren't threats to the bank so far away, but he puts his hands on her all right, and they leave together in another car." The chief looked at the camera. "We think this is important evidence," he finished, and I had to agree that if you were a policeman looking to hang Wade Long for murder, you pay attention to the way the man holds the woman by the shoulders with both hands, how he turns her and leads her out of the picture. Blurry or not, you start to think, "Wade and Stacey Long," and when a car turns past the camera ten seconds later, you figure the two people inside aren't going to lunch.

"Could be anybody," Wade says to the same reporter as he leaves the police station. "You wouldn't recognize your own self in that movie." He's dressed exactly as he was at 9 a.m., the faded green T-shirt tucked into his jeans. I half expected him to start tapping his keys as he said, "I ain't done nothing to be ashamed of."

"The FBI has better equipment," the police chief comes back to announce to the camera. "We'll see who's the star of this movie."

Lottery tickets are a bigger draw at the newsstand than newspapers and magazines. So is tobacco. The flavored kind people who read a lot of books put in pipes. Cherry, especially.

I kept track for a week once. Forty-eight of the fifty-four men who bought cherry tobacco were wearing ties. It tells you something about the ways the world divides itself, but there's nothing I can do with the things I've learned.

At 9:05 the next morning, a policeman arranged himself in the doorway like someone used to blocking the fastest way to open spaces. "You Danny Race?" he asked, and when I nodded as I slid my set of papers back into their racks, he added, "I expected so," and kicked the stopper from under the door to swing it shut.

"You an acquaintance of both the Longs, Wade and Stacey?"

"You could say that."

"All right, I'm saying that. You close with them?"

"Not hardly."

"But you've been seen socially with Stacey?"

"Lunch. She works next door."

"Lunch."

"She was afraid of Wade, if that's what you need to know."

"Love hurts," the policeman said. "You remember that park ranger in Virginia, that guy who was hit by lightning seven times and lived?"

"The one who's in the *Guinness Book*?"

"Well, he's not going to make that record harder to beat. He went out and killed himself over lost love. The woman he wanted hauled ass on him. Don't make no kind of sense, does it? He should of known better." He looked up and down the newspapers as if he expected to see Stacey's disappearance on the front page of *USA Today* and the *New York Times*. "That's why I'm here, Danny. In my experience, a man does harm to the woman, not himself."

In the pet store, near the front counter where Stacey worked, is a glass cage containing an enormous iguana. "Can't sell something this big," Stacey explained once. "Nobody wants something that doesn't recognize them as someone it depends on, not for two thousand dollars they don't."

I looked at the iguana every time I walked by the store, remembering the one I had owned, how it had always climbed up and toward heat—lamps, window shades, bookcases. When it had turned lethargic and refused to eat, I'd fed it baby food on the advice of the pet-store manager. For a while, that did the trick—the iguana gobbled jar after jar of pureed vegetables, and then its skin had gone slack, and it seemed suddenly unable to move anywhere except slowly across level surfaces.

"Who the hell told you that?" the veterinarian had asked when I'd carried the iguana, two days before it died, into his office for a miracle. The steady diet of baby food, he explained, had turned the iguana's bones to mush.

I didn't hate the pet-store manager for his bad advice. I hated him for being the last man Stacey Long had slept with before she'd been killed. There was nothing about the man worth dying for.

At the end of my shift, I made sure to walk in the pet store when I saw he was on the floor. "You're Danny Race, am I right?" he said when I placed myself in front of him beside the huge iguana's cage.

"I'm a friend of Stacey's."

"Aren't we all."

I knew the manager's name was Chet Gable, but he'd have to introduce himself without my prompting. Already I felt stupid and lost, as if I'd walked miles since I'd left the newsstand. What did I think, that the man, ten years older than me, small and drab with a voice to match, could be possessive enough to threaten anyone? The police, I was certain, had eliminated him as a suspect as rapidly as they had erased me. I wished I had never done more than listen to his outline of the baby food treatment, when nothing about his voice or his appearance or the words he chose made any difference to me.

"Police talk to you about all this?" I said.

The manager tapped on the glass to get the iguana's attention. "No business of yours," he said.

"Right. None."

He slapped his palm on the glass, and the iguana's head swiveled so fast I took a step back. "You shouldn't come over here all full of piss and vinegar," he said. "Your football days are old news. I'm the one ought to be casing you and your sorrow for never getting what you wanted from that poor girl."

The iguana turned and settled. "You had one of these die on you, didn't you?" the manager said. He took his hands off the glass and stared at me. "Listen, did you read about those poor bastards got killed on that elevator that dropped twenty-one floors?"

"Yeah," I said, despite myself. Six passengers. The story had made every paper we stocked.

"They had a chance to live, you know. Any one of them if he had jumped," he said, "at exactly the right moment, would've been OK. Those other guys would have been smashed, and he would've walked out of there like Jesus Christ his own self."

"There's simple math that says you're wrong," I said, though I wouldn't have been able to come up with the figures if he asked me.

"You saying you wouldn't try to jump?"

"I'm saying it's hopeless once that elevator gets going."

"A man's got to take what's available. He can't let himself turn into shit. That's a sorry thing to do with the one chance he's got."

He stared at me as if he'd finished a book on mind control, but he didn't have to. I'd already decided to drive to Wade Long's and shoot him before the police arrested him. The situation was as simple as anything else that had ever happened to me. I was sure of that because otherwise I would have gotten stuck long ago.

Thirteen days it took, but somebody rooting through trash dumped off a back road eight miles from the mall found a body. "Most likely the missing woman," the police said, though they had to admit they didn't know for sure, and they were lucky to have any dead body at all.

It was Stacey all right, though it took a day to confirm it through her teeth and whatever else they use in these cases. I waited another day. I gave all the gawkers their chance to drive by and get waved along by the police, the chief saying he would get to Wade Long, who knew enough not to run, if a few more things fell into place.

I parked my car in the only place Wade could have pulled off the road. I imagined how it would be to tug a blanket-wrapped body out of my trunk and managed the job in my head until I gave the body the identity of somebody I knew and stalled.

What I had to do, because I'd come to believe I was obligated to do nobody harm on the chance they had a decency disguised by obnoxious behavior, was convince myself Wade Long was the sorriest shithead ever born, because if someone like me could kill a woman I'd lived with, there was no hope for the world. But as soon as I stepped over the guardrail and skidded down the hillside, I knew that fifty feet from the highway, the world belonged to the brutal and the instinctive who drift us darkly toward the recklessness in ourselves.

Where the ground went level again, it ran bare and narrow as if it might have been the towpath for a canal invisible behind the brush. It was a flash-flood ravine, the kind of crevice that turns, after a spare tire or two, into a landfill, and I followed the footholds for those who scavenged this illegal dump, cleaning up after the slingers of broken televisions and lawnmowers, mattresses and bedsprings, a sort of filter for trash, for the anger that snaps a spine or seals shut a throat.

Somewhere down in the gully, I expected the yellow tape of crime scenes, but aside from the skunk cabbage and itchweed and three kinds of ferns being trampled, the site looked like anyplace else where sumac and locust would try to start a forest as soon as nobody showed up for a couple of weeks. I tried to imagine the body of Stacey Long lying here, the blanket she'd been wrapped in undone, but all I could see were people alive and well and unmindful of what they were trampling underfoot as they drank beer and listened to music on battery-driven boom boxes while they picked through litter.

There's a college in the next town over from the mall. Even if you don't sell cherry tobacco to the professors, you know it's there just by sitting in the bars. A mile outside of town and the customers are all locals, men like Wade and me drinking cheap drafts, or if we're feeling poorly, using those drafts to chase whiskey and make us think we're about to get lucky with some woman in jeans who's not carrying the extra pounds of greasy food and all-day television.

In town, after 9:00, kids in designer clothes with trendy haircuts start filling up the three bars. It's time to move on or get depressed, watching twenty-year-olds from another state acting like they know something Mommy and Daddy and Professor Pipesmoker haven't told them.

But those girls make you want to sign up for a couple of classes. I've seen Wade tail-chasing a few times, and he looks so pathetic I've kept my mouth shut until I can escape to where every woman in the bar lives within five miles of its front door. None of those girls from New Jersey or Maryland read the local papers. They don't know how easy a man like Wade can be set off to violence. Last week they held a rally up there on their big lawn—five hundred of those girls holding candles and chanting, "Take back the night." It makes me wonder which of those beauties will end up bagged in a gully because she thinks the world's changing.

I'd seen Stacey the morning of the day she disappeared. I'd unlocked the newsstand door, and she was setting out the toads and lizards. "If I give you ten dollars," I said, "could I set all the crickets free?"

Stacey smiled. "Danny," she said, "something else will just eat them."

"Not right away. Not with kids and their mothers watching."

"What would these hungry guys do then? You'd have to set them free, too."

"One thing leads to another."

"Always, Danny," she said, looking past me toward the mall entrance. When I glanced back, I saw a man in a muted, pin-striped suit. He turned toward the window of the card shop and tucked a few strands of his silver hair back into place. "Yours or mine?" Stacey asked, and when the man studied himself a second time, I said, "I'll give him quarters for change," thinking that if she stood beside the toads and lizards the man in the suit would ask for a roll of quarters to empty that box of crickets.

Under the counter, inside a copy of the *Harrisburg Patriot* the owner updated every Friday, was a handgun he kept. When I left work at 5:30, I slid it into the inside pocket of my blazer. It felt so heavy in my pocket that I thought the jacket was hanging lopsided, that Wade would notice and then throw himself on me or run, either choice guaranteeing no harm to himself. Each time I had imagined myself shooting Wade, he didn't move when I aimed the gun. He stood his ground and said, "Fuck you."

Wade had a double-wide set back on three mostly wooded acres his grandmother had given him for a wedding present. I'd dropped Stacey off one day a month back when her car wouldn't start after work, and I'd asked her about the fenced-in, cleared stretch above the trailer. "Wade says it's a surprise," she'd said. "But what else could it be but horses?"

I remembered that now because Wade was between the trailer and the nearest fence, and he didn't have horses behind it. "Lookit who come to sightsee," he said as I walked toward him, stopping a few steps away to get my breath settled from the uphill climb. "I'm raising llamas," Wade said. "I'm tired of doing ordinary shit."

I looked at the animals and thought I was in a zoo. They were so foreign that they made everything else seem artificial as well. When the police arrived, they'd think they were in some sort of theme park, that there were other exotic animals that might lunge out of the woods to do them harm. Already, I knew it was a mistake to let Wade talk, even a sentence or two. It would have been easier, I realized, to have run him down with my car.

"They're something, Wade," I said. "I'll give you that."

"Think I'm stupid?" Wade said. "You selling Pick-Seven tickets to suckers and thinking you're smarter than everybody. They're just customers, fella. They don't make you a genius."

"It wouldn't matter if I didn't work there," I said. "I'd rightly agree to that."

Dark clouds were scudding up from behind the patch of pines his grandfather had planted before he'd died twenty years ago. I needed to get this done before rain gave me a reason to say "another time."

"What's up, Danny?" Wade said. "You got yourself some work needs doing?"

"Delivery boy, maybe. I'm not exactly sure."

"You the pizza guy for the do-gooders?"

I needed to stop talking because justice meant only what I was willing to do. "I'm not a support group," I said. "This isn't AA for despair." I understood that if I pulled out the gun, Wade would shoot me with it.

The wind sprayed a mist across the hillside. I had to choose which foolishness I could live with. "You know anything about llamas?" Wade said. He blinked as if the rain was falling harder where he stood, ten feet from me. He folded his hands together and cracked his knuckles.

"No," I said.

"Danny, what the hell you know about anything?"

I looked back at the stand of pines that was fading into the weather's early twilight and said, "Moss grows on the north side of trees."

Wade snorted and shoved his hands into his jeans pockets. "Bullshit it does. Moss grows where it's dampest—north, south, east, west—all around the damn compass. You Boy Scouts—next you'll be telling me you can't rip the tag off your mattress."

Suddenly he yanked his hands up, waved them at the llamas, and said, "Danny, you haven't the balls," so exactly right, I could say nothing. One llama looked our way, and the other five all turned and stared, though it seemed they weren't registering the two of us. "You need passion, Danny," Wade said, "and let me tell you, the dashboard light is beaming so bright anybody riding with you knows there's a need for refueling."

"But I can fill up again and keep going, Wade. I'm free to get somewhere else."

"You got the wish-I-didn't-have-my-freedom blues. You should have stayed in the navy and let somebody decide everything for you. This way you know you're hopeless—the other way you could pretend things would be different if you ever got yourself back on land."

The rain settled into steady. I only owned one other sport coat besides the blazer that was getting soaked. Wade could toss his T-shirt on the floor of his double-wide and put it back on tomorrow morning. "What happens to the llamas if the FBI says they recognize you?" I said.

"I tie them out back of the pet store. I lay the guilt for their demise of that prick who was pumping Stacey. I know for a fact I don't have to leave any by the magazine stand, though honest-to-God, Danny, I wish it was you fucking her cause I don't rightly know what's in that manager made a woman spread her legs."

"I can't say I know either, Wade," I said, and both of us laughed.

"You want to show me your popgun?" Wade said.

"No."

Wade fixed my eyes with his. "That's good. Keep some things to yourself in this world."

I nodded, but the handgun seemed ludicrous as a battery-powered dildo. The owner of the newsstand couldn't possibly expect to be robbed. Who would risk himself on the store least likely to have a decent take in the register? And then Wade turned and ran at the fence, yelling, "Stop staring, you stupid fucks," the llamas bolting silently until they reached the opposite fence where they turned sideways and looked back at Wade as if they could feed and water themselves every day until he'd served his sentence.

The next day the FBI-enhanced picture made the police think the district attorney could convince a jury Wade and Stacey Long were the blurry images moving between cars. I asked for night shift. It would keep me busy until 10:00. By that time I could pretend I've been somewhere and I'm coming home to watch the news and fall asleep like people who aren't angry every minute they're not busy with something. Wade hasn't been in the papers since he was arrested and couldn't make bail. He'll have to wait until his trial to get quoted again about the injustices of circumstantial evidence.

What I've learned is the women who work late all park together under two lights. Each night I come out and see their dozen cars clustered and the rest, twenty or more, scattered throughout the darkness in the mall lot.

I've started parking among the women. It spooks them a little to see a man jiggling a key at a lock when they come out in pairs or groups of three. What do they think when they see me there? That I'm parked among them for my own protection? That I'm a boyfriend or a husband of one of the women in a different group?

Do they slide their keys between their fingers like they've been taught in self-defense class? Do some of them reach into their purses for cans of Mace or electric prods? Or do they recognize me as that guy who sold them a lottery ticket a few days back, somebody so familiar he couldn't possibly be dangerous?

SOMEBODY, SOMEWHERE ELSE

——

The tourists who come year round expecting flames and giant cracks in the earth are always disappointed. The ones who come in summer see how the trees are still green not so far away as another town. The ones who come in winter see how grass grows where the soil is warmed from below by the fire. All of them take their photographs where things look worst to show to relatives and friends.

My name is Harold Plezik, retired two years from Penn Modular Homebuilders, and the rest of us who live here, my wife Melinda and fifteen others, they seldom walk out to where the fire has crept. They say there's no curiosity for what's been seen for most of their lives, long past wanting to scold those camera bugs aloud.

The last to leave is what the seventeen of us are called, but that's just out and out wrong, since we're not leaving Centralia, not any of us scattered along Troutwine Street and beyond. Not that the press has shown up for these past five years, as if our story has ended or is inching along as slowly as the underground fire that ruined Centralia so long ago my children, full-grown for years now, were still under my roof.

Everybody knows the story, or they should. Centralia is the town that was burned out from underneath, the seams of coal below us and places nearby smoldering now for going on fifty years. Those newspapers, they'll be back, for sure, when there's half a century of fire, but that's four years off, forever for a reporter. And to tell the truth, we look to be diminishing, trickling away to senior centers or death, nobody here as young as me and Melinda, past sixty now.

And the houses, too. We're on our own inside the last eight of them, the rest long gone. Just the bare spots still mostly to be made out where they stood, and the shrubbery and such left to go wild in rows as strange as the telephone poles going nowhere on streets entirely deserted.

A ghost town, some would say, though I think it will never get to be that, what with the government taking down the houses as soon as the owners get committed by their children or die. Somebody would have to rebuild Centralia to make it a ghost town, put up a thousand houses with nothing inside but memory.

Here's one, for instance. There was a time when the *National Enquirer* came to town expecting to see hell right up on the surface. They were disappointed to find just steam and warm earth, but they got the story they wanted by setting a pile of trash on fire to get flames in their pictures and claiming you could fry an egg on the sidewalk as if all of us who used that sidewalk wore some sort of magical insulated boots to retrieve our mail.

That's all you need to hear about that, and frankly, I've had enough of telling people about the history of Centralia. Once upon a time, that sort of talk was for those who'd been taught to unravel things and investigate and pick around papers in libraries and courthouses. These days I want only to talk about the here and now of flesh and blood still standing on the earth that's been left unbroken, the underground fire moved on, following coal seams, the experts declare, that will last for a century or more.

For example, the man and the girl I came across yesterday.

I'd crossed Route 61 where it's been blocked by a levee of earth for going on twenty years. There's plenty of dead forest out beyond the highway, the trees a dozen shades of near-white from the fire passing beneath them, but there's still green a short hike away, and that's where I was headed because I have a doctor who's told me to get out of my house or they'll carry me out.

There was a car parked with its tail end right up to that roadblock, facing out as if the driver expected to be boxed in by a crowd of sightseers. Not that unusual except the car was parked on the other side of the dirt levee where what was left of the road hasn't had traffic for twenty years. Still, I didn't pay it any mind but to wish whoever owned it not to be a man taking pictures of his wife where I could see, or worse, a teenager drinking beer with his friends and trying to set paper on fire by laying it on the ground.

It was neither, but right off I wished it was one or the other because there was a man wearing a ball cap and a thin young woman hand in hand ahead and off to my left, the man pushing aside branches as if he was looking for a secluded spot to get laid, privacy there because the world's moved on. And then I could see that it wasn't a thin woman at all, but a girl of maybe nine or ten, not anybody who belonged where he looked to be leading her. I cut toward them, all three of us in the green part of the woods where undergrowth, in mid-summer, had sprung up thick.

There wasn't even a path to speak of where the man and the girl were walking, though when the man noticed me, he turned and began to double back, and I started to take note of his shadowed face, looking for what the police always call "distinguishing marks." "Hey there," I called from what used to be porch-to-porch distance where Melinda and I still managed to live on Troutwine Street.

"Hi," he said, but he didn't stop, no reason to, perhaps, if all we had in common was being in the same place. He glanced down at the girl and kept his eyes there. She didn't look up, but I thought he tugged just a bit harder on her hand.

For a few seconds, I kept my eye on them, and then I followed after, considering on shortening the distance between us. I wished, for once, I carried one of those skinny phones everybody owns now, but I stayed close enough to maybe make me more than curious in that man's mind. And then I thought to speed up to take a look at a license plate at least, but by then they were in the car and he pulled around the barrier just high enough to keep me from seeing whatever numbers and letters he had on that plate until he was far enough away to turn them to the fuzz I see at a distance with the glasses years past being the right prescription. The plate was a Pennsylvania one. I could tell that by the colors, but I didn't even know the make or model of the car except to remember it was maroon and small.

I took myself three slow breaths and stood on the shoulder where the cracks from thirty years ago lay as open and dark as old promises. A young couple got out of a blue car parked near the old playground. The girl could have been the child's older sister. Sixteen maybe. Thin. A beauty. The two of them stared at the rusted pipes with no idea, I was sure, of what had been there. I felt as if I'd eaten something turned wrong in the heat. I walked back into the woods where it was green and circled around for an hour as if I was guarding something.

"You see families all the time over that way," Melinda said when I returned and told her about the man and the young girl. "You said he answered when you spoke. He said 'hello' just like anyone would. That makes them sightseers. Their kind have the run of where it's burning."

"This wasn't family business."

"You think a man is evil because he's walking in the woods with a young girl?"

"He wasn't her father. You can tell fathers by the way girls her age walk with them. They look at the man. They lead. This girl was following."

Melinda considered on that. She took her time picturing before she finally said, "Resisting?"

"Reconsidering."

"You can't be sure."

"Sure enough."

"Then report it. Go to the police and tell them about how you know the man had plans for that girl." Good advice, but there was nothing I could do for that girl now but hope.

For most of his grown life, my father sold insurance to miners. The cheap kind—low payments and lower benefits. The business had dried up with the mines, but he kept his office in Ashland, just down the road where a statue of Whistler's Mother looked over the downtown like something washed up in a great flood. Growing up, I'd asked about that statue, but my father simply said, "It's always been there," and after a while I didn't care whether or not Whistler himself had something to do with Ashland. After all, I didn't live there, and in Centralia, we had the fire to take my attention when I was starting high school.

There's books about how the thing started in a landfill and all the rest that followed, how the powers-that-be argued about responsibility and cost until it was too late. I never read them. What's the point of a book when the story's in your own back yard?

And when the word spread any way it could, the world coming to gawk at a town on fire didn't do a thing to help us, not even when Elsie Turkovich died in her basement a quarter mile from us. She didn't have a carbon monoxide alarm like many of us had acquired by then. My father's company balked at paying. "It's not an accident if someone sleeps downstairs in Centralia," they said. My father stopped selling. He was embarrassed.

After that, it seemed to him, most days, that his life was like that coal seam, that all of whatever was inside him worth a damn just needed air to burn. He'd lived long enough to believe he'd prefer a few years or even months of flame to the eternal smoldering where there was so little oxygen any other fire would just go out.

He must have felt that way right up to his death, unable, near the end, to even get from one room to another without the humiliating walker. Maybe it was worse for him knowing the fire hadn't changed anything because he'd been forty years old when it started, and he'd known for years what he was about.

Though he never claimed he hadn't had a fair chance, the excuse, he told me, of the poor-in-spirit, who put too much stock in the Beatitudes. He kept his mouth shut forever against the shame of admitting he had thoughts in that direction. And when he died, he made sure he was in the hospital so people with authority could testify he'd had a natural death.

Here's something to consider: A while back our mayor was on television. *The Daily Show.* They sent out this fake reporter whose job it was to make a fool of him.

A mayor for twenty people in a burning town. Hilarious. The audience laughed. I wanted to kill that fake. "Maybe when he gets cancer someone will make fun of his wearing a hat to cover his bald head," I said.

Melinda frowned just the small bit she does for a piece of fruit gone quickly soft on the kitchen counter before she said, "Hush, it's just a show."

"He was on our street," I said. "On Troutwine. In Lamar's house for a big joke. I hope it's the kind that disfigures him."

I made myself wait two days before I went out to where I'd seen the man and girl. Nobody had gone missing in the local paper, but for all I knew he'd driven here from a hundred miles away like somebody smart about being evil would do.

I wasn't fifty feet from the road before I caught sight of my first tourists.

Three of them. A woman my age. Two much younger. "We came to see the fire," the older woman said. "We didn't know anybody lived here."

She let me know she was the mother of the female half of the married couple already at a distance from where we were standing. Her daughter and son-in-law were over by the edge of where the trees were still green, and the man, who looked to be thirty or thereabouts, had his feet set wide apart as if he was trying to straddle a border. "You live around here?" she said, and I nodded, but she didn't ask me to pinpoint. "All this is burning?" she asked instead, swinging her head left to right in a way that included the still healthy forest.

"Where the trees are white," I said.

"Big as that?" She gestured toward her daughter. "You hear that? The fire is all over out here."

I turned away. Let her go home wherever that was thinking places the fire had passed were still on fire as if coal could regenerate itself. I made it a point to cross into the shade before I reached the couple, but they were already headed toward a spot where coal was exposed and steaming. I walked a hundred yards until it felt as if I couldn't be seen by them. There was a fallen tree that made for a bench. When I sat down the woods seemed as private as a bathroom with the door locked.

For an hour I listened.

My son Daniel was in the living room when I came in the door. "You have that look," he said at once. "What's up?"

"I had to talk to tourists."

"If you go out there, that's what you'll see, Dad. That's who's in the woods—tourists."

"You sound like your mother, but neither of you go out there anymore. Not so many nearby now. There was more fun for them when the fire was closer to town."

Daniel had moved when the government was offering money for our houses, when there was a rash of the red Xs that they spray painted on the front to let the bulldozers know which ones were ready to raze. It was like Passover in reverse. The angel of death came for those houses in a bulldozer.

"Mom told me you saw the boogie man a few days ago."

I glanced toward the kitchen where Melinda was fussing with making lemonade. "A particular kind."

Whatever was in my face turned him serious. "Ok," he said. "I'll grant you it's possible."

"Possible enough to keep me fretting I didn't take after him."

"What makes you the Good Samaritan all of a sudden?" Daniel said, and I thought of that child getting back into the maroon car, whether she knew by then that there couldn't be any puppies or kittens or whatever that man had promised to show her in a place like Centralia where children hadn't lived since before she was born.

"It's not all of a sudden. Somebody doesn't get that many chances to come across those that need help."

"Everybody needs help, Dad. If you want to be part-time Jesus, just admit it."

"You can't expect others to do what needs to be done."

"That's just the government. That's us where nobody cares."

Melinda stepped in between us with the lemonade in tall glasses half filled with ice. If we didn't finish our drinks within minutes, they would turn to dishwater with the melting. "The police is government," I said, not letting her barge in between us with words.

"They're close by. That makes a difference."

"We don't own our house bought and paid for all these years," I said. "That's government."

"They don't put you out."

Melinda said, "Now the both of you drink your drinks. There's more where they came from. This is visit time, not debate."

Daniel took a sip, and I could tell he wasn't used to lemonade being on the sour side. "You could see the future when I was a kid, Dad. Eminent domain is just the end of it coming. There's nothing to be done any more except to let it run its course."

"All the more reason to pay attention to what's terrible."

"There's nothing to do about that either, Dad. Not now anyway."

"You know what I wish," I said, staring at Melinda as I spoke, "I wish I was the sort of man who could kill such assholes as that fellow in the woods, do some subtraction from the evil side of things."

"Stop it, Dad," Daniel said, but Melinda was the one staring at me now.

"You imagine yourself becoming an executioner, Harold?" she said. "Mind you, he hasn't killed anyone we know of."

"Yes, he has."

"God doesn't see it that way."

"God has it wrong then."

"You best be keeping that talk to yourself."

"I am. I have worse I'm thinking."

I had my palm read once by Mrs. Yanoviak, who lived across the street until she died when I was near forty, about the time Daniel moved and the houses were torn down as soon as they were unoccupied. Within weeks. Like filling in a grave before the mourners are out of sight.

Mrs. Yanoviak held my hand in hers and concentrated as if there might be a difference between the lines on my palm and the ones on every other human hand. I was twenty-two at the time, three years under my belt with making modular homes and married to Melinda with Clarice on the way. Old lady Yanoviak, she stared and said, "You need to have yourself checked now that the baby's coming."

She went on for a few minutes, but all I was listening for was the prophecy of my lifeline, whether it was long enough to keep worry away for the next fifty years. "You'll live a good long time," she said. "It's plain as day."

"Methuselah," I said.

"Don't you be thinking that way," she said. "God shortened us for a reason back then. He'd learned that seventy years was enough for people to prove what was in their hearts."

When I brought up Mrs. Yanoviak after Daniel left, Melinda and I were standing on the front porch. She shrugged. "You and me lived here long enough to lose our illusions," she said. "If that's a good thing, then we're full of goodness."

I sucked one of the lemonade's nearly melted ice cubes into my mouth and held it there until it disappeared. Years ago, after Clarice and Daniel had grown and gone, I'd learned that having little was what could keep people together. Without the kids in the house, we'd been subtracted down to ourselves and the idea that it was important to stay no matter what.

It hadn't taken long to begin to lose some of both of those things. The town nearly emptied. We were fools now, people the government didn't bother asking to pay. Passing fifty, Melinda and I grew leery of each other's bodies, seeing the age in ourselves reflected so harshly, we stopped wanting to touch.

"We live where we know who we are," I said at last, sounding so awful to myself I expected Melinda to hiss.

She took my lemonade glass from my hand, the last three ice cube slivers drifting in the puddle at the bottom. "You look up and down this street and tell me who we are, Harold."

Three vacant lots separated us from the two other houses on our side of the street. On the other side were two houses four lots apart. "The Kelmans and the Mischiks have it ok being side by side," I tried. "I expect that makes a difference, seeing a face at a window from time to time instead of all this flat."

"Old man Mischik is all alone in that house of his, and he's ready to croak," she said. "The Kelmans will be like us inside of a year."

I have to say I flinched at the word *croak*. It sounded as if Melinda had said "fuck off," like dying was the sort of dismissal you might give a possum or some other scavenger you know you need but don't want to see. "We're going extinct," I said, "and what's worse, we know it. We're not like dodos or passenger pigeons or whatever else is dead and gone."

"I bet they knew," she said. "Leastways the last ones. They must have looked around and seen. They must have wondered where everybody had gone off to."

"Such things don't wonder."

"Don't you count on that," she said. "Everything with a beating heart knows when aloneness has come to stay."

These girls came out here once, six of them from the university that makes them volunteer. S.A.V.E. they called themselves, the E for environment, and they were dressed to clean up after the tourists as if they were going to work at the mall.

Three more followed. Older ones. Professors maybe, in hiking boots at least, and the lot of them put dirt into dozens of test tubes out among where all the trees are gray and white. Those three were polite about taking what they wanted from us. Studying bacteria, they said, when I approached them, but they didn't explain how that could matter to somebody, and they didn't ask me one word about my living there.

Melinda asked to come along when I went for another walk the next day. "I haven't been in a while," she said, and I let her have her lie.

We crossed where St. Ignatius used to stand, the building long gone, but its cemetery and two others close by still there, all three resting places untouched by the fire when it passed by. Melinda made me walk straight through it as if she believed that path would somehow settle me. Even the tombstones farthest to the edge, ones worn down a bit by the acid rain, were still in place. "Everybody's at peace here, Harold, no matter the fire. You know there's God when you see something like this," she said. "The living have to take care of themselves, but he's looking out for the dead."

I examined the stones by the fence, all of the death dates as old as the two of us or older. "They all died before the fire," Melinda said. "It didn't touch them, not any way at all."

We walked out to a cluster of sinkholes where the smell of sulfur made us watch each step. What looked to be a family was out ahead of us, and there was a child running across a patch of exposed, steaming coal. A boy, something to be glad for. "You want to head over to the living woods?" Melinda said. "Show me where your troubles began?"

I watched that boy run for a moment. He waved at his parents as if he was on a ride at Disneyworld. "The outsiders used to be afraid of us," I said. "They'd think that we could go crazy with our anger, hurt one of them or worse because bum luck frees you to do most anything."

"That's so much foolishness, Harold," she said. "You don't know the minds of others."

The boy's father knelt and placed his hand on the earth, but his wife kept walking. "Nowadays they know better," I said. "If we were going to do harm to them, that time has passed. Now they know we could only hurt each other and probably not even that."

"Like normal folks," she said, and I nodded.

"Like the beaten."

"You can't talk like that," she said. "Not with how we're here and not leaving ever except by carrying."

I touched one of the large stones I'd seen tourists use as chairs. It was warm, but not hot, and I slumped down and went silent for a minute, long enough for her to say, "Harold? Where'd you go off to?"

"I'm right here."

She stood behind me and placed her hands on my shoulders, kneading them softly until I raised my head and looked at her placid face. "I thought maybe you took me wrong there when I was meaning to be cheerful," she said, and when I shook my head, she leaned down and kissed my cheek.

"We're the Centralians, Harold," Melinda whispered into my ear. "We're from some place."

The paper comes late half the time, so we were finished with toast and cereal the next morning when I heard the deliveryman's car pause at the box. Because Melinda was still in her nightgown, I went out, so I was the first one, coming back through the kitchen door, to see the lead story. How there'd been a body found in the woods ten miles from here, out past Ashland. A girl, the police were saying, who looks to be between eight and ten.

I sat for a minute, holding the paper face down, my stomach working like I had the flu coming on, and then I pushed up from the table and threw up in the sink.

"Harold," Melinda said. "Harold?" and I turned the tap to wash my breakfast away, seeing that girl's face so plain I might as well have her photograph on the mantle.

Melinda turned the paper over. "It can't be the same girl," she said. "They don't say anything about what state they found her in."

"You mean decomposed?" I said. "Like he took her those ten miles before he felt the world was empty enough to do what he wanted?"

"Just hold on with your thinking," she said, up and going into the living room to turn on the television. "They've had half a day to find out. You sit here and watch with me so I can keep my eye on you."

It took twenty minutes of talk about a new movie, a diet plan, and another new gadget to plug in your ears before the Wilkes-Barre area headlines came on with a picture of a girl named Muriel Haskins from over to Pottsville, another ten miles beyond where they found her. Melinda took my hand in hers and squeezed. I could hear how she was holding her breath, but I knew at once that it wasn't the girl I'd seen that day.

I waited until Muriel's picture was replaced by a photograph of a badly damaged car before I said, "It's not her."

"One small blessing," Melinda said.

"Not hardly. He just bided his time until another one let herself be used."

"You don't know for sure it's the same man. It's not likely he'd let himself do such a thing so close by after you saw him."

"Then there's two of the devil."

Melinda turned the television to mute as if she'd heard a car in the driveway and was listening for a knock. "You saved one, Harold."

"An accident."

"That's how most saving gets done."

I dressed and drove to Ashland, and when I said I had information related, maybe, to the killing, I saw expressions change to something other than welcoming just before one of the policemen asked me to take a seat beside his desk.

"What sort of information?" he said, and I lowered my voice as if I had a secret to keep from the others.

He took my name and all that sort of thing after I finished narrowing his suspects down to maybe half the owners of small maroon cars in Pennsylvania. "You find that girl I saw," I said, "and she'll know something more."

"That's possible," he said.

"She must live around here."

"That's possible as well."

"Around here," I said. "'Around here' like that meant something. God damn but I must sound like some old idiot spouting off."

"Anger is a gift sometimes," the policeman said.

Anger is a gift. I'd read that somewhere growing up and then, years later, had heard somebody spouting that very line on a CD Daniel played at deaf-inducing volume, repeating the phrase as if he'd just thought it up.

"Yes, it is," I said, believing it now, and I wished for anger rather than the soul-killing surrender that waited for me each morning like a hangover. There were more days than not when the self-indulgence of sorrow absorbed as many hours as a full-time job.

I rose from my chair, but the policeman stayed seated. Well," I said. "I'm sorry I don't have more for you."

"You can only tell me what you know. You're not required to know more than that."

And then it came to me that the man in the ball cap had spoken. "He said 'hi,'" I blurted. "The man in the woods. He spoke to me."

The policeman leaned forward a bit, both elbows on his desk. "What did he sound like?"

I sat and thought, listening to that memory for nearly a minute. "Like anyone," I said.

The policeman nodded like that was exactly how every suspect sounded. "That fire over your way creeps along at its own good time," he said.

"Slower these days, it seems, or off to make somebody else's misery."

"Like most folks do," he said, and his lips opened slightly, as if a smile might work its way to the surface. When it didn't, his face froze into acknowledgement. "It makes you wonder sometimes. There's coal all around here. For miles in every direction."

"Daniel called," Melinda said before I even recounted my trip. "He's heard."

"When it's on the television, he listens."

She handed me the phone. "Just hold this a minute," she said. "You need to think twice before you call him."

I held the phone as if it was a glass of lemonade. "It seems like we don't know what's happening to us except when the heart of it's passed us by," I said. "We only know what's dead and gone."

"Let's hope not."

"For sure, we can always do that."

"It's some relief."

I thought of that girl in the woods taking my hand as soon as I offered it, and I wasn't glad for that because it would be better if she cried to show me she'd learned something. "You ever want to be somebody else?" I said.

"Like who?"

"Somebody somewhere else."

"There's no point to that sort of wishing. It's like hoping you'll sprout wings."

"There's plenty wasting themselves then," I said, and I pressed *memory* and 1 for Daniel's number. Clarice, if I decided to call her in Colorado so far away, was 2. If Melinda had programmed numbers up to 9, I didn't know who they'd be for.

Last fall a girl drove up from that university of the volunteers. I recognized her parking sticker when she pulled into Lamar's driveway. More mayor jokes, I thought, but when she left, Lamar told me how she'd interviewed him the right way. He was beaming like he'd met his granddaughter, full grown after twenty years. "For a magazine they do down there," he said. "Pictures and all."

I have a copy of that magazine on a table beside the couch. Lamar gave it to me a month back, thick and glossy like you wouldn't expect from a college. Our house is in one of the pictures, and so are the sinkholes out by the woods where that ball cap man was taking that girl.

It's been a month now and nothing more. Melinda claims a goodness in that, but I sit with this daydream of finding that man and taking him back to where the fire burns hottest under the soil. "I want you to dig yourself a hole where the fire is," I say every time.

There's always a rifle in my hand, and the man's hands shake so much I am almost happy. "You can't just dig like this where the fire sits," the man says. "You don't know how close it is."

"Then there's no telling how far you have to go before we find out."

When I told Melinda that way of my thinking, she turned afraid for my soul. Her very words.

It's just thinking, I told her. Remember that boy from down the street who the papers and magazines said fell through the earth and almost went into the fire? It was an old sewer put in years ago that was just covered over with planks instead of being capped. They just rotted out is all. They had him going half way to hell, a good story, like the ones in the Bible where everything happens for a lesson. But if you live through it, you know the extent of the lies and such, the stories people tell to comfort themselves.

THE OUT-OF-SORTS

———

The story wasn't on any of Stu Werner's assigned pages. He copyread sports, but he paid attention to every line of the article about the woman who'd kept the police at bay with three poisonous snakes because that woman was his mother. Though they weren't described, Stu could picture each of those snakes, distinguishing one from the other by the colors and patterns his mother had pointed out half a dozen times when he visited and she guided him to the large glass tank in her living room to look at the copperheads.

According to the article, the police had kept their distance. His mother had swung them, all three in one hand, as she gave the officers an earful. The stand-off, the police reported, had lasted nearly an hour, a long time to handle poisonous snakes. And time enough, apparently, for a cluster of cops to show up from all over the county. "Once the call on the radio said she was swinging snakes, pretty much every cop from anywhere nearby showed up," the police chief said. Stu could imagine the whole lot of them, each more useless than the next to take care of the situation. If she hadn't been bitten on the arm and the face, they might still be standing there, a policeman admitted, "But once we saw her in distress, we used the Taser on her to get things under control."

There wasn't a word about how the police handled the snakes, but there was a paragraph about his mother's state of mind, how she'd seemed incoherently angry, the kind of attitude the police associated with drugs or alcohol. "The woman appeared to be intoxicated," the article said, "but our first job was to make sure she didn't die from those bites."

All that because someone had reported excessive noise. The Walczyks, her neighbors in the double house where she lived, the ones who said, "We were just fed up with her rock music coming through the wall like thunder."

The newspaper office where Stu was sitting while he read was a large loft apartment furnished by nineteen desks and twenty-one chairs, the extra two creating a makeshift waiting room beside the secretary to the editor's desk, a place where family members with obituaries sat for a few minutes before submitting their homemade eulogies. Where people fidgeted while clutching wedding announcements or self-written articles about the achievements of their children. Some people were determined to bring their news personally, and though everything they carried, most of it semi-literate, would be rewritten or discarded, their earnestness prevented him from joining in the jokes that the rewrite woman made by reading a few sentences she introduced by saying, "Listen to these howlers: 'He was the proud founder and owner of an erection business. He was a distributor of a variety of condomints.'"

Near the end of the room farthest from the editor's office was the desk Stu shared with two sports stringers who filed stories only on weekends—high school football and basketball mostly, unless there were championship games in soccer or field hockey, sports that drew the interest only of parents and friends of the players. During the summer, he'd discovered, he had the desk entirely to himself.

His supervisor, Ralph Herrold, was two desks away, his workspace surrounded on three sides by head-high partition walls that he decorated with photographs of his two dogs, terriers that wore bandanas or sweaters in every picture. "I was here before computers made everything so easy," he'd declared early on, and Stu called him The Master to his girlfriend whenever he had one, the name followed by verbs like *sucks* and *blows*.

He'd had three girlfriends in the eleven months he'd worked at the newspaper, but there had been several months between each one, enough that Stu had spent more time without a girl as with one. There was no telling, he thought, the third one gone for a month now, when he'd find a fourth.

Down near the end of the article, in the paragraphs continued on page eight, was the information that the snakes were being held at the police station. "They scared me to death," the police secretary was quoted. "Nobody told me, and here they were when I came into the office this morning."

"We're stuck with them," the chief said. "They're evidence." There would be follow-ups, for sure. His mother had been charged with reckless endangerment and disorderly conduct. Stu wondered about resisting arrest being tacked on, but the reporter, Jack Ferrence, didn't mention it. Ferrence would love having this story, one that could last a few days, one that everybody would follow, curious about just how crazy someone might be to use copperheads as a hand-held weapon. Whether something like this would go to trial. Whether the snakes would be taken to court so a jury could see the weapon in question.

And sure enough, the case was already morning show material on the radio, the deejay and his female sidekick laughing at 7:15 when they used the morning paper as a source for jokes. "The funniest story since Santa Claus got shot with a bb gun in the Christmas parade," the woman said.

Nowhere in the article was there a mention of his mother's medical condition. She'd lapsed into a coma for twelve hours before awakening. From the anti-venom the doctors had given her, not the bites themselves. Like everything that happened late at night, it had taken a full day for the news to reach the morning paper.

There was silence about his mother at work that afternoon, not the usual joking about the erratic behavior of people who made the paper, the reporters telling stories over coffee and Cokes. Stu knew that if nobody had recognized the name, they would have mentioned the three fingers of Medusa before the day was over.

When he asked Ralph Herrold for an extra half hour at dinnertime, Herrold didn't demand a reason. He stroked his mustache with his thumb while he tapped three fingers of his right hand on his desk, creating a tiny drum roll. Stu looked at the terriers, unable to tell them apart when their scarves were the same color and pattern. A few seconds went by until Herrold said, "Well, Werner, we'll see you at 7:45 then."

"People come by more than they should," his mother said as soon as Stu walked into her hospital room. She looked at the ceiling and sighed before she added, "I know why."

She stared at the ceiling for so long, Stu glanced up as well. Nothing was there, not even a maze of cracks. "They're professionals, Mom," he said.

"That doesn't mean they don't want to take a look at the snake woman." At last, she looked at him. "You're the only person I know who's showed up. I half expected Jesse to come by worried about his snakes."

A long shot for that scenario, Stu thought. His mother had never talked about where Jesse was from or how they'd met, but for years, men had followed his mother home from the bar where she served tables. Not the worst men, she would say, coming into that place. "Imagine if I worked at the Top Dog or Knuckles, the sort that come in there. Wife beaters, that's who goes in there. And worse. I just get the lonely and the out-of-sorts."

Stu pictured the empty glass tank. Those snakes had always seemed to keep their distance from each other, coiled in different corners or under the flat, angled stone or the chunk of gnarled driftwood. It was a large cage, as big as a coffee table. For more than half a year the tank had sat across four chairs moved from the dining room. "I haven't sat on those chairs for years," his mother had said. "It won't hurt to get some use of them." The chairs faced each other in pairs like they had in the dining room, but the arrangement still looked unstable to Stu, who was sure that all of the clothes Jesse had hung in his mother's closet would have fit inside that tank. Jesse had told her he'd be back for the snakes, but it had been two months and no sign of him.

"Here," Stu said. "Maybe this will brighten the day." He'd brought a card he'd picked out after searching three shops before work. "Just hanging on?" it said on the cover, a python with a sad face dangling from a tree limb.

"There's nothing like a good meal to cheer you up," it said inside, the smiling python wrapped around a man in one of those hats that city slickers always wear in jungle movies. *A pith helmet*, Stu suddenly remembered. Even the name sounded like a fool would wear it.

His mother smiled. "I couldn't find a copperhead card," he said.

"You should write one then," she said. "I bet it would be as cute as this one." She handed the card to him as if it had grown heavy. "I get my own room because the police want to keep an eye on me," she said. "If one of theirs had been bitten, I'd be in the penthouse."

Or dead, he left unsaid. The room was absolutely bare of decoration. If his mother left, dragging the bedclothes out the door with her, it would be ready for the next patient immediately. He propped the card on the empty nightstand, the sad-faced snake peering toward the door.

The next morning, Stu was still in bed when the radio deejays mentioned the follow-up story. "It's like a *Snakes on a Plane* sequel," the deejay said. "*Snakes in a Living Room*." His sidekick laughed as if she'd heard something hilarious.

At work the night before, Stu had avoided examining the local section of the paper because Herrold or Ferrence or one of the others would have known what he was looking for. But now, Stu retrieved the paper from his doorstep and opened *Local*, finding the article filling three-fourths of a column on page three. "Snakes to Appear before District Judge," was the title, but except for the first sentence and the last sentence—a hearing was scheduled; the snakes would be presented as evidence—every word was lifted from the first published story—the snakes, his mother's name, the details of the stand-off. Jack Ferrence might have spent fifteen minutes on the article, pasting in paragraphs until he filled enough column inches to allow for a real estate ad beneath it.

Stu didn't mention the article when he returned to the hospital. If the hearing was scheduled, the police knew his mother was out of danger, that she was going to be released.

She had the newspaper lying on the nightstand beside his card. "That reporter, he's never once said anything about who I am or what I look like or what I have to say. Not once."

"That's true."

"What kind of reporting is that? People think I'm stupid or crazy or a major lush. They imagine me all bedraggled like a bag lady. You should write the story, start it way back when your father left." She paused as if she was considering going farther back, even before his father had left when Stu was in high school, before he told Stu, one morning at breakfast, "I need to go before I get too old to have a second chance."

"And of course Jesse would be in it," she went on, "and how I came to know those snakes and how much of a pain in the ass the Walczyks are for complaining, us in a double so they're right there on the other side of the wall. Inches away and yet they call the police. It's a wonder they don't need ten more cops in just this town with so much lack of communication."

Like she had the day before, his mother looked at the ceiling, but Stu kept his eyes on her face. "You read those articles and wonder what happened to the snakes after they used that stun gun on me? You and I both know those cops would have run for it if I'd dropped them after they zapped me."

"Probably."

"That's because I put those snakes away before they fired. They didn't use that stun gun because they were afraid for me with the bites and all. They used it when I put down my weapon."

"They emptied the tank though."

"You can bet your ass they didn't get near those snakes. They brought in somebody with the know-how, a pet storeowner or somebody like that, to gather up the copperheads. That reporter never says a word about it and expects everybody to think the police took care of everything."

"You can say that when you go to court, Mom. How you surrendered."

She touched the bandage on her cheek and then the one on her arm. "They were there to take me to the nut house," she said. "That's what would have happened, right? They looked me up and saw who I was and came to take me away. I recognized one of them who drove me there last year when I had that dark spell before Jesse came along. I didn't want to go back. I wasn't hurting anybody but myself. Those pricks next door should have just told me to settle down."

"They said they asked you once before a week ago."

"That's what makes them pricks. They think asking once makes them good neighbors."

His mother was right, Stu thought. The police kept records of everything, including women who'd been hospitalized for depression if they'd had to drive them there. "You were afraid. You thought they would hurt you."

"Those snakes just panicked is all," she said. "If the cops had just stayed put instead of always inching closer, I would have been fine."

She touched the bandages again, this time in a way that made Stu think she might tear them off and throw them. Her gestures were so repetitive he felt heavy, as if he wouldn't be able to stand if he sat in the chair beside her bed. "You relax for a few minutes, Mom. I'll be right back."

Stu rode the elevator to the ground floor and walked into the cafeteria to get coffee. His shift at the paper started in an hour, and he hated the coffee that perpetually brewed there.

At three o'clock, the cafeteria was nearly empty, just two women sitting with cans of soda, their backs to each other four tables apart. Heat lamps shone above covered trays that held hours-old, unseen food. Stu poured his coffee quickly and sipped it as he rode back up to his mother's room.

When he sat the heavy paper cup on the nightstand, he picked up the newspaper. "Let me show you something," he said.

He turned to page five, covering his mother's story, and laid the paper out on the bed. "Watch this," he said, taking a pen from his pocket, and he began to mark the errors.

Extra capital letters on *enchilada* and *tortilla*, as if the names of international food were proper nouns. Titles not italicized, spaces missing or too wide between words, margins uneven. His mother looked pleased. She squinted at the margins and the gaps between sentences and words. "I showed May Walczyk the paper once. I told her to read a page from the local section and a page from sports and tell me which one had the most problems. She didn't see anything wrong. 'It's the newspaper,' she said. 'Why would they make mistakes?'"

Stu folded the paper and replaced it on the nightstand. He tugged the get-well card wider so someone might see the happy python inside. When he dropped his paper cup into the wastebasket, the mouthful he hadn't finished splashed against the side of the can.

"Somebody came by while you were gone," his mother said. She seemed happy to have kept that news from him for fifteen minutes. "I'm not going to jail, sweetheart. And not the loony bin either."

"Good."

"At least not yet. I have a hearing in a week, but the lawyer they sent over said I'll likely be 'looked after' when all this is said and done. They have a name for it, the lawyers, but I'm to be babysat no matter what they call it."

"He was in and out of here fast."

"She. No more than a girl. Is that how you get your start being a lawyer, taking care of people like me who don't have money?"

"In her case, at least," Stu said. "Anyway, you'll be in your own house, that's what's important. Everybody but her or whoever they send will be trespassing."

"Will they now? They'll think I'm fine and dandy in a month or two?"

"A little longer, maybe."

"It'll be like going to college. I'll have to go to class for years, and then they'll give me a send off like I learned something to be proud of."

"College wasn't bad. Classes were the easy part."

She darkened. "People think that you got kicked out for being stupid," she said. "It breaks my heart."

"It was my call."

"Yes, it was. You and your hard head. I didn't know whether to be upset or proud."

Stu's roommate had snapped the arms off the chairs in the lounge on each floor of the seven-story dorm. Methodically, from highest to lowest. "Cheap shit," he'd said. "If these were any good, I couldn't do it."

Stu had followed him, sitting on couches while Brad Moser flexed his arms as if the chairs were exercise equipment. At four a.m., Tuesday, not one person was awake. When Moser was finished with the chairs on the first floor, they walked outside and Moser smoked a cigarette while Stu looked at the sky. "This place is so full of people who are sure they know something," Moser said. "I don't think they know shit."

Moser tossed his butt down and fobbed himself back inside, but Stu stayed outside. Breaking the chairs had been asinine, but Stu had been so fascinated, he was still excited. Ten minutes later, he remembered he didn't have his key fob. That was why security, making its rounds, could identify him as being awake and just outside the damaged dorm at 4:30 a.m. "The student was uncooperative about his reasons for being outside," the report said. "When the extensive damage was ascertained, he became a suspect."

"I couldn't break the chairs like that," Stu had said. "I'm not strong enough. That's all I have to say."

"I saw another student with the suspect when I passed the dorm earlier," the report went on. "Only one room light was on in the entire dorm, and the location was ascertained to be the suspect's room."

When they'd questioned Moser, he didn't deny anything. He just said, "Prove it." His biceps were huge. He was wearing a sleeveless t-shirt.

Stu had been suspended. "No matter what we can prove, we know you were an accessory," the Dean had told him. "At the very least, you didn't do anything to stop it."

"I didn't break anything," Stu had said. "If I'm a witness to a crime, I don't get arrested for refusing to testify."

"You should want to help security officers. They make sure this place is like home."

"Whose home?" he'd said, and taken the fall. A month later Moser quit school after failing three courses.

It didn't matter that Stu had been suspended from college before he finished two years and didn't return. He'd gotten 59 out of 60 on the editing test at the *Daily News*, the highest score ever by an applicant. 56 was the previous best, he was told. And passing was 50, as if catching five errors out of six was acceptable. He'd missed *February 29, 2005*, and he was still angry about it because *29* was more like a trick than a problem. It wouldn't come up. Nobody would make that mistake, not in a year that didn't have the extra day.

Ralph Herrold had told Stu that somebody had spotted the *29* in the past, but that person missed six other mistakes, even making an error out of something correct. "He works here still. Ask him about it," Ralph Herrold had said, pointing to Chuck Yarnell, who proofread the local section so badly Stu had stopped talking to him after a week.

Jack Ferrence's next article, half a column long, had only one new sentence—the date of the preliminary hearing. To be sure, Stu laid the earlier article beside the newspaper and matched the lines. Identical. Every other word was pasted in.

That night, as Stu was eating a barbeque sandwich by himself just before seven o'clock, Ralph Herrold sat his coffee cup on the table. "Eating alone is bad for your health," he said.

Stu regretted coming into one of the two restaurants that were only a block from the newspaper office. He usually walked another three blocks, sometimes more, to places where his co-workers weren't likely to go in the forty-five minutes they had for dinner. "Not as bad as hot dogs and French fries with company," Stu said, the meal he'd seen in front of Herrold as he'd walked past him and two reporters before taking a booth as far from Herrold's table as possible. .

Herrold didn't smile. He wrapped both hands around his mug in a way that reminded Stu of how he'd been told to sit in first grade while the teacher read a story to the class. "You unhappy at the *Daily News*?" he said.

"Sometimes." The word didn't seem to surprise Herrold, who nodded once without losing eye contact.

"*Sometimes* can seem like *frequently* to others," Herrold said. "Or even *always*."

"Clear as this water," Stu said. He held up his half-filled glass in what he thought was a comradely way, but Herrold stayed fixed on his face. The water rose and fell in tiny waves until Stu laid the glass down on the table. "The *sometimes* are when I see how many mistakes get by other copyreaders. I want every section of the paper to be perfect."

"It's not healthy wanting everything to be perfect," Herrold said. "If everybody was like that, where would we be?"

"In a better place."

"You sound like a funeral director. You give it some thought and you'll see that it's just the opposite."

The last time Stu had spent an evening with his mother before Jesse left, Jesse had taken the snakes from the tank and held them in one hand while he drank beer from a can he held in the other. "Just like in them churches," he'd said, laughing, those copperheads writhing in a way that made Stu stand up so he was better prepared to move. Jesse held them until he finished the beer. His mother looked happy to be standing beside a man holding three snakes within striking distance. Her expression didn't change when Jesse laid the snakes back in the tank. "To think," she said.

"Those snake-handlers in church get bit some times," Stu had said. "People die."

"Really?" his mother said and bent down to peer through the glass as if she'd never thought about it.

The snakes were slithering into places that seemed sheltered—two in corners and one under the overhang of the stone. Jesse smiled at Stu in a way that made Stu think he wished Stu hadn't mentioned those snakebites. "Could one of those kill me with its fangs?" his mother said.

"No," Jesse said. "Not likely."

"Not likely." Stu's mother repeated the phrase like she was committing it to memory. The snakes settled. Within seconds, they looked bored. Stu thought they welcomed Jesse lifting them out because it was the only time they ever acted like snakes, their bodies rippling, their eyes alert, tongues flickering.

"You ever consider just letting them run loose?" his mother said. She'd been drinking beer with Jesse since Stu had arrived two hours before, and Stu had begun to worry that a six pack mixed with her depression medicine was a bad idea, or worse, that she'd stopped taking the medicine, expecting the beer to brighten her mood.

"In the house?"

"Yes. That's who they are. Right? Things that would find their own homes."

"That's crazy. There's nothing to eat in a house like this."

"But that's not why you won't let them loose."

"It doesn't matter why not. We're done talking about this."

His mother tapped the glass, but the snakes didn't react. They acted like nothing mattered except to be picked up and carried.

After the snakes were put down, Ferrence finally interviewed somebody again. "We took them to court," the police chief said. "Their part in this was over."

"Thank God for that," the secretary said. "Two weeks of those things coiled up in that glass box sitting on the floor like that. I thought they'd get out for sure."

They were about three feet long, the article said, and when the diction began to sound like somebody besides Jack Ferrence's, Stu Googled "copperheads" and discovered that Jack Ferrence had gone on line to the first site available. "Copperheads are venomous pit vipers. Copperheads account for more cases of venomous snake bite than any other species. Fortunately, their venom is the least toxic of our species. Bites from copperheads are very seldom fatal; however, a bite may still produce serious consequences."

Ferrence hadn't bothered to change the syntax. "Coppeheads will not usually bite. However, the bite will be readily used as a last defence."

He'd even spelled *defense* like the British, as if the copperheads had been imported from London.

Stu saw, before he clicked off, that there was an ad on the first page of the site: "Having a picture of the copperhead on a mug or coaster is a great way to keep a reference image available to use for the next snake you encounter." Stu had never seen even one snake except in the zoo or the pet store or his mother's living room. He imagined himself being better off to have a photograph of Ralph Herrold on his mug. One in which he was holding his sweater-clad dogs.

Once Ferrence went back to writing his own words, there were errors. *It's* instead of *its*. The plural of *lawyers* with an apostrophe as if their position earned them an extra punctuation mark. The kinds of errors fourth graders thinking about video games might make. Chuck Yarnell hadn't corrected them.

The next-to-last paragraph finally quoted his mother: "I'm sorry this happened. I don't want people to be afraid of snakes."

"She didn't look as crazy as people following this story might think," the article ended, "but there's no doubt this is the wackiest story of the year so far."

At least his mother was living at home again, sentenced to a year's probation and mandatory alcohol rehab, when the news of the snakes' death reached her. "They could have given those snakes to a zoo or some such place as that," she said. The bite on her face, Stu noticed, was nearly healed. It looked as if there wouldn't be a scar.

"They do the same to dogs that bite is how they figure it, Mom."

"Those snakes had names," she said. "Hal and Ed. After my brothers, God rest. A car crash and the man's cancer, who would have seen that coming? The accident can happen to anybody, but the cancer, at thirty-four? Ed just didn't believe he could have a problem like that so young."

"I think that kind is for the young, Mom," he said.

"That's leukemia. That's for boys and girls both."

"There's more."

"Then it's a wonder any of us are left standing."

Stu nodded. All the evidence pointed that way. "I got to know those snakes," his mother said. "They were easy to tell apart. And they acted different. You know. That third one I called Jesse. He thought it was cute, but he didn't know my brothers are dead. And him just thirty-six and maybe seeing me looking older everyday."

Stu stayed quiet, waiting to see which direction his mother's talk was going. She hadn't had a drink since her run-in with the police, and she seemed wound up. "Jesse, he'd pick them up and say, 'Don't this beat anything you've ever seen?' You remember him saying it was just like those people in those churches you hear about, how those snake-handlers think they're closer to God with poison right there in their hands."

"Yeah," Stu said. "I heard that, for sure."

"He made me hold one," she said. "He said it was a test of my feelings for him. 'You just wait,' he said. 'You'll be different after.' He was half right about that. I was the same person, but I saw him differently. That's one test of love. I know what he saw in me was going dim, and he thought maybe this would brighten it."

After he left his mother's house, Stu looked up snake handlers. Seventy-three people had died handling snakes in church the year before. Right below that statistic was the Bible verse those snake handlers cited: "In my name they shall cast out devils; they shall speak with new tongues. They shall take up serpents; and if they drink any deadly thing, it shall not hurt them." Mark 16:17–18

Stu knew that snake handlers were supposed to not drink alcohol. He knew they thought doctors were unnecessary. His mother handled snakes because she knew how, not because she believed in anything.

The next day he visited again, and his mother showed him an incorrect headline and an incorrect picture caption in the Sunday paper, the edition Stu never worked on. "I'm starting to see these," she said. "Pretty soon I'll be picking at those bitty things you see. Why, this boy in the picture must wonder how he got into the wrong uniform."

"He won't see it, Mom."

"Why not? There it is plain as day and he lives right here at the college where the paper must come every day."

"Those kids don't read the local paper, believe me. They don't give two hoots about what happens here."

She brightened. "So they wouldn't know I was the snake woman?"

"No. They never heard of her."

"They're not missing much, but it's nice to know I could walk around that place and nobody would be the wiser."

"They don't think they live there," he said. "They think they're on vacation."

"People don't know what it's like having the police force their way in on you."

"It got out of hand, all right. It was overreaction."

"They like it, those men," she said then, and she glanced at the empty glass tank in a way that made him believe she missed those snakes like people miss dogs they've had put down. "You think that's true?" she went on. "The police like to force themselves on people."

"Sure," he said. "Some part of anything is always awful."

She went to the tank, and when she reached inside, he held his breath because there was a chance she was going to scoop at the dirt and pebbles like she expected to dig up eggs or fling handfuls of the stuff around the room.

A moment later, she held out three small coins. "I put these in among Hal and Ed and Jesse," she said. "I've had them since before you were born. Your father and I went to Canada, and we kept some change when we came back, who wouldn't, to show we'd been some place. There's one that works like a dime and two that work like quarters, but it's been so long who knows if they'd buy anything now."

Stu held them. All the times he'd looked at the snakes and never noticed the coins—the snakes were like a magician's hands taking his eyes away from where the trick was taking place. "I worked them down in there pretty good," she said. "I didn't want you reaching in there like you'd found buried treasure."

"Your father was partial to telling people we'd been to a foreign country. He thought it made us special. He wanted to keep their dollars, too, but I spent them at the duty-free store right before we crossed over."

He touched the edges of each coin as if there were clues to discover about his father, and his mother smiled. "I enjoyed drinking from those Canadian bottles," she said. "It didn't seem like we'd paid anything for them using that foreign money that looked like pretend."

He laid the coins back in the tank, dropping them the last six inches as if those snakes had returned, as if he hadn't noticed they were coiled in the shadows. "I've been back to work a week now," she said.

"Good."

"Do you think I'm still attractive?" she said then, and Stu knew that no man had come back to the house with her after work that week.

"Sure."

"I'm forty-two years old, twice your age. Every one of those years means more to a woman. The girls you've been with might not know that yet, but they will."

"You're fine, Mom," he said, and when she didn't answer, his words sounded like something a doctor would say to a patient, leaving "for now" unspoken, keeping the important words to himself.

The morning radio hosts latched on to the story about a judge being dismissed from office for using a penis pump during trials. "Pump it up," the host said, and his sidekick, laughing shrilly, exclaimed, "A big, big case! Guilty as charged."

After breakfast, Stu sat with the eight pages of the front section, the ones Herrold corrected. The first two pages were almost entirely wire service articles, but on page three Stu made the small loops for *delete* three times. He twice placed the carat for *insert* and made the horizontal parentheses of *close up space* four times. Twice he drew the parallel lines for *align*. There was a capital letter error and two en-dash signals required.

Small errors, but by the time he was finished, he'd found forty-one errors. Page seven was full of syndicated columns; page eight were wire-service stories continued from pages one and two. Thirty-nine of the errors had come on the four pages that hadn't been proofed before they arrived.

After Herrold left for dinner that night, Stu tacked the four worst pages over the dog pictures surrounding Herrold's desk. Herrold would know it was Stu. Who else could do the work so well?

Stu was sure he'd be fired. Another man would have laid those pages on the editor's desk, but Stu was used to being by himself by now.

THE PROPER WORDS FOR SIN

———

My son loves to watch me spray the DDT. "Good," he says, as I walk backwards, the cloud of mist following me around the house.

He hates bugs, even ladybugs and fireflies, the ones other children collect and carry in jars until they die. It's gotten to keeping him inside more than a boy of near twelve ought to be, one about to finish sixth grade with a sister going on fourteen who brings home all the problems that come with that.

"If we lived in the South," I remind him when he wears me out with his squeamishness, "you'd find out what insects can become without weather to discourage them."

He shudders at that. For real. Like Alfalfa or one of those characters hamming it up in the *Little Rascals* reruns he watches, everything exaggerated so a dog would get what they were up to if it took a mind to watching television.

What's made it worse is this spring, our new neighbors, the ones who arrived in March the day Kruschev's picture was on the front page because now he was in charge of the Soviets, are bookish. Forward about it, especially the father, who is all the time making a reference to something he's read, even if it's something we all know about from doing, telling me, a milkman, about the danger in what every family ought to have on its dinner table. "Cream," he says, making the word sound like *cancer*. "You know, don't you, what that can do to you?"

While I'm spraying, he comes across the street without an invitation, like we've been friends for years. "This isn't good for anything," he says to me. "It's as bad as fallout."

"It's a miracle, is what it is," I say.

"A miracle will be if we're all still here in ten years. People forget the simplest things right in front of their faces. The food chain. Remember?"

I nod because I know I have to unless I want to look the idiot, but a little more comfort and a bit less nuisance seem a small thing to ask from this life, and there are scientists who know more than Kevin Naugle who use the word *miracle* when they speak of DDT.

"Your boy will be accelerated, I hear," he says now, being what Naugle calls affable, and I nod at that. "And your daughter," I say, thinking that's what Naugle wants to hear.

"They're Sputnik children," he says. "The Soviets have shaken us awake."

We have something to agree on. Accelerated means pushed hard in science and math, ten percent of next year's seventh graders taking algebra and physical science, launching them toward college-level courses by their junior year. "If it helps the country, I'm all for it," I say, though I worry for my boy among the brainy.

"Your boy won't be a milkman," Naugle says. "Those days are about gone." I don't know exactly what Kevin Naugle does in his shirt and tie all day, but my wife Mildred has given him the advantage by telling him how I earn my bread and butter. It makes me want to say a man in a tie standing outside at eight o'clock on a beautiful late May evening is a sorry thing, but I keep that to myself. My boy and his daughter have hit it off, a good thing, maybe, though I have my qualms.

* * * *

Naugle's daughter looks to be a handful. Dressing in what looks like two sizes too small, her hair combed over one eye like she wants you to think she's mysterious. "She just wants to look like a movie star," my wife says, making excuses as soon as she hears me saying she looks like she's hiding.

"Is that in style?" I ask, and when she says "No," I say, "Ok then."

Even my daughter Elise jokes that her brother's little friend needs to act her age. "She's twelve going on sixteen," she's said more than once, though

I'm here to say that girl, Carol is her name, has a voice on the phone that makes me wish I was twelve. It's musical, which sounds silly to put into words, but there's nothing else for describing it. "Is Billy there?" she says, sounding like she's starting up the do-re-mis, and I call him, finding myself using my after-church voice just so she knows how civil we are here.

When Billy takes the phone, he waits for me to leave the kitchen before he starts to talk. I hear her laugh, and I imagine that girl talking about rock-and-roll singers and such, turning Billy's head away from the things boys ought to be doing.

"You should have boys as friends," I've said. "You should be practicing baseball in between your league games."

He plays shortstop most games, where one of the best players on each team plays, but he never practices, swinging a bat only just before and during games. It's been a year since he caught balls with me in the yard. It's his final summer before Pony League, when pitchers throw curve balls, when batting practice is a must. Already, he acts like this will be the last year he plays a game that he's always been good at.

Tonight, Billy writes on the pad by the phone while he talks, taking notes as if he was in school. After he hangs up, I notice him lift the dictionary off the shelf in the den and start up the stairs. I ask him right out what he wants with it now that school is down to its last week. "Looking up things," he says. "Carol's so smart. She knows all these words."

"Like what?"

"Words I never heard of."

I wait, but he doesn't go on. After he closes his door, I try to make out the words by what's come through on the next page of the note pad, but aside from seeing the words are uniformly long, I can't make them out. I think of that girl, her brains and the way she shows herself, and I think: fornication, cunnilingus, and fellatio.

I've seen that girl in her room. She leaves her drapes open. I've seen her unbutton her blouse and flash her new white bra, and when she lifts it off her chest, her small breasts are so firm looking there's no question she doesn't need the bra for anything but keeping her nipples from showing through the tight sweaters and blouses she wears. I think of my son down the hall, how he might be watching, how she might be doing this for him, that she's been giving him the proper words for sin so he knows what he has to pick from, starting with voyeur and this girl undoing her clothes like somebody who enjoys it.

While I watch, I think that maybe my son is right this second undressing for her, though I've never seen her glance this way. Could someone be so convincingly naïve? The angle is such that she's hidden below the waist, but he'd be visible and so would I if I turned on the light and let her see it was a man watching her and what she could expect to see in return if she kept at her behavior.

* * * *

My wife is home all day, but she doesn't spend time with the neighbor women. Mildred has the television to keep her company, and I'm home by three, what with the milk going out early like it needs to. So she turns it off at 3:30, as soon as some woman gets into difficulty on *The Secret Storm*. I usually watch a few minutes near the end, wondering how much misfortune can settle on one person, but when school ends, there's Billy sitting beside her like somebody's wife when I get home. I frown at Mildred, but I wait until the beautiful woman who might have multiple sclerosis waits for the doctor's report.

"He's not sitting here all day," Mildred says at once, so she knows what I'm thinking. "It's half an hour. It's good for the boy to see he's well off compared to some." I give her a look that reminds her it's summer and the middle of the afternoon, a time when only housewives or old women are watching, when a boy should be judging the flight of a baseball off a bat.

* * * *

"So many things can go wrong," he says at dinner after two weeks of watching, making him sound like he's been watching *The Secret Storm* for years instead of taking in only ten afternoons of claptrap.

"Trouble is like insects," I tell him. "It's everywhere. That's why we have the DDT. You'll see. In a few years you'll hardly see a bug. They're licked. They just don't know it yet."

"No, they're not. They can adapt faster than we can kill them."

"Who are you talking to? You're not getting this in school, that's for sure."

Elise smiles like she has a secret. "What has you in stitches?" I say.

"Before he got so smart, Billy was getting himself in a sweat about bugs getting born straight out of dog dirt. You know old man Miller next door has those two retrievers, and their yard is full of it."

I look at Billy, who's glaring at his sister as if he wants to dump the bowl of green beans over her head. "Spontaneous generation," he says. "Smart people believed in it once."

"Where'd you hear that?" I ask.

"Mr. Naugle. He says Aristotle thought he proved it. He had good reasons to not get it right. He didn't have microscopes. He watched mud and feces with just his bare eyes."

"He watched feces, did he? There's a job for a man in a shirt and tie."

"Can you imagine anybody believing that for even one second?" Elise says. "You'd have to be a total moron."

"Shush now," Mildred says, but she gives Billy a puzzled look. "I thought Kevin Naugle was a man of science. He sounds more like a fundamentalist."

Billy shrugs. "It was Mr. Naugle's idea of a joke, Mom. He had me going for a while. He was scaring me. He knows I hate bugs, and he had me starting to think they could come from anywhere that was warm and damp and dirty."

"Never mind him," Mildred says, but Billy acts as if she hasn't said a word, so I know he's past the embarrassing part of the story.

"You know what's scary for real?" he says. "It doesn't matter that bugs don't come from mud. All the DDT in the world can't kill them because there will always be some that can live with the poison, and then their children will be even harder to kill."

I take a bite of meat loaf. I don't have to argue. I'm not the one who's afraid of insects. Mildred isn't eating. Her expression hasn't changed. "I still don't understand why anybody would tell a story like that as a joke," she says. "It's like saying Zeus is watching us and has decided to change us into spiders or trees."

"Who's Zeus?" Elise says, and Billy looks at her triumphantly.

"You're the moron," Billy says, though when all she hisses, in return, is "science boy," not raising her voice, it sounds like the worst sort of dismissal.

* * * *

Most mornings, once I'm in the truck and on my route, work calms me. I love the first hour of driving when it's still half-dark, even in summer, and there's hardly even a car to pass. There's so much promise in that emptiness and light, as if life has shifted for the better, and I think that maybe some morning the first person I see will look changed, and I'll know from now on things will be different.

And there is a pleasure in retrieving empties and replacing them in the milk box slots with glass bottles full to the brim. There are still people on the route who prefer glass, and I imagine them to be people I want to know. Milk's better in glass. It's not a thing improved by convenience. I've been drinking milk from bottles so long I wouldn't want it to come another way. And all that wax on the paper cartons—it gets onto things. And a man like Kevin Naugle would remind you it makes more trash, though you don't need science to see it's a waste. I tell myself to mention it the next time I see him, create a little bit of friendly agreement, but then I think of him predicting the end of milkmen, and I know I won't say a word.

Just one customer cancels during July. A man like Naugle would take that the wrong way, ask me when was the last time someone was added to my route, but I don't see much of him, and then some good things happen to the country near the end of July, not the least of which is NASA gets started so the US can get serious about beating the Soviets. "About time," I tell Billy while I drive him to his last Little League game. "Now we're cooking with gas."

"It's not a race, Dad," he says, looking out the side window as if he's never seen the road we live on before.

"The hell it's not," I say, but he doesn't answer.

By ten days later, when Eisenhower announces that the Nautilus has gone under the North Pole, meaning the Russians know we can send a submarine anywhere at any time, Billy has a habit of going over to the Naugles every day to listen to records with the little firecracker. I can hear those songs coming across the street from their screened-in front porch. I can see the both of them moving around, but I can't hear their voices, even between the songs by the Everly Brothers and Elvis and Buddy Holly.

They keep their voices low or maybe they don't talk, but part of the problem with hearing is Elise and her friends stand in the yard every afternoon swinging their hips to keep hula hoops twirling. "That's something they're too old to be doing," I say to Mildred when *The Secret Storm* is over and Billy is across the street.

"They're just being girls," she says. "They're only fourteen."

"It's not their age I'm talking about," I say, and she brushes past me.

"You keep your eyes in your head, then," she nearly spits.

And then, for three straight days, Billy stays in the house after *The Secret Storm*. "Your friend go to summer camp?" I ask him.

"No," he says.

"What then?"

"She wants to be by herself."

I give him a nod of acknowledgement. "You'll be seeing a lot of girls in a few weeks."

"We're not boyfriend/girlfriend, Dad," he says. "You think you know something, but you don't."

* * * *

After another month of him holed up in his room or across the street, I'm happy when school starts again, but on the second day of junior high, Billy comes home from school with a story about being humiliated on the bus. A senior, he says, took his gym bag and opened it, pulling out his brand new gym suit, the one with a dog's head on the t-shirt and a matching one on the shorts. He tossed it on the floor and held up the once-used jock strap. "Medium," the boy read from the label inside the waistband, and then he said, "Your little prick and peanuts couldn't fill this."

My son quotes the boy like I'm a policeman. I'm surprised Billy humiliates himself a second time and wish he would summarize, or better, keep the whole thing to himself. "Sit in the front of the bus," I say. "You can't fight boys five years older than you are."

"I don't want to fight him, Dad," he says. "I want to kill him."

"I understand," I say, but my son's tone is so even he sounds like somebody who wishes I kept guns around the house.

"You don't," he says. "What if Elise had her bra tossed around the bus? What would you tell her to do?"

Cover yourself, I think, but I shake my head slowly and say, "It won't happen again. You'll see. Boys like that won't even notice you if you keep to yourself."

"32B—that's what that guy would yell out about Elise. He'd tell everybody how big her breasts were."

My son starts to cry. Twelve years old now and he sobs in a way that makes me want to say "Grow up" as if I am somebody who doesn't give a damn whether his son will hate him after he hears those words.

I don't know my wife's bra size, let alone my daughter's. Small, medium, large—the sizes for men and boys are easy, but to have your body measured so explicitly is an awkward thing to get around. "That's not going to happen to Elise," I say. "Don't you worry about that."

* * * *

The next afternoon, he doesn't come home after school. "He's watching American Bandstand with Carol Naugle," Mildred says.

"Is it a special?" I ask.

"It's on every day, George. He's been going over there for quite a while, if you haven't noticed, and now that school started, he asked me for permission. Here, see for yourself."

She turns the television back on, and I watch two lines of boys and girls clapping their hands while couples shuffle between them. "He wants to watch kids dance?" I say.

"I'm happy he's taken to this. Maybe he'll learn to dance," she says. "This one's called The Stroll. I think all you have to do is look cool walking when it's your turn."

When the record ends, a slow song begins, and the teenagers pair up to embrace. "I like this one," I say. "I've heard this somewhere."

"It's Tommy Edwards," she says. "It's really popular." I watch the couples as the song plays until Mildred gets up from the chair and turns it off.

"That's enough for one day," she says. "It's for kids, not for us."

"I know where I've heard it," I say. "Elise plays that song. She sits in her room and sings along the way she does to Pat Boone and Johnny Mathis and all the rest."

Mildred frowns. "I thought you meant that you'd heard it someplace else."

* * * *

In the middle of September, Naugle's daughter misses school for a week, something neither of my children have ever done. "That's twice in one month," I say.

"She's sick," Mildred says on the fifth day. "Maybe she has horrible cramps. You know what happens to girls at her age."

I can hear American Bandstand playing in the basement. I listen for a moment, trying to hear if Billy is shuffling his feet to the music. "Maybe she doesn't have the get up and go to look the world in the eye."

"What's that supposed to mean?"

I twist a finger near my right temple and grimace, and my wife says, "She's just growing up. If you paid attention to your daughter, you'd know."

"I don't see Elise staying in bed all day."

"That's foolishness talking, Jack. If ever I heard it." She looks toward the basement as if she expects Billy to be eavesdropping. "You should hope your children don't pay their father any mind when it comes to knowing what's in the heart," she says, and I spin and leave the room before I find myself telling her if she opened her eyes she'd see the world didn't look anything like what she pretended, and to say otherwise made you a moron.

That night Billy calls me downstairs where he's been hiding himself every night now that there's no phone calls. "Dad!" he shouts. Dad!" As if a fire has started, I think, hurrying down the steps to where he's standing beside his chair, turned away from where the television is showing what look to be photographs of the evening sky. I follow his eyes to a millipede half way up the wall. "Spray it," he says, but I know better than to fill the room with a cloud meant to discourage crawling things. I take a Kleenex from the box Mildred keeps on an end table and pinch the millipede into a small blot surrounded by tiny legs.

Billy turns slowly, examining the walls. "There's more, right?" he says.

"You can count on it."

"I can't watch tv down here then."

"Just when it's dark. They don't come out in daylight. They know what's good for them. What with the lights on, I don't know what got into this one."

On the screen, a man in a dark suit is pointing at a model of the solar system. "It was huge," Billy says.

"For a millipede," I say. "He probably thought he was a tough guy when he was behind the wall."

"He should have stopped there then. Being big gets you into trouble." When Billy goes on, explaining that he wishes he wasn't so tall, I tell him he's lucky, that he'll fill out and be strong and glad for it.

"No," he says. "That's the problem. If you're big, you're always expected to be tough. If you're small, you have a choice."

"Tough comes with being big," I say, but looking at him, I don't believe it at all, and my son shakes his head at once.

So he turns off the television just as the man in the suit holds up the model as if it is a brand new baby, and God's truth, I'm happy, for once, with his squeamishness because he's watching WQED, the education channel in our city. I remember watching one of their shows for a few minutes once and wondering who would sit down with something that was so much like school. Somebody like Kevin Naugle, I think now. Somebody who was still dressed for work even though it was dark outside.

* * * *

On Monday, Billy goes directly to the Naugle's house after school, and that night, when I answer the phone, I hear "Mr. Enright. Hi, there," that girl's voice as musical as ever, nothing like somebody should sound after she's been sick so long.

I've never heard that girl's voice clear enough for words except on the phone. When I see her outside she always waves, a small, fingertip-flutter like she's saying hello as she stands over a crib. I think about that music, whether she will always sound like that. Maybe a girl's voice changes like a boy's sometimes, though my own daughter sounds no different, beginning high school, than she did in sixth grade.

They talk for half an hour, as long as one of those science shows on television, and an hour later, when I go into the bedroom, there she is big as life undressing like she hasn't been out of sight for a week.

Carol Naugle is a 32A—the number comes to me as if it's been shouted down the aisle by a school bully. The girl is as thin as my daughter, but her breasts are smaller, and unless there is a size less than A, I know what is printed on the bra she slips off.

All boys must watch like this, I think. They look in windows for a glimpse of the world to come. They hope for their sister's door to be ajar, for the perfect timing that places them outside that door at the moment when a blouse slides off shoulders, when a skirt drops to the floor. I saw my sister just once like that and never said a word to anyone, but I listened to all of the stories told by classmates in junior high school, especially the week-by-week story one boy told throughout eighth grade about watching his neighbor, of sitting in the dark and waiting because that girl, thirteen, undressed at 10:30 every night.

While that girl reaches for her pajamas, I slip down the hall and go to my son's room, but Billy is in bed with his eyes closed. I wonder how fast he can get into bed if he hears me coming, but when I walk closer, I think he's really asleep, that Naugle's daughter is putting on a show and he's not watching. It makes me remember Elise saying "science boy," the phrase sounding terrible. When I look across the street, I notice, for the first time, she has a television in her bedroom.

* * * *

As if he's caught something from that girl, a week later my son stays home from school for three straight days. When I come home the third day, he's watching *The Secret Storm* with Mildred as if it's summer. The women on this episode seem to be an especially sad lot. One is pregnant. One had cancer. And one has a husband who's set fire to her house. That woman is screaming for the firemen to search inside the burning house for her husband, who she thinks is asleep, when the show ends, but we know he's out drinking in a bar to set up an alibi. "Isn't that something?" Mildred says, standing and going upstairs before I can tell her that the husband will be caught for sure, that no sin is left unpunished in these shows.

Billy smiles when the show ends, and I think for a moment he's been fooled into thinking the husband is trapped inside the burning house, getting what he deserves, but he tells me the boy who opened his gym bag the first week of school was in a fight on the bus while Carol Naugle was absent and was beaten up by a boy who sits in the last seat, alone, every day. "Cy Griffin," Billy says. "He never talks to anybody. He never has a book in his hand. All of a sudden he has Bill Markle over a seat and is punching his face. He broke his nose, Dad. He must have. It was all bloody. The driver stopped the bus and told them both to get off, and everybody could see Cy punching him some more by the side of the road."

Some goodness comes to the world, I think, but my son is flushed with telling me. "It was like he was killing him, Dad. It was great. I was hoping he'd throw him under the back wheels."

I say, "Slow down, there. He got his beating. That's enough."

My son makes boxing motions with his arms, uppercuts and hooks. "You know what Cy Griffin is?" he says. "He's like a genius or something. When he reads a book, he remembers every word."

"Photographic memory?"

"Yeah. There's a better word for it. I thought he maybe couldn't even read because he never had a book, but it's just the opposite. A genius and a fighter."

"Why didn't you tell me this when it happened?"

"It's only been a week, Dad. I told Carol. It cheered her up to hear about somebody getting what they deserved. She went back to school the next day. You saw."

He tells me he's going across the street. "Three days off. I thought you were really sick," I say.

"I was. But I'm better now."

"Who's on American Bandstand today? Elvis? Buddy Holly?"

"We stopped watching last week," Billy says. "Carol says it's stupid to watch people pretend to be singing." Before I can ask what they do instead, he's gone.

* * * *

"Here's a story for you," Naugle says, coming across the street when he sees me doing my last spray before the weather turns cold. "A long time ago, where they grew mandarin oranges in southern China, the farmers had problems with insects. Nobody ever heard of DDT, but they paid attention, and after a while they decided to hang bags of yellow ants in the trees. They laid bamboo bridges form tree to tree to let them spread, and those ants ate the insects that ate the oranges."

"If it was that easy, there'd be something eating mosquitoes."

Naugle doesn't change expression. "The Chinese protected frogs; they revered the praying mantis. You can figure out why."

"I get it."

"They had a certain kind of leaf they put into books that kept bookworms from destroying them. They got things done without poison."

"For all that, the Chinese don't seem to be doing very well," I say. "They're miserable and Communist at the same time. And the ones who live in the South, they have malaria to deal with. DDT will save their lives."

"You know what will come of that?" Naugle says. "More people than the world can stand. Malaria has always been like birth control in those places."

* * * *

"What are you doing in here?" my wife says, startling me. I never thought she could approach the bedroom without me hearing her. She switches on the overhead light, and I squint like a man who's been in the dark for longer than a few seconds. "I was thinking," I say. "The dark helps me to concentrate."

Her eyes go to the window she's looked out a thousand times, the view so familiar I trust she won't recognize which part of it I was watching unless the girl has entered her room in the past ten seconds and begun to undress.

"You should go for a walk then. The darkness along with moving your body is better. Standing here is like watching a turned off television. You've seen this so many times it might as well be blank."

"I guess. But every once in a while I like to look outside at night."

She doesn't smile. He lips are set tightly straight across her face—like the lips of a stick figure, I think, like one drawn with just one line from side to side.

She moves past me and pulls the drapes shut, adjusting the ends so they meet exactly. "As soon as the lights are on, these go shut," she says. "Otherwise I feel naked."

"How do you feel when you go outside and there aren't any drapes?"

"You know what I mean."

* * * *

"There was a show on television today about DDT," Billy says. "You know what the letters stand for?"

"No idea."

"Isn't it a brand name?" Mildred says.

"Dichloro Diphenyl Trichloroethane," Billy says, sounding like he's giving an answer on the *$64,000 Question.*

"No wonder they changed the name then," Mildred says.

"It's white crystal, Dad. It doesn't have any odor or taste. It doesn't dissolve very fast but at least it breaks down quickly in the sun."

"'At least'?"

"So the poison goes away faster."

"I'll spray on a cloudy day next time."

"We should know what everything is made of, Dad. It's important."

"Like soap?" I say. "It works. We're clean. That's enough to know."

"For everything. You don't know whether or not some soap isn't as good for you as another."

"We know milk is good for us," I say. "So we drink it."

My son shakes his head, and I feel the fear that precedes rage, like when I'd lost my job with the highway department because a county commissioner had been voted out of office. "Mr. Naugle says we shouldn't be so sure about milk. He says it's only a matter of time before the world wises up."

"Good luck to your Mr. Naugle when his bones start to break."

"Carol doesn't drink milk."

"She'll regret it," Elise suddenly says. "She'll get a hump like old Mrs. Shelby down the street."

"She doesn't eat meat either."

Elise taps her slice of roast beef with her fork. "What does she do, graze?"

I smile at her. "You like that song 'It's All in the Game'?" I ask.

She makes a face. "That's so old now. I wish the radio would quit playing it."

"How about you?" I say to Billy.

"I've never heard it, Dad."

Elise makes another face. "It's been number one for a month. You're as weird as your little friend."

That night, when Naugle's daughter calls, Billy hangs up in a minute. "What's wrong?" I say, as he heads for the door.

"She wants me to come over, Dad."

"That's new."

"The telephone isn't good for some things."

As soon as he leaves, I go upstairs, but neither of them enter the girl's bedroom. I listen for Mildred for a moment, and then I walk to Billy's room and open my son's drawers, looking under his sweaters and t-shirts and underwear, hoping to find a lingerie catalogue slipped upstairs or maybe a Playboy borrowed from a friend whose father subscribes. His shirts look large enough for me to wear, and yet I outweigh my son by fifty pounds, perhaps more. They make him look even skinnier, like a bag of bones, the phrase coming back to me from my own days in seventh grade.

I don't find anything. Not in his drawers or under his mattress or deep in his closet. It's the room of a nine-year-old. The dictionary by the bed is the only odd thing in the room, and I carry it into the hall where there's light, open it, and leaf through until I reach pederasty: *Sodomy between males, especially as practiced by a man with a boy.* I turn to Sodomy: *Any sexual intercourse held to be abnormal, specifically anal intercourse between two male persons.* I imagine my son sitting in bed to read this, and then I try to imagine a twelve-year-old boy looking up Naugle's science words, even if they were delivered by the sweetest telephone voice in the United States. Sodium fluoroacetate is at the top of sodomy's column: *A powder used as a rodent poison*, the dictionary says. And then comes sodium hydroxide, hypochlorite, and hyposulfite, and I think of Cy Griffin memorizing definitions like this, put the dictionary back, walk outside, and cut through the back yard into the housing plan where Billy has told me he and the boy he'd thrashed both live.

I pass eight houses before I see anyone outside, and then, just as I hear music, I see two boys and a girl who look like they might be seniors in high school. My son has said the tough boy has a DA, and both of these boys do. Cy Griffin, he's told me, has a Marine cut. Both boys are tall and thick, football player types who'd rather spend their time working on cars and drinking beer and chasing girls like the one sitting on the steps beside six empty bottles. The steps run up to a small porch like the one attached to every house on this street, all of them built within a few years of each other less than ten years ago.

I think of one of these boys being pounded and give credit to Cy Griffin for being truly frightening. And I can't imagine my son, in five years, resembling either of these boys, let alone Cy Griffin.

I pass thirty-three more houses, but no one else is visible, and when I step out onto the street and turn left toward our street, I exhale like I've just managed a gauntlet of muggers.

Soon Naugle's daughter misses another two days of school. "Check the calendar," I say to Mildred. "It's not what you say it is." She puts a finger to her lips, but Billy goes upstairs as if he doesn't hear me.

Before midnight, an ambulance pulls into Naugle's driveway. Mildred and I watch from the window. The lights are on in the daughter's room but the drapes are closed. We follow the shadows of what must be the attendants, and then Mildred goes to Billy's room. When she doesn't come back in a minute, I know he's awake and watching.

"She swallowed Drano," Mildred says when I get home from my route the next day. Billy sits beside her on the couch; Elise is rocking in the chair Mildred bought for herself when she found out she was pregnant for the first time.

So I was right, I keep myself from saying, that girl someone who gets sick just from waking up in the morning. I look at Mildred to gauge whether or not the girl is alive, but Billy volunteers, "She won't be able to eat like a normal person, not for a long time or maybe ever."

Mildred sighs in a way I think the women who watch afternoon television would appreciate. "There's no fixing the damage something like that does," she says. When no one else speaks, she adds, "She'll need watching."

"It's so creepy to think about," Elise says. "She'll always be weird now."

I go outside to walk in the yard, and I'm surprised Billy follows me. We end up at the edge of the back yard where we can look past the junipers toward the housing plan where Cy Griffin and the gym bag boy are just home from school like my children. Billy stares between his shoes for a minute while I wait. "There's no bugs," he finally says.

"It's the DDT," I say, but my son shakes his head.

"It's just getting cold," he says. "That's all it is. They'll all be back—like baseball."

"Maybe she'll heal," I say. "There's probably not much experience with this sort of thing to predict from." When he doesn't answer, I ask, "Can she talk?"

"Talk? She can't even eat now."

"There's two pipes going down, aren't there?"

"She was going to have to move again," my son says.

"They've only been here six months."

"That's just it. She wanted to stay here."

"A child doesn't get much say in something like that."

"She's not a baby, Dad. " My son stares away from me. I see his hands are both clenched and think, for a moment, he is fighting the impulse to attack me.

When the girl comes home a few weeks later, Mildred walks over with a casserole, but Billy goes downstairs to the television, leaving the lights off as if he wants the millipedes to attack. I watch the girl's room, and there is a light on, but the drapes are drawn, and that light is so dim I know it is leaking in from the hallway, that the girl is lying in the dark with the door open so her parents can look in on her every time they pass by. There isn't going to be any privacy in that house for a long time, that's for sure. No doors being closed by children.

I think of Kevin Naugle preaching about poisons yet keeping Drano in the house, pouring it down his sink like he's forgotten where the water goes. You can unscrew an elbow pipe in a few seconds. You can get yourself down under the sink and work at it. That's where you'll find the clog. Every time. And then you pull the gunk out of there and reconnect the pipe and everything's good as new.

Drano is for the lazy. A pipe's one thing, not a million like bugs. You can't squash one of them and walk away smiling. Kevin Naugle has no sense about anything. You have to pick your fights and take the best tack. It's how we get along in the world. It's how we make do.

We get what we deserve, I think, imagining Kevin Naugle discovering the evil in his science, his sins of pride being punished through his daughter. And I'll admit it's an evil thought in its own self, but then there comes riding up the knowing that I have troubles in my own house and all of them well deserved. So there is no gloating about any of what is in my head and won't shake loose. I remember that girl's musical voice, and that is something, and I can believe, at least for a while longer, that some sort of better luck might befall us because otherwise we'll have to childproof our house like we're parents to sons and daughters who cannot help themselves.

A ROOM OF RAIN

———

"You come away from that television set and watch this show right here in your own back yard," my mother shouted through the screen of the open living room window, but I waited until the commercials came on before I went outside.

"What show?" I said when I reached the back porch. I couldn't make out anything special because it was raining, a drizzle, the kind that I walked in fifty times a year without an umbrella while she lectured me about how I'd have pneumonia before I knew what hit me.

There she was standing in it, her hands out to the side like she was a little girl who had the day off school, like I did, for Veteran's Day. "Come over here beside me, Bradley," she said, using my full name like she did when she wanted me to know the words were important. I didn't mind. The rain, thin and soft, felt good. "Isn't this the cat's meow?" she said, but after a few seconds I was thinking about how the commercials would be over in a minute, maybe less, while she took my hand and said, "I have a surprise for you." And she walked me, I swear, just seven steps before the sun came out. There wasn't a cloud in the sky. Not one.

"Well?" she said, and I ran back into the drizzle and then out on another side, only six steps until I was in the sun again and could see around the edge of it to where she was standing. It was raining only in our yard, and not even the whole yard at that, just the part up against the back porch on the side where the Daigenaults lived.

I know what you're likely thinking, getting ready to go back to your own television shows, but even now, fifty years later, you can find our rain mentioned in those books full of lists of the biggest and smallest and oddest things to ever happen to anybody on this earth. The World's Smallest Rain—there we are because we ended up with the witnesses you need because while we walked around that rain, my mother told me she'd already called the airport where somebody was always interested in the weather. "You had your nose glued to that tv, but I kept watching out the kitchen window while I talked to them to make sure it hadn't stopped. They're on their way. It took some convincing, let me tell you."

She had her camera, too, the little Kodak she kept handy by the phone "just in case," and she told me to stand inside the rain. "Now outside," she said, and I positioned myself with one foot in and one foot out as she laughed and snapped away before she stepped back and took the whole thing in from the Daigenaults' yard.

We had ourselves a room of rain outside. And it lasted for more than two hours, long enough for the weather people from the airport to examine that shower for almost an hour before it dried up and let the sun shine on all of our yard, including that small, damp part as big as our kitchen.

"Aren't you glad you listened to your mother?" she said when it was all over.

"Yes."

"A boy who didn't listen would have stayed glued to the television and missed the whole thing."

I thought about the old movie I was watching when she called, the Dad from *Father Knows Best* all made up a long time ago to look like he'd been burned and scarred. He was supposed to be a World War II veteran, and by the time my mother called me outside, I could see what was happening, he and this homely woman going to a cottage where they turned better looking when they were inside. I wanted to know how it all worked out, whether they stayed inside that little house the rest of their lives in order to look handsome and beautiful or if they really knew they hadn't changed at all.

The weather people decided the small rain was somehow connected to the air conditioner in the Daigenaults' house, but they didn't say how, and there was no way to prove themselves right except them saying, "What else could it have been?"

"A miracle," my mother said. "A sign." But just like the weather people, she couldn't prove it unless something strange happened or the rain came back in a different part of the yard.

She watched the yard the next day. She tried not to let on, but I saw my mother leaning over the sink to look out before I left for school and, that night, how she kept herself in the chair she never used because it sat in bad light for reading in order to face the back window in the living room.

Me? I switched on the television because I didn't expect something so weird to happen twice. If nobody had ever heard of such a thing, it wasn't going to happen again any time soon. And if it did, a tiny rain like that, and it fell somewhere else, that would ruin it, like a new set of quintuplets getting born and all of them living. Nobody would care about another batch like the ones in Canada my mother and father had gone to see just before my sister Eileen was born, holding me up to look at all five dressed the same in Quintland, the place where they came out to play while people watched. My mother talked about them so much that when I was in first grade, I asked to go back so I could see them again with Eileen. "They're not being shown anymore," she said. "You'll just have to remember as best you can."

My father believed in the weathermen. "The Daigenaults," he said, "they're always running that air conditioner of theirs like it would kill them to break a sweat, and here it is November and Armistice Day already, and we're not at the equator even if snow would be a surprise in January. You mess with your weather long enough, you start to get the world into wrongness."

"Veteran's Day, Bob," my mother said. "They changed the name four years ago."

"You can't change something by calling it a new name," my father said. He never complained about how hot it was when we moved south just over a year ago. He knew my mother wanted an air conditioner. She'd lived her whole life, like all of us, up by Cleveland, and she wasn't anywhere near being used to Louisiana.

"There's no way that bitty thing could make it rain for hours."

"Who did? God?"

"Maybe so," she said. "Maybe we've been picked out for a special something we need to be ready for."

"You keep wishing, Gladys," he said. "Next thing you know, we'll be in heaven."

She looked at me. I'd stopped eating. "Bradley stood in that rain with me," she said. "If you'd gotten wet, you wouldn't talk like that."

"I believe that part, Gladys. But you didn't see God. I know that for a fact. The Daigenaults don't even go to our church."

When the television station called my mother and said they wanted to film her standing in our back yard, I asked to stay home from school, but my father took me down the hall before he told me "absolutely not." My mother didn't follow us. "This isn't a good thing, Brad," my father said. He was knotting his tie, tugging so hard I thought he could choke himself.

"Being on television is the coolest thing in the world."

"Never mind what you think. You ponder what I've said for a minute and you'll see." He tugged the knot, centering it between the tips of his collar before he buttoned them down. "All harnessed up," he said while I counted seconds in my head, but he started to leave just before I reached twenty-two, so I quick-said, "It's been a minute, and I don't see what's wrong."

He laid his hands on my shoulders and squeezed while I stared at the blue tie that split his pressed white shirt. "Then you'll just have to watch and learn."

That night, after I'd told my teachers at school to stay up late to get a look at my mother on the news at eleven o'clock, I settled down beside her to watch while my father sat in a chair off to the side where he could see without looking like he was paying attention. "An unusual story this evening," the anchorman said at 11:28. The segment was right at the end, after the sports and the weather. *The Last Word*, they called it. On the screen my mother was standing exactly where the rain fell, and she held out her hands the way she had, looking up like she expected the rain to begin. "It was real, all right," she said. "The weather people came and saw it all before it went away."

They showed the Daigenaults' air conditioner unit where it sat next to their house. "Conditions appear to have been perfect for a man-made shower," the announcer said as she looked up at the sky for a moment. "This is Ellen Garleaux for *The Last Word*. Good night."

My mother was angry. "I told them that wasn't true," she said. "I talked to them for fifteen minutes and said how you could see the rain didn't reach to the Daigenaults. I showed them my pictures as proof and said it was a sign of something we just had to wait for."

"It was good," my father said, and I knew right off what he meant by that.

"Good I got fifteen seconds for seeing such a thing? And not a mention of me talking about Brad. I even mentioned you."

"Even better then they shut you up the way they do."

"You know what I wish about all this?" she said then, and when my father didn't speak, I said, "What?"

"That Eileen had lived to see that rain. She'd have laid herself right down on that grass and let it soak right in. She'd have thought it was a dream come true."

My sister Eileen had been a Comet-Girl. Twice a week she went to Gym-Starz in Cleveland, where a woman who once had been the second alternate on an Olympic team trained girls and boys to flip and tumble and balance in ways that frightened me and my mother but thrilled my father. He'd signed her up before she started kindergarten because, he said, "She's a natural."

I'd seen Eileen do cartwheels like other little girls, but my father was impressed by the way she danced with him when he played the jive music he loved. As soon as Eileen heard Louis Prima or Cab Calloway, she ran to his arms and he'd lift her over his head while she squealed and shrieked, jump, jiving, and wailing like Louis Prima himself was twirling her. My father would toss her up and catch her. He'd swing her in a circle, her legs outstretched so her body was nearly parallel to the floor, and when he was exhausted, she'd ask to do it again.

There were only a few boys among the dozens of girls at Gym-Starz. The ones Eileen's age were called Meteor-Boyz. If I had been different when I was four, my father might have signed me up, but by that time I already grew tense as soon as he lifted me, and my fear made me cling to him. "He's so careful," I heard my father telling my mother, the word sounding like "stupid" when he said it.

For a few weeks, he asked me to relax, and then he didn't ask, dancing alone with a bottle of beer in his hand, my mother long ago letting him know she wasn't interested in any dancing except where two people held each other close and moved slowly to songs about love's joys and heartaches. Maybe five nights he danced by himself before Eileen, almost two, began to beg him to throw her around.

"There were good times before our troubles," my mother would say. "You have to remember that."

I always acted like I did, but even though back then my father traveled less and Eileen was there, seven years old, I remembered how there weren't any visitors but grandparents. Nobody my parents' age ever sat on the living room furniture. I'd visit my friends and imagine their mothers and fathers coming to our house for dinner, what they would talk about while we ate. That last summer in Cleveland, it would have been the *Andrea Doria* colliding with another ship, and all those passengers drowning when it sank. Or Egypt taking over the Suez Canal and acting like they wanted to start a war, both things happening near the end of July.

Those news items were on television, and my mother watched the early edition at ten o'clock the nights my father was on the road somewhere. She let me stay up because it was summer, but Eileen had to be in bed by nine. She said, "This is for grown ups. Are you big enough to watch?" and I would sit beside her, hoping this would be one of those nights when she wouldn't turn it off after the sports and weather, an old movie keeping us on the couch until midnight.

It was August 1 when Eileen drowned, and the television didn't come on again until September when we moved. Whatever happened with the Suez Canal took care of itself without us knowing about it because we didn't get a newspaper and there wasn't a radio in our car. The house was so quiet I started talking to myself out loud, the grass nobody cut for a month up past my ankles, the pool turning as algae-filled as the scum-covered pond at the end of our street.

All those people on the *Andrea Doria* who'd drowned? I wondered if they were at the bottom of the ocean or if somebody had pulled them up like my mother had done for Eileen.

"My sister is dead." I said that sentence to myself every day for weeks, but as soon as we moved, I didn't say it any more, and it was like I'd never had a sister except when I saw her clothes hanging in the closet in the room next to mine. Each time some strange boy or girl in my new school asked me if I had any brothers or sisters, I said, "no," and it was true.

My mother, a month after we moved to Louisiana, began to sleep in the room that Eileen would have used. "It's just gathering dust," she said. "Nobody will ever visit with us way down here in Louisiana where nobody ever heard of us."

My father didn't say anything except "As long as you keep her things in there where they belong."

But right away, when there was an open house at my new school a month after we arrived, I found out my mother was prettier than the other mothers of kids in my class. Most of the mothers were fat or wore clothes that didn't fit them just right like my mother did. I watched those mothers for an hour and decided that my mother was dressed as if she expected to meet somebody, that she dressed each day with hope.

By the time of the tiny rain, we'd lived in our house for more than a year, and I was at the junior high, where boys and girls from four different grade schools came together, something I thought would make it easier, more kids to find friends among, more kids who felt like they didn't know anybody because three-fourths of them were from some other place.

It was worse. Four times as bad, and that was just among the seventh graders. There were five other grades in that school, including seniors like Bryce Daigenault and his friends, the girls with them looking more like my mother than the girls in my classes.

And right after school began, there were tryouts for a football team for boys in seventh and eighth grade. My father, when he heard about the team, took me to the baseball field that was sitting empty at the end of our street and threw passes to me. "Relax your hands," he said every time I dropped the ball. "You're fighting it instead of catching it."

The football was new, a regulation one. Until then I'd been happy to chase after the half-size, soft ball my mother had given me when I started first grade. "You turn your head like that, you're going to get a face-full, and then you'll be sorry," my father said. "What are you afraid of?"

I shook my head and said "Nothing," but he threw the ball harder, and I batted it away without even trying to catch it.

"You must get this from your mother," he said. "The closest she's ever come to relaxing is when she's asleep. She's the same now as she was when you were born. Are you?"

"What?"

"The same. You're twelve years old already. You want to grow up and be stuck with who you are right now?"

Half the boys in seventh grade tried out, but I didn't. When I was watching television instead of going to the first practice, my father took the football and poked a hole in it with a screwdriver before he dropped it in the wastebasket. "We won't be needing this any more," he said.

I walked to my grade school, six blocks away, for that first year and then to the junior-senior high that was right next to it. I didn't have to sit beside anybody on a school bus like the kids who'd gone to the other three grade schools did when they started seventh grade. Nobody knew I had a sister who'd drowned. Nobody ever ran to catch up with me as I walked, and I always made sure I didn't catch up to anyone else.

When it rained in our yard, after my mother was on the news, there were kids who slowed down as they passed our house, but there was nothing to see. Our house was the same. They stopped looking in a few days. It would have been better if our house had burned down and our charred and soot-covered furniture was sitting in the yard.

Then it was time for report cards and teachers talking about Thanksgiving, so everyone forgot about it except Bryce, who always held out one hand, palm up, smiling like he'd never get tired of that gesture, no different than a simple wave.

On *Father Knows Best*, Bud was having problems with a girl. "Pretty soon you'll be worrying about the same thing," my mother said, but Bud looked old, like Bryce Daigenault, who was a senior in high school and drank beer on his back screened-in porch when his parents went away.

"How old is the Dad?" I said.

"Robert Young? I don't know. Older than your own father, I'd bet."

"He was in a movie the day it rained in our yard."

Just then the show ended with things turning out ok like they always did. "What?" my mother said. "On television?"

Commercials came on, one of them about a car dealer in a town I knew was close to where he lived now but I'd never been to. "He was ugly in it."

"That can't be. It wasn't Robert Young then, especially if it was an old movie."

"Yes it was. He was ugly in the movie, not for real."

"Those old movies are always on. You'll see it again some time and you call me over to take a look. I'll come running."

"It was ancient. Pretty soon it will be something nobody will ever want to watch anymore," I said. "Robert Young doesn't look like anybody's father. I bet you wouldn't be married to somebody that old."

My mother put her hand on my knee the way she did when she wanted to change the subject and be serious. "Do you worry about us?" she said. "Our family?"

"No," I said, trying to stop her from talking because another show was starting.

"What does worry you?" she said. "School? Girls?"

"I don't worry."

"You sound like your father," she said. "And he's not even around."

I was lying. But I couldn't take it back. "Worries are for women," I said, and she slapped my face.

I didn't move. I could feel how my cheek was flushed where she'd struck me, but I acted like she hadn't touched me, putting my hands in my pockets. "I know you don't mean that," she said, getting up from the couch. "I know you in your heart."

She walked up to the television and switched it off. "Maybe next week Bud will have a different problem," she said. "Maybe his little sister will die." She had her back to me. I watched her for a minute before I left the room, and I never saw her move a muscle.

The Saturday morning before Thanksgiving week I heard my father go into the room where my mother slept, and I listened for a minute to hear if he opened drawers or closets or even sat on the squeaky bed, but I didn't hear anything. It was as if I'd made a mistake, that he wasn't in there at all, and I slipped into the hall to look through the open door.

He was standing beside the card table my mother had sitting beside the bed. There wasn't any other furniture in there except for the bed and

a lamp, and I could see there were photographs laid out on the table, the
ones from our two hours of tiny rain, and I wondered whether he'd found
them like that or he'd spread them out to examine.

When he turned, he didn't say anything, looking back at the table and
the bed as if he needed to see them again in order not to forget what was
there. Right then I wondered whether he'd ever been in that room since my
mother had begun to sleep there, whether he was trying to learn something
from those pictures and didn't want me to know he was studying them.

"I don't know what that business was all about," he finally said. "You
think you've seen everything and you haven't."

"It seems like."

"I wanted us to start over when we came all the way down here," he said.
"Do you know that?"

"Yes," I said, although I thought, at that moment, that he meant just
himself.

"Things change, and you think they're different, but they're not," he
said. "Does that make sense?"

"Yes," I said, meaning it this time, and he nodded like he'd expected
me to agree.

He opened the closet, and I saw that every item was one of Eileen's
Gym Starz outfits. All of Eileen's regular clothes were gone. He ran his
hand along the length of them until he touched the last outfit on the right.
"Here's what I bought for her for the day she joined *Andromeda*. Just one
size bigger because she was so good I knew she was going to move right up."

When I didn't say anything, he stared at me. "*Andromeda*," he said. "You
know what that is—the girls' traveling team, the one that has their scores
kept and goes to other towns all over Ohio?"

"Yes."

"You know all about it? You ever look that up in a book to know what
that constellation looks like? You ever look up in the sky and see that
beautiful girl made of stars?"

I started to leave, but he grabbed my arm and held it so tightly I winced.
"What's in your closet, Brad?" he said. "Toys?" For a moment I was sure he
was going to drag me into my room to look, but he let go, closed the closet,
and disappeared down the hall.

Eileen hit her head is what the doctor said. She was likely unconscious when she went into the water. She could do back flips and she could swim. And that day, while I followed my mother as far as the kitchen door, watching her talk on the phone for what she said, later, was "a minute, maybe two," Eileen had probably tossed herself backward off the edge of the pool and slipped as she pushed off, tumbling backwards so awkwardly that her head hit the side of the pool.

"Bradley was right there where I could see him," she told my father, "so I thought Eileen was right nearby because she'd been told."

My father had glared at both of us—my mother for being negligent and me for being obedient. I was so afraid of everything that I always obeyed. I knew exactly what he thought. If I'd run off like Eileen, I would have seen her fall and she'd still be alive.

The day after Thanksgiving was warm, and Bryce had a friend over who was throwing a football around with him in his back yard. After a while Bryce signaled him to run farther for each pass until he ran half way into our yard, the long spiral landing softly on his outstretched hands, but tumbling off and bouncing against the house. "Good hands," Bryce shouted, and the other boy, as he picked up the ball, sneered at me as if I'd laughed out loud.

"You think you could catch it, twerp?" he said.

"Maybe."

"No chance in hell," he said, and I watched as he took a few steps closer to Bryce as if he was distracted rather than shortening the distance because he couldn't throw the ball that far. When he finally let it go, the ball wobbled and nosed into the ground at Bryce's feet. "Johnny Unitas," Bryce said. "Have another beer."

When I heard somebody laugh, I saw there was a girl sitting on the Daigenaults' screened-in porch. The boy who'd dropped the ball looked back at me and said, "You think it's funny, you little pussy? Huh?" I didn't say anything, but I wished I had because there was no way that boy could come back and beat me up, not a twelve year-old in front of Bryce and that girl.

When my mother stepped onto the porch a moment later, I thought she might have been listening by the window, trying to learn what my life was like by overhearing a part of it at a time. "Your father's leaving," she said. "Go outside and tell him goodbye."

For years, she had told me to give him a hug when he was about to leave, but that afternoon she didn't, and maybe because she said something different, I didn't get up at first. Just for a few seconds, but my mother noticed because she said, "He's your father" before she turned back into the house.

My father was already out front beside the car. His suitcase was on the front seat, and he was closing the passenger-side door. "I'm off," he said. "Back to the old grind."

"See ya," I said, but I stayed by the door, holding it open with one hand in a way that I thought would make him say, "You'll let the flies in."

He had a tie looped around his neck, but it wasn't knotted, and his shirt was still open at the collar. He glanced down and held both ends of it with his hands as if he'd just remembered to tie it, but then he let go and walked around the car, opened the door, and got in without speaking again.

That night, after I watched television for two hours straight without my mother telling me to shut it off, I went outside at ten o'clock when the news came on, taking a beer out of the refrigerator and replacing it with one from my father's case in the pantry. I walked down to the baseball field, sipping the beer, but it tasted awful, and by the time I got to the field, I poured half of what was left on the ground by home plate, so what I was carrying was nearly empty, and I could imagine feeling different.

I cut through all the back yards on our side of the street to get home, dumping the rest of the beer on the Daigenaults' lawn and tossing the can into the trees that bordered their yard. The can snagged on some branches, scraping against them before falling, and when I heard a sound from the Daigenaults' porch, I thought I'd been seen, that somebody was about to stride across the lawn to run me into the woods to retrieve that can.

I ducked down, but nobody stepped off the porch. I heard a girl's voice, soft, nearly purring, and I crept closer, making out Bryce and a girl from the high school in the dim light that seeped through the Daigenaults' blinds. "We see you out there," Bryce said. "You can stop acting like it's hide-and seek."

I stood up. The girl and Bryce both had their shirts off. There were beer bottles on a table. The girl was fat in her stomach and her breasts, without a bra to hold them up, sagged like she was older than my mother.

"It's rain boy," Bryce said. "You want a beer?"

The girl laughed. "You getting a good look?" she said. "You a little peeper?"

"You should have waited a few more minutes," Bryce said. "You would have seen everything."

The girl didn't laugh this time. She hooked her bra on and buttoned her blouse. "You're a real shit," she said to Bryce. "You and your skinny pervert neighbor."

Bryce winked at me and took a long swallow of beer before he turned and followed the girl into the house. "Hey now, baby," he was saying. "Hey now, baby." He didn't close the door, but I thought if I took even one more step closer Bryce would come back out with a gun and shoot me, still smiling like we were friends.

When I turned, I stepped into the flowerbed Mrs. Daigenaut had planted the length of the house in the back. Three of the flowers were bent under my shoe. Even though it was November, they'd been in bloom for two weeks and were fading, but for a moment I stared at the broken stems before I started to run, slipping, and catching myself just late enough with my hands that I knew there would be a grass stain on my right knee.

Inside the house, I rubbed at that stain for a second before giving up, and I thought of all the stories I could tell somebody like Bryce if I didn't run away like a baby. My life was full of them, and not only the small rain. My sister's dying in our back yard swimming pool while my mother answered the phone that rang just as she unlocked the gate to the fence that surrounded it. "You stay right there," she said, and I did, following her inside and listening to her talk while Eileen drowned.

"Who were you gabbing with that was so important?" my father asked the day after the accident.

"Grace Yerger," my mother said. "She called me."

"And you had to run back in and answer like it might be the President calling from the White House."

"The phone rings and you stop what you're doing to answer," she said. "That's the way it works, Bob. How else is there to find out who's calling and what they might need?"

"Grace Yerger calls every day, and it's always about church and some do-gooding she's up to."

"Not every day."

"You two yakking it up so you didn't even hear Eileen splash. If it had been Jesus his own self, I wish to fuck you'd have let it ring."

"You don't mean that," she said, and my father stared at her, taking one deep breath before he said, "I'd rather be in hell than have my daughter dead."

When I walked into the living room, my mother was sitting in the chair that faced the back yard. "I was just watching the news, and when I shut it off, I sat here to think for a while."

"What about?"

"I hate the South," she said. "Here it is almost December and as warm as April. It makes your thoughts get crooked. The trees and such never get a chance to rest." She looked at me. "Bradley, does it seem like that to you? Keep you up at night?"

"No," I said.

"Because you're young, likely as not. You might turn out to be Southern, and I wouldn't care for that."

"I lived ten years in Cleveland," I said. "That's long enough to remember winter forever."

"That's good," she said. "Weather's important to who you are. I was thinking it won't ever snow like it rained for us. Not here in this yard. If we get that special weather, it will be just like before."

I didn't know what to say next. I sat with my back to the window and waited for her to go on. "Your father is such a realist," she finally said. "He doesn't imagine the world is anything but what he sees."

I wanted to talk, but I had to swallow the way I did when we had to sing by ourselves in front of the class for a music test at school. "Are you listening to me?" she said, and I heard myself say "Yes" in a voice so high I sounded like a girl.

"Your father thinks I don't know what he does because I'm not there to see." I waited, listening to the way air whistled when she breathed through her nose, thinking maybe there were words in there. "He travels a lot," she said. "Are you following me?"

"Yes," I said, my voice back down to boy-sounding.

"So you know?"

"Yes." My mother didn't speak then, and her breath was like mine, quiet because she'd opened her mouth and let the air come silently to her.

"Your father has a friend in town," my mother said. "You understand what I mean by a friend?"

"Yes."

"Do you now? Just like that?"

I nodded because I did, just like that knowing my father had a woman like Bryce Daigenault had that girl on his porch, that right that minute he might be with her in another room, believing he was happy.

I sat up straight and waited, but after a while I knew she was looking out the window rather than looking at me. I didn't move or turn my head. There, in the dark, I knew she'd tell me if something happened outside.

After a while, when she didn't say anything else, I thought my mother, sitting like she did with her legs resting across a soft, cloth-covered stool, would fall asleep in her chair. I didn't want to be awake and see her asleep like that, someone for whom it didn't matter where she slept. But for a few more moments I sat there and decided she was thinking about the rest of her life and whether living in that house with my father was something she could manage for even a few more weeks.

She should have told me to leave the room, but maybe she wanted me there because I reminded her of the miracle we'd shared. It rained only on us for two hours, and everyone knew the rain was real and not made up like spacemen and Bigfoot and the Loch Ness Monster. I could stand exactly like my mother had when I first saw her in the rain. I could lift my head up and keep my eyes open and remember how her blouse stuck to her body and showed how beautiful she still was, as if that rain had chosen her to fall on.

And what I wanted to tell her was how terrible it was that my father was always going to come back.

THE WORST THING

———

You don't expect to know murderers when their stories make the newspapers. Not if you're normal. Not if you own a house surrounded by other well-kept houses.

But there she was on the front page, Amy Bender, a face I recognized, and she'd killed her own baby, one just a minute old. Given birth in her bathtub and let her newborn daughter drown. Told her boyfriend to take the body outside and throw it in the garbage, making sure it was good and covered by whatever else was in the can.

It's hard to read these things. I know I stopped a few times that first day of her news and sipped coffee. I ate a third chocolate-iced, custard-filled doughnut, what I haven't done for ten years or more. And there I was just retired, two weeks into the first summer that wouldn't end the last Monday in August when school took up again.

Those fourth graders would get along without me. The school had hired a woman who was younger than all three of my daughters, and though her age didn't bother me, it mattered to me that I'd been the only male teacher at Governor Snyder Elementary School, and now there it was—all women again, kindergarten through fourth grade at the school named after the one Pennsylvania governor who'd ever come from our county. Like the old days, the '50s, when I reached seventh grade before I ever met a man in school.

"You won't even know you've retired until September," my wife kept saying, but Connie was wrong. I felt like I'd died, like I'd been buried and the dirt piled on. "You just need something to keep you busy," Connie said, and there was some truth to that.

She'd been a teacher too, thirty years and out four years ago even with the three girls of her own to tend along the way, somebody content with weight-control swimming classes, book club meetings, and three days a week of volunteer work. She'd taught Spanish at the high school in the same district where I'd taught, and she'd counted down the last fifty days on a big sheet of paper she stuck to the refrigerator with magnets. "It's different there," she'd said of the high school. "Not as hopeful. Even the good kids are hard now."

For years people had remarked that the two of us were inside-out: Connie at the high school like a man, me with the young like a woman. And then, these past ten years, that sort of thinking slowed down and nearly stopped, muted like all the opinions about gender and race and ethnicity that people learned to at least keep to themselves.

But that baby-killing woman, that Amy Bender, she'd had a boy in my class last year and a girl the year before. I remembered those two children, both of them terrible students, the kind you know won't finish high school, the girl likely to be pregnant by sixteen, maybe sooner. You're not supposed to think that way about nine and ten year-olds, but there's no denying experience.

Right then, as I read about their mother while I crammed that extra doughnut down my throat, I wondered where those children, just ten and eleven years old, had been when all this was going on. And that article, as if the writer understood what any reader would want to know, answered that question on page two: Tennessee. I'd thought the boy had just followed his sister to the middle school, but in fact his father had taken him. The girl, too, though the whereabouts of her own father remained unknown.

"There's something that calls for the word *piacular*," I said to Connie.

She made the face she uses every time I mention one of the rare words I'd started studying during the last three days of school when there was nothing left to do but collect books, fill in report cards, and show a movie approved by the principal before following my class outside, rare-word dictionary in hand, for what the school called "Field Day Olympics."

"Ok," she said now, "get it over with."

"It's an adjective that means 'requiring atonement.'"

"*Piacular*," she said. "Nobody ever uses that word because it doesn't mean anything to anybody."

"You've been telling me for years to get a hobby," I said.

"It's not a hobby," she said. "It's just you reading one book you bought when we were in Harrisburg for Memorial Day."

"Reading's a hobby."

"No, it's not. It's just what anybody does who has a brain. Book club is a hobby."

She gathered up the box the doughnuts had come in as if she needed to get the last two away from me. "*Aboulia*," I said. "Have you ever heard that word spoken?"

"Of course not."

"It means 'loss of will,'" I said. "It's a perfectly good word. It's not the word's fault nobody knows it."

"Yes, it is," Connie said at once. "If the word was any good, people would use it." She moved my place mat and squirted Windex on the glass-topped kitchen table, beginning to wipe it down.

"Sometimes they get used. There are words in that book I bought that I've actually heard of."

"Name one," she said, not moving to her side of the table, which looked spotless though she'd eaten one glazed doughnut herself.

"*Karoshi*. It's Japanese."

"I don't speak Japanese."

"It means that you die from overwork. You wear yourself right out."

"Those Japanese must have a lot of teachers," Connie said, "but you don't need for them to give you a word for what you already know. You're like somebody who watches reality shows and knows the names of the people who get thrown out in the first few weeks."

"Bloviate," I said. "I read that word in the newspaper last month."

Connie replaced the Windex in the cupboard above the stove, and for a moment I thought she was going to give in. "Not our newspaper," she said at last. "That's a big city newspaper word."

During July, I went once to Connie's swimming class and twice to her book club. If I had been alone, I would have left swimming after five minutes when I found out we were doing something like treading water, only easier because we had little inner tubes to keep us up so we could walk in the water as slowly as a bride coming toward the altar. Worse than that, the bodies of all the men were horrible, like premonitions I didn't need to see

"You can't quit everything after one try," Connie said, and I agreed, choosing to go back to book club because it was twice a month instead of twice a week, so I had time to convince myself it wasn't as boring as I'd thought it was listening to women talk like Oprah, acting like saying "I was so moved" meant the writer had accomplished something special.

When I returned, though, the library where the meeting was held served refreshments, and I was stuck holding a cup of green tea and watching women eat honey-bran muffins dusted with sprinkles colored red, white, and blue for the upcoming holiday. The woman who led the discussion sat so straight that two crumbs from the cake on her fork fell across the swelling of her breasts and lay there, balanced, while she ate as if she were being tested and points might be deducted for bending over the table or allowing her left arm to leave her side. It was only when she lifted her napkin to her lips after three bites that she noticed the crumbs, brushing them into her napkin, then taking a new one to press to her lips after two more bites.

"You get your own things to do then," Connie said when I vowed never to go back. "Don't ruin it for me."

The drowned baby case reappeared in the newspaper the following week. A trial date had been set for the beginning of October because Amy Bender, after confessing in detail, had retracted her statement and intended to plead not guilty. "They'll say she's insane," Connie said.

"It says in the paper that the boyfriend is sticking by his story."

"The guy she told to throw the baby in the garbage?" She tore her doughnut in half and put the uneaten part back in the box.

"He'll testify. He'll say she knew what she was doing."

The boyfriend had kept the body instead of dumping it. He'd tried to bury it. "Like the proper way," he'd said, though that turned out to be inside a plastic bag and under a pile of leaves when he couldn't make a hole in the ground deep enough with his hands. According to the newspaper, he was mentally challenged.

"Retarded," Connie said. "Why don't they let reporters use real words? They almost sound as bad as those things you come up with from reading your book."

"*Leighster*," I said, and though Connie shook her head in a way that said, "Stop it." I went on. "That's the word for 'female liar.' See? We need that word to get this situation just right."

"Is there a word in that book for a man who lies?"

"Not so far."

"There won't be. Think *bitch*."

"This isn't about politics."

"A liar's a liar then. Female's got nothing to do with it."

It seemed to me that it did, but until I found an archaic or rare word for a male liar, I had to let it go. "It sure sounds like that boyfriend's retarded," I said, moving on as best as I could.

"It makes you wonder when you walk in the woods," Connie said. "There's no telling what's there. That could have been you finding that child with all the walking you do. You should be keeping an eye out."

"There can't be another dead baby so soon in the same town. It's crazy to think that way."

"No, it's not." Connie looked out the window as if she were thinking about going for a walk. "So what do you think," she said, "isn't this the worst thing possible?"

"There's always worse," I said, though right then nothing came to me.

"The pessimist," she said. "Like you can come up with something awful nobody's even thought of yet."

"Somebody will do it for me. All it needs is a name."

Connie turned toward me again. "Get something besides doughnuts when you go for your walk," she said. "Get something healthy for once."

When she got up and left the kitchen without wiping the table, I finished her half-eaten glazed. Doughnuts don't keep, let alone one broken in half.

The last time I'd seen Amy Bender in the flesh was at the school spring open house the year before. She'd shown up right at nine p.m., the time everything ended. The last of my students' parents was leaving as she came through the door. Some of the other rooms were already dark, the teachers gone. "It's some job you have, isn't it?" she said, staying near the door where the students' "Skeleton Stories" were posted on a bulletin board.

"Do you have questions about your son's progress?" I said. She bent down and peered at the stories. "Roy's doing fine," I added.

When she straightened, I thought she was going to approach my desk, but she stayed beside the door. "You don't have to lie to me," she said. "My kid's dumb as a stump. He gets it from his Dad."

The light went off in the room across the hall. She turned to watch Mary Cressinger close her door and disappear down the hall, and then she took two steps to the side and checked the bulletin board again. When she bent down to see the lowest row of stories, her skirt rode up her thick thighs.

"Here it is," she said. "Roy's masterpiece."

I knew what she was seeing. Her son's story was three sentences long, all of them beginning with "skeltens are . . ."

" . . . skery as a monster."

" . . . skiny as a witch."

" . . . spooky as a ghost."

"He got one right," Any Bender said, but she didn't say whether it was spelling or semantic accuracy she was talking about. All of the adjectives and nouns her son had used had been listed on the blackboard before the children wrote. The next shortest story had six sentences. A small skeleton, skinny as an icicle, had walked into school and eaten so much pizza in the cafeteria that it had turned into a fat boy.

"Where do they get all these ideas from?" she said. "Do you tell them stories?"

"We read."

She stared at Roy's story a second time. "Will he be bringing this home before too long?"

"It's his to keep after they all come down next week."

"Good," she said, and finally she stood up straight and looked directly at me. "Roy's happy here, right?" she said. "He don't act sad?" When I nodded, she didn't say anything else.

Connie was right to tell me to cut down on the doughnuts. I'd started walking for the exercise but always ended up stopping at the grocery store, just over a mile from our house. Going that direction meant I had to pass the school where I'd taught, and for over a month, I'd made a right angle turn on the sidewalk, not saving even one step by cutting on a diagonal across its parking lot. But one morning in August, when the playground was empty, I veered up the grassy slope and slipped through the gate in the fence that ran a few feet above the street. Nostalgia, I thought, a way to look in the back windows where my room had been located while I saved a bit of time and energy.

That was my intention until, just before I reached the fence on the opposite side, I noticed a condom beside the sliding board. A used one, stretched and limp. Something that must have been dropped there the night before because surely the custodian or a mother bringing her small child to the playground would dispose of it immediately.

I looked at the sliding board and tried to picture the couple. I lay on the slide to feel what it would be like to be the girl on her back as she draped her legs over the sides. The boy, I thought, would have had to have pushed her up the slide because it seemed impossible to reach her if she were lying near the bottom.

From where I lay, I was facing the rear of the school. A janitor worked nights during the school year, but his shift changed to daylight in the summer. He could have been watching me right then. Maybe he checked from time to time as a sentry against men who might be loitering to watch children play.

I sat up, bent over, and lifted the condom carefully between the tips of my thumb and little finger, the small weight of it reminding me of how my mother had always made me spit my chewed gum into a tissue and wrap it before I could throw it away.

I looked under the see-saws and the swings before I carried the condom to the trash barrel by the gate, but the ground beneath them was bare. I peered into the trash barrel, but all I could see were soda cans and the empty bags that had held potato chips and pretzels. I dropped the condom, and it looked so terrible draped across a soda can that I reached down and stirred the cans until it was covered. I had to fling two ants off my fingers when I was finished.

For the next three nights, I rented movies to watch with Connie, timing them so they ended late enough that we went directly to bed. It was all I could do not to tell her I was going for a walk at eleven o'clock. And though I passed the playground earlier each day, it was another week before the yard was empty when I approached it. I walked past every piece of playground equipment, but there was nothing but ordinary trash on the ground near any of it.

By the time September began, with both of us home in the middle of the morning, we sought out different rooms. I read for an hour. Then I just sat there with my feet up, thinking about watching television, but embarrassed to turn it on at 10:30. Because she didn't read except in bed, I had no idea what Connie could be doing, and when I finally came out of the spare room at 11 o'clock, she was putting on her jacket. "It's my day at the day-care center," she said. "I'm having lunch with Ellen Foster before we sign in for our five hours."

"I'm having lunch by myself," I said, "before I go crazy."

"We've never lived together like this," Connie said. "It's different."

"We've always only had summers together, three months at a time."

"Those were vacations," she said. "This is our regular life."

"You mean you can't stand having me around all day."

"Not exactly."

"I bet there's a word for that version of 'not exactly.' I bet married people invented it while they waited out their last days together."

"Maybe you could substitute," she said. "Work off some of that energy."

"Maybe not."

Connie frowned. I could have told her I'd already thought of that and decided it was impossible, that the classroom had to be mine or I didn't want to be there. It was like having children. I could love my own three daughters, but I could never adopt. It sounded like selfishness, something to never say.

A week later, when I shuffled out of the spare room at 10:15, she told me to get in the car. She drove for ten minutes and pulled off the road in front of a house so new the yard around it was bare earth. There was even a wooden plank to walk on in order to reach the front door. "Come inside," she said, producing a key "Take a look."

The house was small—two bedrooms, one bathroom—like the one I'd grown up in with my older brother. "What do you want me to see?" I said.

"This is a Habitat house. We were going to start painting the inside this weekend, but the construction foreman said to give him a few more days."

"You want me to help when you're ready?"

"It would do you good."

"How many are there of you?"

"It varies," she said, and I knew that meant the number was small. "This isn't book club. We're doing something here."

"I think I'll go to the trial," I said. "The baby killer's. It starts in a week."

Connie nudged a leftover sheet of wall board into the center of the room where we were standing. "I hope it lasts as long as OJ's"

"That's not likely," I said.

"Neither was his. It was open and shut, and look what happened."

"I want it complicated. I want it to be like school. You'll be happy to know I put in my name for substituting."

"Good," Connie said.

"They'll probably not even call me," I said. "They had three young women last year who substituted, and all of them applied for my job. One of them got hired, so the other ones will try to keep their hands in."

"Those other two have moved on," Connie said. "That's how it happens. But don't expect to be called right off the bat. You know that teachers never miss school the first few weeks. You just have to wait until reality sets in on them."

"I'm counting on it. That trial is right around the corner."

"Maybe not. It will take a while to choose a jury for something like this," Connie said. "You might be teaching again before they find twelve people around here who haven't already decided they'd like to drown that woman themselves."

It took three days to pick the jury. I stayed home after the first half day of listening to routine questions that eliminated dozens of people who said, flat-out, they'd made up their minds or they would always believe the word of a police officer more than that of someone who wasn't.

For a minute, outside the courthouse, I stood among a small group of men who'd been dismissed, all four of them stopping to light cigarettes.

"That bitch gave herself a Polish abortion" I heard one say, the death of that child become an ethnic joke.

There was a parking ticket under the windshield wiper of my car. Ten dollars, it asked for. "Pay within 48 hours or be subject to an additional fine." I looked at my watch and saw it was nine minutes over the two hours the meter allowed. I noticed no one in uniform on either side of the street. It must have taken a few minutes to record my license plate number. I subtracted until I decided there was an asshole on the job, somebody who started writing up the ticket while the last minute or two counted down on the digital timer. But when those smokers walked past me still laughing, I thought I deserved to be fined for saying nothing about cruelty.

By the time they'd chosen a jury it was Friday. Monday was Columbus Day, something I realized only because court was closed. I walked to the grocery store, and for a moment I was surprised that the school parking lot was full of cars and yet mothers with small children were in the playground. In-service day, I remembered. A way, besides relaxation, for teachers to use a holiday.

At the grocery, a mother of one of my final-year students stopped me by the bakery. The boy I'd had acted shy when he saw me, like the fathers of the children I'd taught, rural men who came to conferences wearing ball caps and bowling jackets. She had three more children with her. "Eight, six, and seven months now for the little girl," she said.

"You have your hands full," I said, and she didn't smile when she answered, "That's for sure."

"I wanted all my boys to have you," she said. "Their father flew the coop after I started showing with the baby, and they could all use a man." I watched, alarmed, as the baby squirmed in her arms, arching back so violently that she seemed likely to tumble to the floor.

"I didn't expect the little one would see you at the blackboard," she said. "Last time we met I was big as a house, but I thought you had enough juice left for the boys."

"Forty years," I said. "A nice round number."

She looked puzzled, and then she pulled at the baby, repositioning her. The boys had disappeared into another aisle—magazines, I thought, candy. "Well," she said, "we all make do, don't we?"

"Most."

"Is that so?" she said. "I didn't know there was another choice." The baby was chewing on her collar. One of the boys, the youngest, reappeared carrying a cheap plastic toy. "Put that back," she said, and when he answered, "Want this," I pushed my cart toward the case where six varieties of muffins were displayed. When I passed him, he slapped at the cart. "Want this," he said again as if I might pay for it. When I turned into the next aisle, not stopping, the baby began to cry.

You'd think you would have heard everything nearing sixty-five with forty years of teaching inside you, but I sat in the court room on Tuesday and heard the coroner testify that Amy Bender had stuffed toilet paper down the baby's throat. A wad of it. Blue. To make sure that baby would die and not somehow breathe in water like it had gills.

The defense lawyer didn't cross-examine, but there was a murmur in that courtroom. And I knew I'd made a sound in my throat and let it loose. Something between a moan and a cough. It didn't sound like anything I'd ever uttered, but the judge looked right at me sitting by myself off to the side, nobody near me.

Which was something else I wondered about—why hardly anybody had come to watch and listen. Now that the crowd of prospective jurors had disappeared, it was like a funeral with just the minister and family. As if the dead had no friends. As if maybe those few were there by obligation, seeing to it that things didn't fall apart, the dead just discarded like there was a plague or a war.

The next day two policemen testified, but after the business about the blue toilet paper, their stories sounded so tame I thought the prosecutor had handled things wrong, that he'd given up the punch line before telling his awful joke. By the third day, when a psychologist claimed that Amy Bender was sane and then spent a few hours being questioned by the defense lawyer, anyone could tell the district attorney was sprinting toward a verdict.

On the fourth, and as it turned out, the last day of testimony, there were exactly twelve spectators in the courtroom, as if we formed another jury. I was younger than most of them, and I wondered if the older ones attended trials as a hobby, whether they sat through DUI hearings and divorce proceedings the way some people sit through television.

Someone here, I thought, must be related to Amy Bender, but there was no telling who. The three men were older than I was. Two women were of an age that could make them her mother, but neither of them sat alone.

In the morning, the boyfriend testified. He spoke like a child. "I was scared," he said. "I knew Amy had hurt the baby bad." He looked straight at the lawyer as if he was being photographed for a driver's license. "I gave it a nice place. I said a prayer for it."

"What did you say?" the district attorney prompted.

"A prayer. You know. Now I lay me down to sleep. That one."

"Thank you."

The defense lawyer made it seem as if that boy wasn't so dumb he might have planned the murder, that he might have thought to pray when he realized what he had done. This is what it is to be court-appointed, I thought. Seeing to it that Amy Bender wasn't just thrown into the river inside a sack full of stones while an audience applauded.

Amy Bender testified right after lunch, the only defense witness. "The baby was born dead," she said. "I panicked." When the public defender asked why she had said otherwise when arrested, she answered, "I was so afraid, I got confused."

There was a moment before the district attorney rose from his chair to cross-examine, and I spent it looking at Amy Bender, who had the first signs of gray beginning just above her ears where her hair was cut nearly as short as a man's, even the longest part of it barely reaching the collar of the jacket of her tan pantsuit. The gray-haired mother—the phrase sounded like the beginning of an essay about the weary and impoverished. It was more than hair color—she was soft in a way that made her shapeless. She had a belly on her, and I thought it was possible she was pregnant again. This woman looked like a grandmother, and yet she was thirty-three years old.

Had she shown gray eighteen months ago? I wasn't sure, just as I didn't remember how fat she'd been in the belly. And now she wore a pantsuit that looked new, but out of style. It made me think of a woman I worked with who'd worn pantsuits every day, a wardrobe of them, settling on a fashion so comfortable that she didn't notice when other women left them in closets and finally in boxes beside the Goodwill bin. It made me think she wanted to cover every part of her body.

Connie was paint-spattered when she walked into the house at five o'clock. *Habitat*, I thought, and saw that she'd painted in one of the shirts I'd still worn for teaching last spring. "I thought you just worked on weekends," I said.

"Old people can paint on Wednesday," she said. "It's like jury duty. Haven't you noticed?"

I hadn't. I couldn't remember the face or age of any juror. "What?" I said. "You think everybody on the jury is retired?"

"Old people decide who's guilty and who's not. We're justice."

"You declared her guilty before the trial started."

"That's why we're needed," Connie said. "So at least some people get what they deserve."

I didn't go back for the verdict the next Monday morning because the phone rang at 6:45, and by 8:30 I was a teacher again, welcoming third graders into the room beside the one I'd taught in. The eight-year-old boy I'd seen in the grocery store sat in the third row. "Caleb's brother, right?" I said, and the boy looked around at his classmates to see if they'd noticed.

"Yes," he said.

A girl raised her hand. "You're Mr. Steinmetz," she said. "My brother had you, too."

To my relief, they settled down to reading and stayed quiet through social studies and spelling. At lunch, the radio in the teacher's lounge announced that Amy Bender had been found guilty. "The jury was out less than an hour," the newscaster said.

By afternoon the class was restless, and so was I. I looked out the window and saw the playground. A woman had strapped her small child into what my students, despite my reprimands, had always called "the retard swing," and she was pushing it in small arcs. There was another hour, and all that was left was a lesson in fractions. Half the class was whispering to each other in pairs. "Hold on a minute," I said. "What do you call it when you say you're sorry for something wrong that you did?"

Three voices chorused, "Apology."

"What do you call it when you're so angry at the person who apologized that all you can think of is 'You should be sorry.'"

"Mad," a girl said, and I shook my head.

"Pissed off," a boy called out, and the room hushed, waiting to see what I would do.

I shook my head again, but they were stumped. *"Antapology,"* I said, and I printed it on the board.

"Cool," said the boy who'd offered "pissed off," but I could see that most of the class was already drifting.

"I want to tell you a story about the worst thing that ever happened," I said, and they sat up like the jury had when Amy Bender had testified.

"It's a short story," I said. "A baby is born. A little boy. But his mother is a witch, and he is so beautiful she never feeds him, and pretty soon he's so skinny he's almost dead."

"That sounds like Snow White," the girl whose brother had been in my class said, "only with a boy."

"But if she doesn't feed him, he won't get to grow up, so he won't even have a name."

The girl frowned and glanced around the room as if she expected somebody to take her side. "No witch is that mean," she said. "She'd at least wait until she found out if she had a good reason to hate him."

"That's what makes it the worst," I said. "She doesn't want to wait."

I walked down the aisle, brushing the tops of their heads with my hands as I spoke. "She doesn't want to wait until he's in school. She doesn't want to wait until he can talk and tell stories, too."

The last two rows bowed their heads as I approached. I'd never had such silence in a classroom. It seemed a miracle that they had lived. "There's a word for that," I said. *"Ugsome,"*

"That's not a word," the girl said, but she looked around the room to see if anyone had heard it before.

"Yes, it is. I found it in a book. It means 'really horrible.'"

"Like when you say 'ugh' when somebody pukes?" Caleb's brother said.

"Worse than that," I said, and then I stopped. For a minute, I'd been eager to speak, but now all of my forty years of teaching checked my tongue. Now that I was back in the classroom, I wanted to be called again.

They watched as I spelled *ugsome* on the board. "Sometimes there's only one time for a word to be used," I said, and they all stared at the blackboard. "Once you use it, you'll never hear it again."

Nobody spoke. "Now," I said, "I want you to write the end to that story I told you. Make it turn out the way you want it to."

A girl began to cry. "What if it's too late to save the baby?"

I looked at the blackboard before I answered. "Here's one thing I didn't tell you," I said. "Even though he was so skinny, that boy was still beautiful."

The girl smiled. Then they all began to work. Twenty-six third graders concentrated, their heads down and pencils moving.

THE VISUAL EQUIVALENT OF PAIN

How many times have I heard some guy say, "I want to kill the bitch"?

For sure, more than I can count on my fingers. But not lately, not since I turned forty and had fewer friends who got drunk and ranted. So it sounded ominous when Frank Wertz, fifty-one years old, made that declaration less than two hours into drinking nothing but beer, long before he had the excuse of his brain turning to mush.

Frank Wertz was hating his ex-wife so much in words, he looked up at the sky as if he wanted God to hear better. Sam Pagala and I looked up too, taking in all those ancient patterns, suggestions from the imaginations of people so long dead, it felt like we were sharing something important for a minute the way a six pack works on the ordinary.

We were standing in Frank's back yard a year after Sharlene had left him for a man she'd been sleeping with for months. A year. It had been so long, he caught us by surprise with his threat. He had the windows open and the speakers near them so the "misery mix," tunes he'd burned onto a CD especially for tonight, pumped into the yard. It had started with a song Sam and I didn't know called "I Hate Everything about You," but once that was over the rest of the tunes sounded familiar: "The World is a Ghetto," "Backstabbers," "You're So Vain," all the angry songs from 1972 when Frank would have been sixteen or seventeen like us and maybe muttering aloud to his high school friends about what he wanted to do to some girl who'd turned down his invitation to the prom. On either side of us, the neighbors' houses were dark, but we'd started so late it was nearly time for someone to call the police, something that Sam, with twenty-eight years on the force, had pointed out half an hour earlier when Frank had taken the cooler of beer into his back yard.

There had been six of us before we'd followed Frank outside, but three had considered their drives home, what it took to manage without incident, and opted for leaving. Sam and I lived in town, a mile or so, a few stop signs and streets narrowed by parked cars, routes we'd managed through years of drinking with Frank, who loved to host in the summer because it meant he could choose the music that worked as a soundtrack for his stories about camping and canoeing, hiking trails where the state park explorers never ventured.

Those stories always came last, a signal that the night was slowing down, all of us holding our last beer, because, among us, only Sam was an outdoorsman. So we could leave, the rest of us, mid-excursion, without insulting Frank, those of us who took our hikes on treadmills in local fitness centers and used rowing machines if we wanted to paddle without worrying about how deeply or swiftly the water ran underneath us.

Frank kept a set of free weights in his basement, a weightlifting bench set up so the stereo washed directly over him as he lifted without a spotter. He didn't tell stories about what he could bench press or dead lift, and that made his stories about isolation and danger easier to take, something like Sam restraining himself when the world's weaknesses were the subject, talking more about places and people than he did about the crimes. We all knew Frank could double our bench press limit; we all knew Sam had seen the results of gunshots and knives and knotted stockings.

What else we had in common? We were the three men among us whose marriages had failed. It seemed natural for the others to break off and go home, like those huge chunks of ice that tumble off the edges of glaciers and drop into the ocean.

Sam had been divorced twice, which seemed to show he'd made his peace with failure. Shortly after Sharlene had left, Frank had asked Sam and me what had ruined our marriages. "Fucking other women," Sam had said at once, smiling.

We'd been in Frank's living room with the television tuned to a basketball game on mute. The image flickered in my peripheral vision because I'd moved to a chair that faced away from the screen. Frank and

Sam looked past me half the time, keeping track of the game, but now Frank stared at me, waiting.

I glanced back at the television. A commercial for a telephone company was on, the one with the nerdy guy repeating, "Can you hear me now?" a slogan I'd heard customers repeat inside the library every day for nearly a year, making me hate them. Frank held his stare.

"Boredom," I'd finally said.

Frank nodded and drank from his beer. "Sure," he'd said. "Sure fucking thing."

Now Frank looked at both of us. "I'm in a terrible fix here," he said.

I hoped Sam would offer advice, even something useless like "Give it time," but all he did was bring his bottle to his mouth like there was something left in it besides an excuse for silence.

"I feel like I've shrunk. You know, like people can tell I'm smaller the way anybody over thirty looks when they're doing one of those shit jobs like stocking shelves or delivering pizzas. You know, you see them in the fucking grocery store all hunched over beside a cart full of cereal boxes or canned soup; they're fucking disappearing right there as you pass."

"The sky does that to you," I said, and right away I wished I hadn't because Frank looked at me in a way that made me turn my head.

We all stood there then. Sam's car was behind mine in the driveway, so he needed to leave first. There was no way I could be the next to speak, but I felt lucky not to be Frank.

"So many stars," Frank said, finally shutting up about Sharlene. He kept looking skyward, but after being his friend for ten years, I knew he didn't think anything was there but animals like or unlike us. "Some of them are looking our way," he said, "but they sure as hell aren't raising the dead and tending them like sheep."

His voice went hoarse, the way talking takes your words after a while on the late night road to silence. "You ever smack your head hard enough on something to see stars?" he said.

"Yeah," Sam said while I was trying to remember if I'd ever actually done that or just seen the stars hovering around the heads of a hundred comic book characters who'd banged their head on something.

"You know what those are? They're the visual equivalent of pain."

Sam didn't say anything and neither did I. The misery mix ended, and suddenly the back yard was so quiet I remembered watching the stars at the Buhl Planetarium in Pittsburgh when I was a boy, how the chairs tilted back like I was at the dentist, and this voice spoke as if it were talking from the sky, giving instructions about distance and time while I gave in to wonder.

The next day I was at the hospital, regretting the night before and feeling sorrowful about my prospects. The barium shake I was forcing down tasted like the terrible strawberry of the bubble gum that drops out of the machines in convenience stores; I had half a cup to go when I saw Sharlene standing in the doorway.

She looked at the cup in my hand. "You having an upper GI?" she said. "Yes."

"You have a problem?"

"Let's hope not." I'd complained about heartburn to my doctor. Every day, I'd said, not saying anything about how I'd kept thinking I had a heart problem until I got so used to it I knew it was something else.

Women in uniforms—the fetish-site phrase came to me as she took a step into the room. For a moment my apprehension was muted by the distraction of her body. She wasn't a beautiful woman, but she was a woman a lot of men would think about wanting to get into bed with if they saw her. A young-looking forty. I thought it was because she'd never had babies, but she looked fit, like if you unbuttoned her nurse's outfit and saw her stomach, that it would look like a girl's, smooth and flat and slightly-rounded as it takes the start of that breath-taking curve under the waist band.

Maybe it was because Frank was past fifty like I was and Sam was, so she had the advantage. "All these machines," she said. "They can see every last inch of us."

"I bet."

"Sometimes I think I'll see somebody's soul. You know. It has to be someplace inside you; it's just a matter of time before we'll be able to see its condition like any organ's." I didn't put much faith in that possibility, the best reason I had for going through this exam. "You'll do good on your test. You'll see."

"I hope you're right about that."

"Your color's good. You'd be surprised how much you can learn from just that one thing."

"I would be," I said. "There's no doubt about that."

She looked behind her into the hall where I couldn't see and then back again. "I have to go," she said, though I could tell she hadn't seen anyone, that she'd just run up against the end of things to say about my health.

"Of course," I said. "You're working and I'm just visiting."

She smiled, but she'd already taken two steps back, her body outside the door. I could hear something on wheels coming down the hall, but the sound stopped before anything passed by the space I could see. She paused for a few seconds, resting a hand on the doorframe before she spoke again. "What's the weather like on Hudson Street?" she said. "You know."

"Cloudy."

"I'll bet."

"Then you know already."

"I guess that's true."

After Sharlene disappeared, I had nothing to do but listen closely to the burning in my chest, what had brought me to the hospital after it had reappeared every day for three months. I'd looked up the choices for what I felt and where that discomfort was located. Acid reflux was the best, the kind of problem that's just an embarrassment. The other choices were ones that would change me forever—ulcers, or worse, cancer. They called up every eating and drinking vice I had, from greasy food to all-day beer. And it didn't miss my notice that cancer of the esophagus had a miserably high percentage of killing you within five years.

Two days later, I had good news. All I had to do was be sensible when I ate, buy a giant-sized bottle of Tums, and prop myself up in bed. I thought of celebrating with a cheeseburger and fries, but I roamed the aisles of the grocery store looking for items that said fat-free. *I can do this*, I said to myself, though the choices were bleak, the packages covered with the words *baked* and *lean* and *soy*.

I microwaved the best of the lot—low-fat chicken with Chinese vegetables and rice—and settled down in front of the noon news. *Breaking News* was flashing on the bottom of the screen, the announcer describing the kidnapping of a woman from the hospital where she worked as a nurse. "Believed to be her estranged husband," the announcer said. "At gunpoint."

There was a stand-off in progress as I began to watch, and when the overhead shot zoomed in, I knew enough about the make and model of the car to eliminate all of the other nurses and put Sharlene inside that green Plymouth with Frank.

There was concern about the woman's condition. The police were there in force, still talking with "the suspect" when the on-site reporter declared a shot had been heard. The announcer described the police movement as "cautious advancement." I poked at the broccoli and carrots and tiny, brittle pieces of chicken with my fork until an ambulance pulled up, and I could see Frank and who I figured for Sharlene being taken away.

I sat in front of the television for another hour, but there weren't any more updates. I kept wanting to open a beer, but I stayed downstairs with my cold, ready-made healthy dinner, and stared at the soap opera that ended and was replaced by another. I looked away then, focusing on the hundreds of CDs I had arranged on two shelves that were built into one wall of my basement above the television. Frank loved the way they were ordered from soft and slow to loud and aggressive. "By fucking mood," he'd said once. "What a great fucking library for sound. You ought to do this where you work and let people know where the books are for when they're sad or happy or pissed."

"The best books cover everything," I'd said.

"That's a short shelf then," Frank had said. "That's one you could empty with one hand."

For a few minutes, I thought I wanted to play something aggressive but sad, but all of the titles made me think of those times in a music store when I'd gotten depressed and decided there was no point in ever buying even one more CD.

I didn't want to slip into wanting to throw them through the window into the yard, something I'd done once with half of my collection of vinyl, relieved, the following morning, to find only a handful of the records had skidded out of their sleeves. So I walked out the back door and away from anything of my own I might harm.

For a while I just hiked fast, surprised how long it took to get away from houses. As I walked, I imagined my wife unfaithful, her making a choice for the other man. The humiliation. My anger.

I've kept a gun in my house since the day I moved in with my wife and two sons. The gun, I told Helen, came with owning something so large, the need to protect it. When she threatened to throw it into the river, I explained to Helen that it was taped to the underside of the bed where the boys wouldn't see it, but my hand could find it coming out of sleep to an awareness of an intruder.

Once the boys were grown and gone, Helen hadn't complained about the gun being there. She never mentioned it or anything else she disapproved of until she'd filled her van with boxes and suitcases and stood in the driveway with the van idling to say, "It's all yours, Harry. Now you can put your pistol under your pillow like James Bond."

Facing traffic, I thought I was going to imagine shooting her, but nothing showed up in my head. Nothing whatsoever except the darkness of anticipation, what it might be like before being born.

Big thoughts. That's what my father would have called my ideas— getting into territory for which you're not equipped. "You're getting things inside that head of yours that it's not large enough to hold," he'd say. "All this mooning around won't get you anywhere."

My father had done the same thing as I did when I was thirty years old—built a house in the country and seen it surrounded in five years when three farmers sold their land to developers. The year I was nine, just before building began the second summer we lived there, he'd taken me through what he knew would be the last crop of corn. It was August, the corn as high as it would get. He must have known I'd be frightened walking among the stalks in the dark.

The field was full of rustling and scurrying noises that made me stop to look down so often he said, "The things that live here aren't interested in you, Harry."

After a while we came out of the corn into a bare space where rocks were scattered. Some of them were enormous, ten feet long, six feet thick. "How many tons do you think they weigh?" he asked.

"Ten," I answered at once, and when he said, "Guess again" I knew my answer was foolish.

"A hundred."

"Maybe."

"A thousand."

My father climbed onto the largest stone and lifted me up so we could see over the top of the corn in every direction. "Look at this," he said, but all I saw was corn all the way to faint lights where I thought the houses on our street had to be.

He kept standing there, not speaking, and I slid down to scramble over the rocks as if I was exploring another planet. A minute later, I stepped on a stone that shifted under my weight and turned my ankle. I sat on a boulder and held it. "Oh Christ," my father said, climbing down. "Put your weight on it. Walk it off."

I worked to keep from crying and limped into the corn, following him. I kept falling behind, and he would slow for a few seconds, but never stop. I was panicked. If I lost sight of him I thought I would be lost forever.

It took a long time to get through the corn. Maybe half an hour with me hobbling like I did. When we emerged and saw the six houses on our street, I sat down where our lawn began and listened to the pain flooding up my leg. Now that I didn't have to keep up, I wanted to crawl to our back door. "See?" my father said. "See what you can do when you have to?"

A rustle in the field I was passing snapped me out of remembering so fast I nearly lurched sideways onto the highway. Just some animal, I said to myself, but I kept an eye on the swaying weeds until the traffic thinned enough for me to cross the road. The news report at five o'clock said Sharlene was dead.

Frank had sex with her before he shot her, the newspaper said the following morning, and Sam confirmed it. "In the fucking back seat," he said. "Like they were at the drive-in or something." I stood in the doorway to the kitchen. Behind me, on the counter, a package of skinless turkey cutlets was thawing. "Frank's going to live," Sam said. "He's through with playing martyr."

Sam's tone made it clear he would have had some respect for Frank if he'd outright killed himself, but I was stuck on the last minute sex and what either one of them might have been thinking while he fucked her.

I thought of Sharlene in her uniform, the way I'd looked at her the day of my upper GI. I felt like I'd pulled that gun from under my bed and shot her myself.

There was a mystery beyond the old story of loss and anger. "This will settle him down," she might have thought, but I knew it was foolishness to guess at something like that, a kind of secondary rape that made me uneasy with myself.

"He let her fix herself after," Sam said. "She was all buttoned up. It was the autopsy that showed us what went on just before. I have to tell you it lowered my opinion of Frank a considerable notch or two."

Like always, Sam didn't speak to the damage a bullet in the head does, and I was thankful for that even though I knew a little about how an exit wound might look in a situation like that. He toed the carpet with his shoe, rubbing it in the way you might scuff out a small anthill you want to discourage. He watched his foot as if he expected something to move, but it was a carpet in the middle of the living room I never even sat in since Helen had left. "When you were married," he said, "did you ever think Helen was cheating on you?"

"No," I said at once, and Sam nodded like he wanted me to see he'd never thought that about his wife as well.

"What a thing," he said, "thinking another man was inside your wife. It wouldn't sit well."

I thought he was trying to work up an excuse for Frank, that there was justice in what he'd done despite Sam's years of being unfaithful, but then he said, "Imagine if Frank was married to the Virgin Mary. How things would have turned out."

"That wasn't him," I said. "That's over and done with."

"Yes, it is. And so is this."

"He made a choice."

"He fucked up is how I see it," Sam said. "Majorly. He had no claim on her."

I could tell Sam had tried to find something valuable among the mess of this and failed. I didn't blame him. Frank had been a friend, but now he was lost to both of us. The only difference was Sam had tried harder to hold onto something, so maybe that explained what he said next, beginning with "I can't abide this. Absolutely not."

I looked it up after Sam left, the thing Sharlene had mentioned about how
the soul might be examined. What I found was that in 1907, a doctor
named McDougall had put dying patients on a scale, noted their weight
to a fraction of an ounce and waited. Joyfully, he measured one less ounce
when they were dead, proof, he thought, that the soul had escaped to
heaven or hell.

The hardest part for McDougall was waiting. Each time he wished
hard for weight loss, and then he began to watch the chest of each dying
man, sure this magic flew from the heart. There was a blur, he thought,
when the body lightened.

As a control group, McDougall tested dogs, who lost no weight
whatsoever, the air around their dying unchanged. I thought of Helen,
what she'd make of the shooting when she read about it in the newspaper.
When I couldn't shake it, I called her.

"He's your friend," she said. "It passed through my mind that maybe
it was your gun he used on her."

"You liked Sharlene," I said. "I thought you might want to talk."

"Ok, Harry," she said, but it sounded like she wanted to hang up until
she paused and started again, using a tone I hadn't heard the last few
months we'd lived together. "Here's a story that might explain a few
things."

She paused again. "I'm listening," I said.

I heard her exhale, and then she started. "In England, once, there
was mechanic who worked on airplanes, and he found this pin in the
lift mechanism that didn't fit quite right. Instead of spending the time
to find another pin, he sawed that one off a bit to make it fit better. You
know what happened?"

I was sure I knew, but I said "No."

"The plane crashed. Sawing that pin reversed the effect that thing was
supposed to have. It made the plane go down."

"I get it," I said, and Helen stayed quiet so long I thought the phone
had gone dead.

"Really," she said, as deadpan as a judge.

"Yes," I said. I didn't elaborate, but I knew she meant for me to
understand that the mechanic had committed something worse than sin
because he'd ruined other people rather than just himself. That's who hell is

for, she was saying. Not for ordinary sin, or else everybody would be there, people like me who made promises to themselves they never kept, the usual kind about bucking up under pressure, being someone who controlled his weaknesses and didn't fall back on alcohol for comfort or excuse.

Right then I wondered if people could ever be happy together. I'd never heard anybody talk about it over drinks. If such a relationship existed, it was something between you and a woman you loved.

I'd seen Frank once in the three days between that night in his back yard and the murder. He'd walked into my office in the library. "You have time for a beer?" he'd said.

It was just after one o'clock. "At four thirty," I said. "Sure."

He'd nodded like he knew what I'd say. The way he looked around the office made me reconsider the globe I had on a shelf, the drawings of famous old libraries. It was like being a politician with photographs of presidents on the walls. You had to hang old ones up there or else visitors would judge you by the faces you displayed. "You ever get discouraged by all this?" he'd said. "Not being able to keep up with all the books?"

"No."

"What do you think makes people keep writing stuff? There's already more books than the world will ever need and not enough readers for them."

"I hope that's not true," I'd said.

"It's a museum is what it is," Frank said. "I'd go crazy if I had this job." He watched me for a few seconds until I said, "Why's that?"

"It's not what you think," he said. "It's not because I don't read. It's because you're by yourself, and even if somebody's here, there's always silence. Libraries give me the willies. There's not even one of those radios coming out of the ceiling. Christ."

"To each his own," I said, a stupid thing to say.

"Fucking-A it is. I could hit somebody in here. I could smack one of those shushers. Don't you ever want to do that?"

"No," I said, though it was a lie.

"Shhhh. Even when I was a kid, I hated anybody who said Shhhh in school. Who the fuck did they think they were, a goddamn teacher? And I sure as hell hated the teachers that said Shhhh."

"There's places that need to be quiet," I said.

"Shut the fuck up," Frank said in a way that spoke to the past and the present. He grinned then, the way a boy happy to get away with something would.

Frank's eyes skipped from side to side as if he wanted to see somebody looking at him, one of the men still young enough to fight if he called him out because he disapproved of him talking out loud in a library. In another few seconds, I thought, I'd have to tell him to quiet down and then he'd say, "Sorry, ok" or "Who says?' or "Fuck off," deciding which way the afternoon would end.

"When you were growing up, did you ever see a librarian who was a man?" he said, quieter now, nearly a whisper, so I knew he was calming down.

"No," I said.

"I always thought you needed to see what you might become," he said. "You notice what's what when you're a kid, and it sticks to you. Nurses are all women; secretaries are all women; your teachers in grade school are all women, what everybody sees like that."

"Not always."

He looked around the room as if he wanted me to see the evidence that only a certain kind of person sat in a library, that there was something about the old men with their newspapers that proved his point so that when he shrugged and left without saying anything else, I'd have something important to remember.

My story with Helen was as familiar as the road you take to work each morning, the one you barely notice as you weave through traffic and listen to music you would never buy and play inside your house. I hadn't been angry or jealous. I'd said, "Whatever you want," like a man who hadn't loved her for years.

Which made me wonder about Frank, how someone could feel so strongly about someone that he had to destroy her. And himself. Or maybe it wasn't hard at all if your anger rose from such love. What did I know about intensity, the life that follows from it?

He put the gun to his chest when the time came. And he fired, I'll give him that. He blew out a lung and under other circumstances than being attended to immediately, he would have died.

But there they were, the police and the paramedics called in with hope for his wife already dead in the car. So I'm thinking he hadn't the nerve, that he gave himself a chance with where he placed the gun. That he wanted to save face in front of that firepower they had pointed his way.

But Sam Pagala knew better, what with being there, and so did I, just hearing it from him. If Frank wanted to die, all he had to do was point that gun at the police. It didn't take a bullet in his brain or heart, just the thought of it aimed at those uniforms.

And isn't that the issue here? Didn't he want to show them? It seemed an awful thing to think—that carrying an anger like Frank's might be a good thing in a world where people fall away from each other so easily.

You can't have that, I told myself. Absolutely not. But it took me a long time to shake it, thinking there was a misery inside of getting along with everybody that was just this side of hell.

ROGER THAT

———

Roger Wharton, the man who lived next door, recited the names of all the vice-presidents in order: William King, John Breckenridge, Hannibal Hamlin, Andrew Johnson. He was a whiz. Schuyler Colfax, Henry Wilson, William Wheeler, Chester Arthur. The only time Pete Logue and I knew Wharton wasn't making up those names was when a president got assassinated and somebody we'd heard of took his place.

"Roger that," Pete Logue said when Wharton finished up with Lyndon Johnson.

"Before you have your dads buy you encyclopedias, you come talk to me," he said, moving on to the categories for books in the Dewey Decimal System while we finished the Cokes he'd opened for us in his kitchen.

As soon as school ended in June, Pete Logue and I, the only boys on our street between the ages of eight and fourteen, did just that, drinking his Cokes while we listened to him recite on Wednesday and Saturday afternoons. I was eleven, Pete was almost thirteen, so neither of us could do anything but spend time together unless I wanted to play with seven-year-old Jimmy Meenan, or Pete tried to make friends with fifteen-year-old Victor Hutka, who had sideburns, a mustache, and a car he drove without a license.

Roger Wharton lived by himself in a house that stood between mine and Pete's. "He came with the neighborhood," my father said. "He and his wife Susan in that big house with no kids to use it."

My mother had explained, once, that the Whartons had moved in when they were still under thirty, expecting children, and when they didn't arrive, stayed on, filling their eight rooms with souvenirs from traveling during the six weeks Wharton took off each summer from his job. "His dental practice," my mother said, a strange way of putting it, especially since our whole family was his customers.

We'd lived on Cranberry Street since the year I was born, four years before Susan Wharton had died in a car accident, falling asleep at the wheel a thousand miles from that house, her husband walking away, my father said, without a scratch when they were broadsided on the driver's side. Seven years now he'd been alone in that house, so his wife was a photograph to me.

"It was after his wife died that he started to come up with all these lists," she said. "It's like since he stopped traveling, he had to collect something, so he started in on whatever he could accumulate."

"Something he doesn't have to cap or clean or polish," my father said. "Something he doesn't have to take care of. Nobody needs to know these things." He drove a truck, spent a hundred nights a year or more sleeping somewhere else. "I know the names of the roads when I see them; I know where they go. Wharton couldn't find his own back door in the dark."

"He's an educated man," my mother said, looking out the kitchen window at Wharton's weed-filled, uncut lawn, the burned-out shrubbery he hadn't replaced since I could remember. "It's not in his nature."

"He's long ago gone to seed," my father said, and that was the end of it until the next time my father noticed one more unkempt thing in Roger Wharton's yard.

He didn't seem to know that Wharton's shrubbery looked better on the side of the house that faced Pete's room. It was all rhododendrons over there, which I took to mean they were hardy and needed no care to blossom every May while half the azaleas on our side had failed and worse, the junipers had overgrown and split, parts of them sagging and brown, the rest of them towering green above the roof line. My father, looking from our porch, said he thought Wharton must feel guilty every day when he saw his yard looking like a mouth full of cavities, something you couldn't get anymore unless you drank Coke and ate candy all day.

What I never mentioned to my parents was the tone of Wharton's voice changed when he was reciting lists. The rest of the time he sounded like a dentist, someone who knew the secrets you kept. I thought about how he could see how careless I was about brushing my teeth, that I never flossed.

His dentist voice was the kind that sounded like a grandfather, a man used to seeing others, even adults, as children. But when he did lists, he sounded like a kid. He never sounded like a man his age, like a father, Pete's or mine or anybody's I knew. It was what made me think, sometimes, that my father was right to dislike him.

"Listen to this, boys," Wharton said one afternoon as we drank Cokes in his living room, the two of us sitting on his couch while he pulled a chair up close to face us. "Collective nouns. You know what they are?"

We both got that look that comes with not doing homework the night before an oral quiz. "A school of fish," he said, and we nodded.

"Everybody knows that one," he said, "but try these on. A pace of asses. A shrewdness of apes. A knot of toads. A bale of turtles."

We waited, but that's as many as he listed. Pete shrugged, but I was enthralled. *A shrewdness of apes*—who thought up this stuff? And where did Wharton find it?

"Roger that," I said, because these were exactly the things I wanted to know. The only list I knew was all the letters for Morse Code, the dots and dashes from a to z. I'd been in Boy Scouts for six months. Pete had quit two weeks after I joined, and by now he couldn't remember any letters except the dot for e and the dash for t.

"Boy Scouts," he said the week after he quit. "Have fun."

But he had to admit Wharton was infallible. Even when we picked the category, South American countries, instead of letting him decide, he named them from Argentina to Venezuela. We asked for the names of everybody on the Supreme Court, and he gave us a roster we had to trust, since we didn't know anybody but Whizzer White, an old football player my father talked about for two days when he'd been appointed the year before by Kennedy.

My favorite was all the bones of the body, the way Wharton showed us just where everything was located, having us touch ourselves in a sort of Simon Says of anatomy. "Pick a spot," he said, and we put our hands on our shoulders (clavicle) and near our eyes (lacrimal). We slapped our hips (pelvis) and our thighs (femur). "You could learn them all," he said. "There are only 206."

Pete put his hands behind his back and shoved one inside his pants. "Tailbone, right?" he said, keeping his hand there.

"Coccyx," Wharton said. "There's a real name for every part of you."

That was the day he walked us down the hall for the first time. "That's my weekend bedroom," he said, "and this is my weeknight room."

He didn't open either door. But there was a third bedroom that was full of the kinds of souvenirs I loved—multi-colored, glittering rocks; slices of tree trunks smoothed and glazed; a hundred different shells, all of them larger than anything I'd ever dragged home from the beach. I'd been in dozens of shops that sold stuff like that, but all I'd ever been allowed to buy were postcards. One wall was covered by a bulletin board plastered with what looked to be fifty bumper stickers thumbtacked in rows, each with the name of a national park from Arcadia on the left to Zion on the right.

"I had a teacher once who had us memorize the national parks," he said. "I did it in one night and then had to wait two weeks to take the test. I'll bet you boys haven't been taken to ten of these so far."

"Roger that," Pete said, and I hoped Wharton wouldn't ask how many national parks I'd been in because the answer was zero.

Two weeks after school was over for the summer, I had my annual checkup at Wharton's office. My mother drove me and waited in the lobby. "It's just a cleaning," she said. "You haven't had a cavity in three years. Why would you get one now?" I thought of all those Cokes, whether Wharton had a mouth full of cavities himself from drinking them when Pete and I weren't around.

Instead of reclining half way like it always did, the chair tilted me back to nearly horizontal. I tensed, half gagging on spit even before anything got started. The dental assistant, who looked like she was just out of high school, had a tag that said Marie, and she stopped reading my old x-ray report when she heard me clear my throat.

She patted me on the shoulder. "Something new since you were here last," she said. She leaned close, her breasts so near to me without touching that I thought she must have practiced this in school, how to stand so that her breasts didn't brush against patients lying on their back. Someone had graded her, maybe, or at least given her advice.

When Wharton walked into the room, he was wearing a surgical mask and a loose green smock, but I could see the top of his blue tie and the collar of his white shirt. "How's that smile of yours doing?" he said through the material that was the same color as the smock.

"Ok, I guess."

"You guess? Marie says it's perfect. Let me take a look, just to be certain. Open."

He was done with me in a minute. "Good until next time," he said.

"Roger that," I said to myself. I looked for Marie on the way out, but I didn't see her in any of the rooms. My mother smiled as she made my next appointment. "Perfect," she said as if she'd been consulting with Marie. "Thank you, Roger," she said then, and I turned to see that Wharton was standing in the doorway. He had his mask pulled down; it hung near his collar.

"My pleasure," he said.

"I hope I'll get as good a report next week when it's my turn."

"Of course you will," Wharton said. "You keep after yourself."

"What do you think a man does in a house alone?" my father said a few nights later as we finished the slices of pie my mother had served us.

"It would depend on the man," my mother said at once. She'd cut herself a piece of pie so thin it looked like an icicle on her plate. "His circumstances."

My father glanced at me as if we shared a secret. "You know who I'm talking about, don't you, big guy?"

"Mr. Wharton," I said, though I knew what my mother meant, that there must be millions of men who lived in a house alone.

"There," my father said. "Wharton. That puts a face on it. What do you think he does? He never has visitors. You never see him outside."

My mother pushed the pieces of her pie crust into a small pile that looked like something you'd put a match to. "He reads. He watches television. There's plenty to do besides entertain."

My father grunted. He liked to have people around when he was home. He'd invite other couples for barbeques or a group of men to play cards.

"Who wants to sit around?" he'd say. "When you're not working, you should enjoy yourself. When I have the yard in shape, I want people to see it."

"He probably has hobbies," my mother offered.

"Hobbies," my father said, making the word sound like smoking or drinking or shooting heroin. "What hobbies do you think a man alone all the time has?"

My mother sighed, but she didn't answer. I went down both sides of our street, listing the names for all twenty-four houses, but none of them except Wharton's had a man living alone in them. "Reading," she said. "Reading's a hobby."

"Reading?" He looked at me again. "Big guy, you think all that reading you do is a hobby?"

"No," I said.

"See?" my father said. "There you have it."

"What do you know, Bill? It's possible a man can enjoy things that you don't."

"He's a man who does nothing is how I see it. When I'm home I have things to do here. Fixing things. A yard to tend to. Wharton either lets things fall apart or hires out."

"He's a dentist, Bill. He has the means. What would you do if you didn't drive half your life and work around the house the other half?"

My father had a thin smile fixed on his face, the kind teachers used when nobody knew the answers in class. "Danny's a visitor," my mother went on. "He and Pete are over there all the time. Roger's not a recluse."

"That's my point," he said. "That's my point exactly." He pushed his chair back and stood without looking at either of us.

"Bill," my mother began, "you're wrong," but my father had his back turned by then, disappearing through the side door into the yard.

My mother gathered up the dishes and stacked them in the dishwasher. "Your father," she said. "Sometimes."

I nodded. I was sorting through all of the points my father could have been making, but none of them made me think "Roger that."

That summer, when my father was on the road, my mother started serving TV dinners. I loved them, especially the roast turkey with the stuffing that looked like a piece of bread turned brown by spices and the salty gravy. "You'll get them as long as you don't tell," she said early on, and I didn't. I knew my father despised food that came ready made. Paying to have somebody do the work you can do by yourself is how he put it. My mother could cook, so why wouldn't she?

My mother would make one for herself and give me the meat and potatoes part after she acted, each time, as if she might eat the thin slice of roast beef or either one of the two small pieces of fried chicken. All I had to do was take my time and wait in order to get doubles of the parts I liked best. She'd eat the peas or the corn or the mixed vegetables and the little piece of cake or cobbler that came with each meal. "I'm always making a pig of myself when your father's home," she said. "He thinks people never change, that I was thin when he met me, so I'll always be thin. If he was home 365 days a year I'd turn into a big fat blimp."

I smiled when she said something like that because it meant the meat and potatoes were coming soon. TV dinners didn't have enough food "to keep a bird alive" my father would say, and he was right about that, but my mother would say, "For a man who's so fussy about everything, he doesn't tend to his own belly."

The first month of the summer, my father made two one-week runs, and my mother fell into the habit of walking to Teresa Savage's house, eight doors down, to play cards after dinner. "Pete can come over, but that's all," she said. "I don't want you wandering around the neighborhood when I'm not home."

I didn't mind. She served ice cream with every TV dinner, never making a bowl for herself, but letting me slip a couple of spoonfuls in her mouth after I put chocolate syrup all over it. "Mmmmm," she said. "If I let myself scoop it into a bowl I'd eat myself sick. Now you and Pete stay out of trouble."

Before she left, she always made a big show of throwing the foil trays away. "No dishes," she said. "That's a bonus. You run the rest under hot water and let it sit out. And you make sure all this goes in the trash before your father gets home and sees what we're up to."

One Wednesday afternoon in mid-July, Pete came out of his house with his hands behind his back. "I got something for us to do besides drink

Cokes with Roger That," he said, and he showed me his father's rifle. "It's just a 22," he said. "It's a pop gun."

I held it like I'd seen men carry a gun in the movies. I felt like I was guarding something, that I needed to keep an eye out for problems.

He put his hand in his pocket and pulled out four bullets. "What do you think?" he said. "Want to shoot at something?"

"What?" I said, looking at the trees across the street.

"Birds," he said. "You can blow a bird to bits with this."

It seemed like something neither of us could do. Birds were small and kept moving unless they were far away. "Ok," I said, confident we'd be done in a couple of minutes, the four bullets used up. It was Pete who would be in trouble if his father kept an exact count of his ammunition.

I was right. By the time I was taking my second shot we'd missed three birds, and all I was thinking about was where my bullet had ended up because the bird I'd fired at was sitting on a branch above us, and there were houses a hundred yards away.

The last bird that looked like a target was on the ground fifty feet from us. I was relaxed by now. Pete couldn't shoot worth a damn either, and when I pulled the trigger the bird flapped once, then righted itself and staggered a bit before hopping "You hit it," Pete shouted. "Jesus, look at it."

He walked toward the bird, and I had to follow. It looked as if I'd nicked its wing, turning the bird clumsy. We were ten feet away, but all it did was run. Except through a window, I'd never seen a bird from this close, and I was suddenly terrified, handing the rifle to Pete and letting him stand over the bird, a robin, as it slowed down.

I wanted it to fly, but only one wing opened. I didn't need somebody's father to tell me that bird was going to be killed by something before too long.

Pete spun the rifle around his finger like it was a baton, and it slipped off onto the ground before he could finish a full circle. "I got it around twice in my room," he said. "It looks so cool."

The bird had settled now, like it had given up. "Your Dad's going to be pissed, isn't he?" I said.

"I'll clean it," Pete said. "I watched what he does. He'll never know, and I only took four bullets. There's no way he's counting that close. Dads never know anything unless you're dumb. Your Dad's the same way. You could get away with anything if you tried."

"No, I couldn't. He's always checking up when he's home."

"That makes it even easier," Pete said. "You only have to be good when you know he's coming." Pete picked up the rifle and twirled it again, finishing a circle before it caught and dangled. "See?' he said. "I'm going to practice until I can end up with the gun pointing at something when it stops, something cool like that." He looked at the bird and the surrounding trees as if he was searching for more targets. "I still can't believe you hit it. How cool is that?"

Two nights later, when my father came home before dinner, we went to one of the drive-ins my father loved. There were seven of them within twenty-five miles of our house, and all of them showed movies we could have seen indoors three months before, but my father said movies were meant for places where he could relax after he'd been driving for a week. What that meant was he could bring a cooler full of beer and a bag of potato chips, but my mother never complained, and neither did I because she always bought us Cokes and popcorn from the counter beside where the bathrooms were, and we watched with him until the second feature ended.

In July that meant one a.m., yet there, when we came home, was Roger Wharton walking back to his house. He was wearing shorts and a tight t-shirt that made him look as skinny as Pete and I were, but nothing clicked because I was groggy with near-sleep, until my father said, "What's he been up to, you think?"

My mother said, "Who knows?" but my father left the car running and nobody opened a door while Wharton, without looking our way, crossed his yard and entered his house. "A man needs to be trusted," my father said.

"You can't expect everybody to be like you," my mother said. "That's not fair."

"There's fair and there's necessary, Arlene," he said. "You get to choose, but a man on foot this time of night is something I'd call odd."

"More people should walk," she said. "Half the world is fat these days."

"You want three guesses to see if you don't start thinking what I'm thinking?" my father said.

"Bill," she said. "Save it for later."

"Maybe I shouldn't," he said. "Maybe it would do some good to talk out loud."

He turned the key then, and I followed the two of them into our house. When I heard my father talking in their bedroom, I was too tired to go to their door and listen.

Pete sighed, but he still went along on Tuesday when Wharton called us over after he saw us in Pete's yard. It felt different being in Wharton's house after supper, and we hadn't been there ten minutes before I had to use the bathroom. When I came out I could hear Wharton talking to Pete in the kitchen. "How many animals that went into space can you name?" he said, for once not listing them.

Pete said, "There was a dog and a monkey, for sure. A chimpanzee, too." He sounded like he was in school, like he was bored and was looking at the clock just before it said 3:15.

"Yorick was first. We sent him up. And then Patricia and Mike. They were all monkeys of one kind or another, and we recovered all three. And then the Soviets sent up Laika. Remember her? The dog? The Communists just let her go around and around until she ran out of air and died."

"That's the only one I ever heard of," Pete said. I could tell he was ready to leave. He'd been complaining about Wharton since July began, sounding the same way he did about Boy Scouts six months ago.

"Gordo," Wharton said. "Sam, Belka, Strelka."

I tried the doorknob of the weekend room, and the door swung open. I kept listening for Wharton's voice while I looked inside. It was full of pictures of Wharton's wife. In the living room, the pictures were of him and his wife together, but here she was by herself in every one—a wedding picture, a couple where she was even younger. As Wharton kept talking, I tried to guess which picture had been taken last, narrowing it down to two in fall foliage that didn't look like trees from anywhere near our street. She'd died in October. The day before, I thought at once, or at least no more than a week before. They might have been developed after the funeral when Wharton picked up the camera and found a used up roll of film inside. I closed the door and tried the knob of the weekday room. The door was locked, and I began to sweat. I was sure the other room was meant to be locked as well, that if Wharton knew I'd opened it, he'd never speak to me again.

I finished my Coke and we left. By now it was nearly dark. "I'm glad he doesn't get to look in my mouth," Pete said. "Molars, bicuspids, incisors or whatever. What's he doing right now, you think? Memorizing the stars?'

"That's impossible."

"No, it's not. There's always some weirdo who knows something nobody else does. There has to be a map. You know, with names on it."

"Who would name all the stars? There's a gazillion."

We both looked up at the same time and immediately looked down. We laughed. "Roger that," Pete said, but a moment later he was wearing his angry face again. "Anyway," he said, "what kind of dentist has a refrigerator full of Coca Cola?"

"He gives it to us," I said. "Maybe he doesn't drink it."

"Get it?" Pete said, sounding exactly like my father at the dinner table, like he knew something I didn't but I was expected to learn.

"My dentist doesn't want to be friends," he said at last, and because the only thing that came to mind was "Why not?" I didn't answer.

"My dentist has us sit up in a chair," Pete added.

"He just started," I said, regretting the story I'd told him about Marie and the new chair. "Maybe he's just trying it out."

"What's a man think about when he has women half lying down like he does all day?" Pete said. "I bet he takes his time with their teeth while he gets an eyeful."

I knew what Pete meant. I thought of Marie, the assistant, and what she would look like lying on Wharton's dentist chair.

"Mrs. Starrett goes to Wharton for her teeth, and she's an eyeful," Pete said.

"Yeah," I said. I'd heard Pete's father say that all the time about the woman who lived on the other side of Pete's house. She'd just been married. "What an eyeful," Mr. Logue would say when she crossed her yard. Even when her husband was walking beside her, Mr. Logue would whistle under his breath.

"Your mom's an eyeful," Pete said. "You don't notice because she's your mom, but trust me, if you were somebody else, you'd think so too."

I thought of the pictures of Wharton's wife, trying to decide if Pete would think she was an eyeful, but when I wasn't in Wharton's house, I didn't think about asking Pete, and he never said a word about her.

My father was sitting on the porch when I got home, and he noticed me in the doorway. "Bring me another one of these, would you, big guy?" he said.

I carried the beer outside and handed it to him. "Have a seat," he said, smiling. There were three empty bottles standing beside his chair, which was unusual because my father was the kind of man who slid his returnable bottles into the case he kept in the garage as soon as he finished each one, a habit I thought he'd acquired so either my mother or I didn't count how many beers he'd had.

"You getting along?" he said.

"I guess."

"You're getting towards grown up. I come home and I hardly recognize you sometimes."

"That's good, isn't it?"

"Six of one, half dozen of the other," he said, and he took a long swallow of beer.

He pointed his beer at Wharton's yard. He looked like he was thinking about digging up the dead bushes and taking the mower to the lawn. It was the look he'd give my room when the bed wasn't made and there were board games and clothes on the floor. The look that started my hands moving. He'd cleaned up one time when I was eight. He'd made my bed while I sat in a chair and watched, tugging the blanket so tight it looked like a board, and then he'd picked up two handfuls of model cars and thrown them in the trash. The only thing I did right that night was refuse to cry.

"Is it a mess inside?" he said.

"No."

"You sure about that?"

"Everything looks clean."

"I've got half a mind to check for myself," he said. "It doesn't follow from what I can see."

"Trust me," I said.

My father didn't shift in his chair, but when he didn't say anything for a minute, he looked different, like Richard Hoak looked when his report card said he'd failed fifth grade, changing into somebody I wasn't going to know anymore.

"There's limits, Danny," is what he finally said. "You and your mother both need to learn that." He picked up the empties and carried them into the garage. When he didn't come out, I thought he'd opened a warm beer in there, drinking it fast before he stepped out again and went to the refrigerator for a cold one.

I heard the screen door groan, and my mother, holding it open with her elbow, said, "What's that father of yours doing with himself in the garage? He's been out here forever already."

I threw up my hands and tilted my head like I'd seen actors do in a hundred TV shows when they pleaded ignorance, but my father reappeared before she could ask another question. "You're leaving again tomorrow," she said, "and here you are mooning around out here half the night."

"It's my job," he said. "What do you want me to do?"

"It's more than two weeks this time," she said. "You have a boy who's almost twelve. You know what that means?"

"You bet, Arlene," he said, lifting her arm and brushing past her. "You bet I do."

My mother didn't follow him. She caught the screen door with her hand and held it open like she expected me to come inside. I sat in my father's chair and looked at Wharton's raggedy bushes for almost a minute until I heard the door close.

By the time I got up the next day, my mother had gone to the store, and she served TV dinners for lunch, something new. "I bought you a whole slew of them. Your father's going to be away for a long haul. Teresa's invited me for bridge. I know it's a Wednesday and the afternoon, but things don't always have to be the same. I want you to promise to stay right here like it's night." She squeezed my shoulder. "Help yourself to a bowl of Neapolitan," she said. "That will get you started, and then ask Pete to come over. I haven't seen you and him together much lately. Did you forget how to use the phone?"

I watched her walk down the street until it curved and made her disappear, and then I ate three scoops of ice cream, washed out the bowl,

and waited ten more minutes before I headed over to Pete's house. I had a
couple of hours before she had any chance of finding out I'd left the house,
and if she called, I could say we were watching television and didn't hear
the phone, which was in the kitchen.

Mrs. Logue waved as I came through the back door without knocking
like I always did. When I walked into Pete's room, he was standing at
the window with his back to the door. He was staring so hard I thought
I could touch him before he heard me, and I tiptoed half way before he
said, without turning, "Either stop there or get ready for this."

"What?" I said, hurrying up beside him.

Wharton's weekday bedroom was on the side of the house where the
rhododendrons had gone halfway up the windows, but from Pete's room
we could see right in, and there was my mother kissing Roger That. The
bushes cut them off at the waist, but as soon as Wharton's hands went
underneath my mother's blouse, lifting it so I could see her bra, I sat down
on Pete's bed and stared at the clock radio, waiting for the minute number
to flip over from three to four.

"It's ok," Pete said. "I've never seen anything. You can't see from here
except when they're standing up."

The four dropped into place, and I pulled the radio toward me,
yanking the plug out of the wall. I wanted to throw something, but Pete
said "Whoa," and I just held it stuck at 1:44, the numbers dark but still
visible.

"It's not my fault," Pete said. "I didn't want you to know unless you
found out for yourself."

My mother went to Teresa's for cards three nights while my father was
gone. Each time I hurried to Pete's house to make sure he was watching
television instead of my mother. His parents watched with us like they
always did, but when Mr. Logue walked down the hall like he was going
to the bathroom while commercials were on, I counted 1001, 1002, 1003,
imagining him slipping into Pete's room for an eyeful before I got to 1100.

The day my father got back, my mother had dinner on the table, but
he just opened a beer and said he wasn't hungry. "I ate fast food at one
o'clock," he said. "Two Big Macs fill you the hell up. I need to wash the
road away."

After my mother and I ate the battered-fried fish she made, I followed her out to the porch where my father was sitting beside four empty bottles. "I have half a mind to clean up that yard of Wharton's while I'm home," he said. "It keeps me from enjoying even one minute out here seeing that mess."

"Relax, Bill," my mother said. "By tomorrow you'll be ready to take care of your own things." She handed him a fresh beer, but my father didn't lighten.

"What do you think, big guy?" he said. "There's always the names of the books of the Bible to learn, right? Genesis, Exodus—there you go, you can finish them off just like that."

"Bill," my mother said.

"It's a hobby," he said. "Leviticus, Numbers, Deuteronomy. See?"

I thought of Pete Logue watching Wharton undress my mother, and I wondered if she had ever been completely undressed before she disappeared onto the bed. For sure, Pete had seen my mother naked from the waist up.

"Seashells, driftwood, and lots of colored stones," I said, and my father looked at me. "That's the start of a list of things in Mr. Wharton's bedroom," I said. "You should see all the stuff he has in there."

"What sort of man has boys in his bedroom?" my father said, staring at my mother.

"Moccasins, belts, and a whole shelf of key chains," I said. "There's hardly any space except on the bed."

My mother looked stricken, but I knew there was no way, even though she was the only one of us who knew what was in Wharton's weekday bedroom, she could correct me.

"You know what I'm talking about, Arlene?" my father said, but my mother just shook her head slightly. For a moment, just then, I was ready to say I'd seen all those things from Pete's room, that I'd never been in any of Wharton's bedrooms, but my father was so angry I began to add all of the pictures of Mrs. Wharton, the ways in which she was dressed, the swim suits she wore. It didn't seem like lying. Even if nobody slept there, all of those items were in bedrooms.

My father stared at me. "You trying to tell us something?" he said. "Is there something we need to know about this goddamned dentist?"

I glanced at my mother, but she had an expression that reminded me of the one on that wing-shot bird. The only way I could stop talking was to run to my room.

As soon as I threw myself on my bed, I heard my mother say, "No, Bill," but then the front door slammed and I popped right up to see my father appear in Wharton's yard, shouting for him to come out because they needed to tend to some business right this minute.

Wharton, when he stepped outside, said, "What's this about, Bill?"

"You know exactly what it's about," my father said, taking two steps forward, closing up the distance between him and Wharton, who stiffened, but didn't step back.

"No, I don't, Bill. You'll have to tell me," Wharton said.

"Your bedroom," my father said. "Ring a bell?"

Wharton looked over my father's shoulder, and I knew he expected to see my mother in one of our windows. Maybe, in fact, he expected her to call out to my father, asking him to come back inside. I waved so he would see me, and when he looked back at my father, he turned into Roger That, explaining about the ways he was helping me learn. "I have a lot of things a boy likes to look at," he said. "I thought you'd appreciate it, Bill, you being away so much. Curiosity, active learning, association, metaphor."

"What's he talking about?" my mother said from behind me somewhere. I hadn't heard her step into the room, but when I didn't turn, she came up close, laying her hands lightly on my shoulders so I knew she was looking across the lawn at the two men she slept with.

My father hit him then. He drove his fist into Wharton's stomach, folding him up. My mother clutched my shoulders as Wharton wheezed, making a noise that sounded like Pete's dog whistle, something imagined more than heard.

And then my father looped a roundhouse right and caught Wharton flush on the ear, spinning him into the spotty azaleas. "You stay away from my family," my father said. "Understood?"

My mother stood behind me then. "It's ok," she said. "I promise."

In my room that night, I saw Roger Wharton's hands under my mother's blouse, the way his face had pushed between the cups of her bra just before I turned away. Breastbone, I said to myself, though even I knew the real name was sternum, something that seemed made up so doctors could learn the bones without thinking of the body parts they wanted to touch.

What list had Wharton reeled off for my mother the first time she was in his house? There were thousands of lists, but none of them, I was suddenly sure, were something a man would tell a woman he wanted to undress. It would have to be later, when they were dressed again, when they were in the living room with all of that junk that cluttered Wharton's shelves and tables, getting in the way of the pictures of him and his wife. The names of dentist tools. The names of healthy foods. My mother would listen like I did. She would remember parts of those lists even if she didn't give a damn about any of them. And then the idea that he would recite a list to her sounded so foolish, I knew he'd never say a word about the animals in space or the vice-presidents, that those lists were his hobby, what he did when he was alone or in the company of boys.

WHERE WE LIVE NOW

———

Saturday

"Shut that thing up," the prick kid says. He holds his phone at arm's length like he's taking a picture of himself and then slaps it back against his ear.

The loud baby and I are on the other side of the loud TV, way across the room. The loud baby is laughing. I wait for him to finish his call, then I go Thelma and Louise on him. I owe somebody's swear jar a fistful of quarters. An older guy I've seen around never takes his eyes off the bass fishing on TV. I really want to put the prick kid's face through the window. A couple of salesmen make a point of coming over, the guy from parts flirts with Lyssa. I'm a regular; the prick kid is just passing through.

The prick kid flips his phone shut and walks to the Michelin display like he has a friend meeting him there to inspect tread patterns, but all he can do is inhale that rubber smell from new tires for a while until Roy, the service manager, says, "Ellen, you're ready to roll." Roy has another invoice beside mine, but he makes silly faces at the loud baby, and I'm paid and carrying her out the door, tires aligned and brakes adjusted for next week's trip to Punxsutawney, before Roy says "Bobby Crowe?" as if the room is packed with strangers.

Ten minutes later, when I tell Edwin the story, he puts his finger to his lips. "The baby will be saying 'goddamn' and 'go to hell' before she learns to walk." He doesn't repeat "prick" and "asshole," not even in a whisper.

Sunday

Right before noon, a commotion starts at the big Presbyterian Church two doors down. An ambulance and the police, all that fuss meaning more than a heart attack. "Whatever it is, we know them," I say.

"Let's hope not well," Edwin says, but that doesn't hold water. I take Lyssa outside with me and let him decide whether or not he'll follow.

The ambulance leaves, but the police stay, going in and out, so I let myself drift their way until Cheryl Walcott, from next door and a churchgoer, comes outside still dressed like she's ready to pray. "In the church," she says before her voice drops to a whisper. "With God watching."

I look at two cops, a scattering of people, all of them a stone's throw from the concrete steps climbing to the main entrance where a yellow crime-scene tape is up, and wait for her to tell me the story.

"He shot her right there in the pew where she sits during the sermon. Marched right down the aisle and fired twice and killed her on the spot, anybody could tell."

"Who?" I finally have to ask, and Cheryl squints at me as if she's just discovered she's mistaken some out-of-towner come to gawk for her neighbor.

"Denise Erhard" she says. "Her ex-husband Clay put two bullets in her before a couple of fellows wrestled him quiet." She looks at me as if she wants me to cover the baby's ears. "In this very town and him a teacher of our little ones to boot."

The church almost shimmers in the overhead, early May sun that is just starting to send the steeple shadow toward Cheryl's Victorian three-story. This time of year, the shadow will be over her house before three and over ours less than an hour later. By Memorial Day, the shadow will reach us around five like a sundial that says it's time for dinner.

Cheryl looks so much like she wants me to hug her that I say, "Teachers have shot people before."

"What's next then? A doctor? A pastor?"

"Them too."

"A teacher," she says as if she hasn't been listening to either of us. "Me with three girls, the oldest wanting a clarinet."

"You should be thankful he wasn't like one of those lunatics who shoots everybody. You all got to go home with your families," I say, and when Cheryl just stands there, I add, "It's like in those nature films where the lion pulls down the weakest while the rest of the herd thunders away, safe for another day."

Cheryl comes back to life. "Ellen Stark," she says, "somebody else might slap your face for saying that out loud."

While I make sandwiches for lunch, I repeat Cheryl's story, and Edwin reminds me how, when the Erhards had separated a few weeks before Lyssa was born, he'd told me how that meant there were only three other couples in town where both partners had graduated from college, and we knew two of them. "The third," he said, "is a rumor," and I didn't know whether he meant us living together like we did without a license or there was a couple he didn't know. Now, holding his turkey sandwich, he says, "He's not the first. Going to college doesn't keep you from being a killer."

"You sound like one of those profilers you watch on *Criminal Minds*," I say. "The ones who figure out the reason killers slaughter people."

"Those criminals always kill more than one. They have to establish a pattern."

"What does a woman do to get herself to be the first one shot?"

"There's only the one thing," Edwin says, too certain to be right.

"He's an ex-husband," I say. "There's no sense to that."

"It doesn't matter if they're separated. There's a man out there who's thinking he could have been the one dead and soon to be buried if Clay Erhard had a different way of settling things."

"Well, you can't be an ex-husband," I say, and when he just chews his bite of turkey and bread instead of answering, I watch him and try to imagine how he would kill me if I slept with another man. No gun, of course. Not Edwin, even in our town full of guns. And no blood from a knife. He'd have to smother or strangle me. He'd have to touch me and be close, and then I know all he would do is leave before I say, "I remember from when we were in grade school he wasn't a good-looking man and she was pretty."

Edwin takes another bite and talks while he's chewing. "You were nine or ten."

"Exactly. Old enough to see that he was an ugly prick."

Monday

The newspaper uses the whole front page with the story, including sidebars about the killer and the victim. The reporter spends half a column emphasizing how Clay Erhard isn't some outsider, going on so long I'm half surprised he doesn't say Erhard isn't like some monster in one of those old movies with titles like *It Came from Beneath the Sea.*

But right there on the front page is the ugly prick in a tuxedo. Like he got to pick which one they print. Like the police let him search the house until he handed it to them and said, "Here, this is how I look."

His bald head and glasses. Dressing up to conduct the grade school band like he's Leonard Bernstein at Carnegie Hall. At least I won't see the likes of that when Lyssa is squeaking and honking on something or other for parents who film the show on their phones.

There are a few details Cheryl didn't mention. How Erhard was seen pacing outside before the service. How the minister shouted "No!" just as Erhard leveled his gun. And some she did, like how he walked down the middle aisle and fired two shots. How other congregation members grabbed him and held him after the shooting. And some I almost know from living here my whole life: How Denise Erhard was both the organist and choir director. How the ugly prick has taught for more than twenty years at the elementary school. How Denise, fifty-two years old and now dead, taught music at the elementary school in the next district for thirty years. How the church was 180 years old, the oldest thing in town except for an inn turned gift shop on the next block down.

I stop when I get to the part about how the ugly prick will be given a psychological evaluation. "Some lawyer will say he's crazy," I tell Edwin.

"He was at the time," Edwin says, like he expects Clay Erhard to dance around murder.

"He doesn't sound crazy," I say. "It says here he called her a filthy bitch."

"They put that in the paper?"

"SueAnne Waltman, the minister's wife, says she heard him plain as day from where she was sitting two rows behind."

"That doesn't mean it gets printed. They should just say he responded with obscenities."

"You sound like you're auditioning for the grade school concert," I say.

"I bet he said worse. I bet SueAnne Waltman, a preacher's wife, couldn't bring herself to repeat the real words."

Edwin loops his tie into a perfect knot to remind me he has to go to work half an hour before I do and doesn't have time to argue about the dead, but I read him another quote. "You just feel this tremendous grief and try to process what happened. We are considering closing the church for a month out of respect."

"That's Pastor Waltman," I say as Edwin plants a peck on my forehead. "And here's one from a county commissioner who lives twenty miles from here: 'This is devastatingly tragic for the community. What a shame this sinister deed took place inside a church.' Who is that guy anyway? He talks like he lives inside some old book."

Edwin sighs. "I bet nobody mentions that if enough have guns, some will use them on others."

"On a wife, you mean?" I say.

"Husbands too," he says, "wives, children" as if he wants me to hate him.

"We don't have guns," he adds, taking that steaming pot off the burner before it boils over.

And then he's out the door before I can tell him that I'd bet Erhard didn't think things were over until he fired his gun. Then he knew he'd closed both sides of his life, the past and the future, each of them useless. That's what he meant to say, at least, though his words printed in the paper were "I had to end it, that's all."

The selfish prick. Thinking like God.

Tuesday

More of the same on the front page, but room now for a car crash with nobody dead. Still, those two photos of the dead and the living side by side. I look at the ugly prick's picture and think about Jason Fields and the way he looked at me when I told him I was pregnant with Lyssa. Apprehensive. Frightened maybe. And then relaxed just before he said, "We can deal with this" as if he'd just remembered where the jack and spare tire were stored. He even squeezed my shoulders like I was his aunt hosting a reunion dinner.

What he didn't do was ask how I felt.

And what I most remember is the way, a few days later, Jason looked when I said I was keeping the baby and I wasn't there to negotiate. Angry. Like all it took to make him want to shake me was fatherhood.

"That's crazy," he shouted over his shoulder, stomping toward his pickup. "There's no way."

He didn't touch me. I'll give him that. But when he came back around after an hour and I held my ground, I watched him start doing the pick-up-and-go. After he had his stuff stacked in the bed of his truck, he walked to where the woods began, his head down, hunched over, the low sun turning him into a silhouette. He picked up a thick, fallen branch and swung it against the trunk of a tree three times before he dropped it and jogged to the truck. For sure, I kept my eyes on that rusting pickup until it disappeared. "Change locks," I wrote on the to-do list. Right on top where I printed the things that couldn't wait.

I moved in with Edwin two months before Lyssa was born. I'd once upon a time gone out with him for a year before he'd gone off to college and I'd started driving back and forth to the community college for my associate. "I'm willing," he said, sounding like Mr. Barkis in *David Copperfield* when we read it in ninth grade.

The truth? I was grateful, but I wasn't surprised. I've known Edwin since the first day of kindergarten through when he opened his insurance agency four years ago and then up to the minute he made the offer.

I'd even worked on his teeth, what with me being a dental assistant for five years and Edwin, twice each year, sitting in the chair. He's careful with his teeth. I know that from finding so little plaque, it's mostly a polish with him, the curettes and hoes waiting for somebody who comes in after he's got a coat of tartar going deep into his bleeding gums.

But since just before the baby and now, for six more months, I've kept the books and greeted patients, the baby nearby. Arbogast, the dentist, has promised one year, which seemed generous until the year is nearly expired and a month from now I'll have to trust a sitter and add that expense if I want my old job back, the retired assistant who's filled in already hinting she might quit before the year is up, returning to the front desk because she wants to be off her feet, even if it means 25 percent less pay.

Wednesday

Since Lyssa turned four months old, right about the time winter began to break, Edwin and I take her somewhere on Wednesdays because, as if we need two Sundays in Forestville, everything closes in our town. Selling insurance like he does, Edwin needs to stay in step with the Wednesday close, and Tom Arbogast has had his office closed mid-week at least since when he filled my first cavity.

Outside of town, along Route 6, everything's open all hours, seven days a week, so we stop for burgers or pizza before we go to the park or a few miles north to Lake Alice, but I'd thought of Punxsutawney and their famous groundhog Phil last week, and when Edwin said he'd never been, same as me, we made a date.

Punxsutawney, when we get there after ninety minutes, is so plain looking I almost think the whole groundhog thing is a fairy tale concocted by dragging any old groundhog in from some farmer's field. "Phil's hole and the rest is right in the middle of town," Edwin says, driving without asking directions. "We've both seen the groundhog's stage a dozen times on television. We'll recognize it when we get there."

A couple of blocks prove him right when they lead to the town square. The place is nearly deserted, which gives us plenty of time to stretch our legs and carry Lyssa, awake after the ride, her diaper changed, toward a carved wooden groundhog that is Edwin's height. I balance Lyssa and take a picture of him with his hand on the shoulder of his new friend.

"All these years and we've never been," he says.

"Us and a whole lot more," I say, but he's already moving toward the shiny, cartoonish statue of a groundhog in a tuxedo, red bow tie, and top hat who's waving a friendly paw. Lyssa ogles that groundhog's buck teeth, remembering, maybe, the oversized tooth models from Arbogast's. Edwin snaps pictures like we're at the Grand Canyon until three boys, each of them wearing souvenir top hats, come up and surround the cartoon statue to pose for their mother.

Near the souvenir shop a man in a red shirt and top hat is speaking while he holds a gray groundhog that looks drugged. We've missed part of the talk, so I don't know if it's Phil or an understudy. "Phil's favorite meal is dandelion leaves in early spring," the man says.

Edwin looks excited, like he wants to hold the real Phil in his hands and ask whether next winter will be hard. "We need a hook like this to get tourists into Forestville," he says.

"Nobody will care about a cartoon tree," I say, and when Edwin frowns, I add, "A lucky thing, for my money."

Lyssa reaches for Phil with both hands. She laughs. Three women are taking pictures with their phones. Another is talking to somebody on hers, saying "totally fat" and "funny cute." She is wearing a top hat like the ones in the gift shop window and on the heads of the three boys.

Edwin seems dumbstruck. I take Lyssa inside the gift shop and buy her a small, stuffed groundhog. When we come out, Lyssa pushing the groundhog into her mouth as if it's made of candy, I say, "What do you think that guy in the hat says about groundhogs to people he knows?"

I expect Edwin to talk weather forecasts. Instead, he says, "He keeps his mouth shut. Groundhogs are pests."

I think I've missed Phil biting Edwin, but I keep on. "Like a minister when he's socializing," I say.

Edwin looks at me like he's been praying in secret his whole life. He takes another picture of the guy in the top hat. All the way home, I have to keep myself from saying that the groundhog's shadow shows or it doesn't. Then it's over. The only complications are the road conditions driving back to Pittsburgh or Erie or wherever people come from to stand in the cold at sunrise.

Thursday

Because it's a murder, nobody thinks to make casseroles or fruit-filled breads to drop off at the nearest relative's house. Anyway, there's no immediate family who live in town, so there's nothing to do but show up for the viewing, murmuring condolences to strangers with hugs that seem selfish, as if something has been earned through simply surviving.

Edwin says he can't close early, but Sally Arbogast, Tom's daughter just home from college, offers to sit in for me at the desk and keep an eye on Lyssa when I leave at three o'clock and promise to return by 4:30. I walk the six blocks back to the church by myself, thirty-four houses until ours, and with each one I pass, I pretend I can know people by the houses they live in. I want to think that siding and shutters and the spotted or spotless windows explain how the owners act, but the houses refuse to add anything to what I already know about the people who live there. Even ours looks like the start of some Penn and Teller trick, a false front that says "ordinary" that will vanish while my gaze is drawn away by clever patter or gesture.

The door to the sanctuary is still yellow-taped. They have Denise in an open casket in what looks to be a social room downstairs. I notice her hair is styled like in the newspaper photo. And I notice how much weight she carried, enough, I think, for Edwin to be wrong about dying for sex. With her being childless, it's just two sisters and her mother receiving the sorrys. The old woman is in a chair with a high back, the daughters standing on either side like slaves. If there are friends of the ugly prick filing by, I bet they've been sworn to silence by their wives.

I sit on a folding chair like everyone else. Moved to the basement, even the funeral itself can't shake the anger and fear from its grief. I examine the men for copycats. I watch the women for helplessness. As if Denise Erhard was victim zero, as if by attending her burial a plague would begin the way it does when those tribal women I've read about wash the body of an Ebola victim.

Cheryl catches up with me on the way out. She walks with me toward Arbogast's because she says she needs some air. "So close," she says. "There will never be a way to feel safe again."

"Local let us down. I'll give you that," I say.

"That's Ralph Sauers across the street mowing his lawn. He's only a block away, and he could be as crazy as Clay Erhard. Buddy Fields getting his mail next door to Ralph could be angry enough to do something crazy."

"You should have more faith in human kindness," I say, and it sounds like I've been staying up late reading.

"The town must be having bad dreams," she says. "Everywhere somebody must be waking up sweating."

It's like listening to a fortune teller. No matter how silly, Cheryl sounds confident, her voice as assured as a news anchor. "I have something to ask you," she says. "We have to do more than a few loaves of zucchini bread," and by the time we get to the office, Cheryl has made a push for me to hit up a big chunk of Forestville to donate to a scholarship in Denise's name.

When I tell her I'll canvas fifty houses for contributions, she smiles as if she believes a few thousand dollars might pay for a resurrection. "Saturday morning," she says. "You can have Arbor and all those tree streets where there's the most money. Take that adorable baby. She'll make you our best money raiser."

Friday
The paper comes after both of us have left in the morning, so I don't see it until after five-thirty when I get home late from Arbogast's because I had work to catch up on. The funeral is on page one with a photo of pallbearers carrying the casket a few minutes after Cheryl followed me. From now on, I think, everything will be about that ugly prick crying crazy.

Edwin is in the living room eating Cheerios like a boy come home from grade school wanting a snack. He eats nothing but the old fashioned plain kind for breakfast every day except Sunday, when I make omelets that he orders by opening the refrigerator and picking three things for me to chop and slice before sprinkling them over the whipped, thickening eggs. "Hungry?" I say, but he scoops up the rest of the cereal and drinks the milk from the bowl before he says anything.

"It feels like we've lived here forever," Edwin says.

"You're tired of having me around?" I say and add a laugh.

"I mean all the time in Forestville."

"Twenty-eight years," I say.

"That's every day of our lives. That's the same as forever."

"That's not much of an eternity."

Edwin looks at me as if he's seeing all the ways I could be somebody he's disappointed in. He puts the bowl down on the coffee table and tells me the best guess for my age when I die is eighty-three, and I notice he has his actuarial tables open on the floor beside the couch. "Fifty-five more years," I say.

"On average," he adds, "but every time you go off and run alone like you do you lose a fraction of those years. It's like smoking. Or gaining weight."

"And here I am ready to change into sweats and do just that," I say.

"Whether you run by yourself isn't a question anybody asks in my business, but maybe they should. A woman running alone is a threat to herself. The danger outweighs the benefits. The numbers say you'll run into the devil out there some day."

"It's still too cold for him," I say. "Anyway, he was in church last week, so everybody recognizes him."

Ten minutes later I hand him the baby. "There's no more reason to be afraid now than a week ago," I say.

Lyssa starts to whimper. If she begins to cry, Edwin will hand her back and expect me to stay inside. "Logic doesn't live here," he says, but Lyssa settles.

"What?"

"There aren't any words for where we live now."

I don't tell him how foolish this sounds, but I say, "Where does a music teacher keep a gun?" Forcing a shrug. Adding "In a house like this, where?" as I open my arms, palms up to lift an answer from him.

"No kids," Edwin says, "so there's a spare room turned into an office."

"A desk, a computer, and a gun in the closet."

"We don't know."

"Maybe up high so she never even saw it. His secret waiting to be told."

"And her secret, too," Edwin says, angry now. Like I'm accusing him of having a hiding place.

"Or not," I say, and close the door behind me. I walk the three blocks north to where the houses thin before I start to jog. In 100 yards, by the time I reach the dirt road that winds up to Lake Alice, I'm loose enough to stride where it's not muddy. Edwin tells me to go to the high school and run on the track, but he should worry about the young girls who are parked with boys in trucks once the road is passable. Fourteen, even thirteen—I recognize some from their appointments, though they pay no attention to me. I recognize the trucks too, some of them driven by young men already out of high school.

I try to do a mile, but it's mostly uphill going out, so I stop before the steepest part and walk, catching my breath. At the crest, before the road winds down to the lake a mile farther on, I can see the steeple of the Presbyterian Church through a space where the trees make way for the creek that feeds the lake. Nothing else of Forestville shows. Other towns have a courthouse or a bank for the building that can be seen from a mile away. We have a church where a woman gets murdered during the sermon.

Earlier today, seven different patients told me it's staying open, that the tape is coming down and there's a service on Sunday

Saturday
Some of the women on Arbor and Hemlock and Spruce invite me inside when they see the baby. I never go farther than just into the living rooms because sitting down will keep me from doing the thirty houses I think can be handled in the three hours I give myself with Lyssa riding on my back in the carrier.

I finish twenty-three houses in two hours, four with no answer, and I tell myself twenty-five and done until next Saturday because Lyssa is squirming and so am I.

House twenty-four, at the end of Hemlock where the forest begins its run all the way to the county park a quarter mile away, is Fred Vogel, a widower who lives alone. He comes outside like he needs to keep me away from his house, stares as if he doesn't recognize me. Frowns. His lips are tight, and he works his mouth as if he's turning over a melting sourball with his tongue. "Your little one looks like a papoose back there behind you."

"It keeps my hands free."

"You've seen pictures, right? Squaws with their young on their backs."

"She seems to like it."

"My Ethel, God rest, always held ours in her arms. She wanted to know how they were doing every minute."

"Times change," I say and regret it at once because Fred squints and looks me up and down like a side of beef.

"You hear them?" he says, not taking his eyes off me. "The birds?"

"Sure," I say.

"I love hearing English in the morning from my backyard birds. I remember you now. You've lived here all your life so you know what I mean. It's good to know they're citizens, born here like the ones before them and the ones going back to when Ethel would take our daughters out in the yard and tell them the names from bluebird to swallow, all of them chattering without any damn accents." His mouth flexes. The sun lifts above the tree line and this small-town prick and I are caught in its light.

I mean my nod to be neutral, but I see Vogel's glance move to where

I've left footprints not quite vanished from when I cut across from the neighbor's yard to save a few steps. When a siren opens full-throated on the nearby county road, I try to translate its accident. Squalled from among the bright new leaves, the cries of those birds who chirp in English sound nervous. "Just because a man's a damned fool doesn't make me want to give money that will get handed to somebody I might not know," Vogel says and goes back inside.

I take a breath and cross the street to stand on the lush lawn that surrounds the Harshbargers', who have given me a check for fifty dollars. Lyssa is so quiet I unstrap the carrier and work the thing off my back, lifting it up in front of my face. She opens her eyes and looks at me, hands reaching, as always, for my glasses, and I lean in close to feel her breath on my face, letting her tug the glasses loose. We are standing on thick grass. When she drops them, there will be no chance they can break, but the future seems so empty and bleak I think that if I look at Lyssa, she'll read such fear in my eyes that she'll be tugged toward it as if the future possesses the gravity of Jupiter.

Sunday
Instead of making omelets, I go to the service at the church. All these twenty-eight years, most of the last one living two doors away, and I've never been in the sanctuary. The pews have cushions, something I've never imagined because the Lutheran I did attend until I was fourteen only had padding on the kneelers. Right away I see that Lyssa is the only child under six in the church. As if the young are checked at the door like coats

The second pew on the right is roped off the way I've seen them reserved for funerals and weddings. On either end there are two wooden posts painted white with a white velvet cord hanging loose between them. Because it's the only completely empty pew, I sit in the one right behind it. There are so many people behind me that I sense, for a moment, how Clay Erhard might have believed that someone would stop him as he walked up the aisle or that all those steps would give him time to change his mind, something to have faith in right up until he pointed the gun and fired.

Although no one is there to play the organ, there is singing, but I rock Lyssa to the hymns' rhythms, and she seems to nod off. But when the church goes quiet and the minister begins to speak, asserting that the church will never close, not ever as long as there are those who seek its comfort. "Think of what science has shown us," he says. "Tarantulas leave behind footprints of silk."

A ripple of appreciation goes through the congregation, and Lyssa stirs in my arms as the minister launches into his sermon, reading Bible verses that make it seem like Easter. "Respond," he says. "Relieve. Restore. Rejoice." So much like a slogan I half expect him to add "resurrect." When his voice swells with volume and then pauses for a moment for a practiced effect, Lyssa fusses as if she expects my voice, but I let myself disappear. She begins to cry.

Lyssa stretches herself and screams. Pastor Waltman doesn't resume. He looks my way as if he can't go on unless I carry the loud baby outside or someone slides into the pew beside me and asks do you need help, can you carry your child, can you stand and walk, can you please, please, please allow us to worship in peace?

The loud baby cries as if Pastor Waltman has been describing hell. She is so loud the congregation expects an apology, maybe, when I get up and go. Pastor Waltman is smiling at me, calm. A shepherd, I think, holy and purposeful, showing everyone I am the woman who has forgotten how to be a mother.

There are murmurs behind me. I reach into my purse and find the small, stuffed groundhog, but the loud baby turns her head to see what all the whispers are about behind us. When she cries again, she could be telling all of them to shut up. But then I decide she is trying to get them all to sob and scream.

THE KILLER'S DOG

When she knocks on his locked screen door, Frank Fawcett's sister, who hasn't had a dog since the two of them were teenagers, stands beside a full-sized German shepherd on a chain leash. "Dog-sitting," Maureen says, and he's glad to see she has the leash wrapped around her wrist.

"For how long?" Fawcett says through the screen's fine mesh.

"Maybe a while. Can I bring him inside? I bet you think he's a beast to hold, but this chain is just for show."

Fawcett has a dog-hating wife who Maureen knows is at work at the mall, so he understands she expects him to give in. "Only in the kitchen," he says, going ahead to drag chairs in front of the door to the living room.

"You don't have to worry," Maureen says, "He's a whole lot less messy than you are," and to prove that, she tells the dog to sit, then lie down, and it obeys like it's being paid.

"So who's too sick to keep their dog?"

"Sick's not the problem." Maureen looks at the dog as if she expects it to answer for its owner. "Hutch is in jail."

"Hutch?" Fawcett says reflexively, but he recognizes the name because within the past week, two bodies have been found buried on Hutch's property, alleged drug dealers missing for nearly three weeks when they were dug up. "You'll have the dog until it dies then."

"He might get off with a light sentence. The dead people were scum. It was self-defense."

"He buried them."

"Wouldn't you?" Maureen says. "No matter how it happened, dead people are hard to explain." She glances at the window, and for a moment Fawcett imagines somebody evil following her, somebody obsessed with revenge and settling on Maureen as a surrogate, but she doesn't appear nervous when she turns toward him again. "Maybe you remember meeting Hutch a couple of weeks ago at Cindy's party?"

"Fourth of July?"

"That's the one."

"He'd already killed them by then, right?"

"Yeah. It looks that way."

"Jesus, Maureen. Don't tell me you're best friends or worse with this guy."

"Friends is all," she says, but Fawcett wonders if it's a lie coming so easy, that if he asks around he'll learn more about his sister than he can live with. "Nobody else has room like I do, or they already have dogs of their own." She drops the leash, but the dog doesn't move. "His name is Marlow. I've heard there was a detective in some old movie with that name. Hutch must have thought that was ironic or something. You know, sorting out the good and the bad."

"He's never said?"

"Nobody asks Hutch why he does what he does."

"I hope you're wrong about the detective. If Hutch got that name from reading Conrad, that would be way more interesting."

"Conrad? Whatever. Your one year in college made you just smart enough to think you could be on *Jeopardy!* or something?"

"Everybody knows *Heart of Darkness.*"

"Now you're just being an asshole."

"It's just reading. You went to college longer than I did."

"I went to a school that showed you how to do a job. That's not college."

Maureen is thirty-one, her next birthday a month away. She'd gone back to school at twenty-eight, declaring that she had to be somebody else by the time she turned thirty. It had sounded like a judgment when she'd announced that at his thirtieth birthday party because he'd worked at McDonald's for six years by then, a manager since he was twenty-eight without any further possibility of change from that day on unless he resigned. Now, she glances at her watch and says, "Hey, it's five. Turn on the news. I've been keeping up with Hutch and you should too."

Fawcett doesn't tell her he knows Hutch has been on the news nearly every night for six days, four of those the lead story. There are rumors of more bodies buried on his property. Indications there might be a national serial killer story in the making, though so far there's been nothing confirmed except the familiar tale of a drug deal gone bad.

"See?" Maureen says after the newscaster says nothing is new in the double homicide case. "Such bullshit. People just want the story to be worse so they have something to talk about. They wish he'd killed twenty people as long as none of them were friends or family."

As soon as Fawcett powers down the television, Maureen tells him she wants him to learn something about Marlow. "All we have to do is walk a couple of blocks," she says. And don't worry, your neighbors won't recognize the dog and start calling 911."

A half block down the sidewalk, when Marlow drifts in front of her, she yanks the leash until the dog retreats and falls in beside her. "Hutch gave explicit directions. The dog never leads. If you let it walk in front of you, it thinks it's the master."

"Makes sense," Fawcett says, imagining Hutch choking the dog until it understood the advantages of obedience.

"Remember when we had Blaze and she was always dragging us along, sniffing at everything?"

"We were kids."

"Mom and Dad should have trained her. We had her for twelve years, and I never heard any of this." The dog turns its head toward a power-line pole, and Fawcett watches as she tugs the leash like she's inscribing an exclamation point on the air and the dog faces forward, leaving the temptation of scents behind.

At the corner, the light red, she says "Sit," and Marlow drops its hind legs like they've turned to sponge. "See? Isn't this great?"

"Elise will appreciate that the dog didn't leave a trace."

"She'll find a single hair on her carpet and think she'll have to hire somebody to steam clean it."

"You're only looking on the dark side."

"You should have kids. You should have a real house." After they cross, she turns and lets the light go red again, saying "Sit" as if Fawcett needs his opinion of the dog reinforced. Marlow sits. "Hey," Maureen says as they cross again and head toward Fawcett's house, "HIV Positive is playing at FloodPlain Saturday night. If I see Elise there with you, I'll admit I'm wrong about how uptight she is."

"She's on late shift through Saturday."

"HIV Positive has gotten huge since your last time. Once upon a time you were the guy telling everybody to get tickets."

"That was two years ago. Anyway, it hasn't been that long since I went."

"Yes, it has. Get your ass in gear or else I'll start thinking she's trained you to sit like a dog."

Even though the band plays five shows a week within a two-hour drive, Fawcett hasn't seen HIV Positive for more than three months. The last time he went, he thought something had moved on, the style of music maybe, the nature of the venue falling on hard times in a part of town college students and white collar workers avoided. A singer in an orange prison jumpsuit was something, maybe, you could only get excited about once or twice. "OK," he says. "I'll give it one more shot. If the dog can sit through an entire set, I'll buy all your drinks."

"Maureen stopped in," Fawcett says at once when Elise comes home at 10:30. He's already in bed, thumbing through a copy of *People,* which Elise says she subscribes to for her job. "Because I need to keep up with celebrities," she's told him. "So I can make small talk with customers. His alarm, for the fifth night in a row, is set for five a.m. because he has the early shift, overseeing four hours each of Egg McMuffins and Double Cheeseburgers.

"She the same as always?" Elise says, an edge in her voice.

"Actually, she was different."

"How's that?"

"She's been changing for years," Fawcett says, deciding to omit the dog. "Ever since nursing school."

"You keep saying that and pretty soon you'll believe it."

"I made spaghetti if you're hungry."

Fawcett sees Elise soften. She drops down on the bed, kicking off her shoes, and flicks at the *People* with her fingers. "Now we have things to talk about, right?" she says. "Thanks for the spaghetti, but I ate Arby's on my break. I wished for a steak with each bite of my regular roast beef."

"One more day of the sunrise shift."

"And one more day of nights. We'll go out next week. We'll have a meal without any buns involved."

When Fawcett comes home late the following afternoon, Elise is already gone. There isn't a note, nothing about how, with a few hours to inspect, she's noticed dog hair, so maybe there had only been the two thin strands he'd found and walked outside after Maureen left. Hutch was such a perfectionist, maybe the dog waited until it was outside before it shook loose a cluster of hair. He has time to take a nap before he showers and heads out to show Maureen he still has stamina.

As always, when he first gets to FloodPlain, Fawcett's first beer goes down fast, and he buys a second before stepping away from the bar, but already he feels bloated, as if he's guzzled a super-sized soda at work. Fifteen minutes later, the beer in its plastic bottle going warm in his hand, he knows he is going to watch this show sober, but not without the bottle because it seems impossible to stand among the crowd with empty hands. Like a chaperone, he thinks. Like some high school teacher watching half-buzzed students grope each other at a post-football dance. And despite Maureen's enthusiasm, the crowd is nowhere near capacity, and there are even groups of men using both pool tables, their girlfriends sitting on chairs watching them instead of working to find a great place from which to watch the band.

When he's jostled from behind, Fawcett doesn't turn and complain. When he's shoved again, hard enough that he has to take a step to catch his balance, he braces himself and keeps his eyes forward, ashamed. For a moment, as he waits for a third shove, the one that will shout "Fuck you" in his ear, he thinks about leaving, then puts that choice away because he would be more easily beaten outside.

The shove doesn't come. Those shoulders turn into accidents. And when he shuffles his feet enough to shift sideways and inspect for trouble, there isn't anybody within six feet of him. He sees Maureen near the stage, a beer in each hand. The man beside her, tall and burly in a leather jacket despite the club's heat, is holding a phone to his right ear, one finger pressed to his left, and Fawcett decides they are together even before the man closes the phone and Maureen passes him one of the beers. Fawcett watches her for two minutes, but she doesn't turn around and check the crowd.

The room goes dark then, sequenced red and blue lights flashing across the stage while feedback from a guitar being passed near an amp rises and falls like the voice a killer alien might have as it lunges from its space ship. Fawcett brings the beer to his lips to keep from retreating. It tastes like saliva, warm and frothy, the remnants of an unwanted kiss. It's a relief when the singer, stepping through a roiling cloud of smoke, yells, "How the fuck are you?" and everybody in front of Fawcett roars as he begins to scream. Even now, with his head shaved instead of sporting the blond Mohawk he'd displayed at the show three months ago, the singer, this time in a blood-red jump suit, seems so familiar the performance feels likes it's being beamed onto an enormous screen from a DVD.

Fawcett moves up, getting far enough into the crowd so he's among the two hundred or so who seem to be into the show, holding up their phones to take pictures or record something to put up on YouTube. "You can't slack off anymore," a woman in matching black leather pants and halter top beside him shouts his way. "You never know what's going to be posted, so every song matters."

He tries to believe that, but the other third of the audience isn't paying much attention. And when the singer drops to his knees and moans out the chorus, Fawcett wonders if anybody in the audience is thinking James Brown and expecting somebody to step out with a cape to wrap around the imaginary prisoner of love.

When the song ends and the singer pauses to drink from a plastic milk carton, the woman leans closer and says, "Everybody's been telling me your sister's great with Marlow. Hutch sends his appreciation."

Keeping his eyes from her cleavage, Fawcett looks at her face more closely, but a name doesn't surface and he opts for "The dog sure does listen."

She looks annoyed for a moment before she smiles. "For sure, Hutch is the original Dog Whisperer."

Hutch's girlfriend—Fawcett recognizes her now. Jackie something. A woman eager to display her extraordinary abs. On stage, the singer is running through so much patter that Fawcett decides he's already drunk, that if there is beer in that milk jug, a second set might never happen. "Hutch has a lawyer who knows his shit," she shouts as the music begins again. "A deal's going to get done. We'll all be together again before you know it."

He can't remember her last name, but Fawcett recalls every word of his first conversation with Jackie, the girlfriend. "Seriously. You work at McDonald's?" she'd said when they met at the Fourth of July party.

"Yeah."

"A grown white man?"

"I'm the manager."

"That's better. For a second there I thought you were retarded."

He'd imagined how she'd talk to somebody she knew. To Hutch, maybe. When they were in bed together, that dog told to sit beside the bed because it made being fucked more exciting. Everything about her was so exaggerated—her clothes, her makeup, her body—he thought she'd be scarier than Hutch with a gun in her hands. Hutch would put a bullet into his brain; Jackie would shoot him in the groin and then maybe give him the stigmata before she dropped him with one to the chest.

He sees Maureen turn and wave after the fourth song, but by the seventh, Fawcett, needing a break from the din, lets his bottle drop to the floor and moves to the side door where a bouncer says, "You leave, you're gone for good."

While the singer roars, "Fuck me, I'm fucked up anyway," Fawcett nods and exits.

Outside, the music muted enough that he can hear the high-pitched ringing in his ears, Fawcett stands near three women who are smoking. They're laughing at something already said among them, and then they inhale in near unison before one of them speaks, nodding toward him, her words smothered by the shrill whistle of his tinnitus, and they laugh again.

He makes a handgun from a finger and his thumb and points it their way, squinting down the length of the barrel as if he wants them to raise their hands. They stiffen and stare, uncertain for a moment, and then the woman who talked raises a middle finger. Fawcett remembers other hand gestures, their pantomime of contempt or longing. Instead of employing one, he drops his gun and waves before walking toward his car. Halfway there he turns, and he sees that the women are re-entering through the side door.

A few days later, when he meets Maureen for lunch, Fawcett is relieved the dog isn't sitting beside her. "There's a crate," she says. "Jesus, Marlow's not a seeing-eye or something."

"I thought maybe you could say, 'Lie down all day' and Marlow wouldn't move."

"You know what, Frank? You're not a funny guy, but I'm going to ask Hutch if I can keep Marlow."

"If he's convicted, you won't have to ask."

"So he's comfortable. It's no different than working with patients. I'll still ask. It's the right thing."

Maureen has been a nurse for nearly two years, which right now, seems obscene, even if she is the kind of nurse that is more like a secretary, filling in forms while the patient keeps a thermometer under his tongue. She knows the heights and weights of hundreds of people she sees on the street. She knows what medications they take and how often. She knows which patients the GP she works for has referred to specialists because they have something way worse than the flu or a strep throat.

Worst of all, she knows his private statistics. It means that at least once a year, he has to listen while she takes his blood pressure, telling him "140 over 85, a little high" and adding "slow down on all the chips and bean dip" as if he's a boy running at the public swimming pool.

"Hutch doesn't believe in doctors," she'd said when he'd asked her if he was that GP's patient like practically everybody else he knew.

Just like she denied ever seeing Hutch at the fitness center where she worked before she'd decided to go back to school. "I would remember Hutch being there, trust me. I remember too much about those days. I was about sick of fitness. There's enough vanity there to sink the Titanic."

"Darwin at work in the twenty-first century," Fawcett had said.

"Whatever. Those shits used to look at me like I should beg them for it."

"If you worked the counter at McDonald's, you'd get the same scummy eyeball, only it would come from lardasses waiting for BigMacs and fries."

"But they'd be doing the wishing instead of thinking it was me fantasizing."

Now, though, she wants him to know she has Hutch photos on her iPhone. "Here," she says, "check these out. He's in three of them."

In the third one, Fawcett is in the frame with Hutch, who is smiling as if he welcomes Maureen taking his picture. "You want me to believe he's normal, right? That he's that close to me and yet I'm safe as can be?" He doesn't add that those pictures make him suspect there's more to her having that dog than being willing.

"Look at you," she says. "You look like a stick man standing beside Hutch."

She's so accurate, he doesn't answer, but as Fawcett examines the pictures, he understands that the photograph of Hutch he's seen on the news doesn't show the thin, manicured sideburns that seem to float on the sides of Hutch's face, that the televised photo isn't as current as his sister's. He pulls a fourth photo up and Hutch disappears. "So now you remember?" she says.

"I always remembered. This is just the rerun."

"That other guy—go ahead and back up and look again. See him there on the other side of Hutch. He's a prison guard."

"John, right?"

"Yeah. John. You remember everything then? They're best buddies from way back. And here Hutch is under his lock and key until the trial at least. It's like a movie or something."

"Next you'll tell me there's going to be a prison break."

"Really, you should stop with all this worrying. You're not on his radar. You're not into drugs; you don't even drink the hard stuff. A beer drinker who goes home early would be way down the list of people he'd want to get back at if he was on the street."

Fawcett scrolls through ten more photos without seeing himself. "It looks like that's the only one I'm in."

"What did I just say? You'd be in more if you hadn't left before it got dark."

"Elise wanted to watch fireworks at the park."

"She dropped you off and picked you up like she was your mother."

As if Maureen has sent him, the next day John eats lunch at a McDonald's table. "What's the point?" Fawcett thinks, but he waits until John is nearly finished with his Big Mac before he pours himself a large soda and wanders over to where John sits by himself. "Hey there," he says, "I'm Maureen's brother, remember me?" and when John smiles, Fawcett sits down. "I saw you yesterday, too, in Maureen's pictures from Cindy Viker's Fourth of July party."

"Do I look wasted in all of them?"

That has to be scripted, Fawcett decides, and keeps on. "You do; Hutch doesn't."

This time John takes his time to answer, polishing off the Big Mac and wiping his mouth with a napkin first. "Hutch had things on his mind right about then."

"I bet he did," Fawcett says.

John eyes him for a moment and then relaxes. "Hey, if you're wired up about Marlow living with your sister, lighten up. There's no strings attached to that shit. The only reason she has the dog is because she's been out to Hutch's enough to be family."

"So there's no place like home?"

"She's not into drugs, if that's what worries you. Hutch wouldn't have junkies and shit driving up like he was running an ATM for whatever gets some fool high."

"Maureen thinks you're funny."

"Then I wish she was my sister," John says, and Fawcett watches him pick up Big Mac lettuce shards off his tray and eat them. "Seriously, man, she's got her shit together, and no rudeness intended, I'm out of here. I have to guard more than a bunch of burger flippers."

"You never can tell," Fawcett says as John slides his garbage into a bin, but when John leaves without turning around, Fawcett slurps down the rest of his soda so fast he feels chilled, a headache beginning to form behind his eyes. If anybody is timing, he has six minutes left on his break, so he walks to the employees' entrance to get some natural air. As always, the ground near the door is littered with cigarette butts. Worse, there's a glare from the sun that makes his headache flare, and he lets the door swing nearly shut again, breathing in the warm, humid outside air through a space so narrow he feels like he's drowning.

He's ready to retreat, but he notices two couples standing between their cars, and something about how focused they are on each other nudges him to suspect he might be witnessing a drug transaction, that the couples, all four of them with the pallor of indoor living, even in August, work in pairs to make their dealings safer. He keeps one foot wedged in the door and leans back, watching as they exchange McDonald's bags as if they've had their orders mixed up, silently together, then dividing again.

Anything is available, Fawcett thinks. Nothing else moves in the lot, nothing in the two backyards behind it, a set of swings in one that he's never seen a child using all summer, a deflated small plastic pool near the back door filled with a jumble of toys, including a tricycle and a fat plastic bat for swatting whiffle balls. Somebody has gathered the toys and consolidated them like a half dozen unpaid loans, but the pile hasn't been touched since April. It's as if a child has died in that house, some terrible exhaustion set in on the parents. The toys had lain scattered all winter, covered completely or partially by snow, resurfacing during warm spells before being covered again.

The cars drive off, leaving only the ones parked by his employees. Fawcett props the door open with an unopened box of napkins and walks to where a grease-stained KFC bag lies between where the cars have been parked. It is full of bones. Because there is no sign of ants, he knows one of those couples has dumped it. He flings it into the dumpster.

He counts to fifty, and when nothing else moves he lets the door swing shut before he gives into the impulse to get in his car and leave.

Each time the double-murder story comes on, the station shows the same photographs behind the news anchor, Hutch over the right shoulder, the dead man and woman over the left while the anchor begins with a summary of the case. Fawcett expects that routine, but for once Elise is watching with him, and she's impatient. "It's like they think nobody has watched the news for two weeks giving this recap of the grave and how long they think the bodies were in it," she says.

"I guess," Fawcett says, although Elise sitting there makes him recognize that the report needs only three or four new sentences to be featured, that regardless of what he hears, he still keeps his eyes on the photo of Hutch, the executioner, and the indecipherable tattoo on the side of his thick, defensive lineman's neck. Absolutely, Hutch had to have been stunned that the husband and wife tried to steal from him, that they believed him somehow vulnerable to the threat of a gun in his own house. That such a realization drove a fury through him.

"That vicious bastard was at that party I dragged you away from," Elise says. "Your sister, too."

"Yes, he was," Fawcett says, and something about her tone makes him want to tell her about Marlow, how well-trained he is. He takes a breath, deciding.

"You know what I think," Elise says. "No woman would be friends with somebody like Hutch. They'd either avoid him or fuck him."

"Can you hear yourself?" Fawcett says.

"Loud and clear. What part don't you believe?"

The news has switched to weather before Fawcett, without saying another word, gets up and goes to his computer.

Fawcett follows the MapQuest directions he's printed out and parks a hundred yards away from where he sees the driveway to Hutch's house begin. He keeps an eye on the house as he cuts through the woods because nobody could be inside except someone who would see him as an enemy. Six acres Hutch owns, the newspaper has said, and the state game lands bordering this side assure Fawcett nobody lives anywhere close behind him, something that makes him uneasy as soon as he's farther into the woods than anybody stopping to take a piss.

The house, even though he's seen it on the news, surprises him. The wooden siding is newly stained, and so is the deck that runs the length of the back of the house. And though he can't see inside from a hundred feet away, he appreciates the meticulous landscaping that surrounds the house. The way a forest of rhododendron gives way to a strip of azalea and finally to a variety of ferns and a low swatch of unfamiliar thick green leaves that provide ground cover to the edge of a stream a few strides from where he stands. Even in August, with three weeks of neglect, it looks like something to photograph. Something, he suddenly thinks, that reminds him of an enormous, poisonous flower. Something that would be less threatening if the deck was collapsed, the door off its hinges, the house surrounded by a field of goldenrod and milkweed.

He turns his back to the house and moves farther into the forest where yellow crime-scene tape flutters like an obscene flag. The earth is still piled in a mound beside an open hole as if somebody might need to lower himself and look for additional clues. When he leans over to look, Fawcett feels lightheaded.

He spends fifteen minutes examining the ground where he walks, his steps as short and slow as those of his grandfather, who uses two canes. He remembers the cemetery where he has visited his mother's grave for fifteen years, how, after a year or two, the earth mounded over the freshest burials settles and the grass blends, and he is able to cross those plots without feeling disgusted with himself. Hutch, the newspaper had reported, has lived here for six years. If he had buried others three or four years ago, the sites could be anywhere.

When Fawcett finally gives up the search, he's so far behind the house and so disoriented, he can't be certain it's the one that belongs to Hutch. He tries to make out his car, but the road has disappeared. He stares at the ground near where a rash of thorn-covered bushes clusters into a dense thicket. For a moment he believes that he can make out the shape of a grave, the feeling so strong, he lays a hand to the earth, imagining the bones beneath it. He rakes at the soil as if he might distinguish how recently it was disturbed, and then jerks his hand away when he hears a dog bark.

Hutch out on bail, he imagines crazily. The merciless and his well-trained dog. Or his sister, he thinks next, though he remembers that Marlow never barked while she visited.

The dog barks a second time, and though he can't make out whether it's closer now, Fawcett feels the sweat of his foolish panic in his armpits, and when he skids a few steps, turns and searches, the sweat comes from his scalp when the car isn't visible

There's a third choice, he tells himself—a neighbor on the opposite side, somebody living on a large plot of land like Hutch. Everybody in an area like this would own a dog. Maybe two. All of them big.

A buzzing begins in his ears, something like the tinnitus that stayed with him for two days after only forty-five minutes of HIV Positive. The sound makes him want to stick a finger into each ear and dig. As if he's just sat through a double feature without leaving his seat, heaviness sets in behind his eyes. He feels unsteady. A year ago an earthquake struck 200 miles from here, the first in over forty years, and he'd been fascinated, listening to things he owned rattling on shelves and tables, feeling the house vibrate as if a road crew was blasting away rock from a nearby cliff to widen the highway.

Now he just feels sick, nausea amplified by the certainty that if he's confronted, he'll beg and plead, not even capable of fleeing. It's just you being an idiot, he tells himself, but he slips behind a tree as if he can sense a sniper nearby. The dog sounds closer when he hears it again, and he tries to reason with himself. The dog doesn't belong on Hutch's property any more than he does. There's no reason for it to come after him. He backs up three steps, looking through the trees, and though he sees nothing and the dog doesn't bark again, Fawcett keeps retreating as if the dog has gone mute in order to stalk him.

He's backed up twenty paces before he pauses to search for the road again, and this time he picks out the car. He doesn't look back while he walks toward it, keeping his eyes on the Prius and wishing he'd driven his SUV instead of this weak, effeminate thing, telling himself one more minute, then thirty seconds more, then ten, and ducking early as he scrambles to open the door and push the start button, hearing nothing as always but having to trust that the car is running.

He drives to Maureen's, but instead of telling her about being at Hutch's, he tells her about talking to John. "You mentioned Hutch to John?" she says. "You know that John works for him, don't you?"

"He deals?" Fawcett says.

"Like me, I mean. Now that Hutch is inside, John does favors for him."

"Sort of on spec?"

"You're all the time so judgmental. He's not unlocking the doors or anything."

"I don't care what he's doing. It's him saying you're family and me thinking that doesn't mean you're anybody's sister."

"You're in asshole mode again. No wonder you don't have any friends."

Fawcett grabs her shoulders and twists her to face him. "It's not being an asshole to ask that question." He feels her try to free herself, and his fingers dig into her, insisting, but he's controlled enough to remember Marlow, who stays sitting, his head cocked as if he expects something.

She winces when his fingers find bone and says "OK," but he holds his grip until she seems to get chilled, shivering a bit, and starting in with "If you have to know this, I'll tell you."

His hands open and lie across her shoulders the way he remembers his high school coach's did before he sent him into a game. "Expect success," that coach had always said, at 6'7" always looking down at Fawcett.

"Hutch and I were together for a while but not long."

"How long is not long?"

"Two months, maybe less. It was like something you'd do at summer camp and move on. He was intense." She looks away, searching the room until her eyes rest on Marlow. "And it turns out I'm not."

"Good."

"Hutch said he didn't want me, but he trusted me." She looks into his eyes again, and he holds them. "He said I'm rare."

"How long ago?"

"Two years. Right before I got the job at Dr. McElroy's."

"Why don't I know this?"

"Who am I with now?"

"No idea."

"That's why," she says, and steps back as if she's unlocked herself, moving toward her bedroom.

She's already to the door before he thinks to say, "Have I ever seen the new guy?" but only the dog looks back as if it's forgotten something before she pulls it shut and he hears the lock click.

The next morning, his day off, Fawcett shows up at 8:30 when he knows she's getting ready for work. "Peace," he says.

"What's that mean? If it's an intervention, hurry up. I have to leave."

"How about I give Marlow a day off from the crate?"

Though it's forced, Maureen laughs out loud. "Go ahead. Take him for the day. You look like you need yourself some company that doesn't talk."

"That sounds correct. I should paste a star on you."

"Fuck's sake, Frank. You talk like that to the dog and he'll forget who you are."

"He doesn't know me."

"Right now he remembers who you were yesterday, and pretty soon he'll decide that was somebody he could learn to hate."

"That what you've decided?"

"I'm moving in that direction, Frank. Self-righteousness is a disease. Pretty soon you won't be able to treat it."

"Give me the leash and a couple of Milk-Bones. If Marlow rips my throat out in the car, you can tell everybody you were right."

Fawcett drives to the riverfront walk, two miles of narrow sidewalk that runs along the floodwall. Twice he yanks the leash, and the dog falls back the same way it did for Maureen. There's a pleasure in knowing that people passing him must think he's trained that dog. Hutch has made it as perfect as a dog could be, so compliant that Fawcett can imagine Marlow witnessing the killings, sitting as Hutch dug a grave large enough for two bodies. What it had taken to make a dog sit in spite of excitement or curiosity or fear.

When two attractive women approach, Fawcett pauses and says, "Sit," as if he needs to insure their safety as they pass.

Marlow sits and he lets the chain leash go slack. When the women get within what might be striking distance, the dog doesn't move. "Wow," one of the women says. "How does that ever happen?" She kneels in front of Marlow, her skirt tight against her thighs, and rubs him under his chin. "You're such a good dog," she says as if she could fall in love with obedience.

The other woman, her blouse cut low enough to distract Fawcett, begins to apologize. "Janelle is so into German shepherds," she says, but Fawcett has already returned his eyes to the kneeling woman, imagining what she will say after they move on, starting with superlatives for Marlow's behavior that might spill over into praise for his owner.

He watches them walk away and waits for the woman who hadn't knelt to look back, a sign the kneeling woman has mentioned him. When neither turns, Fawcett wonders what command for "attack" Hutch has taught the dog. Whether Marlow has learned another command that overrides anything said in anger or fear. For now, Marlow stands beside him for another half a minute until the women are so far away they could turn around for any number of reasons than evaluating a man and his dog.

CREDITS

——

"Things that Fall from the Sky" appeared in *Green Mountains Review*, Fall 2016.

"Gun Comfort" appeared in *Santa Monica Review*, Spring 2017.

"What was Good for You" first appeared in *Lake Effect* 19, 2015.

"A Day like Any Other" appeared in *Talking River Review*, 2012.

"Story Stories" (*Hayden's Ferry Review*) and "The Nazi on the Phone" (*Cimarron Review*) first appeared in *For Keepsies* (Coffee House Press, 1993).

"Callback" (*Willow Springs*) and "Darwin in the City" (*Cimarron Review*) appeared in *Emergency Calls* (University of Missouri Press, 1996).

"The Stone Child" (*Black Warrior Review*), "Zombies" (*The Journal*), and "Natural Borders" (*The Idaho Review*) appeared in *The Stone Child* (University of Missouri Press, 2003).

"Wire's Wire, until It's a Body" (*Sonora Review*) and "The Lightning Tongues" (*South Dakota Review*) appeared in *Sorry I Worried You* (University of Georgia Press, 2004).

"Somebody, Somewhere Else" (*Cimarron Review*), "The Out-of-Sorts" (*CrazyHorse*), and "The Proper Words for Sin" (*Black Warrior Review*) appeared in *The Proper Words for Sin* (Vandalia/West Virginia University Press, 2013).

"A Room of Rain" (*The Journal*), "The Worst Thing" (The *Missouri Review*), "The Visual Equivalent of Pain" (The *Kenyon Review*), and "Roger That" (*CrazyHorse*) appeared in *A Room of Rain* (Vandalia/West Virginia University Press, 2015).

"Where We Live Now" (*Cimarron Review*) and "The Killer's Dog" (*Cimarron Review*) appeared in *The Killer's Dog* (Elixir Press, 2017).

Sorry I Worried You won the 2003 Flannery O'Connor Prize for the Short Story.

The Killer's Dog won the 2015 Elixir Press Fiction Prize.

For Keepsies was nominated for the National Book Award, PEN/Faulkner Award, *Los Angeles Times* Book Prize, and National Book Critics Circle Award.

The Stone Child was nominated for the PEN/Faulkner Award 2003.

The Killer's Dog was nominated for the Pulitzer Prize and the Story Prize.

"The Proper Words for Sin" was a finalist for a 2006 Pushcart Prize.

"A Room of Rain" was cited as a Notable Story by *Best Nonrequired Reading 2009*.

ABOUT THE AUTHOR

———

Gary Fincke is the author of seven short story collections, including *A Room of Rain*; *The Proper Words for Sin*; *Sorry I Worried You*, a winner of the Flannery O'Connor Award for Short Fiction; and *The Killer's Dog*, an Elixir Press Fiction Prize winner. His stories have appeared in such magazines as the *Missouri Review, Kenyon Review, Black Warrior Review*, and *CrazyHorse*.